THE DECISION

A Novel By

Mary Syreen

*To Brenda and Sharon —
So nice to meet
you on Kauai!
Mary Syreen*

1/24/01

Published by:

Lakeside Press
6331 Mountain View Lane
Anacortes, WA 98221

For information, contact Lakeside Press, 6331 Mountain View Lane, Anacortes, Washington, 98221.

© 1999 Copyright by Mary Syreen

ISBN 0-9645798-4-7

Library of Congress Number 99-095233

Cover: Miss Print
        Oak Harbor, WA
        (360) 675-2002
        Charly Elm - Graphic Artist

First Edition

Printed in the United States

ACKNOWLEDGMENTS

This book would not have been possible without the advice and assistance of Kevin J. Cox. His proficient contributions, as always, were immeasurable and he deserves more credit than this short paragraph offers. I will be eternally grateful.

To my daughter, Marilyn Cox, who gives me encouragement to follow my dreams.

To my editor and friend, Linda Keltz. Your example makes all of us better people. Thank you!

To my readers who call or write to ask when my next book is coming out. You put frosting on the cake!

To my friends who give so much support and to all of you who buy my books, I do thank you so very much.

Also by Mary Syreen:

CONSEQUENCES

THE MANIPULATOR

THE DECISION

THE DECISION

CHAPTER ONE

Maybe, just maybe, the sun didn't always shine in Miami. It would have helped to have a dark and rainy day like his mood. One last walk along the beach, one last glance at Jaki's condo. How many days. weeks, months will this hurt continue? Nate asked himself.

This was not exactly the way he had his life planned. Ask him a couple of weeks ago and he would have said, "Jaki and I are leaving together. Of course marriage is in the picture." Now he could still hear her laugh. Her, "Are you kidding? Leave all this?" She wanted him once, or did she? Was it all just a game to her? Of course she wanted to be rich. Who didn't. But he was sure she didn't like the way she got her money. He was sure she hated Richard and the things he made her do, the little kids she taught how to be porn stars. She told him she hated Richard, that she only went out with him to keep other guys away, that the condo was a working arrangement. He believed her until that day, the day she laughed.

"Leave all this. You must be out of your mind."

One week ago, a week filled with hope: Was that her call? Was the little pink envelope from her? A week filled, at long last, with dispair. She didn't call or write, or accept his calls, or answer her door. He finally admitted to himself that it was over. That his move to Los Angeles would be solo. And he had to go. It was part of his deal with Vinnie. He had asked to go. He wanted out of the organization, but Vinnie said never.

"No one leaves. You knew that when you wanted in. Richard made it plain. No one leaves."

1

And now Nate knew that no one leaves alive. He had seen how the organization operates. He remembered the packages he had delivered. Packages wrapped in black plastic and duct tape, reinforced with nylon rope, and he knew what the packages contained. No, no one left the organization alive.

"I'll send you to L.A. with my cousin Dino. You can work with him. He's a good guy, do all right by you," Vinnie told Nate. And at that moment Nate believed Jaki would be delighted to go with him .

Nate glanced up at Jaki's window. Did the drapery move? Was she watching out her window? Would she step out onto the deck and wave to him. Motion him to come up, to wait for her. Changing her mind, she would go with him.

In your dreams, Nate chided himself. Only in your dreams. Get a life! She only wanted what you gave, never you. Had it always been that way?

He kicked off his thongs feeling the warm sugar sand between his toes. Even at five in the morning the sand was warm. Soon it will be too hot to walk on without some kind of covering on one's feet. Nate watched the little sandpipers, marveling that their tiny legs could hold their bodies, as they ran to the edge of the water and pecked in the sand for food. As the waves caressed the shore the little shorebirds, their soft-tipped bills full of food, raced the water to the dry sand, only to begin the regime all over again. He heard the unmistakable signal that a pelican had spotted breakfast and then the cry of the laughing gulls diving on the pelican ready to take the catch away. The big bird prevailed and the fish was held tightly in the dispensable pouch disappointing the gulls once again. Yes, Nate knew even from the smallest bird to the largest animal and especially man, it definitely is the survival of the fittest.

Would he survive without Jaki? Of course. He did what his mother had taught him many years ago. Make a list, put the positive items on one side, and the negative on the other. The side showing the negative things about Jaki took almost a full page. After writing "beautiful" he couldn't think of much else to add to the positive side. Not any more.

THE DECISION

He turned and watched as the sun began to color the sky, rising gently on the horizon chasing the darkness away welcoming a brand new day, and to Nate, perhaps the beginning of a brand new life. The sun owns Miami or for that matter, all of south Florida. Make no mistake, the sun controls lives, deciding how long one stays on the beach; when AC's are turned on or off; the type of clothing one wears; when to wear your Ray Bans; when to shop; and even what to eat. The sun controls our emotions. Nate learned that early on when he arrived in Florida. It dominates the lives of Floridians as no other master can, calling all the shots. He noticed the footprints he had made earlier had disappeared as the waves embraced the shore. How quickly they were gone without a trace. Would he be erased from Jaki's mind as easily?

Stop! Stop right now. She is out of your life he told himself. Good riddance. Concentrate on her selfishness, her lies, her sleeping around with just anyone, her practically living with a married man and loving it, smirking and bragging at the amount of money Richard spent on her; her stealing; the list could go on and on and he began to feel better. His mother was right. That is a good way to get someone out of your mind and your heart.

Nate jogged back to his car. Never pays to leave a car unattended long in Miami. He knew that. How many times had he "borrowed" someone's car for an hour or two, returning it fairly close to where the owner had left it making the owner question his memory. He drove slowly back to his condo with only a token glance at Jaki's place. His clothes were packed, fitting nicely into the beige luggage accented with red and blue stripes around the ends. Distinctive, one of Jaki's recommendations. She did like to be noticed. The rented condo boasted very few of Nate's possessions and now that he was leaving it was no matter to him that he had acquired little. No extra baggage he told himself.

He took a quart carton out of the refrigerator and drank the last of fresh squeezed Florida orange juice, the cold liquid comforting his dry raspy throat. Salt air always did that to him but the joy of being on the beach more than made up for any discomfort. Grabbing a bagel and slathering it with the last of his cream cheese, he finished his breakfast and glancing at the wall clock deciding it was time to hit the road. As always he didn't organize his time to miss the major part of Miami traffic but who cared this morning? It's the last time he would face it and could L.A. be any worse?

The condo would be used by the next person who would carry out Vinnie's orders. Although he would deny it, Vinnie had become the biggest crime boss on the east coast. At an early age he had caught the eye of Salvador Vacalli who ran all the unions, in secret of course. No one admits to a Mafia or that one person has that kind of power. Nate knew it was true. Vinnie, smarter and more cunning that those he controlled, married Vacalli's daughter thus securing his place in the organization forever or as long as he remained Ardella's beloved husband. And he took marriage seriously. He and Ardella produced four children and Vacalli, who had doubts about his only child marrying, let's face it, a common crook, embraced Vinnie for the happiness he gave Ardella, and the offspring to perpetuate the Vacalli bloodline. He made Vinnie his number one man and Vinnie's intelligence prevailed, the organization grew under his tutelage expanding in areas that even Vacalli would find offensive.

Vinnie never strayed from his matrimonial bed, became a youth baseball coach, church deacon, the pillar of society. That he sometimes caused someone to become missing, or silently influenced every major decision or election from the White House on down to, some would say, dog catcher, went undetected by Ardella and their circle of friends. After all, wasn't he such a great family man, didn't the Corsicas depict the All-American family, the stars and stripes displayed prominently each day on the spacious grounds of the Corsica Long Island home.

So how did Nate, a twenty-six year old west coast surfer and bartender, become involved in this crime organization? Nate knew the answer too well. Greed. His job as bartender on the cruise ship Golden Sea opened the door to many opportunities. But one he should have avoided as he now knew, was playing Richard's game --- giving confidential information about passengers. Pointing out wealthy women, information he garnered from ship's records that most passengers had no idea was available and shouldn't have been to a bartender, or Nate guessed, anyone since he had to sneak and pick a lock to get it. Course he had no choice in giving out this information. Richard had caught him watering drinks and stealing tips from co-workers and when Richard offered to keep the information about Nate's dishonesty to himself in return for Nate helping him, the two became buddies, or so Nate believed.

When Richard offered him a job in Vinnie's organization pointing out the advantages - great travel, a car, condo, big money and living in southern Florida - Nate was eager to go. From the beginning he knew the organization bordered on the fringe of dishonesty but, hey, Nate hadn't been a Boy Scout for years and someone would get these perks, why not him? The dishonesty, in reality, was crime in its worst form, drugs, child porn, murders, graft, money laundering, prostitution, forgery and all this done with a smile by very average-looking fit-right-in-the-community people. Vinnie even insisted that Nate get a part-time legitimate job. So Nate found work in a surf shop and taught the sport on weekends, if he had time from his other duties - delivering drugs, exotic birds or whatever Vinnie or Richard assigned to him. Nate gave the impression of a real "beach bum" only interested in surfing and girls. No one ever questioned his "other" activities. No one knew about them.

Except Jaki. But then she had a job in the organization as well. She directed the kiddie porn videos, and hated it or so she said. Nate and Jaki were in love, both wanted out of the organization, wanted to live the kind of life most observers thought they already did, and to raise a family.

Until Richard. Richard with his rich wife's money he freely spent. He bought Jaki a luxurious condo along Miami's finest beach, a race horse, beautiful clothes and jewelry. "Leave all this?" of course she wouldn't. How could Nate even dream that he could compete with someone like Richard?

As Nate expected, he entered the commute traffic on Miami's freeways. And as usual he wondered why snowbirds and retirees seemed to think they had to shop, sight-see or make appointments at that time of the morning. Two hours later, driving would ease for them as well. He snapped the locks on the doors as automatic as fastening his seat belt, and perhaps safer. Already he noticed the "supposedly worker" thumbing for a ride or a casual "innocent" jogger catching the morning rays, getting in a few miles before earning a living, or so it looked. Nate knew many of the thumbers and joggers were opportunists, waiting to pounce on some unsuspecting traveler. Steal whatever, use the car, and in some cases kill the occupants. Nate knew this scenario well. They would never fit into Vinnie's organization. Too blatant. Too often caught. Vinnie demanded sophistication, intelligence, casualness. One of Vinnie's men walking into a bank would never pull a piece or take a hostage. His way was a quiet talk with the manager urging him to call home to speak with his wife who would tell him she had a gun at her head or their child's head. Vinnie's men would have such a disguise that five minutes later walking into the same bank any of Vinnie's men would not be recognized even by the manager. Organization! That's what it is all about. Nate knew this. And it's spread from coast to coast.

Nate's car, a white medium priced, four-door, three years old with a spacious trunk ---- always a spacious truck, and forgettable. After all, how many white cars are there in Florida? Probably more than half the cars on the road are white, Nate guessed, and not only in Florida. Nate dressed in a forgettable way as well. Beige shorts and tee shirt, no logos, Keds, and even though he would have liked the Ray Bans or Gucci sun glasses, he opted for the department store brand, a suggestion from Richard. He blended in. Even his hair, not long, nor short, light brown, and he was five-feet ten, 165 pounds, average. Just the way Vinnie wanted. If someone described Nate, and later someone would, he would say, "Oh, kind of average looking, his hair not too light, not too dark, eyes, well, couldn't really see them, he wore dark glasses, the kind you see everyday at Wal*Mart. He was maybe somewhere between twenty-five and thirty-five, maybe younger, maybe older. Looked like a guy you see everyday, nothing special."

THE DECISION

Leaving Miami, Nate chose the coast highway AIA getting glimpses of white sand beaches and the Atlantic Ocean along the way. At Fort Lauderdale, he veered over to highway 75 and Alligator Alley, by-passing Deerfield Beach where Richard and Marian lived. Nate wanted no chance meeting with Richard since two days ago he had spilled all of his frustrations and deceitfulness to Marian. Nate marveled at her calmness when he admitted his part in Richard's deception. He told her Richard knew that she was very wealthy before he "accidentally" met her on the cruise. Perhaps she knew all along that she had married a manipulator. Nevertheless Nate was afraid to see Richard again. He knew Richard never forgot, never forgave.

Highway 75. How well Nate knew this route. How often he had delivered "packages" to the wealthy in Naples, then took Highway 41 to affluent Sarasota, on to Bradenton where he could always "borrow" a ride if he had to change automobiles for any reason. Then back to 75 all the way to Valdosta, Georgia and another job for Vinnie. In fact, Vinnie had outlined several deliveries for Nate along the way to L.A.

"No rush, take your time and enjoy the country, nothing perishable," Vinnie told Nate. The "packages" were placed in the trunk of Nate's car sometime during the night. Nate never saw nor heard when this happened, had only been told to leave the car in the designated parking space between the evening hours of nine to midnight. Plus open the trunk only at delivery points. Packages were marked for customers and "make no mistakes, otherwise take a month or so vacation, only call ahead when you'll be in Houston and Denver. The guys there don't want drop-ins," cautioned Vinnie.

Valdosta and just a few miles away, Little Miami. Then another few miles and he made his first delivery. A small white box decorated with butterfly cutouts. Looked like a very colorful birthday gift. Perfect for a young girl. However, a few drops of the "gift" and the recipient would celebrate nothing ever again. Nate knew if the cargo was discovered in his car he would not be celebrating anything for a very long time, either. He drove very carefully, never speeding, obeying all traffic laws, always observing his

7

surroundings. Never give the highway patrol any reason to pull him over. Nate chose Valdosta for his first night's stay. He picked up a few pounds of pecans and his very favorite snack - boiled peanuts.

As he approached Macon the next morning, Nate's thoughts drifted to a time three weeks earlier. Was it only three weeks when he saw Rudy bury his dog alive, when he saw Carmen, very pregnant, very frightened? She's a kid, only a kid. What is she doing here with this monster he remembered thinking? Nate focused on his driving. Still the face of Carmen burned in his mind. He took the exit to Highway 49 and the decision forever changed his life.

CHAPTER TWO

"What are you doing here?" Carmen stood in the trailer doorway, dressed in large baggy man's jeans, a man's short-sleeved blue and white stripped shirt - looking much the same as she did the only other time he had seen her. Her eyes showed apprehension and alarm as they darted around the yard and then back to Nate. It seemed as if she held her breath and stood very still like a young doe all of a sudden caught in the headlights of a car. Would she bolt and close the door? Cry out?

"Carmen, don't be frightened of me. You aren't afraid are you? You remember me don't you, the cupcakes and coffee?" Nate looked into her eyes imploring her to relax, trust him.

"What do you want? Rudy isn't here," she gripped the door so tightly her knuckles were white.

"I want to take you away, so you don't have to live here anymore. So you can keep your baby. You want to keep your baby don't you? I'll take care of you. Please trust me. I won't hurt you," pleaded Nate.

When he mentioned keeping her baby Carmen glanced to the yard outside the trailer. There were two dozen or more mounds that a casual visitor might think were raised garden spots. Nate knew that they were graves. After all, he had seen two of them filled and he was sure another would be dug for Carmen's baby whether or not the baby died. Otherwise, where is her first child? Why isn't she preparing for this one's birth? She told him three weeks ago, "The baby won't need nothing." Nate absolutely knew what that meant and what Rudy had in mind. Rudy would not tolerate a baby for one minute.

"Back to Miami?" asked Carmen. "I know people would help me there."

"No, never to Miami," said Nate. "That's the first place he would look and everyone there knows him. We can't go there."

"He will find us no matter where and kill us," Carmen murmured. "He's a terrible man."

"He won't find us," explained Nate. "I'll take you with me. It's thousands of miles from here. You hate it here. You're scared all the time. Think of the baby." Nate pleaded and asked himself why is he doing this. Why not just walk away? She's nothing to him, he reasoned. Except she's Rudy's captive, she has no choices and for some reason he could not leave her here.

"We have to hurry. I saw his truck in town and he could be coming back any minute. Come on. Right now!" demanded Nate.

In a split second Carmen made up her mind to trust Nate. What would one more beating be if Rudy found her and this may be her only chance?

For months she had tried to think of ways to escape. She played scenarios over and over in her mind, but never did she dream Nate would come along. Always she had run through the woods but she never seemed to get past just running, running, running.

"All right. I'll get my things. I have some clothes and...."

"We have to hurry. We'll get anything you need along the way," Nate kept his eyes on the driveway. If Rudy should come home right now what could he use as an excuse for being here? In that instant he knew he would race to his car for his Smith & Wesson. He would kill Rudy rather than let Carmen stay here and he was sure Rudy would try to kill him.

But no truck came up the driveway.

Carmen disappeared into the trailer retrieving her shoes, some well-worn brown slip-ons, and a faded denim bag tied with a shoelace. She hesitated at the doorway casting a glance around the trailer. What should she take? Is she forgetting a treasure from her past? She ran back in, stuffed something in her bag as Nate took her hand pulling her towards the car.

"Come on, we don't have any time to look around," he admonished.

"I know, only I'm scared. Are you sure? I haven't any money, can't buy food or gas," questioned Carmen, obviously frightened. She wanted to get away, even a hundred miles, any distance. This was her only chance and she knew it. Only, only... What if Nate didn't mean what he said? What if he got tired of her, tired of spending money for her food like Rudy, what if? But anything was better than being here with Rudy. If Nate got her a few miles away she would call Oprah . Oprah always helped people, gave them a second chance, believed them. Oprah would accept a collect call wouldn't she?

Carmen had tried getting away once before several months ago. One day when Rudy left for his, it seemed, daily trek to his favorite bar in town, she walked down the dirt driveway not knowing how far to the main road. A road where she hoped to hitch a ride. The dogs followed her and after two miles or so she saw a cloud of dust in the distance and knew Rudy was returning. She ditched her bag under some bushes knowing there was no way to explain why she had taken it on a casual walk. She willed herself to take deep breaths, calm down and pretend that this is a very ordinary thing to be doing.

Rudy stopped his truck a few feet in front of her. The dogs stood very still, tail between their legs, shrinking from Rudy. Their body stance showing craven fear.

"Open the tail gate, Carmen," demanded Rudy. He then snapped his fingers. The dogs immediately jumped into the back of the pickup. "You," he snarled at Carmen, "get in." But before she could climb in the cab, Rudy pulled the truck forward, nearly knocking her to the ground. He continued driving very slowly while yelling for her to get in. She ran to keep up but couldn't reach the door handle, the thick dust almost choking her. Rudy, tired of this game, stopped the pickup and Carmen managed to crawl in, coughing and wiping dust from her eyes.

"Where do you think you were going?" Rudy snapped out the question.

"For a short walk and the dogs kept going and I didn't know what to do and if they could find their way back... I'm glad you came along," sputtered Carmen. "I was scared we walked so far." She hoped she sounded contrite. Oh, God, let him believe her. Don't let him lose his temper and beat her and the dogs. Especially Goldie. Good old Goldie who just sat on the doorstep most of the time. Yet today seemed almost her old self, jumping and yelping, eager to go with Carmen down the driveway. And King, the silver-tipped German Shepherd, protective of his territory, yet reduced to a fraction of his fierceness around Rudy. The newest dog, Killer, a ferocious Doberman Pincher, at first snarled at Rudy which was a big mistake. Rudy named him Killer because he had been trained to attack on command. Rudy bent the dogs to his way and controlled them with a look or snap of his fingers. The dogs stayed near Carmen as if they could feel her fear of Rudy. Still, they obeyed him and only played when Rudy was away.

Rudy bolted from the pickup slamming the door and dashed to the trailer pulling off his jacket as he headed toward the tiny bathroom.

"Tomorrow I'll show you where you can walk. Well, here," Rudy walked to the kitchen window pulling Carmen along. "See that hump. You start there and walk all the way around the garden and no other place. You end up back there."

Carmen knew the hump was her baby's grave. Rudy is doing this on purpose, she thought. He is punishing her for the walk.

He never said that the hump was the baby's grave and she never saw him put the baby there. But she knew. Gazing out the kitchen window after Rudy had returned to the bathroom, Carmen wondered for the hundredth time if the baby had been a boy or girl. She never saw it on the day it was born, only heard a small cry and then she slept. She dreamed she held a small bundle wrapped in a soft blue blanket, she touched the baby's cheek, smooth soft skin, black hair like hers. Then she had awakened. She looked for the baby, the blue blanket. Nothing. Only the woman who had given her the shot.

"Where's the baby," a drowsy Carmen asked the woman standing at the sink washing dishes.

"There is no baby. You know that." The woman kept her eyes averted and continued washing dishes.

Yes, Carmen knew that. Knew there was no blue blanket. Nothing for a baby because the baby would not be there, alive or not. Carmen hoped it had been born dead.

Rudy showered and shaved, put on his "go to town" clothes, splashed after shave over his face and arms.

"I'm going out and we'll continue our talk where you can walk tomorrow but for now only where I told you," he snarled.

"Should I fix supper for you?" Carmen tentatively asked.

"I won't be home. You can open a can of soup for yourself and feed the dogs." And with that Rudy slammed out the door and roared away in the pickup.

The dogs watched him go. As soon as the pickup rounded a small curve and climbed over a knoll, Killer began running, his long legs bounding over the dirt road, chasing the pickup. Carmen called, "Come back, Killer," but he kept running. Carmen became frightened, Rudy would shoot Killer when he saw him following. But Killer didn't follow Rudy. He ran to where Carmen had hidden her bag. He carried the bag in his mouth and ran just as fast back to Carmen.

"Oh, Killer, you are wonderful." Carmen hugged the dog, all the dogs. They licked her arms, her face, snuggled against her. It was as if they conspired against Rudy in protecting her. They were her best friends. Her only friends. She never tried running away again ---- only dreamed about it.

"I'm ready," Carmen brought her thoughts back to Nate and the present. "Can we take the dogs?"

"No, but don't worry. They'll be okay. Dogs are smart. There just isn't room and......."

"I know." Carmen took a last look at the dogs and it seemed as if they were smiling. It can't be, she thought. Dogs don't smile. But it made her feel better. It seemed they were saying "Go!"

CHAPTER THREE

Carmen took a deep breath and willed her heart to calm down. It seemed to be thumping as loud as a bass drum. It felt like it would jump out of her skin. Nate leaned down and opened the car door for her. As she climbed in she glanced at Nate. She was scared: what if, what if, what if. The words pounding in her head.

"Don't be frightened Carmen, but keep down in the seat until we get a few miles away," Nate smiled at her while asking himself again why is he doing this? Why take her away, why let himself in for such tremendous problems? She is pregnant and under age. Is this kidnapping? Can he trust her not to run and call the cops?

She scooted down in the seat her stomach nearly reaching the window, "Okay?"

"Yeah, that's fine, it won't be for long," answered Nate.

At the end of the driveway Nate noticed a man he had seen earlier still working on a fence. Good thinking that Carmen was out of sight. Nate reached across her and waved to the man who stared at the car and sort of waved back, continuing to watch.

How to handle this? Nate asked himself, then decided to drive a couple of hundred feet, stop, back up a few yards, and then continue on. He hoped it gave the impression that Nate wanted to ask the man a question then decided against it. At any rate the man could not see Carmen nor Nate's face since he wore a wide-brimmed cowboy hat pulled down covering most of his face. A hat he planned to keep only another hour or so. He had learned the disguise lessons very well.

Later when the man described the car and driver, and he would, he could only say "Couldn't really see his face, but he seemed a friendly sort of fellow. No, couldn't really see the license, covered with mud though I don't know when he coulda got that, dry and all. Kind of car? White's all I know, coulda been a Pontiac or Buick, or one of them small Caddies, can't rightly say. Kind of average, both the car and the man."

Nate drove slowly through the small town. "Rudy's truck's still at 'The Bar.' Wouldn't you think they would've picked a better name for it?"

"Can he see us? Does he know this is your car?" Carmen's voice trembled.

"No, we're fine. No one's around so don't worry."

"Is it really called that? When he said he was going to the bar I thought he meant a bar." She gave a small giggle, the only time Nate had heard her give any type of humor.

"Nate?"

"Yes?"

"You could let me out anywhere. I could hitch a ride. It doesn't matter where I go."

"Look," Nate glanced at her, exasperated at this new notion, "I'm not letting you out anywhere. I told you where we're going. If you truly don't want to go with me then I'll take you to a shelter, probably find one in Atlanta. Then who knows what would happen to you. But, if you stay with me, that's it. I'll take care of you until you can really take care of yourself. Just say what."

"It's just that I don't know why you're doing this. I'm scared."

"You would be more scared if you got out and hoped for a ride. You can sit up now we're out of town."

"What if you get tired of having me around. Spending money, buying all the gas."

"Let's not think of the worst thing that may happen. Let's think good thoughts. You're away from Rudy, I have someone to ride with me, the sky is blue, and there's a McDonald's up ahead. Hungry?"

"Yes. All right, I'm with you as long as you want and thank you." Carmen began to cry. Tears of happiness, fear, apprehension, and panic. All kinds of emotions tumbling out with the tears.

Nate let her cry. He knew her mental state was under high pressure at the moment. How could the last two hours not affect her? Her emotions ran the gamut from excitement to fear. It would take awhile.

At last she said, "I'm okay now It's just that I wanted out of there so long. Forever. And I gave up hoping. I'll do anything for you. I'll kill for you, stand in front of a bullet..."

"How about for now try eating a Big Mac and fries? And maybe a chocolate shake?" Nate smiled as they pulled up to the Golden Arches drive-in window.

Nate liked watching the way she shoved the french fries into her mouth. It seemed very nice to do something for someone. Someone who deserved a better life.

"When we get to Atlanta, you get new clothes," he told her. Her eyes brightened. "You need something of everything and then we throw those things you have away."

"Okay." She leaned against the seat and closed her eyes. She only awakened when he parked the car next to the shopping mall entrance outside of Atlanta.

Shopping with Carmen was considerably different than shopping with Jaki. Carmen immediately went to the sale rack. Jaki never bought anything that had been marked down. Carmen glanced at the price tag and asked Nate, "This okay?"

"Buy three of everything, " Nate told her.

Not many maternity clothes made it to the sale racks, so they went to another section. They hurried, both knowing any public exposure could be dangerous. Rudy could have friends or at least acquaintances in many places. True, not many would have seen Carmen but why take chances? Nate doubted that Rudy would make law enforcement officers aware of Carmen's disappearance, but he knew Rudy would have a network of other information available, some well known to Nate.

"Carmen, I know you need more than clothes, but buying everything in one place is a mistake. Let's go to Burdines and get the rest." Nate looked around, totally cognizant of his surroundings. He did this without anyone realizing they were being observed. He felt safe, no one paid attention to them although there were some glances at Carmen's baggy jeans and shirt.

In Burdines he bought a small piece of luggage and a matching makeup case. Carmen's eyes glowed as she reached out to stroke the imitation leather handles. This kid hasn't had much of anything lately, Nate thought. Passing the cosmetic counter he noticed a free-gift with purchase promotion. He bought a bottle of Estée Lauder Beautiful cologne and got the free gift ---- a red cosmetic bag holding two lipsticks, eye makeup, hand lotion, a mirror, comb, and a small bottle of Pleasures cologne. You would have thought he had given Carmen the winning lotto ticket.

"We'll drive another two hours or so then stop for the night. Do you want to put on some different clothes?" asked Nate.

"Okay."

"How about when we stop for gas and we can get rid of your old stuff too."

"Okay." She chose a yellow-flowered top, or smock, she told Nate it is called, black pants that he was amused to see had a stretch panel over her stomach. Carmen laughed when she lifted the smock and showed him.

"I've never seen anything like that before," she said.

"Me neither. They're cute," Nate smiled at her. He put her old clothes in a nearby dumpster while she packed her new clothes in the luggage.

"We're on our way to Chattanooga, I have to make a small delivery there but we won't make it today. You look nice."

"Thank you," tears again. But not for long. "I can't tell you how much..."

"You don't have to, but tell me how did you get with Rudy in the first place?"

"It was such a dumb thing to do," Carmen began. "All of us in Cuba wanted to go to Miami. That was our dream, something we all dreamed about. Talked about it forever. Our goal."

"Miami fine. But why with Rudy?"

"It was all a nightmare and I don't think any of us had any idea what could happen."

"Tell me."

"Well, my brother was always a rebel. Anything to upset our parents. And they expected so much from him. More than from me. He even wanted to be called Carl instead of Carlos and Dad hated that. Anything American made my parents upset. Dad was Cuban and Mom came from Russia with grandma and grandpa, and all Communists. The Party was everything."

"When you say 'was', are your parents .... ?"

"Dead. Killed in a head-on car crash about four years ago on the way home from a Party meeting."

"So then you came to America?" asked Nate.

"Well, not then. It isn't easy to get here. Carl was fifteen and I was twelve when they died. Carl moved in with a friend's family and I lived with an aunt and uncle. They were members of the Party and strict. Mom and Aunt Lizel had both worked in an office of some kind. I never knew much about their jobs, but my aunt still worked when I lived with them."

"How come your grandparents left Russia?"

"To work for Castro and The Party. There were quite a few Russians around us. Carl hated them and I didn't know much. Carl went to this group of Freedom Fighters and everyday planned to get away from Cuba." Carmen told her story in a monotone as if it had happened to someone else.

"Carl even talked about going with the boat people, but no one would take him. Older guys, tough guys, guys that weren't too welcome in Cuba got to go. Then one day Al Renn, who used to be called Alberto Alverez, came back from Miami and set up a meeting to talk to some of his friends and show some slides of what Cubans in America were doing. Carl was going and I begged to go with him to hear Al tell us, I guess, what we all dreamed about," Carmen paused and looked out the car window remembering that day three years ago.

"Al told us how wonderful it was to live in Miami. Then he showed the slides. All the Cubans had jobs, three girls working in a restaurant, smiling; a fellow driving a new car, smiling; a model, smiling; a guy dressed in a snappy suit being boss of some blacks and white guys, smiling; a party on a beach all eatin' hamburgers and hot dogs --- American food --- and all smiling; a volleyball game on the beach, the players smiling. Everyone successful and happy. Everyone smiling. That's what we all wanted.

"Al told us we could all be like the people in the slides. He could take us there. Five thousand dollars each. Where could Carl get that kind of money. Where could I, where could anyone? But Carl did, got enough for him and most of mine. He stole from anyplace he could. I stole from my aunt and uncle. They always kept quite a lot of money hidden in the house but I knew where and I took it.

"Al took fifteen of us on his boat. It all looked like any other day with a group of friends out for a boat ride. Only we kept going on to one of the Keys --- I don't know the name of it --- never found out. We didn't know at that time that Al did that all the time. He grew up in Cuba, not far from us, and we thought he was helping us get a new life, the kind of life we dreamed about." Her voice became bitter, eyes filling with tears.

"A new life all right, we were sold right there on the dock."

"How did he manage that?" Nate asked, taking his dark glasses off and wiping them on his pant legs.

"Here, I'll clean them." Carmen reached for them and used the bottom of her smock to get the smudges off the lenses.

"We docked in this remote area, no town or anything, kind of at the end of a little one-lane road. There were three or four cars around and, as I knew later, Rudy's truck. But, we were all so happy. All laughing and smiling just like in the slides. Al had told us we couldn't bring anything with us, no clothes and stuff cause it's got to look like a day's outing he said. But who cared? We could buy new clothes with all the money we earned."

"Stop a sec," said Nate. "You have such good English and very little accent. How did you learn to talk like that?"

"All us Cubans know English from school and my parents, especially my mother, drilled it into us. 'Always know what the other person is saying' she told us. I know Russian too."

"Okay, go on with your story," Nate encouraged her.

"Well, Al gathered us in a line and we really thought people were choosing us for jobs, at least I did. And I guess they were, only not the kind of jobs we thought." Carmen brushed her hair back away from her face. She had taken the rubber band that had held her pony tail and now her hair tumbled down below her shoulders.

"Maria, Carolina, Lucia, and Alisha were chosen first. The man who chose them acted like the boss. He spoke first and said, 'Those four' and they were older, around twenty and beautiful. I knew they were headed for New York and television." Carmen sighed remembering the fateful day which had begun so promising.

"Didn't you have any kind of hint things weren't what you thought?" asked Nate, glancing at Carmen. Then his eyes flicked to the rear view mirror, the speedometer, and the gasoline gauge before peering ahead at the highway. An effective habit, always knowing his surroundings.

"Oh, no. We never dreamed it was anything other than what Al said. The guys all went with this couple, a man and woman and another fellow who only stood with them, never saying anything. They took three cars. The couple, around forty, I think, and I believed probably store owners, seemed in a hurry. The woman was nervous and I thought they needed someone in the store right away. Jobs already! I was left and Rudy said okay. I really think he wanted one of the pretty girls. Carl and Al were talking and now thinking back on it I wonder if Carl might have been working with Al. I don't know for sure, they were so friendly. Carl told me to go with Rudy and he would see me in a few days. He went in the last car with another man."

"Were you scared?"

"Oh, no, I was excited. On my way to a job and I believed to be living with a family that wanted me. When we drove a few miles, I asked Rudy where I would be working and he said, 'At my place. It's aways yet.' I kept watching for a nice restaurant or beautiful home."

"Georgia is quite aways from the Keys, how long did it take?" asked Nate.

"Most of the night, but Rudy pulled into an old road and we slept awhile. He had a gun pushed down behind the seat and I saw it when I curled up and put my hand back there to get comfortable. That scared me a little, but he seemed nice enough and stopped at Checkers and got food for us." Her voice was flat and emotionless.

"Sometime in the late afternoon we pulled up to the trailer. I thought he knew someone there or had some business," she paused a few minutes watching a smattering of raindrops on the windshield.

Nate turned on the windshield wipers and headlights. A sudden rainstorm, one of the south's rapid downpours, over in minutes but flooding streets and blocking drainage, was slowing Atlanta traffic to a crawling pace. The only dry spaces being under an overpass. Then as quickly as it had started, the rain stopped and traffic speeded up again.

"Boy, that was fierce," remarked Nate. " I know about rainstorms, but those drops came down in buckets. Look at that field, it's almost a lake." He gestured toward the window. Carmen shivered.

"Cold?" asked Nate.

"No. Only rain seems so cold and one day Rudy made me stay out in it all day and night."

"Why?"

"He said I wasn't warm towards him so he would show me what cold really is. I caught a cold and was sick over a week."

"Nice guy, huh!" Nate gave a disgusted shake of his head. "So things went on like that often?"

"Well, sometimes. When I finally realized the trailer was where I would be living I couldn't believe it. Al had shown us beautiful homes. I sat in the truck and Rudy said, 'Get out, we're home.'" Carmen stared out the window a few moments before she continued.

"The dogs walked up to the truck, Goldie was there then, and King. King wasn't much more than a puppy. His ears didn't stand up yet. Rudy scratched their ears and seemed to like them. When I climbed down from the cab the dogs sniffed at me so I petted them. Rudy said it looked like they liked me 'cause usually they snarled at strangers." Carmen raised her head and gazed at the headliner of the car.

"The trailer was a real dump and, and, almost as soon as we got inside Rudy jerked me into the bedroom taking off his clothes with one hand and pulling me with the other. I didn't know what was happening. I had never done that before. Rudy was heavy and rough, he slapped me when I cried and hit me real hard when he saw blood on the bed."

"I'll kill him," Nate's voice filled with anger.

"I wanted my brother and knew that Carl didn't know what was happening to me. Rudy said he bought me and I had to do what he said. I didn't know where I was. Rudy would go to the store but I didn't go anywhere. The only people that came had some kind of business with Rudy."

"You poor kid, how did you stand it?"

Carmen gave a bitter laugh. "I learned to watch for his moods. Fake my emotions. I kept the trailer spotless and cooked great meals. My aunt had taught me to cook and clean, so I knew how to do that. And I was very careful what I said. One time I said I liked broccoli so he made me eat it for two days. Only broccoli."

"What a jerk."

"He liked to control and I learned to let him. He was kind of proud of my cooking and the way I kept the trailer. So sometimes he would bring guys inside for coffee or once in awhile for lunch or..." she looked shyly at Nate, and Nate smiled at her. "I always wondered if I could slip in their car or truck, but I knew I couldn't. Rudy watched my every move. The guys, too.

"Once when one of the men kind of suggested the three of us could go to bed Rudy took him outside and, and... this is hard to talk about. I never had anyone to talk to before and now I can't stop, but that was horrible."

"Don't talk about it if you don't feel like it."

"It's okay. Only it's hard to think anyone could be so cruel."

"What did he do?" asked Nate.

"Rudy made him get in the snake house."

"Snake house? Where was that and what was it?"

"In back of the trailer. Rudy built it. Heavy screen on the front with a side door and an opening on the top that he could slide back and forth. The snakes couldn't get out. There were three or four poisonous snakes in there. About four feet long. He showed them to me and told me they could kill someone in just minutes. I don't know if that was true or not but they scared me."

"How did Rudy get the guy in there?" asked Nate.

"Through the side door. It was big enough. I think he has put other people in there, but I don't know. Just sometime someone would be there and then they wouldn't and Rudy would get rid of their car. He put the rats and mice through the side door too and sometimes he made me do it. I never acted afraid, I knew better. Kept the rats and mice in a special house outside too. He raised them for the snakes."

"Didn't the guy put up a fight or anything?"

"Rudy had a knife. A real sharp knife and he made King and Goldie stand there and the guy didn't know if they would attack or not. Anyway, Rudy put him in there and went to dig a grave. I knew what was happening. I heard the guy scream a few times and then nothing. After an hour or so, Rudy took him out of the snake house and shoved him in the grave. I don't know if he was dead, but I think he was. I hope he was."

"What kept the snakes from getting out the door?"

"He has kind of a net he puts in through the top with some mice and the snakes crawl in it. Then he slides a cover over it and the snakes can't get away. It's like a scoop."

"So how did he explain away a body and vehicle. Anyone show up to ask about him?"

"Rudy called someone and said the guy never showed and he acted kind of mad about it. But it was all an act. He cut the guy's truck in pieces and buried them too. There are lots of things buried in the yard." Carmen's thoughts went to her baby and tears welled up in her eyes. The hurt would never go away.

"What a creep. Did he ever threaten to put you in with the snakes?"

"No, he liked all the things I did for him I guess. And wanted me alive. But I knew he would if I displeased him very much or tried to get away. He will put both of us in there if he finds out we are together."

"He won't find out."

THE DECISION

Carmen was talked out. Nate knew he would learn more about her life in the days to come but for now he decided to stop in Dalton for the night. She seemed exhausted like a wound up doll whose battery had suddenly gone dead. He took the exit into Dalton and spotted a Holiday Inn with a close-by family restaurant. Nate would have preferred an Outback Steakhouse but he knew anyone knowing Rudy would never go into a family restaurant.

CHAPTER FOUR

Rudy

"Ready to come home with me now?" When Rudy looked at Lisa it could only be called lasciviously. His breath smelled of stale beer and fried catfish. Lisa leaned back in the booth getting a few more inches away from Rudy and that horrid smell. He needed a bath she thought. And though she hated the smell of beer, he had bought her plates of catfish and bottles of wine all afternoon. But, did she need to put out for that?

"I can't, I have to take care of my mother, besides you have someone there."

"She don't count. How do you know about her anyway?"

"I heard." Lisa kept her eyes on her wine glass, then reached for the bottle. It was almost empty but if she could keep him interested a little longer he would buy another one.

"Who from?" Rudy put his hand on the bottle keeping it from Lisa. What a lush but he didn't care. She had a great body even if her face looked haggard and her eyes listless. She had been around the block a time or two he guessed. Now it was time for him.

"Audrey, the girl who used to work here. She's gone now. She told me you had a little Cuban up there."

"So. She's my housekeeper and cook."

"Audrey said she was pregnant."

"What difference does that make to you. We play house once in awhile," Rudy laughed, his hand reaching across the table to stroke Lisa's hair. He liked long blonde hair although he could tell Lisa's hadn't been blonde many days.

"I still can't. My mother expects me home and she needs care."

"Your mama's caretaker. Who's taking care of her now?" Rudy sneered. "Come on, I got you all that catfish and wine, you owe me." He pulled her up from the booth.

"No, I have a boyfriend," she looked towards the bartender who was listening but didn't take the bait. No one tangled with Rudy. Lisa pulled away, "I don't want to go with you."

Rudy stared at her for a long time. "You tramp, you'll pay for this. Sure I have someone at home and she never tells me no. But, I won't forget this and you won't either." He sauntered to the bar, "I'll pay for my beer and the catfish I ate. Give her the bill for the rest."

"I don't have any money. You said order anything I want. You said that when I first sat down. You did." Lisa looked at the two wine bottles --- expensive wine --- and plates of fried catfish and fries. At least a hundred dollars. She didn't have a penny.

"Call your mama and get your allowance, cunt." Rudy slammed a ten on the counter and walked out. His truck tires sprayed gravel on nearby cars and the walkway as he tore out of the parking lot.

"Don't worry about it Lisa. I'll put it on your tab or who knows maybe you'll find another way to pay." Jesse the bartender liked long blonde hair too. "Feel sorry for the little gal up there. Rudy's in one of his foul moods."

"Isn't he always," Lisa smiled at Jesse. She knew, as everyone knows, that there is no such thing as a free lunch. She sat on a bar stool, put a cigarette in her mouth and held her face up to Jesse for a light. Her reflection came back from the mirror. My God, she thought, I'm only twenty-five and look forty-five. It's true what they say --- the kind of life you lead shows on your face. Well, maybe she would run a bar tab someday, but for now let's pay another way. Jesse smiled back at her.

"Carmen, Carmen, where are you?" Rudy shouted barreling into the trailer door. Had she been there she would have heard his truck come to a screeching stop scattering gravel and causing the dogs to jump out of the way. Other times he made the dogs wait at the head of the driveway until he came to a stop and missing them by only a few inches, "To teach them a lesson, they wait for me and don't move 'til I say so." Today Rudy was like a madman tearing up the road to the trailer.

"Carmen get in here I'm telling you," his voice raging and angry. He pushed a chair over, hit his leg on the table which made him more furious. "Carmen!" Where is she? She's always here. He searched the trailer. A walk? He stormed outside walking around the trailer shouting, "Carmen, Carmen." He walked thirty or more yards into the woods, behind and to the left of the trailer. Not here. He called her name over and over becoming concerned. After all, she is pregnant. What if she had dropped the kid someplace? She had never been away before. He retraced his steps back to the trailer and searched more completely, however standing at one end it was easy to see the entire length. She is not in the trailer, he even looked under the bed, though in her pregnant condition she couldn't have fit under it anyway.

Rudy stood in the middle of the trailer pondering Carmen's whereabouts. Searching the closet he found no clothes missing. Everything seemed to be in place in the built-in chest of drawers. Neatly folded, God she is so picky about order he thought. She couldn't be far and what is it with the dogs anyway? They just stand at the doorway looking at him. Even Demon, the three-month-old pit bull who hadn't learned to be as fierce as the other two and stayed by his pen most of the time, took up the sentry at the door. And their look. Rudy knew it couldn't be true but they seemed to be smirking. Joyful almost.

Deciding to search the woods again Rudy took a large powerful flashlight and a machete to trudge further through the thick underbrush cutting away a small trail. After two hours in the pitch black pine woods and dropping his flashlight several times, finally losing it, he gave up the search. He couldn't see beyond a foot in front of his face and further searching in the dark was useless.

Besides he was soaked. He didn't remember it raining this much. Lisa had been quite a distraction. He grew angry at her all over again. The tart! The woods were like walking through a rain forest. Coming back into the trailer he tracked in water and then noticed the puddles he had left earlier. No matter, Carmen would clean it and wouldn't say a word about his carelessness. She never did. She had learned her lessons well. But where is she?

Should he call the hospital? It's a twenty mile ride so how could she get there? He knew the only cab in town had stayed put all afternoon. At least the driver had spent the time in The Bar. In fact, off and on near Rudy's booth with another of the town's "ladies." And Rudy knew any call would be talked about anyway. No, Carmen did not take the cab. She had no money for cab fare anyway, he muttered to himself.

He showered and stood under the hot water a long time. He had been chilled, he thought, to the bone, and he was hungry. This is not like Carmen at all, he grumbled. Her job is to be here. Fix his supper. Still he felt a growing apprehension. Something gnawed at his insides. Tomorrow he would take the dogs and search the woods again. No way could he call the cops. Neither he nor his property could stand the scrutiny of the law. He sprawled on the bed exhausted after the fruitless search. He slept fitfully through most of the night.

At dawn he opened his eyes, reached across the bed and immediately sat up remembering that she is not there. He shivered. The fire had gone out in the corner wood-burning stove and the trailer was cold. Carmen always banked the fire before going to bed to keep the chill away. Another job she had not done. The trailer seemed unusually damp. Another rain storm had passed through during the night and the sun was two hours away from bringing in warming rays. Later in the day the trailer would grow hot and humid, the air still and heavy. But, nights were cold now and a small glow from the stove kept it cozy. He needed hot coffee. She always brought him a cup of coffee first thing in the morning. Cuban coffee, his only acknowledgment of her past.

He pulled on a pair of jeans and sweat shirt, grabbed a pair of socks and reached on the closet shelf for dry shoes.

The shoes he had worn the day before were still wet and soggy. His shoes were on the right side of the top shelf. Carmen kept the trailer so neat and clean. Everything had a place.

Hey! Her bag, that ugly worn out bag she loved. It's gone! She kept it on the same shelf as his shoes. If she went for a walk she wouldn't have taken the bag. What else is missing? What did he miss last night in his frantic search? He pulled her clothes off hangers and emptied the chest of drawers, throwing the contents on the bed. So few. Lucky she stayed pregnant most of the time. She didn't have much to wear. The clothes were all there. All except that old shirt of his she wore everyday and an old pair of his pants --- the only things that fit her now.

But! She kept a photo album on the same shelf and it is not here. The album contained shots of her family and a little kitten Carmen held. Her treasures. He had laughed when she showed him the snapshots, still he knew she often looked at them, an expression on her face hard to read. So, he determined that she did not just wander away. Deliberate. She wanted to leave him. Rudy walked outside.

"Where's Carmen?" Rudy shouted at the dogs, "find her!" The dogs sat near the steps watching Rudy. They know something, he thought. He wanted to beat them; wanted to put Carmen in the snake house; and he would when he found her and he definitely would find her. No one took anything from him. Plenty of guys could testify to that and some women too. Calm down he told himself. Think. Don't let anger cloud judgment. She left someway. She couldn't get far walking. He looked for tire tracks but of course the rain had taken care of those if there had been any. Even his truck tracks were gone, covered by puddles of water or lost through rain soaked gravel. Who came up here anyway. Be rational about all this. Think smart.

Back into the trailer Rudy calmly made coffee, bacon and eggs. He burned a few small pieces of wood in the stove to get warm and as he warmed his hands around the mug of hot coffee he pondered his actions. First he contacted a source in Miami. Check out her brother, although Carl must know at this point the trip from Cuba had not been what the "picnickers" first thought that they would find in the U.S. Rudy learned that Carl had been sent to Pittsburgh to work at robbing jewelry stores; that Carmen had not contacted any of the "picnickers" in Miami; and if and when she did Rudy would be contacted immediately. Then he called the power company. Had the meter man given her a ride? Not scheduled to be in Rudy's area for another two weeks. Somehow she had made it to the main road and then hitched a ride. A very remote chance since there was only one dwelling further along the dead-end road. And, wait! The fellow working on the fence across from Rudy's driveway. He must have helped her. "I'll kill him!" Rudy shouted jumping from his chair, grabbing the truck keys, and slamming out the door. The wheels spun and splashed muddy water as he recklessly drove down the driveway. The dogs only sat and watched. At least the rain had stopped.

Rudy stopped his truck with a jerk and lucky for the neighbor man a small drainage ditch separated the road from his fence. Rudy could have ran right into him.

"Where's Carmen?" Rudy yelled getting out of his truck and slamming the door. "Where have you got her?"

"Who, what are you talking about?" The man stayed on his side of the fence. He knew the reputation of the man up the hill. Rudy had not actually done anything to frighten anyone, but his looks, his size, his manner spoke volumes.

"Don't play dumb. It had to be you, you're the only one around." Rudy demanded an answer.

"Well, neighbor, let's back up a little. I'm Russell Ward and I know you only as a neighbor. I have no idea who or what Carmen is but I'll be glad to help you if I can."

"Carmen is my housekeeper and she's gone. I have every reason to believe you helped her. Took her somewhere. To your house maybe and I'm gonna find out and when I do you will never see the light........"

"Whoa, whoa there," Russell interrupted, "I ain't took no one no place. You got your facts all wrong."

"Mr. Ward," Rudy sneered, "someone came to my place and helped Carmen get away. I think it was you."

"I'd like to know your name so's we could talk together a little better." Russell tightened his hand on his hammer.

30

He knew his slight, five-foot eight inch frame would be no match for the angry big man who, he guessed, was at least twenty years younger so friendliness must prevail. Still his hands shook with fear and his knees felt as if they might crumble any moment. Like walking over a high bridge and looking far down below at tumultuous water.

Rudy stared at Russell. He was a master at reading people and knew Russell told the truth. He did not help Carmen. "Were you working here all day yesterday?"

"Came about ten, left around four-thirty, five, wanted to finish this part but couldn't. The rain kept me in the pickup the good part of an hour so I came back early this morning," Russell began to relax.

"Did you see anyone going up my drive?"

"Well, yes I did. A fellow in a white car went up, I don't think anyone was home cause he came back down in ten, fifteen minutes."

"What time?"

"Around one. I just finished my sandwich and started back to work."

"Did he have anyone with him when he went up?"

"Not that I noticed."

"How about when he came back down?"

"No, don't think so, course I couldn't see very well. Just got a glimpse but I would say no."

"What'd he look like?" Rudy questioned Russell.

"Oh, I'd say kind of average looking, he wore a cowboy hat pulled kind of over his eyes, but his hair wasn't too light, not too dark, he wore dark glasses, not the fancy ones, and he looked to be around 30, 35, I'd guess. Nothing special that I could see."

"Kind of car did he have?"

When Russell described what he had seen, Rudy gave a disgusted shrug. Carmen could be far away by now. Except why? Why would anyone bother with her. She knew no one. It must have been a chance meeting. Someone with the wrong house. Still Russell had said that the man had been alone. Or was he? Carmen could have hid. Maybe in the trunk or crouched down. She's small, except her stomach. But, why would anyone bother he asked himself again. Still someone had. Russell watched as Rudy backed his truck around and drove back up his driveway. Rudy never told Russell his name. Strange fellow, Russell mused. Very strange. Wouldn't want to be in the shoes of whoever took Carmen.

Rudy now had a plan. He needed to learn the whereabouts of anyone who had delivered "packages" to him the past three years. He counted the "garden spots." Twenty-four. Most had been delivered by the same person. He counted once again and remembered five different drivers. It had to be one of the drivers. And why aren't the dogs upset? They followed Carmen like a shadow. He had many questions and he would get answers.

Rudy dialed Vinnie's number in New York. And the answers came!

CHAPTER FIVE

"Been in a motel before?" Nate asked Carmen. He watched her walk around the rooms touching the towels, opening the door of the small refrigerator, straightening the pictures on the wall above the two beds. A generic print showing a narrow rippling river tumbling over rocks to a small pool below, and the other snow-capped mountains with tall evergreen trees. Carmen liked the prints.

"Nope, never have." Carmen answered.

"Ever seen snow?"

"Nope," she continued inspecting the room. "Nate, look, there are small bottles of shampoo and hand lotion. Look at these," She held the small samples in her hands as if they contained the drink of the gods. Her eyes shone with honest pleasure he had rarely seen. He laughed. The joy of seeing someone's happiness at such a little thing made him both pleased at his unselfish act of rescuing her and sad that she had been in that perilous situation in the first place. Then his thoughts grew serious. What is he in for? On a whim he is now responsible for her well-being and there's soon to be a baby. Oh, God.

"Let's go eat then you can use the stuff in all those pretty bottles." Nate put his luggage on a chair and run his fingers through his hair. He was hungry. Still he wondered about his actions in bringing her along. Everytime the questions entered his mind he had the same answer. She needed him. And try as he may to tell himself to find a home somewhere besides with him, he could not. The truth is, he told himself, I want her with me. It made him feel useful and it gave his ego a terrific boost to see her happiness and know he provided it. Never had he possessed such control over another and it gave him a heady feeling. He liked that.

Carmen ordered the cheapest meal on the menu. "You don't have to do that. Order what you like," Nate told her.

"You're spending so much money on me as it is. I want to be careful." She raised her eyes to his, somber, unsmiling, pleading for him to understand how she appreciated his actions and in some way wanted to be less of a burden.

"It's okay, Carmen. Money is not a problem." And it wasn't. Nate would replenish his supply in Chattanooga, one of his scheduled stops, just as he had in Valdosta. Besides he had left Miami with a large amount of cash thinking of Jaki's spending habits. But, as his thoughts strayed once again to Jaki's rejection, he wondered if she had ever ordered meatloaf in a restaurant.

Carmen showered, shampooed her hair, used the body lotion just like any other teenager would do. She's such a kid, Nate thought. Maybe someday all of Rudy's horrid actions will be erased from her mind. He thumbed through the local newspaper, placed free in each room he guessed. Read a pamphlet on area tourist activities and waited his turn to shower. It had been a tiring day, an unforgettable day. A day that he would question his minute decision for years to come.

"Nate," Carmen's voice trembled, "You don't have to stay in that bed," she paused, "I know I don't look so good right now but I know how to do lots of things." She held her breath. It seemed like she had been holding her breath for hours, trying to build up nerve to offer herself to Nate. She was sure Nate wouldn't be as brutal as Rudy, maybe even tender. No matter, though, she had an obligation to Nate. She owed him big time. She knew that and was willing to pay. Pay the way Rudy had taught her.

Nate pulled on his walking shorts and crossed the room to Carmen's bed. "Carmen, don't say that and don't feel that way. You don't ever have to sleep with anyone again unless it's your choice," Nate took her small hand in his and felt her tremble. He smiled at the Mickey Mouse gown she wore. The other one she had chosen pictured

Donald Duck, he remembered. "I didn't bring you along for a sleeping partner. I will never be coming to your bed."

"I owe you so much, " even though her voice was little more than a whisper, her eyes did not meet his and the tenseness in her body gave small jerks of fright. She clenched her hand over his and he could feel stiffness, the anxiety and apprehension. Pure fear emitting from her.

"Oh, Carmen, don't be frightened of me. You're like a little sister to me and don't ask me to explain it, I can't. I just know I'll take care of you," Nate unwound her fingers from his hand, stroked her slightly damp lemon scented hair, and gently said, "Go to sleep now, we have another long day tomorrow and the further we get from Georgia the better it will be." He crawled back into the other bed but it was at least an hour before he closed his eyes.

Chattanooga, a city of approximately 160,000, just across the Georgia border, boasted some of Tennessee's finest museums and lovely southern mansions, several beautiful parks along the Tennessee River and a variety of tourist attractions. But for Nate, he only had to locate a specific flower shop and deliver another beautifully decorated package.

"Carmen, it's better if you aren't with me when I make this stop so I'll leave you at the Chattanooga Choo Choo park...."

"The what?"

Nate smiled, "I read about it in the tourist stuff at the motel and it's close by. There really is a train you can ride on."

"A kid's train?" Carmen asked, "Choo Choo."

"Naw, a real one, people can even rent a car for the night. Sounds fun. I'm not sure but I think I remember my grandma singing a song about it. She said when she was growing up there were lots of silly songs. Anyway, you'll be okay. I'll only be gone a couple of hours tops and we'll pick out a meeting place."

"Okay."

After parking the car Nate and Carmen walked to the train area. Definitely set up for tourists he thought. And a pretty spot for spending a few hours. He took out his wallet and gave Carmen three twenty dollar bills and a ten.

"You can ride the train and shop a little. If you get hungry there's a hot-dog stand or other eating places."

"People seem to be having fun." She looked around and her eyes brightened when she observed people getting off the train.

"See the bench under that tree over there?" Nate asked.

"Where that old couple are sitting?"

"Yeah, well, I'll meet you there. Now don't worry, I'm not sure how long I'll be gone for sure but according to my map the place isn't far."

"What do you have to do? Could I help?"

"No, it's something I have to do for Vinnie. It won't take long." Nate was anxious to be on his way. Delivering "packages" always made him nervous. He would be very happy when they were all out of his car.

"Who's Vinnie?" Carmen was puzzled. Nate had always seemed so open with her and now he seemed to be hiding something and very much in a hurry to be gone.

"Little girl, you don't need to know right now, but, later when I come back I'll fill you in on a few things. Now go have some fun, but listen, don't tell anyone your real name or what you're doing here. Don't mention me at all. Okay?"

"I know, I'll be careful. You'll come back though, won't you?"

"Of course I will," he flicked his finger under her chin, "we have big plans." As Nate walked back to the car he thought why not keep going. Someone could take her to a help house or some place. She's away from Rudy, that's all he intended to do wasn't it? Get her away. She really isn't his responsibility is she? He turned and looked back. She stood where he had left her. Her eyes held a forlorn and apprehensive expression. She raised her hand and gave a small wave. She's scared Nate thought. She isn't sure whether or not he will come back. He made a circle with his thumb and forefinger ----- the universal sign that all is okay. And once again he knew he was bound to her because he wanted to be. His minute decision to rescue her had changed his life forever.

The owner of the flower shop, located on a side street and nearly lost between two larger buildings, made a token attempt at a legitimate business. Nate could see, though, that the glass counters had not been dusted for weeks and several vases held drooping blossoms. The girl behind the counter had apparently just painted her finger-nails since she waved her hand in the air and blew on her blood-red nails.

"Can I help you-a?" The girl had a thick southern accent, "suh?"

"Mr. Rose," Rose? Couldn't he have chosen another name! Rose from the flower shop. Kind of silly. "Where do I find him, he's expecting me."

"Through that door-or." She made two syllables out of door---a way of speaking he had found intriguing when he first arrived in the south ---- and now disliked intensely. He thought it was all a put-on anyway. Kind of a "poor little helpless me" attitude. He believed the girls from the south were anything but helpless. She waved her hand toward the back of the shop still blowing on her fingers.

Nate deliberately dragged his hand along the glass counter leaving imprints of his fingers which he hoped would embarrass the girl enough to clean the shop. He doubted that she would, though, doesn't want to mess up those fingernails. Not her job, I'm not here to clean, what dust? He could imagine any excuse she would give.

Rose, seated at an over-size desk, puffed away on a cigar. No wonder the flowers were wilting Nate mused. The buttons on Rose's shirt , a bright blue with yellow plumerias boldly printed around the bottom, strained to hold together. He obviously wore a hair piece which was styled, if you could call it that, straight down to his ears and was black as coal. His jowls hung in clumps of fat and his face, especially his nose, had little red veins prominently bringing attention to a favorite activity, or so it seemed to Nate.

Rose blew a cloud of smoke in Nate's direction, "Come in and take the load off," he gestured toward an overstuffed chair. All the furniture must be made to hold enormous weight if Rose was an example.

Nate glanced around the room. There were several tall brass sculptures of Civil War heroes, the most prominent being Jefferson Davis, who had been president of the Confederacy during the war. Two small flags were anchored to a pedestal set next to the desk. The Tennessee state flag --- red with a blue edge and a blue circle in the middle displaying three white stars, and the unmistakable Rebel flag. A flag that either brought strong feelings of "those damn Yankees" or an embarrassment that slavery was ever a part of the United States. Nate believed many in the south still fought the war and there were some who thought the south had won. They would never give equal rights to blacks which, of course, many called "niggers."

Seeing a Rebel flag always made Nate uncomfortable; still it gave him knowledge on what to expect. The bigotry and prejudice of the rebels made him choose his words and actions carefully. After all, he wasn't there to right a wrong or take a stand on any issue. A two-faced attitude to be sure, but one that allowed him to get along and get the job done.

As Rose reached for his "gift" he nodded his head towards the front of the shop," What do ya think of my little squeeze out there? Cute huh?"

Nate, grinning, gave the older man a conspiring look and with a wink said, "Good taste."

"Yeah, she's not much for selling flowers but that wasn't what I hired her for anyway," Rose laughed and saliva rolled down his chin. What a pig, thought Nate. But he kept silent seemingly to admire the Civil War mementos.

"What do you think of my men?" Rose asked, his hand sweeping around the room indicating the sculptures. "Jefferson Davis is my favorite. Those soldiers were real men, real heroes. Someday everyone will know that."

"The workmanship is awesome," Nate did the obligatory tour of the room stopping at each sculpture ostensibly showing his appreciation. The artist's work was indeed awesome, he hadn't lied about that, but being from the west coast of California he didn't think the men fighting for the south were heroes.

"This little package here will make my life perk up," Rose fingered the small box Nate had given to him. "Yesseree ole Vinnie always comes through." Rose's eyes grew bright and calculating. Nate wondered who Rose planned to kill, not that it mattered to him, he wouldn't be around. He knew one drop on someone's skin would bring certain death within a six-month period and leave no traces as to the cause. Some would say a sudden heart attack, blood clot, but most would say, "Just his or her time I guess." And since there would be no apparent foul play involved no one would question a death that seemed so unfortunate. Poor, poor, man or woman. So sad for the family and such a fine citizen. Nate brought his thoughts back to the present and realized that he had been staring at the sculpture of Robert E. Lee.

"I can tell you're a friend of the south and Lee was a really great man, really great. Don't come any better." Nate had apparently impressed Rose. If he only knew, Nate thought.

"Better go, got a lot of driving yet today." Nate edged toward the door feeling just a trifle sick to his stomach. The cigar smoke, maybe, but more likely the atmosphere. He hated racism even though he had been forced to participate on many "occasions."

"Say good-bye to my squeeze. She likes attention, only don't give her too much. Wouldn't want any hard feelings," Rose laughed at his double entendre.

"Don't have time to linger. Maybe will meet you again someday," Nate said hoping that would never happen.

"Can't say, maybe we will. I'm certainly glad we met today," Rose patted the box and Nate knew Rose would be sending Vinnie a million dollars for the contents. A million dollars and Nate had two more to deliver. His share for the deliveries was fifty thousand available when he reached L.A. The "squeeze" gave him a big smile with an invitation in her eyes.

"Anything else I can help you with? Some flowers for your lady or anything?" She sat on a stool her long legs crossed showing off golden tan thighs. Her tight mini-skirt had inched up in a bunch and he guessed flowers were not all she sold.

Nate stopped at a vase of yellow roses. Carmen. Maybe she would like a bouquet.

"Those are nice and only fifty dollars," the girl sauntered over to Nate her perfume overpowering any scent of the flowers.

What is he thinking? Nate chided himself, no one should know about Carmen. No one. "I'm only traveling through, thought my mother may like some roses, but now I remember they are traveling." Another lie.

"Well," she drawled, "anything I can do for you?" Her meaning left no doubt.

Somehow Nate could feel Rose's eyes on him. A one-way window perhaps. Not that he even liked the girl but her actions and any response on his part and he may have a drop from the package on his skin. And the girl isn't too bright either Nate thought. Rose knew what she was doing. Nate had a feeling that she may develop some terrible illness. Poor, poor girl, and so sad for the family and such a good worker. So sad.

Nate found Carmen in almost the same place that he had left her---sitting on a bench under a tree he thought maybe a cypress. He stood twenty or so yards away from her watching her observing several small children practicing somersaults. One little boy, Nate thought two years old tops, couldn't make it all the way over and the adults watching as well as the children laughed. The little boy liked the attention and his movements became more exaggerated, a little clown. Carmen watched, no laughter and as Nate drew closer he saw a tear drop. She wiped her eyes and lifted her face to the sky perhaps asking God to protect her unborn child and maybe asking if her other child, the one she never knew, was an angel in heaven. There was such sadness in her eyes it seemed her heart must be breaking. Then a little girl tumbled Carmen's way and bumped her leg on the bench. The little girl began to cry. Carmen reached down to help the small child and just as quickly the crying stopped and the child smiled at Carmen. She smiled back and the little girl reached her arms up to be held. Instant trust. That's what it is, Nate told himself. Exactly. He had questioned why he had stopped for her, why he knew he would care for her. He knew that moment in the park that she emitted instant trust to others and received the same emotions from them.

The little girl's mother came for her and she, too, smiled acknowledging Carmen's help. Nate had seen mothers or caretakers snatch their child away when a stranger spoke to them or reached to touch the child. And well they should Nate thought. Too many times the outreach was not done in a friendly or helpful manner. Carmen, though, was like a beacon, showing the way to safety like the beam in the sky guiding an airplane. Some people had it, some people didn't and it showed in the eyes.

In that minute Nate knew that Rudy would look for Carmen. Rudy would never let her go. Why should he? Carmen only left to protect her baby. Mother-love. Perhaps the strongest emotion in the world. If not for her baby Carmen's life would revolve around Rudy. She had made a bargain. She kept her word.

When Nate approached Carmen the relief in the eyes spoke volumes. So she had been worried that he may not return. And why not? He knew his lifestyle the past few years had taken away any instant trust from his eyes, if there had been any in the first place. You can not steal from co-workers, lie to friends, and manipulate others without it making some kind of an imprint on your personality. Without it showing in your eyes. Still he would not, could not lie to Carmen or be dishonest to her in anyway. Did he love her? In a way perhaps. There was no lust, no sexual desire. But like the feeling he had for his older sister. He would do anything for Kathy, and she for him. No questions. Just a loyalty that if one or the other asked then okay. Hadn't Kathy gone to bat for him many times when his parents questioned his activities? And yes, even scolded him when he needed it. His very best friend. Carmen was like a little sister to him. The same loyalty was there, on both sides it seemed.

"Come on squirt, let's go," Nate took her hand gently pulling her up from the bench. "Have fun?"

"Yes, I'm so glad to see you." She began to sob, then smiled. There it is again. Trust.

"Did you think I wouldn't be back?" Nate asked.

"I did for awhile. Cause I'm a burden to you that you don't need. Common sense tells me that," she explained. "But then somehow that feeling went away and I knew you would come for me. All of a sudden I knew."

Only his sister had believed so strongly in him. And he hadn't seen her for five years.

CHAPTER SIX

The drive to Houston took three days and during that time Nate and Carmen talked about their earlier lives, learning their likes and dislikes just as strangers who become friends do.

Carmen's early childhood paralleled most other youngsters her age except her parents pushed education. Especially her mother. Getting less than perfect marks was not acceptable. Carmen excelled in all her subjects. Carlos, though quite intelligent, baited their parents by doing poorly in a particular subject, then the next month or so he would excel in that area and nearly fail in another. A game with him. Carmen had no such animosity toward their parents but she adored her older brother and backed his every idea. She followed him around like a puppy. Not that Carlos was a bad person, he thought he knew more than he actually did, a typical teenager, and he acted that way.

Carlos wanted the good life in Miami or what he perceived the good life to be. And when he made arrangements to leave Cuba he had no idea about the life Carmen would be forced to live. He had no idea even where she had been taken. He worried but no one knew anything or so they said. He asked around to no avail. Their lives became a turn around of the way they had lived while growing up. Neither knew where the other had been taken.

Nate told Carmen about his years on the cruise ship.

"I was the bartender in charge of the two lounges. And I wanted more money than I earned so I began stealing tips and watering drinks."

"How could you do that? I thought everything was paid by a card or something. I read that someplace," asked Carmen.

"It is, only on our ship we negotiated having the bars separate. Mostly when passengers leave the ship they tip fifty dollars or so and after it's divided up we are lucky to get fifty cents. So having the bar separate we got more tips."

"And you kept them?"

"Not all, look, I'm not proud of it, but we all looked for ways to make extra money."

"I'm not judging you, I think you are wonderful," Carmen smiled.

Nate glanced at her, "I'm not wonderful but that's how it was."

"How do you water drinks?"

"Well, each bottle is supposed to make a certain number of drinks. Say, twenty-five. I had a couple of bottles that I would take enough liquor to make five drinks, fill the first bottle with water or a cheap brand, and have an extra bottle or two to sell. I could keep the profit from the bottles I made. I pocketed two or three hundred dollars a day from that."

"Wow!"

"Then Richard came on board and saw what I was doing..."

"Didn't you hide what you were doing? I would think that anyone could see what you were doing was wrong."

"Oh sure, but he is a con man himself and you know what they say that it takes one to know one."

"Did he report you?" Carmen asked, showing genuine concern.

"No, he asked me to do some things for him."

"Like what?"

"Find out the rich, very rich women on board and point them out to him. So I did."

"How did you know who was rich?"

"You know, it's easy to tell. Look at their jewelry, go through their stuff in their cabins. Look at their passports. See where they have traveled. Checkbooks. Passengers are so careless they don't pay attention to what they leave around and we can get in any cabin.

Course a few we knew from seeing them before. Believe me we know who has money and who doesn't. On a cruise ship money people make a huge statement. Look at me. Look at my jewels. Look at how much money I have. They all show what they have."

"So, did you find one for him?"

"Yeah, a very rich one. Stockholder in the ship line. In fact, one of the owners. The captain had briefed us that she would be on board. I guess they were old friends."

"So, what happened?"

"Richard met her, pursued her but in such a way she was completely fooled. In fact, we all were. He seemed to really care about her and he was, oh, so smooth. I wanted to be just like him."

"Oh, no, you couldn't be dishonest like that!" Carmen said.

Nate gave a short laugh, "No, not much."

"But, not that bad," Carmen the optimist.

"Anyway, they got married when the ship reached Kauai. Richard planned it all. He was quite the manipulator. Only we were all so happy for them. Except the captain. He didn't seem to like Richard and now, I wish I had never had any part of it. But at that time everything was cool."

"What happened. How did you decide to move to Florida?"

"Richard asked if I wanted to make more money, have a prestige job. So I jumped at the chance. And he taught me very well. Only I didn't like all the things I had to do. Watering drinks and stealing tips is one thing but........."

"What did you do?"

"You saw what I did when I came to the trailer that day. That whole place is filled with dead bodies isn't it?"

"I think so. I don't know who they are. Three or four men would bring something wrapped in black plastic and Rudy would dig another hole and in it would go . He called them his mound gardens and he actually planted vegetables on top and used the black plastic to cover piles of wood for the stoves. He laughed about it. A big fun time for him. It made me sick."

They were silent for awhile, reflecting that they had both wanted more then they should have and it had changed their lives forever. Nate, though, thought Carmen an innocent victim. Why wouldn't she have trusted her brother to make life better for her. Nate couldn't be that generous with himself. He knew he had been greedy and willing to do anything to be like Richard. At first anyway.

"How come you don't have a wife or girlfriend or do you?" Carmen asked.

"Oh, I did. A girlfriend I thought would be my wife. She worked in the organization too, we both wanted out, I thought. But then I found out Richard was her lover and used his wife's money to buy terrific things for Jaki and she didn't want to leave all that."

"Still love her?" Carmen didn't want to hear the answer; still she had to ask. She had to know.

"No, not really. I still see her in my thoughts sometime. The way she was at first but then I see her the way she is and no, I don't love her anymore." Nate pursed his lips and his hands tightened on the steering wheel. Bitterness shone in his eyes. "She is just as manipulative as Richard. They deserve each other. The only person that didn't deserve it is Marian, the woman he met on the ship. She is a very nice lady."

"Does she know about Jaki?"

"Yeah, but he can convince her it's nothing. She believes whatever he says. When she got it out of me that he knew all along that she was rich, she didn't even say anything then. I know she still believes in him."

"Too bad, I guess." Carmen stayed silent after that for several miles. Then, "Will you tell me what you are taking to Houston and what you left in Chattanooga?"

Nate glanced at her. Hadn't he promised himself he would be truthful with her. Still he had vowed to protect her as well.

"Carmen, it's better you don't know. It's not that I don't trust you, only I don't want you involved in this at all. I'm part of the same organization that Rudy is in and I have to do certain things but it's better for you....."

"If you don't want to be in it then just quit."

"I can't. I just can't. And it may be better in L.A. I don't know what I'll be doing, but I'll keep you and the baby safe."

45

A promise he would not be able to keep.

Carmen learned that Nate had grown up in southern California. Went to Mira Mesa high school, attended Miramar Community College less than a year, drifted around the California beaches a couple of years surfing all day long, before getting a job with the cruise line. His dad had managed a bank, one that had been robbed so many times that finally security guards were placed outside and thick bulletproof windows installed to protect the tellers. He had made stock purchases from the time he was a young man so now he and Nate's mother lived an enjoyable lifestyle in Palm Springs. An area his mother always aspired to live in.

Nate's mother was a "club woman." Bridge every Wednesday afternoon, volunteer on political campaigns when the candidate oozed wealth. A little bit of a snob. She had always dreamed of a home in La Jolla even though the Mira Mesa home ranked as one of the nicest around and had a view of the mountains. Now she liked having a home with a Palm Springs address even though it was actually a villa in a planned community.

Nate drifted away from his parents and had not seen them for the same five years he had not seen Kathy. He was not at all sure they would like Carmen. Especially his mother.

And he didn't plan to keep Carmen with him forever; only find a safe place for her far away from Rudy. There are plenty of places around L.A. He could send money or she could get a job in one of those places where she could live with the baby. He felt good about himself ---- providing a great life for her. He glanced at her and she had her head back on the seat with her eyes closed.

CHAPTER SEVEN

Houston --- hot, dry, flat. Nate told himself that he would never live here. Buildings sprawling and really as he drove into the city, the streets weren't all that clean. Trash littered in the gutters and much had been blown against the buildings. Then he chided himself, what will compare with the white sand beaches of Miami with its buildings painted in soft pastel colors. The ultimate look of Florida.

He glanced at Carmen who sat gazing out the window deep in thought, or so it seemed. Uncomfortable. He thought back at how she needed to scoot across the seat in a restaurant, her stomach against the table pushing herself up with her hands to even get up from the booth. Her body lumbering as she walked. How long before the baby is due? Carmen didn't know. Hadn't had checkups. He had bought her a supply of vitamins only guessing at what she may need and she ate fruit and drank at least a quart of milk a day. Only today she seemed tired and more quiet than usual.

His meeting with Reggie Morgan and Cliff Arnez was scheduled for five o'clock at the T Bone, an upscale restaurant that specialized in what else? T-Bone steaks. In fact, that's the only thing on the menu plus a large garden salad and either a baked potato or Texas fries. A sliver of cheesecake was offered for dessert. The restaurant was easy to spot. A large lighted twenty-foot high T made the site visible for miles. He drove by observing the area looking for anything that raised red flags. Nothing. Even though he felt secure that Rudy would not find Carmen, he kept her out of sight of people from Vinnie's organization and would take her to a motel before the meeting. The parking area of the T-Bone would handle 200 or more vehicles and seemed relatively busy for this mid-afternoon . Good; Nate preferred getting lost in a crowd. Easier to spot someone who didn't belong and the five o'clock delivery time could be even busier as well on the highway. Early-bird specials brought out the budget minded and commuters leaving the city for suburban homes kept Houston's finest busy with minor fender-benders. In fact, as Nate well knew, the Organization was not above initiating those minor accidents to divert attention from its "business."

Nate pulled into a Holiday Inn--Carmen's favorite motel chain; the tiny bars of soap, shampoo, and lotion giving her a special thrill. Another perk was the adjoining restaurant and convenience store a few steps away. Never knowing how long a meeting may last, Nate purchased small food items and the always milk and orange juice. He arranged for a dinner to be delivered to Carmen and bought her a couple of magazines. He planned to be away only an hour or so, still Carmen needed the security of being taken care of.

Again he noticed how she had to push herself up to get out of the car and her walk resembled a duck, kind of wobbling from side to side. It only looked as if she is as wide as she is tall. He knew that wasn't so. Then a chill ran down his back. What if she had the baby soon. God, why did he bring her along. What will he do? But she needed him. Now more than ever. Still he had been a fool, except, he knew he wanted to care for her. He would never abandon her and he guessed he would always question his actions and the answers remained the same.

Nate parked just a few cars south of the T-Bone door. It was four-forty-five and as he surmised, the parking lot began to fill. He noticed a couple of drug sales going down which surprised him. He had learned his lessons well; he could spot deals being made and even though they would never admit it, crooks have a special look, as do cops. The eyes, he thought. People could not hide the emotions coming from their eyes whether it be hate or love, the truth or a lie. Some, as Nate, had learned to control the eyes somewhat, still he was very, very careful. Richard had taught him and also taught him to become an expert at detection, especially to know a crook or a cop and sometimes they were in the same skin.

He heard, before he noticed, the argument between two swarthy looking men and a younger Hispanic, a couple of automobiles away. The three were standing between two cars and their voices grew louder as they began to move from between the cars. Trouble! Nate knew instantly and decided to stay in his automobile and out of sight. About that instant the restaurant door flew open and a short stocky man came barreling out. Three other men came right behind him but veered in other directions. The short man rushed to the three men involved in the loud, boisterous argument.

"Hey, what's going on here? Watch your language." Shorty spoke quietly but with authority. Reminded Nate of movie star Clint Eastwood. The three men stopped talking, perhaps surprised by the quiet question.

Then one of the two swarthy-looking men, on the same side Nate guessed, said, "What's it to you fatso?"

"What's it to me? This is my place and my customers don't like hearin' that kind of talk," his voice quiet but menacing. Nate could hardly hear him although he certainly commanded attention.

"So what, mind your own business."

"Like I said, my customers don't like it and neither do I. Now maybe I can help you out here. What's the problem Juan?" He turned to the younger man and the other two men exchanged glances, oh, oh, their expression shouted friends.

"The situation seems to be I have some merchandise and these two gentlemen do not wish to pay me the price agreed upon and the discussion is getting a little nasty," Juan explained in a sing-song voice.

"Look mister," Swarthy One took a step towards Shorty, "this don't concern you so why don't you just leave. I don't care if you do own this place, which I doubt, my business is my business."

"Well, my friend, that's where you're wrong, and step back please."

"Get lost or I'll blow you away," his hand moved towards the inside of his jacket.

Shorty whipped out a Smith and Wesson .357 Magnum. Nate knew the model well, he had one just like it lying on the seat beside him under the daily Houston Banner. "Before you make a complete fool of yourself take a look around. To your left you will see my man Benny. Notice if you will, his gun is trained on your heart and then there's Buck, he has a nervous finger, and glance up on the roof, Joe-Boy can hit a dime from there and give you change. Oh, and don't forget, we all have silencers, no noise you know, and all I have to do is raise my hand like this, oops, sorry, that is the signal. Now withdraw your hand and pay Juan what you owe him plus a little extra for my time and explanation."

"Forget it. He's trying to scam us. The dirty son......."

"Please, you are being offensive again," Shorty said a slight grin curving his lips.

"Give it to him," Swarthy Two said, his eyes sweeping the gunmen's positions. The other man handed Juan an envelope. He opened it and riffled through some bills. "Okay, all here."

"Now," Shorty said, "let me tell you about our food and I'll explain how we handle problems such at yours."

"I don't want your stinking food."

"Of course you do. We have two sizes. One a 20-ounce for $28.50, and for the larger appetite, which I am sure you have, there is the 32-ounce for $39.95. Come in and make your choice."

Nate nearly laughed out loud. Shorty was a master.

"Hell, no. Never," Swarthy One said. He was definitely the more stupid of the two, thought Nate.

"Well, then, I will just wave good-bye," Shorty started to raise his hand.

"Hey, wait, stop," The gunmen still had their weapons aimed at the two men. They knew they had no choice.

"Give your weapons to Benny. He will hold them for you. Now if you wish to do business on my lot again please remember to do it quietly and fairly. I provide a safe environment, as you will notice, no policemen. We have a good reputation here but I insist on consideration of my customers. Ladies have very sensitive ears. Enjoy your steaks."

And with that Shorty turned and walked straight to Nate's car. Nate who believed he had been unobserved. Window open, was that it?

"Reggie and Cliff are waiting for you inside. I'll tell them you are out here." Shorty leaned down to speak in Nate's car window and even in that short remark, Nate felt a chill travel down his back to his feet. The quiet voice emitted more fear than a gorilla from a zoo.

Nate jumped. How did Shorty know him? How did he give himself away? He became apprehensive. He thought he had been unnoticed. Just someone perhaps taking a nap or waiting for someone. But Shorty knew him. Just how far did Vinnie's organization reach? How could he have possibly have known him?

Almost speechless Nate could only murmur, "Okay." He wondered what he would discover about Reggie and Cliff. Had they been watching him as well and more important, had they seen him drive by a couple of hours ago? If they had, and they saw Carmen, what then?

Reggie and Cliff came towards Nate. They were about as average looking as Nate. Or as Nate would look in twenty years or so. Both men around six-feet tall, one sixty-five pounds, hair not too light, but not too dark either. Eyes? Maybe blue or hazel. Couldn't really tell, both wore dark glasses, the kind you see everyday at Wal*Mart. Tan slacks, one wore an old sweatshirt that Nate knew could be discarded very easily leaving an indistinguishable tee-shirt or perhaps a sport shirt; the other man wore a long-sleeved light brown shirt that as well could be changed for another look in a heartbeat. Nate knew the men mirrored himself. Very average looking. Vinnie's men.

"We saw you drive up, why didn't you come in?" The man extending his hand to Nate said. "I'm Cliff, this is Reggie. A rose smells sweet this time of the year."

"What color rose my friend?" Nate asked. And the three bantered the correct passwords. Still there is one more test and Nate had opened the envelope containing the answer only this morning--as Vinnie's instructions indicated. "What color is the cacti in Marshal's garden?" Nate waited for the answer. The men, if they were the right ones, had learned the answer only this morning as well.

"Purple." And with visible relief the three knew the correct people had arrived.

"I didn't come in because I didn't want to get caught in crossfire. That short fellow can make a believer out of anybody." Nate explained.

"He has control. Makes it easy for us to do business," Cliff said.

"Here's your gift," Nate handed the small beautifully wrapped box to Reggie who accepted it with both hands.

"It won't explode, Reggie," Cliff said with a chuckle. Anyone watching, and nobody was, would have thought the young man in the car just delivered a pretty gift for a party or some such occasion.

Reggie peered into the backseat of Nate's car. "Where's the girl?" he asked.

"Girl?" Nate instantly became alarmed. Had they seen Carmen? Stay cool man! Let the other men talk. Listen carefully.

"Yeah, seems we heard you have a girl with you. Where is she?" Obviously not in the car, Reggie had kept his eyes on Nate.

Heard not seen. Nate took a deep breath and decided that Jaki could be the girl. "She changed her mind, wanted to stay in Miami."

"You took her to Miami?" Reggie asked.

"She got there by herself. I only wanted to take her away but she wanted the luxury life." Nate told the truth. His eyes said so.

"Luxury life. Are you kidding? What kind of luxury life could she have there?"

"What ja mean. A three-million dollar condo on Miami's south beach isn't luxury?" Nate asked incredulously.

"Who you talking about?" Reggie asked.

"My girl Jaki. Who you talking about? Or I should say my ex girlfriend. She changed her mind. I'll survive though." A gaze off to the distance gave credence to Nate's statement ---- he hoped.

"No, my friend, we're talking about Rudy's little Georgia squeeze. She's gone, man, and he thinks you have her," Reggie said.

"I'm not following you, Reggie, in fact you've lost me completely," Nate remarked.

"You know Rudy, don't you? Of course you do, you've been there so give her back and Rudy may forget it. Where you got her?"

"Hey, you aren't kidding. You'll have to fill me in though. I have no idea who you're talking about or where anyone is."

"You met her. Cute little thing I hear. What's she look like, a Georgia peach?"

Nate could recognize a fishing expedition as well as anyone. "As I remember being in Georgia and if you're talking about the guy in the trailer, I was there only once and for a short amount of time, I didn't know the guy's name is Rudy til you said so. And about the girl, gosh, she was pregnant. I was in kind of a hurry, wanted to get back to Jaki, we were making great plans then. But Rudy insisted I go in for coffee and cupcakes. The girl didn't say much. I was there about ten minutes."

Reggie, whose eyes didn't miss much, kept looking at the back seat . Nate wanted to turn around and look as well but he willed himself to stay facing the men.

"What's that black thing in the back?" Reggie asked.

Nate jerked his head around. God, what had he missed? The sweater! What now? Think quickly man! "Oh, that." Oh what, come on think. "I gave a couple of students a ride to Hattiesburg," he hoped he had gone through Hattiesburg, "and the gal forgot it."

Reggie held it up. Nate died a thousand deaths. Cliff kept his eyes on Nate.

"Why ja go that highway?" Cliff asked his eyes never leaving Nate's face.

"No special reason. Looked more interesting and I'm seeing the country. I have some time before I need to be in L.A. so a few side trips is okay."

"Tell me about the students. We don't pick up hitchhikers you know."

Oh thank you, Richard for teaching me to lie so well. Nate gave a small pledge to do whatever Richard asked.

"They weren't hitchhiking. I had stopped for gas and the man at the station asked if I would give a couple of kids a ride. Their car was broke down and the station guy had to wait for a part. Seemed okay to me, only twenty or thirty miles I think. Nice kids. Had to get back to college." Then he added, "Gave me a little company."

"What you talk about?" Reggie asked. Nate thought him very suspicious. Didn't his story sound okay? What's with these guys anyway. We all work for the same organization don't we?

"Oh, let's see. The guy sat in the front with me and kept turning around to talk with the girl. They talked about the car, not too much to me. Very polite, though, really appreciated the ride." Nate could remember what he said as long as he didn't go into too much detail. The big problem with lying is remembering what one said. Nate said no more about the students. Neither did the other two men. They apparently believed him.

"Rudy is sure you took his girl. Why would he think that?" Cliff asked.

"I have no idea," Nate responded relieved that they had bought his student's story. He began to relax. After all they had not seen Carmen with him.

"Remember her name?" Reggie asked. Always probing Nate thought. Nosy jerk.

"Give me a minute or two and I will. I've been a bartender and remembering names comes with the job. Let's see, do you know it?"

"Yeah, Rudy made sure we knew who we are supposed to find."

"You may have to tell me. I remember the girl but I may never have heard her name."

"Carmen, her name is Carmen," Cliff announced. He had a slight southern accent but then that could be acquired, too.

"Sounds okay to me. So, why does he think I would have the slightest desire to take her with me?"

"A witness saw your car go up Rudy's driveway and come back down again."

Nate laughed. No way could the man at the fence know for sure that the car was Nate's. Nate had made sure of that.

"Well, someone may have seen a car in that area but it definitely was not mine."

"White car, same model, same license number." said Cliff.

"No, my friend. I could agree with a white car, same model but no way the same license number. Someone is trying to pull a fast one." In fact, Nate again told the truth. He had switched license plates and had a couple more to switch if needed. They were fastened securely under the car and completely out of sight even if the car is on a hoist. Richard taught him this trick. Thank, you again, Richard.

"What do you think could have happened to her then?" Reggie asked.

"I would ask if Rudy knew for sure she is gone or if perhaps he is...... well, he may know."

"And if he doesn't?"

"He should look in the woods around his place. She could have wandered off. Seems I remember the trees being very thick. Maybe she fell, or got sick. I really don't see anyone wanting to have the responsibility of her unless she has some friends around. I don't have any idea."

"Let's go in and eat. Arnie likes it when people do business in his lot give him some business too, and the steaks are great."

Nate wanted to leave but could see no valid reason. "Great idea." He locked the car doors and joined the others.

The restaurant and clientele impressed Nate. He guessed four hundred diners and it seemed Arnie greeted each of them. And, as Arnie had told the swarthy men, the steaks were terrific. Booths lined the window area and tables took up the other floor space. Close together it left no opportunity for private conversation which suited Nate perfectly. Nate, Cliff, and Reggie sat in a booth towards the back of the restaurant. it offered a view of the parking area; the comings and goings of people and Nate surmised that this was their regular booth. His car was in plain sight and he could readily see how they knew when he had arrived. Who came in and who left occupied Cliff's and Reggie's topic of conversation. Nate, too, observed the cars in the lot and noticed during the hour the trio spent at dinner that most spaces had changed vehicles at least once. All except the black Lincoln Town Car that seemed to have a valued location. Nate pondered who may drive it. Arnie maybe? It certainly hadn't moved.

The three sat nursing cups of coffee another half hour. At last Nate said, "Well, better go. Think I'll just find a place to crash tonight and look around Houston a little tomorrow. You guys have any suggestions on what to see?"

"Arnie has some tourist stuff in the waiting area, maps and brochures. Take some of those," Cliff responded.

"Right. Maybe I'll see you guys again and if you get out California way look me up, the seafood out there is terrific." And the three shook hands vowing that it would be great to meet again and no one meaning it. Not unlike seat-mates on an airplane who met only once and promised life-long friendships.

As Nate left he noted the license plate number of the Lincoln. TBone#1. So it does belong to Arnie. He stood at the doorway a few moments surveying the parking lot, a habit learned from Richard. As he pulled out of the parking lot of the restaurant, as always, he glanced in his rearview mirror and observed a red Sunbird and white Caddie exiting right behind him. Great automobiles, Nate mused and he had already pulled onto the highway before the metallic green Mercury left the parking lot.

"Believe his story?" Cliff asked Reggie, as he took the last sip of coffee and waited for his change.

"No, too cocky, too flip," Reggie gazed out the window of the restaurant watching Nate unlock his car, climb in and leave the parking lot.

"Come on!" Reggie said , as he left some bills on the table and headed for the door.

"Hey, that's a big tip and I don't have my change," Cliff protested.

"No matter, let's go. I have some ideas," Reggie shouted already half-way to a metallic green Mercury.

The meeting went well, Nate thought, and why not? Richard had taught him to be a skilled liar. Do the little things Richard had said. Scratch his nose, shrug, gaze around the room as if questions were of no significance. It always worked, or so Nate believed. He stayed alert, glancing in the rearview mirror every three seconds or so, then at the speedometer, and casting his eyes back on the road. The red Sunbird had gone the other way but the Caddie was still a few cars behind him. Nate decided to pull into the right lane, check out if the Caddie followed. The Caddie sped by. Nate relaxed but only for a moment. Another car had moved right. This time a pretty green that nearly matched Jaki's eyes. Quit thinking about her, Nate admonished himself. Then he smiled. There was no hurt in his heart and the green color was only a fleeting thought that it matched her eyes. Like seeing yellow and thinking of a lemon or a daffodil. Nothing personal. Or was it?

He moved his car once again to the middle lane and increased the speed. The Mercury fell behind, stuck in back of a slow-moving van. It then moved to the left lane, sped up, then to the center lane only a few cars behind Nate. Hmmm. Nate became alert but not overly concerned. He should have been!

Nate decided to try another ploy. Is he being followed or is it just a coincidence? He moved to the right lane again and slowed the speed considerably. The Mercury moved right as well. Nate quickly pulled to the side of the highway hoping to imply car trouble. He got out of his car and ostensibly examined the tires on the right side. Keeping his head down, but lifting his eyes, he saw the Mercury take a right into a service station. Need gasoline? Nate didn't think so. And there were two people in the car. Although the men's hats were pulled down nearly covering their faces, he believed them to be Cliff and Reggie. Oh, oh, he said to himself.

He could have fun, he thought, and pull into the same station, but then they would be more careful or call in another tail that he couldn't spot as easily. Instead, he pulled onto the highway easing into the middle lane being careful to keep his eyes and face straight ahead never moving his head in the direction of the Mercury.

By now he was close to the Holiday Inn where Carmen stayed. He drove past. Never would he lead them to her. A couple of blocks further on a frontage road, he spotted a Motel 6. Perfect. After all he had told Cliff and Reggie he planned to stay the night in Houston and explore the city the next day. This motel offered the perfect location. And the room had an expansive view of the office and parking. A convenience store on the corner being a bonus.

Just as Nate thought, the Mercury followed him, pulling into a lot across the frontage road. The men parked behind a row of used cars. The office was closed, Nate guessed, since no salesmen seemed to be around ready to pounce on a potential customer. He did not glance that way again. He had seen enough through the reflection of the motel office.

He stayed in his room quite some time contemplating his actions. He decided he could not call Carmen from his room. Even though he would have an outside line, his telephone would reveal a call made. Still, he must talk with her, explain the evening's circumstances. Plus, he wanted Cliff and Reggie to observe that he was, indeed, alone. Nate sauntered to the convenience store casting his eyes about for a pay phone. Outside the store stood the easily identified booth with the blue motto displayed, along with scrawled graffiti describing who loves who and some other graphic suggestions. Nate dismissed the outside phone since it was clearly in the sight of Cliff and Reggie. Inside the store he palmed a twenty dollar bill and the attendant allowed him the use of the office telephone.

"Carmen, listen, there's a situation here that means I'll have to stay in another motel tonight."

"What happened?" Carmen's voice emitted instant fear.

"Calm down. There's no danger, but I think I'm being followed and I don't want you involved."

"Nate, I'm scared. What should I do?"

"Nothing, you're okay. No one knows where you are......."

"Where are you?" Carmen interrupted.

"I don't want to say over the phone, but listen to me now, you're fine. You have food, just stay in and lock the door. Put the security lock on, watch television and get some sleep," Nate tried to calm Carmen but he could tell she was close to tears. "I'll call you early in the morning and come by and we can get an early start."

"But, Nate, who is following you?"

"Carmen, I'm not sure or why, I just want to be careful."

"What if they kill you?" Carmen sobbed.

"Listen, it isn't anything like that. Maybe nothing at all. Probably I'm mistaken, I just don't want to take the chance."

"Chance for what, Nate? I don't understand."

"I know you don't and tomorrow I'll tell you all about it but for now it has to be this way."

"But what if something happens to you." Carmen sobbed and her hand clenched the telephone.

"It won't. Don't worry. You're okay. Stay calm. It's probably a prank."

"If it's nothing why are you staying away?" Carmen asked.

"Just a precaution. You have to trust me on this, Carmen. I'll call you early and we'll be on our way. Now, get some rest. It isn't good for the baby for you to be upset."

"Okay. Be careful." She seemed calmer. The baby meant everything to her.

Nate gave the attendant another twenty, "I made no phone call right?"

"Right." The young man was grateful for the forty dollars. No one would asked about Nate.

As Nate left the store, he tossed his nearly full can of soda in the trash container with the words printed on the side, "Toss in. Keep Houston Clean." Nate had wanted to imply he had drunk the soda in the store and had spent time talking. He put coins in a newspaper dispenser and scanned the Houston Banner headlines. He hoped Cliff and Reggie were watching him.

They were.

"Reggie, it looks like he's all alone. What ja think?" Cliff asked.

"I think so too, but we better hang around awhile. We make a mistake and might as well kiss the world good-bye."

"If she was with him, wouldn't she go to the store with him? Or he would get her something to eat or a can of soda? I don't think he knows anything about her, or cares." Cliff intently watched Nate walk to his room at the motel.

"Did you ever meet Rudy?" asked Reggie. He, too, watched the motel.

"Yeah, once. Meanest man I ever saw. Nasty and mean just for the fun of it. And scary. You ever see him?"

"No." Reggie lit up a cigarette and rolled down a window letting the smoke drift out. "Think he spotted us?" He kept his eyes trained on the motel, watching as Nate climbed the stairs to the second story room.

"Don't think so." He, too, began to smoke. "We were careful and he had no reason to think of a tail."

"Why'd he pull off the road like that? Do you think?" Reggie tossed his half-smoked cigarette out the window. Who cares that a No Smoking sign was prominently displayed in several places among the used cars. "Tell me more about Rudy."

"Don't know. I'll tell you one thing, " Cliff tossed his cigarette out as well, "If he finds the girl and she did run away, her life is gone," he snapped fingers, "like that. And if Nate or anyone else helped her, they're outa this world, too. Rudy's crazy. Walked away from Attica one day. Got out on a fluke. He had a job in the library, learned how to use a typewriter, typed up his own release papers. Got out clean as a whistle."

"How come no one spotted it?" Reggie asked.

"Are you kiddin'? He was such a trouble-maker they were probably glad to get rid of him. And the release form was legit. Same ones they use for everyone. Do you think the warden really cared?"

"He been in Georgia since he got out?" Reggie seemed fascinated by Cliff's rendition of Rudy's life.

"Not sure. Six or seven years and no one will rat on him. He is an escaped felon, so he's careful and very, very scary, let me tell you."

"How did he get involved with Vinnie's organization?"

"How did any of us? Vinnie pays good, goes to bat for us and as you know very well, controls us. It's not a bad life, only I wish we didn't need to keep a legit job. Keep up appearances as Vinnie would say."

"Yeah, I know. I sell cars all day long. Gets old. I sell maybe one or two a week. Couldn't live on that, not the way Enid likes to live. Me either, I guess."

Both men watched Nate as he opened the door to his motel room and switched on a light. Nate stood in front of the window a few minutes giving Cliff and Reggie an opportunity to see him. They did. Nate then closed the drapes and looked at the Mercury from the side of the window. Great! With the small opening he could clearly watch the men and it was like a game of cat and mouse. Cliff and Reggie watching Nate's room, and Nate watching their car.

"What's so important in the package?" Reggie asked.

"Mercury," Cliff tapped his fingers on the steering wheel and wondered how long they had to keep up this boring stakeout.

"Mercury? What's so important about that. You see it all the time in a thermometer," Reggie said. "Take your temp and there it is."

"Not like this," Cliff turned to face Reggie, "this will paralyze and kill. Remo will be paying big bucks for this."

"How much?"

"Couple hundred thou'. This will change a few lives," Cliff laughed, a frightening sinister laugh. He knew where a few drops would be used. He already had the set-up planned. He and Remo, his boss and "district manager." Another laugh. "Yep, this can make millions for us. A good bonus for you, too. Enough to leave the car business if we play our cards right. Move right up in the organization."

"How much do ya need to do all this paralyzing stuff?" Reggie asked.

"A drop or two." Cliff's eyes grew brighter and brighter as if all of a sudden a naked blonde crawled into the car and draped herself over him.

"This little package will make millions for Remo?" Reggie's mind saw bundles of money floating into his arms. The ten thousand he had been promised wouldn't quite do it, if Remo made millions. "Our cut should be more." Greed began to filter through his mind. "In fact," he licked his lips, "why not sell this ourselves and split the take?"

"Are you crazy?" Cliff said, shocked at Reggie's proposal. "Tired of living? And well, let me tell you a few things that will happen if this isn't delivered to Remo in about...." Cliff checked his watch, "two hours. You got kids? You would be tied to a chair and get to watch .... you got a daughter? Don't even think of crossing Remo or anyone in Vinnie's organization. That's the whole reason we're looking for that girl. Someone broke the rules. And no one, no one, breaks Vinnie's rules."

"We could be long gone. Mexico, South America...."

"You know, Kid," Cliff's quiet and menacing voice made a chill go down even cocky Reggie's back. "You even thinking that way isn't too bright."

"I'm not a kid, don't patronize me," Reggie angrily said.

"Don't be stupid either. Remarks like that in the wrong place can get you killed."

"Only kidding. I know the rules, just wanted to see your reaction. If you said what I did I'd have told you the same thing. A test see?"

Cliff continued to observe Reggie. A test. No, Reggie would have run with the mercury. And in just that moment Reggie became a liability in spite of his sharp eyes. No conscience or scruples. So many assets, Cliff thought, but loyalty was not one of them. Cliff had no doubts that when Remo learned of Reggie's desire to bolt, then Reggie would be history. Poor, poor man and so sad for his family.

After an hour, Nate turned off the lights in his motel room. In his mind that hour could have been used to read the newspaper, shower, watch the TV news, and then go to bed. In reality, he never left the window and as his eyes became accustomed to the darkness, he could see the men and Mercury even better. Both men had lighted a cigarette. How stupid, Nate thought. Then he saw one of the men, the younger one, Reggie, Nate remembered, walk across the road to the motel office. Getting a room for the night? No, Nate reasoned, they would have driven the car over. What then?

Nate was right to be concerned.

Reggie met the motel manager, Bill, his nameplate read, and asked if Nate had arrived earlier with a girl. No, Bill said. Only a couple of hours ago and alone. He had unlocked the room himself and the young man, Mr. Olmstead, certainly was alone. Reggie asked if there had been any telephone calls from the room? Bill pressed a few keys on a computer, no, no calls made from that room.

"Is there some kind of problem?" Bill asked, and he became apprehensive. He hoped he hadn't rented to a car thief, or robber, or some other ner'do'well. Had he locked the back entrance? Was he now being stalked, someone waiting 'til the other man left and then with a gun or a knife rob him and maybe kill him. The young man had seemed friendly enough, asking about places to explore in the city, paid in cash which in itself was a bit unusual but, hey, cash is cash.

"What's he done?" Bill asked.

"Nothing really and I may have the wrong person. Friend was expecting a call from a guy driving a car like that and I thought it could be him. Guess not. Thanks." Reggie walked back across the road which had huge chuck holes and broken asphalt. The state sure didn't keep this road up, he thought, as he stubbed his toe on a piece of broken pavement. And, he also thought, it was stupid of Cliff to send him to question the motel manager. Didn't learn anything and when he turned and looked back the manager was standing in the doorway watching him. Great. Now the suspicion was away from Nate and on him. Stupid Cliff.

Reggie's suspicions were right. The manager's attention was certainly on the man walking across the road. He watched as he joined another man in a Mercury. The men seemed to be arguing, one pointing his finger at the other. Hmmmm, maybe he should call and have the local patrolman check it out. The man had certainly aroused Bill's suspicions. That story was as phony as a three dollar bill.

"Let's go," Reggie said, "I don't feel right about that manager. He's watching us right now I bet," he glanced back across the road to the motel.

"You didn't handle it right probably. I shoulda gone myself," Cliff berated Reggie which didn't help Reggie's mood.

"Look, I asked what you said to ask and the answers were no, no girl, no calls, no reason to stay here."

"Okay, we'll go."

And the Mercury pulled out just as a patrol car pulled in the parking lot. The driver of the patrol car followed the two men five miles before turning off. He duly noted the license number as Cliff knew he would. No matter. They weren't breaking any laws. Not then anyway.

Still it was unnerving to be followed by a patrolman and know they were being identified by the dealer license plates on the car.

"There is one plus," Cliff told Reggie," the cop will know we are car dealers or salesmen and we were in a used car lot. Could look like a tie in with our jobs."

And that is exactly what the patrolman thought as he turned off the highway. His cousin Bill's concern just another false alarm.

Reggie and Cliff arrived at their respective homes sure that they had done their duty and that the report they sent to Vinnie would absolve Nate of helping Carmen.

Still, Vinnie did a more thorough investigation. He received reports from several sources including Jefferson Rose in Chattanooga, who agreed that Nate arrived at his flower shop alone. No young girl in sight. In fact, Rose said, Nate showed interest in Rose's own gal. But his gal showed no interest in Nate whatsoever. Of course Rose knew differently, but he accepted her claims of undying love and devotion she gave so willingly. That time anyway. Plus, Rose wanted everyone to know how faithful they were to each other. And how devastated he would be if ever she died. And she would, soon.

Nate remained by the motel window long after Reggie and Cliff drove away. He pondered what the men wanted. Were they interested in Carmen, or was she just a smoke screen when they really were interested in another "package" that he may have. Even if they knew he had another delivery the "package" was hidden so well no one could find it. Richard had taught him how to do that. And, of course, his piece spoke volumes to an intruder. No worry about break-ins. Well armed relieves any stress.

One thing did puzzle Nate ---- since Reggie and Cliff were members of Vinnie's organization and had the same training in loyalty codes as Nate, then why were they spying on a fellow member? Why follow him? They knew the rules. We help each other. Give support. It's almost like a blood-brother oath. So why the secret watch? The brief conversation about Carmen certainly took any suspicion away that Nate had any part in her disappearance. He had barely shown interest in her or so he believed. So then, he thought, it must be the "package." Of course Nate knew something about the danger of the substance he carried. Vinnie briefed him on that. But, perhaps, there is more than what Vinnie told him. What exactly is the danger in mercury anyway, he asked himself. And how did Vinnie become involved in this operation.

As Nate pondered these questions, Reggie and Cliff were asking themselves almost the same thing. How did Vinnie get involved in the mercury operation. What does it mean? And why is there such a huge cost to customers?

CHAPTER EIGHT

Atlanta, three years ago...

Gordon Jeffries glanced at the clock for the umpteenth time since the two o'clock mail delivery. The batteries must be low on that old white-faced wall clock, he told himself. The little hand doesn't seem to move at all and the clicks from the big hand noting a passed minute hardly makes a sound. It must have been more than three minutes since he last looked. It's the excitement and eagerness to get home and tell Grace the good news. He could leave early, though in his thirty-two years at the laboratory, he never had. No need to start now and hear the snide remarks about old guys not being able to keep up. Can't work a full day. Like when his lab partner, Gil, got that ulcer and had to retire. Too old to learn new methods, missed a microorganism which was no big deal, every test is done a dozen times or more anyway, and someone else caught the problem. Still Gil couldn't take the pressure anymore. No, Gordon would not leave early.

Three-thirty! Only three? Was the big hand closer to four? He guessed not. Well, think of something else. Work on the new report. Stay busy and time will go by faster. It did and by six o'clock Gordon had a bottle of Turning Leaf, a chardonnay, out of California that Grace especially liked, under his arm in anticipation of a celebration. Grace would be pleased. How to tell her? Quietly? Let her question, why the wine? Dance around the floor? None of these. He burst through the door shouting, "I won!"

THE DECISION

Grace knew the excitement that Gordon felt. Hadn't they talked about it for months. What ifs nearly every day. Ever since he entered his essay in New York's "Year of the Child" contest. There were ten winners, each to receive five thousand, plus the essay would be published in a book. Any money received from book sales was to be donated to the abused children's fund. The contest had been sponsored by the Corsica Import-Export Compound. Gordon had never heard of that company, but no matter, in addition to the five thousand, he and Grace looked forward to a long weekend in New York City. And at the Hilton, no less.

Frosting on the cake was the publication of his essay for all of his co-workers to see. No more could they pooh pooh his poems or short stories that he tried to get published and failed. Now he could rightfully claim to be a published author.

Grace deserved a vacation, too. She had worked hard raising their three children, helping out at their schools, and then after they were grown, and on their own, she worked as a practical nurse at St. John's hospital. Not an easy job or good pay, still she liked it. Liked the patients and felt she contributed to their well-being. And the hospital staff liked her. Why not? She arrived early to work and stayed late. Just a few more years and both Gordon and Grace could retire and travel. Both looked forward to that.

Life hadn't been easy for them. It seemed whenever they saved a little money, one of the kids needed braces, or a new horn, dancing lessons, or camps. Always something. On top of that, Grace's mother had moved in with them when she became a widow. This wasn't too easy on the kids or their friends and Gordon felt sure that when she died, the tears shed were crocodile. Even Grace had a feeling of relief since her mother had been a demanding person. Get this for me, Grace. Get that! Turn on the TV. Turn it off.

Now he and Grace had been alone four years and looked forward to retirement. The trip to New York just the beginning of travels. They vowed to take short trips more often plus put the five thousand in a saving's account just for travel.

They were met at the airport and whirled to the New York Hilton in a limousine. Their first ride ever in a limo. That afternoon, the couple met the other nine winners and their spouses for a short session and preview of the book. There in the second chapter was Gordon's entry. Oh, how proud, especially when receiving praise from the other winners. He praised the others as well, but oh, how wonderful to be in such great company. And the book! Gold foil cover with black embossed letters, "Children, Our Heritage." The back cover listed the winner's names and a short description of their entry. There he was for all to see. Number two! Number one had the name Ardella Corsica. Gordon heard some mumblings that sure she's the wife of the sponsor, but Gordon thought that she deserved to be first. Her poem depicted the struggle to raise a child from birth to adult. It was inspiring, both Gordon and Grace agreed and so right on.

The banquet and award ceremony, the major event, was scheduled for Saturday night in the Hilton ballroom. Dignitaries from the governor's office, New York City, as well as from the book publishing company attended. And look who we are sitting next to, Grace. The Corsicas themselves!

Gordon believed Grace looked as good as anyone else, except the younger women. Although on closer inspection she did look a little tired. It had been a grueling day. They had taken a city bus tour, went to the top of the twin towers, saw and smelled the Fulton Street fish market, and crazy enough, some friends told them later, to ride the subway. During shopping, Grace purchased a light blue suit for the banquet. She nixed a silk dress Gordon chose, buying instead something she could wear many times at home.

Vinnie and Ardella Corsica were interesting table companions.

And when the two women became engrossed in children talk, Vinnie suggested a switch in places so the men could engage in "men talk."

"What's your line of work, Mr. Jeffries?" Vinnie asked, as he slipped into a chair next to Gordon.

"I, a chemist, Mr. Corsica," answered Gordon.

"Please call me Vinnie. The ladies have become fast friends already and I think we will, too. What is it that you do?"

"Research mostly. Trying to find the cause of illnesses and more important, find cures."

"From Atlanta aren't you?" Vinnie asked.

"Yes, and those of us who live and work there think it's the best place we could be for our kind of research."

"I agree. The Center for Disease Control would certainly be the place to be." Vinnie watched as Grace's fingers caressed the sterling silver bud vase which held one red rose and a small white card marking her place at the table. She then picked up one of the forks balancing it in her hand as if weighing it. Very heavy sterling silver and very expensive, she would have known if she had turned it over and read the name brand. Grace gazed at the other women, all dressed in latest fashion finery and jewelry she was sure were real gems. Sitting next to Ardella, Grace felt dowdy, although Ardella, very charming, was not condescending. She made Grace feel equal in every way. A real lady, Grace thought.

Vinnie's observation of Grace gave him an inspiration. Never one to let an opportunity slip by, he began to court the Jeffries. He knew, for instance, that the Jeffries were only average income. He guessed no more than forty thousand dollars a year, if that. Grace probably used stainless silverware and he would wager that her dishes were those purchased at supermarkets. Buy fifty dollars worth of groceries and get a five-piece place setting for five dollars. Vinnie knew the scenario. He grew up in a poor family. If he played his cards right, and he always did, he could use Gordon. He needed a chemist. He wanted something developed. This may be his man.

Vinnie had to bide his time while the awards were presented and speeches made. Political speeches, although no one would admit to that. Vinnie, as the sponsor, gave the opening speech and duly praised the participants. He made everyone feel successful and touched briefly on each chapter of the book. This impressed Gordon and Grace. A man that busy taking the time to not only sponsor a contest to help abused

69

children, but to speak out publicly about it. What a fine man!

"Well, that's over. Let's go to the lounge for our after dinner drinks," Vinnie suggested.

Gordon's heart skipped a beat. This important man wants to spend his time with us. Grace and me! What memories we have to tell back home.

After a drink, even Grace ordered a martini when Ardella did, Vinnie said, "Hey, we have tickets for the matinee of "Chorus Line" tomorrow and since Ardella and I can't make it, please be our guests. We insist."

Ardella, the dutiful wife, caught on immediately. Vinnie wanted something. Now she understood why she and Vinnie were sharing a table with this couple. Her best friend Lisa and husband Jack, sitting at a table on the other side of the lounge, kept sending questioning signals. Any other time Vinnie and Ardella, Lisa and Jack, shared drinks together. Oh, well, get on with the charm, she told herself. Pleasing Vinnie made life so much easier.

"Oh, a wonderful idea," Ardella exclaimed. Tickets? She knew at the moment that they had no tickets for "Chorus Line" since they had already seen it. She knew, as well, that Vinnie would soon excuse himself to make a telephone call and tickets would magically appear at the Jeffries' hotel room. She had seen this scenario many times. Even if a performance had "sold out" signs displayed, Vinnie could somehow get tickets.

In their early married years, Ardella had questioned Vinnie's power ---- silently, of course. After all, she grew up in the Vacalli household and had observed her father use his power in much the same questionable ways. Ardella learned to be silent just as her mother had been. After all, both father and husband had provided their wives with all the luxuries imaginable. And if you can believe it, both men were respected in the circle of friends the wives chose to generate. Business associates were seldom included in social events unless Vinnie needed something from someone. Now Ardella knew the Jeffries fit that category. She brushed back the lock of hair that consistently fell foreword over her eyes. She felt depressed even though this was her big night. She fought the feelings. Long ago she knew what caused them. She knew, too, why her mother took her own life when Ardella was thirteen. The worst possible time a girl could lose her mother. Daddy came through, though. He hired a surrogate mother/house manager. The maids took extra care and dancing lessons, music, drama, tennis and swimming programs were plentiful.

"Don't you agree, Ardella?" Vinnie's voice brought her out of her reverie. She had missed his statement but she knew her role very well.

"Absolutely!" She wondered what she had just agreed to. No matter. Vinnie knew her day-dreaming sent her into different worlds. He would repeat his decision now that her attention had returned.

"We want to show you our part of New York. Away from the skyscrapers and concrete and take you to the best lobster dinner you can imagine," Vinnie smiled at Ardella. She knew her cue.

"Oh, please, we would love having you and we just won't take no for an answer." Actually she kind of liked Grace and wouldn't mind having the Jeffries as guests. Gordon seemed okay, too, although he showed his admiration for Vinnie a little too openly. Almost fawning over him. Vinnie played it well, though, directing most of his remarks to Grace as if he already knew he had Gordon in his pocket.

"But, it would be such a bother for you, " Grace protested.

"Nonsense, we want you to come."

Grace wondered what happened to the play. Had she missed that part of the conversation? She must pay attention.

"We're supposed to check out Monday morning," Grace explained. She had a habit of pushing her glasses up from the bridge of her nose and she pushed them again.

"Now, here's what we'll do" Vinnie said, "check out time is noon, I know that, but, do it Sunday. My driver will come for your bags about eleven-thirty, you two grab a quick bite, oh, anywhere, the hotel's great, then the matinee, and my driver will be there when it's over and take you to our place. Now it's all set, right Ardella?"

"Absolutely," she smiled at Grace and reached over to squeeze her hand.

They want us, they really want us. Both Gordon and Grace had the same thoughts.

"Besides," Vinnie continued, "I want to know more about your work." He directed his remarks to Gordon and Ardella thought, "ah, so that's it." She and Grace would be delegated to shopping, driving around, or in other words, stay out of the way.

The Jeffries were treated grandly. The matinee tickets came early Sunday morning, somehow breakfast arrived around the same time even though they hadn't called for room service. Vinnie called, though.

"Is everything all right? Eggs the way you like them?" Vinnie sincerely asked.

What was not to like, Gordon asked himself. "This is how the rich live, Grace. They take all this service for granted. I could adjust to this."

"Umm, me too, but how can we pay them back?"

"We'll have them down to Georgia and a picnic in the back yard. Be a treat for them to see how the other half lives," Gordon laughed.

How naive both of them were. How little they knew how Vinnie's world worked.

The Corsica home filled the Jeffries with awe. Their sleeping quarters was not just a spare bedroom but a suite with a sitting room opening to a verandah giving a view of the Atlantic Ocean, bedroom larger than the Jeffries living room, and the whirlpool tub in the bathroom could easily hold ten people, Grace thought. And, Grace excitedly told Gordon, the towels were warm, big, fluffy, and heated. A luxury she had only read about. Theirs was not the only suite.

"It looks like this whole floor maybe filled with rooms like these. Bigger than our first house." She walked around the rooms touching the knickknacks, real crystal; smelling the bouquet of yellow roses arranged in a sterling silver container that when she lifted it nearly made her knees buckle with the weight.

"Do you think they need another maid or something?" Grace asked digging her toes into the thick white carpet.

"Maybe I could be the gardener," laughed Gordon.

"Backyard picnic, huh," Grace poked her finger on Gordon's shoulder.

"They may like it, you know, seem like regular people to me."

"Well, lucky for us, they like us. Did you ever think we would be inside a place like this, let alone stay here?"

They hugged each other, each one thinking what great stories to tell their kids when they get back to Georgia.

The next morning Vinnie suggested a fishing trip in the Sound.

"Oh, dear," Ardella moaned, "would it make you men too unhappy if Grace and I do something else." She receives a grateful glance from Grace.

"Sure don't want to come, Grace?" Vinnie asked, always the considerate host.

"I'll tell you, Grace would do anything rather than fish," Gordon answered.

Vinnie, of course, knew the direction the conversation would go. Ardella did her job perfectly. What woman would have said to the hostess that no, she did not want to spend the time with her? The women decided on shopping and a tour of the area including driving by the schools the Corsica children attended. Private schools, of course, and beautiful. Affluence was all around. The little shops were what Grace called trendy, still she purchased a porcelain coffee mug with a sketch of Long Island. This would remind her of the extraordinary vacation whenever she had her morning coffee, she told herself. The mug cost twenty-nine dollars! In Georgia it would have been less than ten dollars. Ardella made no purchases. After all what could she need or want, Grace thought.

Lunch at the country club gave Grace another insight to affluence. Most of the women wore light suits, silk, Grace thought, and lovely hats. Shoes matched the color of the suits. Oh, my, Grace felt dowdy in her good blue dress and white sweater. To Ardella's credit, she had dressed moderately, off-white pants and a brown blazer. Her shoes did not match either the pants or the blazer. Grace silently thanked Ardella for her consideration. Lucky us to find such nice friends!

The fishing trip went better than even Vinnie had planned. Gordon enjoyed talking about his work and Vinnie was an avid and interested listener.

THE DECISION

"Tell me more about your winning essay," Vinnie encouraged Gordon.

"It's something I thought children needed to be told a long time ago. I have this little character named Markie who had to go to the hospital. The story tells his reactions to all the care and explains each step so children can understand," Gordon was clearly enthusiastic about his project.

"A wonderful idea," Vinnie said, and then continued to ask Gordon about his work. Then after a few minutes abruptly changed the subject to his own business. "I work hard, wanted to give Ardella the beautiful things in life. She deserves them, and the kids do too. She's a great wife and mother."

"I can see that. Grace is great, too. I'd like to give her more," said Gordon.

"We're alike on that. We want the best for our families. All that money can buy," Vinnie waved his arm in the air ostensibly giving Ardella and their children the world. Gordon was silent. His thoughts bordering on the fact that he could never give Grace the luxuries Vinnie provided for Ardella and their children. It made him sad and feeling depressed. Vinnie, of course knew exactly how to play on Gordon's emotions.

"When you have a great family like ours I guess a person would do anything to make life easier for them," Vinnie offhandedly remarked, or so it seemed.

Gordon gazed at the water, then his eyes casually surveyed the boat. The Boston Whaler, especially rigged for fishing, was the type of equipment he had dreamed of for years. And he had noticed a fifty-two foot cruiser tied at the dock in front of the Corsica home as Vinnie untied the Boston Whaler. Ardella had mentioned that they would be taking the cruiser down the sound to the Lobster Trap Restaurant. Nice living, thought Gordon, and more than a little envious. He, too, had observed Grace caress the silverware and feel the softness of the silk napkins used at breakfast. He thought of the paper towels the Jeffries used as napkins and torn in half at that. Come on, he told himself, there's always someone richer, but most people have a lot less than we do. Think of the great things Grace and the kids have accomplished, let alone himself. The kids all have college educations and now on their own with good jobs. All three working in the health industry. True, no doctors, but lab technicians and a nurse aren't bad. Still he felt a trifle depressed. So much was out of his reach.

Vinnie, a master at reading body language, decided to let his major conversation go for now. He had Gordon thinking the way he wanted.

"Hey, look at the size of this bluefish," Vinnie held up the fish he had just caught, then added it to the cooler with several smaller blue fish, plus the striped bass Gordon had reeled in. "We'll have these for breakfast. Ardella is an expert at cooking fish. You guys like fish?"

"Love it. We go to the mountains for trout. The trout in the streams are to die for. We always have it for breakfast," Gordon responded. See, he told himself, we have lots in common. Not so different. Grace and I could adjust to this life style. We already do many things the same as the Corsicas.

"We probably have enough and, let's see," Vinnie glanced at his watch, holding his arm out so Gordon could see the watch as well, just as Vinnie intended, "it's three-thirty and we're about an hour out, time we shower....."

"And clean the fish," Gordon interrupted.

"No, Lester will do that, but I know Ardella will want to cruise by some of the homes to show Grace. Women like to do that. Maybe you'll see one you like. There's a couple for sale."

"Be nice. Can't imagine anything better than yours."

Let him think about homes for awhile, Vinnie decided. "This place we're going is a little further down from here and some pretty high rollers live here. All nice people, though, like you and Grace." Was that a little thick? Vinnie chided himself, don't want him to catch on.

Gordon murmured, "Ummm," then continued to examine the fishing equipment on board. Expensive, he knew, and top of the line in every way. The rod and reel he was using cost over a thousand, he believed. Fishing being his passion, he knew great equipment when he saw it. Someday maybe he might have a boat like this and top equipment as well.

Vinnie watched Gordon almost salivate with desire. He knew at that moment he had him in his pocket. Tomorrow another fishing adventure and he would spring his idea. And another few hours of watching Grace want the things Ardella has, some of them anyway, Gordon will agree to work with him.

The Jeffries wanted to pick up the tab for dinner. Not tonight, Vinnie had told him, "Next time you come." Ardella smiled. Gordon smiled. Grace's heart skipped a beat. Wow! They will be invited back and there is still tomorrow to bask in this luxury.

Ardella planned an outing to a museum, lunch at the club again, and then the Jeffries would leave for Georgia later in the day. Grace savored every moment. She felt lucky, indeed, such wonderful friends. Gordon was very pleased he had given Grace such a fabulous weekend. Still, he wanted to give her more.

Vinnie made his move during the next day's fishing trip. He knew the timing was perfect. He had watched Grace touch the sterling silver bowl that held the bouquet of yellow roses. Ardella had placed the flowers in the center of the table in the breakfast room. The arrangement matched a painting on the wall. This impressed the Jeffries. And the fact that the Corsicas dined in several different rooms impressed them as well. Fabulous home! Grace could not keep her eyes from the incredible furnishings and original art work, or the floral arrangements in every room. Not artificial flowers as Grace used. Everything screams affluence, Grace mused.

Ardella played her role perfectly not aware that Vinnie programmed her actions. An accomplished manipulator, he pressed the right buttons on everyone. She thought that he may actually enjoy Gordon, that perhaps money or influence didn't matter if the friendship was genuine.

A few hundred yards out into the sound, Vinnie asked Gordon more questions about his profession.

"Do you have a lab at home that you putter around in like a jeweler, something like that?" Vinnie asked.

"You bet. Well equipped, too. I guess everyone hopes to discover the cure for a rare disease or find some new medication," Gordon responded.

"Are you working on anything special?"

"Not significant. I try various combinations hoping for a common purpose to discover something profound but so far I haven't discovered anything new. We all hope to find the cure for AIDS."

Gordon baited the fishing hook as Vinnie slowed the Boston Whaler. They were ready for trolling. Catching more blue fish was the objective for the day, or so Gordon believed.

"Have you ever heard of dimethylmercury?" Vinnie quietly asked.

"Where did you hear about that?" Gordon jumped as if he had been shot. "My God, no one knows about that." He stared at Vinnie, fishing forgotten. "It's, it's, well, a big secret in the scientific world."

"Can you tell me something about it?" Vinnie's voice soft and cunning, leading Gordon exactly where he wanted.

"I can tell you this! It's very dangerous, absolutely toxic. Stay away from it."

"You ever work with it?"

"We did a few times, we're trying to find a cure for the poisoning, but so far our lab hasn't. No other lab either that I know of."

"Does it look like the mercury we see in thermometers?"

"Not at all. Dimethylmercury is colorless, like water, but is heavier and has kind of a sweet smell. Where did you hear about it?" Gordon asked, probing Vinnie for an answer.

"Oh, around. Where does it come from?"

"It's a man-made compound and highly toxic. Very rare and only used for research."

"Can you get some?"

"I can't. I'm not in that part of the research and anyone that is has to be documented and if you aren't part of that team then you can't get it. Wouldn't want to anyway. It's too dangerous to work with."

"But," Vinnie continued quietly, "if it is man-made couldn't you get the components and make it in your lab at home?"

"Impossible. First of all, I don't know all the elements and it would be too dangerous. I'm telling you, " Gordon looked directly at Vinnie, "this stuff is so toxic that just a pin drop will kill. Not could kill, will kill."

"What would happen if someone got some on, say, a hand or arm?"

"Just what I said. They would die, man."

"Right away? A week? A month? When?"

"You're really into this aren't you? Well, let me see, from what I know, and really from what I know, it is kind of fascinating. Depending on how much one gets on them, it could take as little as a couple of weeks to six months. The bad thing about dimethylmercury is that by the time the diagnoses comes in, it's too late to do anything to stop its deadly progress. It just keeps eating its way into the body. There's no cure."

"What happens exactly?" Vinnie had anchored the boat, and clearly he was very interested in this subject. He had not put his rod in the water.

Gordon put his rod back onto the bracket and thought for a moment how to explain this substance to a layman, how to make him understand the danger. He believed Vinnie to be a little more interested than a non-scientist should be. Almost like someone being shown a powerful semi-automatic-gun and asking how it would kill. He was apprehensive about Vinnie's curiosity, still, he enjoyed talking about dimethylmercury and felt elated that he knew something Vinnie did not. Kind of an upsmanship, a bringing him up to Vinnie's level.

"What happens if someone accidentally touched a little dimethylmercury? I'll tell you what I know, which is not a whole lot," Gordon said. "First, a person feels a little nauseous, kind of an upset stomach. So they think it had to be something they ate, or a touch of the flu. They get kind of dizzy, stumble, not steady on their feet. They probably think oh, no, did I skip lunch. But, they don't want to eat because of the upset stomach. Then things begin to get blurry, speech is slurred, they just aren't with it. Understand so far?"

"Sure, go on," Vinnie replied.

"So the person gets medical attention. Takes some pills or a shot for a virus. But, as I told you, it's now too late. The person will continue to get worse. speech is gone, the body functions begin to fade, and they lapse into a coma. It's just a matter of time until death."

"But, there's no cure? Death will certainly come?" Vinnie asked.

"Absolutely, and that's the frustrating thing to the medical profession. There is no cure. The doctors can only stand by and watch death get the final say. And watch a family suffer. I don't know why dimethylmercury is even allowed to be made even if it is only for research," Gordon shook his head.

"I want you to make me some," Vinnie quietly said. "I'll give you two-hundred thousand dollars."

"What?" Gordon stared at Vinnie, "You must be kidding. Why would you possibly want it?" If Vinnie had suddenly began to cut holes in his boat it would not have surprised Gordon as much as his asking for dimethylmercury.

"The reason doesn't matter and think of what you could do with two-hundred grand. Think of what you could do for Grace, the things you could buy her ---- things she deserves. A wonderful woman like her."

"I can't do that. It's too dangerous. If it fell into the wrong hands, it could be murder. I can't." Gordon was upset. Here fishing on Long Island Sound, an innocent outing, his new friend had asked for something so completely unethical that Gordon became nauseous, then chills went from his neck to his ankles. "I would lose my job, but, it's too dangerous. You don't know what could happen."

He shook his head back and forth. Never had he been so surprised and upset.

"You wouldn't lose your job. It isn't as if we would hand a brochure out or put up a sign. You would make it in your lab, a lab you could upgrade anyway you wanted. Think of the new equipment you could buy. You must have dozens of things you want. And I know Grace does. I saw how she yearned for things Ardella has."

"She wouldn't want me to do that for her."

"Has she even heard about dimethylmercury?"

"No, never."

"And she would never know. Don't you work in your lab many days and she has no idea what you're doing?

Isn't that so?" Vinnie had heard Grace tell Ardella about Gordon's lab in their basement. And the long hours he spent hoping to discover a break-through to cure some disease. His dream, Grace told Ardella, was not only to make them wealthy, but to help mankind. "Someday he will," Grace had said.

"Yes," Gordon admitted, "but I never do anything like that."

"You mean you haven't," Vinnie took his fishing rod from the bracket, flipped the reel to unwind, and made a cast out in the water.

Gordon's rod remained in the bracket. He watched Vinnie's hook break the water making small circles on the surface. Vinnie slowly moved the hook up and down, reeling in the line a few feet and then letting it out again. Playing the hook and line to entice the fish. The men were silent, both seeming to be intent on whether or not a fish would bite. After a few moments the line jerked and Vinnie knew he had a big one on. He began to slowly reel in the line. Closer and closer it came to the boat. Gordon did not move his eyes from the line and the movement towards the boat. It fascinated him. Vinnie brought the fish in ---- a large striped bass --- beautiful. He held it up, then calmly hit it on the head with a mallet, and put it in the ice chest.

"A big one like that I would never let go. Right bait does it everytime," Vinnie said while putting another lure on his hook. This time a yellow feather with black dots.

Gordon did not respond, but the chill down his spine fairly shouted that he, too, was hooked. Vinnie's words echoed in his mind, "A big one like that I would never let go." It wasn't so much what Vinnie had said, it was his voice, low and menacing, reaching deep inside Gordon's soul. Gordon would make the dimethylmercury. He knew he had no choice. Vinnie had not made threats, but somehow Gordon knew that when Vinnie made a request, it was obeyed.

Vinnie cast the line out once again, "I always catch the fish I go after. It's just a matter of time. Do you want to fish or have you seen enough?"

"I think I'd like to fish awhile. This is the kind of boat I've always wanted," Gordon replied. Both men locked eyes and a mutual understanding prevailed.

"You learn quick and make up your mind quickly as well, " Vinnie remarked. He asked how Gordon wanted the money. Gordon asked when and in what quantity Vinnie wanted the dimethylmercury.

The agreement was made, and at a later time, Gordon would relive the conversation over and over in his mind. How did such a little thing as Vinnie catching a fish make him decide to not only break the law by stealing the components, but jeopardize his whole career and his marriage. Grace being such an honest person, would never understand. For the rest of his life, Gordon would question his decision. But, on this bright September day, in his mind's eye, Gordon saw the new lab equipment he could purchase, the lovely china which would impress their friends, and sterling silver, no more stainless, even though Grace always maintained she liked stainless better. Real diamond jewelry. He had seen her eyes crave the diamond and ruby bracelet Ardella wore. Two-hundred thousand dollars would not buy Ardella's lifestyle, but it would certainly enhance the Jeffries. Still, Gordon knew he could not involve Grace in the scheme. She would never agree no matter how much money was offered. Making the dimethylmercury could, perhaps, be easier than finding a way to explain about the windfall of money.

Vinnie, of course, knew exactly how to do that. Since his company had sponsored the contest, it would be the clearing house for book sales. When a check arrived at the Jeffries' home, it always had a notation that the money was tax exempt and was from book sales. Vinnie explained that the money was tax-free because the entire project was charitable. And wouldn't he know this? He had so many charities, Gordon told Grace. How lucky we met them, Grace would exclaim. That their friends or working associates could never find the book in stores or libraries didn't phase Vinnie. After all, the book stores could not possibly stock every book printed, nor did libraries have the shelf space.

Gordon finally told Grace to stop talking about it, "It's causing too much jealously and making my work difficult."

Being the dutiful wife, she did. Gordon insisted she stop working and find more important ways to spend her time. Join a ladies club, visit museums, up-grade their social status. Grace was not the social climber type, her life had centered around her family, and, she said, the ladies weren't as nice as Ardella. Indeed, their husbands did not need Gordon, so the wives did not conjure up ways to include Grace. They were not unkind, but they were not especially eager for Grace to join the club. She stayed busy with her garden and volunteer work. The amount of time Gordon spent in his basement lab was her only complaint. Every spare moment he worked at something or another. He didn't confide in her .

"You wouldn't understand," he told her," Take a couple of your friends out to lunch."

"This is Saturday, why don't you and I go out to dinner?" Grace gestured.

"Not now, I'm working on something very important."

And he was. Vinnie received the first shipment of dimethylmercury six months after the Long Island trip and eagerly ordered more. Gordon received another two hundred grand.

"My goodness, " Grace exclaimed, "you are getting rich from your article." The Jeffries talked about moving to another home. One with a larger basement.

Then they were saddened when their favorite National Basketball Association team lost its center and coach to some virus. Just when the playoffs were about to begin. Both men "came down" with some unexplained illness. The team had the best record and was a shoe-in to win the NBA championship, but lost all heart and talent when the men died. Rumor, too, was that gamblers had made a bundle betting against this team. Who could possibly predict illness? Who can figure out where a virus comes from anyway, commented Grace.

Gordon remained quiet but in his mind's eye, he saw a large striped bass.

And then the batting leader for the favored World Series team "came down" with a virus. How sad, he was such a fine family man, and role-model for youngsters everywhere. He had vigorously rejected a proposal to strike out in a highly important game. He tried to blow the whistle on the man making the proposal but, sadly, the virus came along. He died several months after he had lapsed into a coma.

A golf pro, sure to win the Masters, seemed to get the flu and then lapsed into a coma; top jockey for the favored horse in the Kentucky Derby died after a short bout with what doctors said was an undetermined virus; the governor of Kansas lapsed into a coma after a trip to Chicago where, some said, he must have contacted food poisoning. All of those patients eventually died. And all in different parts of the country. So there was no connection was there? If big gambling purses were paid, or if laws suddenly changed, or projects, previously rejected, now gained approval, well, then did anyone believe these isolated deaths had anything to do with it?

The Jeffries found a larger home in a more affluent neighborhood with a basement Gordon could furnish with all the latest equipment any chemist would envy. Grace became accepted in a social group she liked; her clothes became more stylish; gifts to the Jeffries' children were elaborate and frequent; life was very good, very good, indeed.

Grace, so proud of her new home, sent invitations to Vinnie and Ardella, but the letters were met with polite rejection. No time this year, but thank you. People who knew Vinnie could have told the Jeffries that he seldom mixed business with pleasure. Only with his boyhood friend, Richard, did he mix the two.

Grace kept the Colonial style home spotless. She rejected all but once-a-week cleaning help. She enjoyed dusting the figurines that she endlessly collected; she liked scrubbing the ceramic kitchen floor which never really needed it; spice racks were constantly cleaned; copper bottoms of kettles were polished until they gleamed; and one day when she could find nothing else to clean upstairs, she decided to tackle Gordon's lab.

"I'm so sorry, honey, I broke one of your vials when I dusted downstairs, " Grace apologized, "but it only contained water and I wiped it up right away, so hope it's okay."

Gordon dashed down the stairs nearly stumbling as he ran to the table where he worked. Oh, God, don't let it be the dimethylmercury. Don't let her have touched it. She always wore rubber gloves when she cleaned, maybe, maybe the vial did hold only water, but Gordon knew he had no vials holding only water. He saw the space which had recently held a sampling of dimethylmercury ---- the empty space. There was no indication that anything had ever been on that spot. Grace had cleaned very well, indeed.

Gordon rushed back up the stairs shouting, "Were you wearing gloves?"

"Of course, I always do," she answered running her fingers through her new smart hairstyle.

"Where are the gloves you wore?" Gordon's voice sounded raspy and his wild eyes blazing.

"What's the big deal? It isn't as if I haven't broken anything before. Good gosh, I used to clean your lab all the time."

"I told you not to go down there. I told you I was working on something not to be touched," screamed Gordon. "Where's the gloves you wore I asked you?"

"Under the sink in my cleaning tray where I always keep them," Grace replied and added cautiously, "Calm down or you'll have a heart attack. I've never seen you so upset."

"Did you scrub your hands?"

"Of course. Gordon it was only water wasn't it?" Grace became apprehensive, he looked as if he would explode running his fingers through his hair like that and screaming.

"Oh, Grace, come on lets get some disinfectant on your hands and arms. And I'll get rid of the gloves. You may have touched something you shouldn't have." He knew the gloves would not have protected her, but, perhaps, she didn't actually come in contact with the deadly liquid. What to do, oh, God, what to do. He couldn't call the poison center. What could he say? Tell them he had been breaking the law in his spectacular lab? Maybe had provided the deadly poison that killed those well-known persons, and in his heart he knew that was true. His only hope was that she had not touched the liquid. He would watch very carefully and at the first sign then.... what? He had no idea.

A week later Grace complained of feeling nauseous. "That potato salad must have been tainted, I'm never eating there again."

Gordon sat quietly for a long time. His eyes were dry but his heart was broken. And when Grace fell asleep that night, he returned to his lab and let the tears fall. "Oh, my, God," he moaned, "what have I done? My love, my very life, my Grace." At that moment he would have given his very life to undo the past three years. But, alas, he knew there was no reversal. His beloved Grace would slip away from him. He knew every indication he would see. Her slurred speech, unstable on her feet, eyes out of focus, and at long last only sleep. Gone forever. His wife, his reasons for living. No, he would not let that happen to her. She would hate being helpless, hate not being able to talk with their children, hate needing a walker, never understanding why she was so ill. No, Grace would leave this world still able to smile, to talk and laugh, to walk and run, to see clearly. He knew how to accomplish that.

And he did. She suffered a sudden heart attack.

"She didn't suffer, we're grateful for that," each of their children said at one time or another.

"Yes," Gordon agreed, "we're grateful for that."

But when a week later the restaurant where Grace had eaten the potato salad was closed because of food contamination, especially potato salad, Gordon went to his lab and smeared dimethylmercury over his hands and arms. He filled the porcelain mug Grace had purchased on Long Island with her favorite hot English Breakfast tea, heavily laced with cyanide and sat sipping the toxic liquid until he fell asleep never to awaken. In his hands he held a fishing manual opened to photographs of striped bass and the beautiful porcelain mug.

THE DECISION

CHAPTER NINE

Houston

"Carmen, listen, get your things together. I'll be there in ten minutes," Nate called the Holiday Inn and this time from his room. He felt sure that he was no longer being watched by Reggie and Cliff. Last night he had observed the parking lot for an hour after the men had driven away in the Mercury. They did not return and Nate managed to sleep a few hours, although fitfully. This morning he did not see any unusual activity in the parking lot or surrounding area. No additional automobiles were parked at the motel; he felt safe.

He hurriedly re-packed his small bag which now held the last package to be delivered. Can't leave it in the truck of the car anymore, he thought. And he always carried the bag with him, even in restaurants. The bag carried his loaded Baretta Cougar .32 automatic. Plus under the seat of the car, hidden from casual view, was his Ithaca Mag 10 Supreme 10-Gauge Magnum, ready to fire. If all else failed, his Smith and Wesson .357 Magnum, ready to fire as well, was tucked under the spare tire in the trunk.

"I'm ready now, I've been awake a long time," Carmen sounded sleepy. "I was afraid for you." She began to cry.

"Don't be upset, everything's okay. Watch for me and come right out. We need to get going."

""I will." Carmen brushed the tears away and splashed water on her face. She put the small bottles of shampoo and hand lotion in her bag and stood by the window watching for Nate.

86

Good thinking, Nate mused, he had paid for the two motels at check-in time and there had been no additional charges. No need to stop in the office. They were on their way.

"We need to make a contingency plan," Nate said.

"A what plan?" Carmen did not understand the word.

Nate smiled. She brightened the day. Her long dark hair was held back in a pony tail that flipped around whenever she moved her head. Her trusting eyes gave Nate a confidence that was a new emotion in his life. Someone who depended on him completely.

"Contingency means something unexpected may come up. Like last night," he explained, "and I felt apprehensive about Reggie's and Cliff's questions. Then when they followed me I wasn't sure what they wanted. So I had to make another plan than what we had said."

"What did they want?" Carmen asked. She shifted around in the seat trying to get comfortable. Her pregnancy was becoming more difficult for her, Nate noticed.

"I don't know for sure. Now, I don't want you to worry, but they did ask about you. Rudy is looking for you and the men asked how well I know you and such."

Carmen gasped and pressed her hands hard against the dashboard.

"Calm down," Nate cautioned. "I threw them off-guard. Pretended I couldn't remember your name."

"Did they believe you?" Very frightened she turned towards Nate and clenched her fists. Her eyes brimmed with tears.

"Yeah, I think so. Seemed to anyway, but there is something else they may have wanted and you know a little about that and should know a little more I guess. Just in case something like last night comes up again."

"Nate, you are scaring me."

"I don't mean to, but I want you to be strong and able to handle situations, " he explained, "and to trust me."

" I do trust you. You always come back for me."

"Yes, and I always will, but if sometime I have to be away from you and can't reach you to tell you, then you have to stay put and wait. Not talk to anyone or tell anyone your name."

"Okay," her eyes opened wider and wider while Nate searched for a way to allay her fears.

"First of all, I have a sister in Seattle, well not Seattle, but close. I'll write to her and explain our situation, then if something happens to me, you send her the letter."

"Nate, what's going to happen to you. I'm scared."

Nate reached over and patted her arm, "Nothing, this is the contingency plan I told you about. Probably we will never need it but we have to talk about this just in case." He pulled into the drive-in of McDonald's and ordered four Egg-McMuffins and coffee, plus a large carton of milk for Carmen. He took a by-pass around Houston avoiding the inter-state highway.

"I'll also give you some money, here." He handed his wallet to her," take four hundred dollar bills and two fifties. I'll get more today.

"Why do I need this?" Carmen touched the money as if it would burn her fingers. She gingerly took the money but seemed repulsed by it.

"I'm trying to explain to you, Carmen. This is in case I have to be away from you a few days, you'll have money for a motel and food."

"Then would I send the letter?"

"Only if I'm away a week. Nothing's going to happen," he quickly added, when Carmen's tears spilled over. "We have to be prepared and then we can handle any situation."

"What is the something else I should know about?" Carmen put the money in the small red zippered bag that was part of the Estée Lauder gift set Nate had given to her.

"You've seen the small packages I've delivered along the way," Nate asked.

Carmen opened her eyes very wide. She hadn't seen the packages. Of course she had known Nate was doing something secretive, but she had no idea what.

"No, I guess you haven't. The packages are something I'm doing for Vinnie."

"Who's this Vinnie again?"

"The boss of the organization I got involved in.... the same one Rudy's in."

"Oh, okay, I remember," Carmen ate the last of her Egg-McMuffin and finished her carton of milk. Nate smiled, she would make a perfect model for the mustache of milk in those commercials.

"The packages contain something very dangerous and expensive. I thought Reggie and Cliff may try to steal the one I have left to deliver in Denver, but, I'm not sure they even knew I had another one."

"What's in it?" Carmen asked, wiping her mouth and putting the empty container and used napkins in the little garbage bag hanging from the radio knob.

"I don't know exactly. All I know is it's dangerous and people are paying big bucks for it. I have a certain password that I use when it's delivered. I call a number Vinnie gave me and leave a message. The person I deliver it to has a password and he calls a number, too. I'm not even sure it's the same number, it's all in code. I don't have a particular day to make the deliveries, just so it's a reasonable time. Vinnie told me to see some of the country but if I stay a couple of days someplace it's okay. He knows and I know the deliveries will be made. After last night I carry the package in the bag in back, the one I take with me everywhere. I also have a loaded gun in there, Carmen, so don't, don't ever open that bag."

"Nate, what are you into? Why do you need a gun?" A question he would be asked again in a few days.

"Protection. I've never had to use it but I know how. And I have another one, a small one, a .380 caliber, that tonight I'm going to show you how to use. You'll carry it in your purse."

"Oh, Nate, I don't want to do that. I'm really scared of guns. I can't, I just can't."

"In your bag then. Chances are you'll never use it. I can almost guarantee you won't, but still, we have to be ready just in case."

"Just in case of what though?"

"Well, for instance if Rudy should show up, I would shoot him before I would let him take you back."

"Oh, no, Nate, that's what Rudy did. Kill people. I know he did. You aren't like that, Nate, I know you aren't."

"No, Carmen, I'm not, and you aren't either, but, I think I could be under certain circumstances. And I want you to be able to protect yourself and the baby."

The mention of the baby made a believer out of Carmen. Yes, she knew, she would protect the baby, especially from Rudy.

"Come on now, enough serious talk for the day. We'll go over what I told you again tonight but for now let's listen to some music. In Texas it will be country for sure. You can take a look at the map and plan where we might be for lunch," said Nate.

"How about Abilene? Doesn't that sound like kind of a nice place?" Carmen pointed to a small town on the map.

"You've studied some American history haven't you? But, I bet you're thinking of Kansas."

"You're right," Carmen smiled, "name's the same, though."

"Abilene, Texas will be our lunch break," Nate agreed. They passed many oil wells in the flat monotonous country and sometimes herds of long-horn cattle. Farm houses seemed to set back miles from the highway and the only sign that a real person maybe around was a mail box with the red flag raised to show the rural carrier that something needed to be taken from the box. The country music radio station gave news up-dates every half-hour, but the world events seemed far away and uninteresting to Nate and Carmen. He kept glancing in the rear-view mirror every five seconds or so and several times he would hide his car in an area to observe passing automobiles. Nothing. They were not being followed. Still there was a wariness that would linger with them throughout their journey.

That night they stayed in a motel just outside Lubbock. They feasted on wonderful Texas steaks, and both acted giddy and silly, relaxing for the first time in days. Nate believed he had dispelled any suspicion that he had Carmen and the further away from Georgia they drove, the safer she would be. He did, however, go over their earlier conversation with her and teach her how to load and unload the .380. She remained uncomfortable with the gun, still he had to admire her determination to do as he felt necessary.

Carmen made no more overtures that he could share her bed and they developed a camaraderie that few people reach with anyone. Mutual trust was there. It had to be.

THE DECISION

They depended on each other. Nate knew he could go to jail for what he was doing; Carmen was, after all, an illegal alien, a minor, they had crossed state lines. He could be in deep trouble if she decided to blow the whistle. As for her, she knew Nate could just leave her. Sure, she now had five hundred dollars, but how long would that last? And the letter to his sister, would that do any good? A letter to someone she didn't know and certainly his sister did not know her. Yes, they had to trust each other. There was no other way. And they did. Each feeling the other was an essential part of their life. Somehow these two very different persons were united. Who could possibly explain why.

Nate drove on, making a decision to cross a corner of New Mexico. An unusual way to reach Denver but in his opinion a safer way. Stay off the freeways as much as possible, he told himself. They frequented the fast-food places during the day and opted for a family-type restaurant for dinner. He never let down his vigilance, keeping a lookout for automobiles he may have seen before; state troopers watching for speeders or some other law drivers maybe breaking; anything just a little out of place. And he kept his eyes on the speedometer, never exceeding the speed limit. Richard had, indeed, taught him well. Never breaking a driving law. Don't get pulled over for any reason, he continually told himself.

As they drove along listening to an almost faded out radio station, the best reception Carmen could find, a special news bulletin told that a leading candidate for New York's governor had died after being in an unexplained coma for several weeks. The man had contacted some kind of a virus and lack of immediate medical attention had cost him his life. The man believed he had the flu and didn't see his doctor. Not that seeing his doctor would have mattered at that point. It wasn't the flu. The announcer mentioned that the candidate was such a great man and this was so sad for the family. The man's death left the field wide open for his opponent who was backed by organized crime although no one would admit it.

"Can you find a better station, Carmen?" Nate asked. "Remind me when we stop and I'll get some tapes. At least we can choose what kind of music we listen to."

91

"Who do you like?" Carmen asked.

"Neil Diamond. How about you?"

"Mariah Carey. She's so cool."

"Picked up some American slang haven't you." Nate said, smiling at her.

Smiling back she answered, "Some. I really want to be American. Not that I don't still love Cuba, but it isn't like this. Only I would rather be back in Cuba than with Rudy."

"You don't have to be in either place. How does Los Angeles sound to you?"

"Will you be there?"

"Of course, I have a job waiting for me."

"Then it sounds wonderful," she hummed along with the radio as she gazed out the car window.

After spending the night in Cimarron, New Mexico, where Carmen bought a clay pot for some in the future flowers, he headed toward Colorado and the delivery of his last package.

But, driving up Highway 25 in Walsenburg the unexpected, but should have been expected, happened. Carmen grabbed his arm and let out a moan, "Nate, something happened. I'm all wet. I have bad pains."

"Oh my God." The car bumped the curb and stopped. Lucky no one was hit but Nate panicked, "What's happening?" he screamed, but not as loud as Carmen screamed when another pain racked through her stomach, quickly followed by another.

A man walking nearby jerked open the car door and shouted, "Why don't you watch where you're going, you could have killed someone .... oh, my God, is she having a baby?" The man yelled, "Call 911, get some help over here."

That drew several don't-want-to-get-involved-but-let's-see-what's-going-on lookers. A policeman came running and then called for an ambulance. A woman cried out loudly, "I'm a nurse, let me by."

Carmen clutched Nate's arm, "'It' coming, it's coming. Help me!"

Nate thought if he could just keep breathing then he would live. But, he wasn't sure he could do that. He put his arm around Carmen, he had to help Carmen. The policeman kept the passenger door open and turned Carmen so she had room to put her legs out the door. "Get out," he shouted to Nate, "let her lie down. The baby's head is coming out." Another patrol car stopped and the policeman made the gawkers move away. "Give her some privacy you morons. Get out, get out, or you'll all be arrested." The lookers moved back somewhat, not really concerned about an arrest. They hadn't broken any law.

An aid car arrived, paramedics jumping out at a run, rushing to assist Carmen. The baby was being born. There was no time to take her to a hospital but the three paramedics, two men, one woman, knew exactly the procedures. Nate stood helplessly by, taking deep breaths. He had a feeling he was supposed to tell Carmen to do that.

"Didn't you have enough sense to get her to the hospital?" the woman claiming to be a nurse asked. "You men have no sense at all."

"All right, that's enough, " a policeman said, "all of you people leave."

"It's a girl," a paramedic said. Nate nearly collapsed, tears ran from his eyes. He was exhausted as if he, and not Carmen, had just given birth to the little girl or as if he had just run five miles at a record clip.

"Your first one?" the policeman asked. "After six it will be old hat. Here, let's just push your car off the curb, think you're okay to drive to the hospital? Lucky you had a good reason for hitting that curb or I'd write you a hefty ticket."

"I can drive," Nate swallowed, "thanks, she wasn't even having pains."

"The first one doesn't usually happen that way. After that it doesn't take long sometimes. But, the first one generally gives plenty of warning."

"I'm still shook, but, I'll follow the aid car."

"Yeah, you better. I see you're from out of state. Alabama is a long ways from here. Heck, you don't have to talk now, better get following your wife and baby. I'll be along later."

Whew, Nate had forgotten which plates he had on the car. Alabama. He remembered Dothan. Stopped there for some terrific fried chicken one time. What else about the town could he remember if the policeman pursued this line of questioning. Nate needn't have worried. He never saw that particular policeman again.

The paramedics had Carmen on a stretcher, wheeling her into the hospital when Nate arrived. He parked right behind them until someone yelled and told him to move his car. He backed up a few yards and then ran to catch up with Carmen . When the paramedics stepped aside to confer with someone at the emergency desk, Nate leaned down and whispered in the ear of a drowsy Carmen, "You're my wife, remember, wife. Don't say anything, just pretend you're too sleepy." God, he hoped she could hear him. Why hadn't they talked about this, that something like this could happen? And if she had been having labor pains, she certainly didn't mention it. And where's the baby?

"Please step over here and fill out some forms Mr...? What is your name? And your wife's?"

"Nate, uh ... Olson. Nathan Olson and my, my, my wife is Carmen. Carmen Olson. She, a, doesn't have a ring because her fingers were swelling." Did fingers swell when a woman is pregnant? Nate had no idea but it sounded okay. Didn't it? And he hoped he remembered to call himself Olson.

The woman taking the information had piercing eyes. She knows I'm lying, Nate thought.

"Who will be responsible for the charges, do you have medical insurance?" She looked him straight in the eye. "Mr. Olson?"

"I'll pay. Cash. I'll need to go to the bank."

"A check or credit card will be fine or if there is a problem, a finance system maybe worked out. You don't have medical insurance do you?" Her voice and eyes told him how very stupid he was not to have insurance. Probably thought it would all be free but, not on her watch. She was tired of all the free-loaders, holding their hands out for the welfare checks and food stamps. That's why they all come to the emergency room so they don't have to get regular doctors of their own. Well, she would ask for a deposit.

"How much can you pay before you go to the bank, Mr. Olson?" The way she said Mr. Olson made Nate cringe. She knew, he was sure.

"How much...." Nate seemed dense, " I need to go see Carmen. Where is she?"

"You'll get to see her, but we need more information first."

"Where's the baby? Is it all right?" Carmen needs the baby. That's what all this is about. So she can keep her baby.

"Mr. Olson, could I have your current address and employer? And for the birth certificate we need your age and your wife's," she raised her eyes to Nate when she said "wife's" then continued, "and her maiden name and several other questions you need to answer."

The witch, Nate thought. "I will be paying cash for her care, and the baby's, we are passing through so we don't have a permanent address or the name and address of my employer, which I don't have. I am twenty-five and Carmen is eighteen," legal age in Colorado Nate hoped, "and her maiden name was Juarez," The only Spanish sounding name he could think of and only that because once he and a group of high school buddies had gone to Juárez, Mexico one summer for a load of watermelons ---- a little pocket money. He must get to Carmen and tell her what he had told that witch of a receptionist.

"Here's two thousand dollars, that's all I have until I get to the bank. How much will this cost?"

"Generally, Mr. Olson, we're looking at four or five thousand dollars if there are no complications. That's why insurance is so necessary."

"I have the money Mrs....", he looked at her name tag, "Johnson. I assure you the hospital will not be stuck with the bill, but now I insist on seeing Carmen and the baby."

"I'll take you there, " another older lady, wearing a green smock over white pants, said. Her name-tag read, "Dorothy--Volunteer."

"Your baby is in special care right now and your wife is in her room."

"Why, is something wrong with the baby?" Nate grew panicky again.

"No, it's a precautionary measure for babies born outside of a hospital. The baby is just fine. A beautiful little girl." Dorothy smiled and Nate liked her immediately. "I think your wife is asleep right now. That was quite an ordeal for her and for you, too, I guess."

"Yeah, I'm not sure I've calmed down yet," Nate responded, "That Mrs. Johnson was kind of a pill."

"She's actually very nice. You just caught her after she had quite a time with another patient's family. She's the one who gets all the abuse from people," Dorothy said. "Do you want to see your wife or the baby first?"

"Carmen, I guess," Nate wasn't used to the word "wife" but in this circumstance it was best to let everyone think that they were married. He had to talk to Carmen. He didn't right away, though. She definitely was sleeping. Small dark head on the light green colored pillow. Strange, he thought all hospitals were painted stark white as he remembered when as a child his tonsils were removed. Carmen's room had walls painted yellow with pretty red, blue and orange flowers painted along a border. The bed linen matched the green of the pillow. Carmen will like this, Nate thought. She had just been brought to the room after an examination. Dr. Orean told him she would sleep several hours and he was welcome to wait with her or the lounge is located down the hall with coffee or tea available. "A volunteer is on duly there and will let you know when your wife awakens, and of course, the cafeteria is on the first floor if you're hungry."

"Could I see the baby?" Nate tentatively asked.

"Check at the nurse's station. She maybe in the nursery by now but, I'm not sure. I didn't do the examination."

As Nate approached the window of the nursery, a nurse waved to him and held up a small baby wrapped in, what Nate thought, was a well-worn blanket. She mouthed the word, "Olson" and it took Nate a moment to realize she meant him. He nodded and she brought the small bundle to the viewing window. Nate stared at the baby girl, the smallest baby he had ever seen. She seems kind of red and wrinkled, he thought, lots of black hair, eyes closed, a tiny little nose, small lips. He didn't quite understand his emotions. Was this tiny little person now his responsibility? Forever? Fear! Why did he do this, he asked himself. How did this happen to him? And what does he do now? Many questions, but no answers.

A volunteer handed him a cup of coffee, "It looks like you could use this. The first child always knocks young parents for a loop. The responsibility is enormous or so they think. Babies are stronger than they look," said Dorothy.

The nurse put the baby in a small crib that had a recipe-size card hooked on the top. The card was bordered in pink and read, "Baby girl Olson, 7 lbs. 2 oz. 20 inches, Dr. Norton." Who is this tiny Baby girl Olson? Who is Olson? The hot coffee eased the lump in his throat, still his voice seemed to be gone. How could such a tiny little thing frighten him so? The baby made a grimace. He saw a small dimple at the corner of her mouth. Gosh, he thought, she's a real person, his eyes never leaving the baby. She opened her mouth, but Nate could hear no sound. The nurse put a small bottle in the baby's mouth. Water!

Nate rapped on the window. "Shouldn't she have milk?" he shouted, finally making his voice work. "I can pay. Give her milk."

Dorothy laughed, "You are so funny. The baby won't get milk for awhile yet and then maybe from her mother. I'm not sure. But," she patted Nate's arm, "she's doing just fine. Have you talked to your wife yet and told her how beautiful your little girl is?"

Your little girl. Nate wanted to shout that she is not his little girl. Carmen is not my wife. I got caught up in a situation I can't control. I want out. I want to be in California, to surf, play volleyball on the beach, go to parties. All this Nate wanted to say. And then the baby smiled, he thought. Right at him. Only a gas pain, explained Dorothy. Just a small pain. The baby probably didn't feel much, she added. Nate's expression clenched at the word "pain."

Fathers, Dorothy thought, and fathers of little girls were worse. More uptight. As if they would challenge anyone to a duel that looked the wrong way at their little girl.

"Come along. Let's see if your wife is awake." She led Nate back to Carmen's room and then proceeded on with her other duties which included delivering mail, filling water glasses, opening or closing drapes ---- any number of volunteer jobs to ease the load on staff personnel. And smiling at everyone.

"Carmen can you hear me?" Nate took her hand, "We have to talk. There's some things you need to know."

She opened her eyes and smiled. All of a sudden Nate believed in miracles. The sun flooded the room even though the drapes were drawn. "Have you seen her? They said a little girl. Is she okay?"

"She's perfect. Looks just like you. Even has a dimple the same place you have one. Right there," Nate touched the corner of Carmen's mouth. "Can you understand what I'm saying?"

"Yes, I've been awake. Too excited to sleep but I pretended to sleep 'cause I kind of thought our two stories should match."

"That's my girl. You're right. I told them we are married."

Carmen looked at her ring finger. "Said your ring was too tight so you took it off. And our last name is Olson. Can you remember that?"

"I never even knew your last name," she replied.

"Your maiden name is Juarez, okay?"

"Where did you get that?"

"I had to think fast. They needed all this for the birth certificate. You have to give the baby a name."

"I've been thinking about that. Do you like Natalie? It's almost like Nate." Carmen glanced up at Nate with those trusting eyes and he knew he would protect her forever.

"Are you sure. It's a pretty name, but you don't have to name her anything like my name."

"I want to."

"Natalie Olson. What about a middle name?"

"Would Carla be okay. It's almost like my brother Carlos."

"That's nice." Nate peered around the room noticing two small floral arrangements. "Where did those come from?"

"I don't know. A lady in a green smock brought them in but I pretended to be asleep."

Nate took a white card from an arrangement of yellow roses and babies breath held in a ceramic baby shoe, "From Deb, Jay and Ryan, the paramedics who delivered your baby girl. Good luck," he read, "And the other one is from the policeman, it says, 'Good luck and Happy Days, you made mine happy,' gosh how terrific. His name is Dan Roland. Can you believe this?" He held up a ceramic cup shaped like an infant's head. The cup held white corn flowers and four small pink carnations. Carmen was enchanted.

"So what now? Do you have any idea when I can see her?"

"Soon, I think they bring a crib in and she stays in here with you. Will you feed her yourself?" Nate became shy all of a sudden.

"Nurse her? Oh, yes, yes, yes. I'll take such good care of her."

"Yes, we will." And Nate vowed to himself that he would, indeed, take good care of both of them.

"Remember what I told you and, oh, yeah, you're eighteen," Nate said, "and we're only traveling through on our way to the west coast."

"I'll remember. Is your name really Olson?"

"It is for now. Yours too. Don't forget. I have to go to the bank and then I'll rent a motel. Do you need anything?"

"My robe and slippers, and I guess Natalie will need things. Gosh, all of a sudden there's someone else to think about."

"I know, but think what we have. This beautiful little person." They looked at each other and laughed as if they were kids and had just found two free tickets for the roller coaster. Nate told her to sleep for now and he would see her later.

The bank first, he determined. He withdrew five thousand dollars on his debit Visa card. Thirty thousand left in that account. Plenty. Vinnie paid very well. He found a motel fairly close to the hospital. It had two rooms with a counter and two-burner hot plate plus a small refrigerator at the end of one. A small table with two chairs and a sleeper completed the furnishings. The other room held a double bed, chest of drawers and a desk. A bathroom separated the two rooms. The double bed was covered with a cotton spread of various colored squares made to resemble a country quilt. The windows had drapes made of the same material. Not bad, Nate mused, and suitable for a several day stay. Carmen would like the looks of the outside, too. White stucco trimmed in blue with flower boxes under each window. Red geraniums and some kind of purple blooms. On closer inspection Nate noticed the flowers were artificial. Oh, well, they look nice, he thought.

Now, on to the shopping for baby things. He had never done this and had no idea what to buy. He enlisted the help of a clerk in the new-born section of a department store telling her he had promised to purchase an entire supply of clothes for his sister's new baby. The clerk only smiled, not believing this far-fetched story for a moment, guessing this was the baby's father and not married and never intended to be. His promise to the new mother, whatever it may be, only an out.

"Everything a new-born will need. Maybe six of everything," Nate said.

"Okay," the clerk responded, "I can do that. My daughter just had her first, so I know what's needed." She began gathering little shirts, and Nate noticed they kind of spread out at the neck. "So the baby's head will go through easy," the clerk explained. Then six onecies, a one-piece stretch garment that snapped down the front and between the legs. Used for day wear and sleeping, the clerk told him. What an education, Nate thought. Blankets, small ones called "receiving" and several larger ones with pretty satin around the edges, plus a couple of loosely-woven material which, the clerk said, were warm and easily washed and dried. Nate couldn't resist two tiny dresses, one with pink ruffles, and the other a blue combed cotton that felt like silk. The clerk smiled.

"Do you need a car seat or car bed?" the clerk asked.

"I guess so, both."

"It's a law that infants and young children must be strapped in when in an automobile. We have both here and they're excellent. I got this car seat for my new granddaughter." She showed a car seat to Nate who actually had never paid much attention to them before.

"And diapers, don't forget those," the clerk added. "Do you want this on your charge card?"

" No, cash," Nate responded, as he peeled out six-hundred and eighty-seven dollars for the purchases.

"These are just the basics," she said. "Since babies grow so fast, you'll need bigger sizes in about three months."

"Oh," Nate looked at the four large bags of baby paraphernalia. This every three months?

"You could have used more, like little shoes and socks, but I think for now you're all set. I did put two bottles and a package of liners, Q-Tips, and some other small items you will need in this other bag. If you need anything else just come back and see me. My name's Phyllis," she smiled and then went on to another customer chuckling to herself and wondering who else the young man will try to fool.

Back at the motel, he spread the purchases on the bed thinking how excited Carmen will be. And surprised that he knew to buy all Natalie needed ----- for three months. A baby is expensive, he muttered to himself.

Nate stopped at the front desk of the hospital and felt a slight hollow in his stomach when he saw that Mrs. Johnson still had duty. But, lo, and behold, she smiled and greeted him warmly. "Well, hi, the new father is back."

"I've been to the bank so how much more do I owe?" Nate, caught off balance by Mrs. Johnson's friendliness, stumbled over his words and seemed almost tongue-tied.

"Not as much as we first believed," she jauntily replied. She had a few papers in her hand and handed one to Nate.

"How much?" Nate took his bulging eel-skin wallet from his pocket.

"We won't know exactly until your wife and the baby are discharged, but since she didn't use the delivery room and the baby didn't require special care long, it shouldn't be more than another thousand," Mrs. Johnson announced happily. "Go on up, the baby is in your wife's room now so you can be a happy little family."

Carmen cuddled Natalie and kept touching her cheek. The glow on her face sent another unidentified emotion through Nate.

"How are you?" he asked, stepping into the room and glad he had remembered to bring a bouquet of pink and white carnations. The vase was a throw-away plastic container, but he had a feeling Carmen would want to keep it forever.

"I'm fine," she smiled. "Isn't she beautiful?" Carmen's eyes flicked up at him and just as quickly back to Natalie. Nate, too, looked at the small bundle in Carmen's arms. He never knew a person could show such blatant love for another as Carmen did to the baby. Sure he had seen looks of love exchanged, and had uttered love and devotion phrases himself, but never had he seen anyone look the way Carmen did at this moment. He swallowed and another emotion sent little jabs around his heart and down his spine. He had never felt those before.

"I got some things for her and if she needs more, we can get them. The Penneys store is just a mile or two from the motel," said Nate, his eyes kept flicking back and forth from Carmen to Natalie.

"Really? What did you get?" Carmen excitedly asked.

"You'll see, you'll be surprised. Does she need anything today?"

"Natalie, Natalie."

"Yeah, Natalie. Such a big name for such a little girl. Look, she's opening her eyes."

"She does that sometimes. Do you want to hold her?"

"Natalie," Nate smiled, "yes, but I'm kind of scared. I might drop h..... Natalie."

"Here, just reach under the blanket, Natalie's blanket," Carmen laughed at the game they were playing with the baby's name, "and then lift her gently. Keep one hand under her head."

"Okay," Nate did as instructed. "Gosh, she's like a feather." He held her a few moments, then placed her back with Carmen. "I never held such a tiny baby. How do you know how to do all that? Like keep your hand under her head."

Carmen's smile faded, "I had a book once, well, I guess a friend of Rudy's was at the trailer, a girl friend, and the next time she came she had this book. It told all about babies, how they grow, and what to expect, from the time they are born up to the age of two."

"That was nice of her."

"She asked about the baby's father and when I told her Rudy, she never came back, and later Rudy took the book from me, but I had read it by then." Carmen touched Natalie's cheek and drew her closer. "Rudy said I didn't need to know anything about babies. It wouldn't be around. I was scared all the time."

"You don't have to be afraid anymore." He squeezed her hand.

"I forgot to tell you the doctor said we can leave here tomorrow. Is that okay?"

"Super, but that's only two days, do you feel all right?"

"The doctor said everything is just fine with both Natalie and me. Very healthy he said, and asked if I had help at home and I told him I did."

"We'll stay at the motel for awhile. It has a small kitchen and it's close by."

Nate pondered his final delivery. A place just outside Denver and he needed to make contact with the recipient to set up a time. His dilemma was, could he leave Carmen and Natalie here or what. Would she feel comfortable staying alone with the baby? The trip could be made in two days if, and this was a big if, the fellow in Denver didn't have the same suspicions as Cliff and Reggie. If he does, of course, the trip could take longer. And, he had to contact Vinnie. That was part of the plan. Still, he didn't want a call to originate anywhere around Carmen. With caller I D numbers now, it made keeping locations a secret, impossible. But, he certainly didn't want Vinnie to begin a search for his whereabouts either. Nate knew the extensive powers Vinnie possessed in almost any area. Right now, Vinnie has no reason to question him and the amount of time he took to reach Los Angeles. Nate liked it that way.

Yes, Carmen said she could stay alone with Natalie. The motel was perfect. Nate's purchases beyond her expectations. She could hardly contain her joy seeing the clothes he chose for Natalie, and the car bed! She had pictured making a bed for the baby in a drawer. And look at all that food. Enough for weeks or so it seemed. Milk, orange juice, sandwich meat and bread, apples, oranges, grapefruit, bananas. Frozen dinners, a barbecue chicken.

"Nate, we can live for a month on this," she laughed.

She held up each item of clothing examining it and carefully placing it in a drawer. She could have won a lottery and not been happier. "The little dresses are darling. Did you choose them all by yourself?"

"I couldn't resist and the saleslady had to kind of put the brakes on me. She said I bought enough for now and that we'll need to get bigger sizes in three months."

"Three months. I can't believe I have her and can keep her."

"Natalie," Nate said, smiling at Carmen.

"Natalie."

CHAPTER TEN

The drive to Denver seemed lonely without Carmen. No one to share the sight of the pink beauty of snow on the majestic Rocky Mountains when the setting sun cast its glow; or the light green of new growth on the darker evergreen trees, like a Christmas tree rimmed with sparkling green tinsel; or the variety of colors in the boulders jetting out from the mountainside; or share the fun of discovering a quaint little restaurant in a remote off-the-highway small town; or laughter when seeing an unusual and humorous bumper sticker on a passing car; or teasing Carmen about a Big Mac and fries, her favorite food. He missed her and yes, he missed Natalie. Already the four-day old baby girl had created a place for herself in his heart.

Near the southern outskirts of Denver, Nate stopped at a pay phone to call his contact and to get in touch with Vinnie. Who first? Vinnie, he guessed, in case there are changes in the delivery schedule or a new password.

No changes, but Vinnie delivered a bombshell.

"You heard about Richard?" asked Vinnie in his distinctive voice that only he could effect.

"No, what?" Nate was sure that the message would be that Richard had left Marian for Jaki. That seemed to be Jaki's plan anyway.

"He's dead. Zap. Had a heart attack in a restaurant last week and then his bereaved wife had a heart attack 'bout a half-hour later."

"What? I can't believe it," Nate exclaimed, nearly in a state of shock.

"True buddy, I'm grieving. Richard was my best friend from grade school. Big shock. I always thought nothing could ever happen to him that I couldn't fix."

"He was a physical fitness nut. Jogged every day, drank all that vegetable juice. He always told me take my vitamins, watch my diet. And all the time he had the bad heart," exclaimed Nate.

"Yeah, but that ain't all. His wife, you ever meet her? Anyway, she lasted longer than he did, so everything in Richard's name went to her and now to her kids," Vinnie said. "There's a big fight goin' on. The daughter had new locks put on Jaki's condo. Jaki couldn't get in, couldn't take anything out. She's fuming."

"You mean everything he gave Jaki wasn't really hers?"

"That's right. Richard kept everything in his name, pretty smart guy. Always thought he would outlive his wife, she was so much older."

"So, where's Jaki living?"

"Back at the place she works. She was one surprised broad when she went to her condo and couldn't get in. The daughter had an attorney there and he gave Jaki a copy of the title and Jaki's name wasn't on it. Nor any of the contents. Not even her clothes."

"You're kidding. I'd think she could have her own stuff."

"Nope. Nothing in the condo. Nada. And seems there is a race horse she thought was hers. Not that either. Or her jewelry. Only what she was wearing. Richard always thought things out. Always looked out for himself." Vinnie chuckled in spite of his sorrow over the death of his friend.

"That he did. So what's going to happen? Think Jaki will get any of her stuff back?'

"Don't know. My guess is Jaki will make contact with you in L.A. Or, who knows, she may find another rich guy in Miami. She'll make out okay but, is she ever fighting mad."

"Anything she can do?"

"Her attorney told her no. She screamed at him, 'Richard bought those things for me' but he told her as far as anyone knew no one had ever seen them together, nothing in writing, no way to show she even lived in the condo if it came to court. He told her to be more careful next time. She fired him."

"Well, I guess one could say what goes around comes around, whatever that means," Nate added.

"I really don't care what happens to Jaki, but I'll never stop missing Richard. And Ardella liked Marian, too. A real bummer," Vinnie's voice was sad. "Richard and I never cheated each other, always on the same side. Like all of us in our organization. Never double-cross. You know that don't you, Nate?"

"Sure, Vinnie. I never held anything but highest respect for Richard," Nate lied, hoping Vinnie would believe him and he wanted the conversation back on Richard, not the organization.

"I don't mean just Richard. I mean anyone in the organization. We're all one and no exception."

"You bet. So have they had the services yet?" asked Nate.

"Yeah, and that was a big brouhaha too. Richard didn't have any family. Only his wife, but her daughter wouldn't have anything to do with services for him. Took her mother's body back to Chicago. So, I stepped in and we had a small service for him and cremation."

"Wouldn't he hate his beautiful body being burned?" Nate remarked.

"Yeah, I thought of that, but, I gotta watch the space. There's no room for all those six-foot graves."

Nate thought of the space in Rudy's yard, but wisely kept that thought to himself.

"So, now Nate, getting back to the organization, I need to ask you some questions."

"Shoot," Nate wondered what next, but was totally unprepared for Vinnie's question.

"Where's Rudy's girl? I've gone over all the deliveries to his place and you're the only one I came up with that could have her."

Nate felt a chill go from his neck down his spine and cause his knees to shake and go weak. What to say? He knew no one had seen Carmen with him, so why the questions and more important, how could he lie without Vinnie picking up on it?

"You know, Cliff and Reggie asked me about her when I was in Houston," Nate said. "That's the first time I heard she was missing. I have no idea what happened to her."

"Ummmm, so you say. Rudy thinks different and will be meeting you in L.A. He asked me for your schedule but I told him there was no place you had to be at any certain time, so if he wanted to see you it had to be L.A."

"She probably ran away or got lost in the woods or I guess any number of things. I have no idea." Nate's throat was dry. Did he sound believable?

"You better be telling the truth. Anybody do anything to another member, well, I guess I don't have to tell you where they end up. You've seen Rudy's yard."

"I know."

"Rudy's not the best person in the world, but, he's part of the organization." Vinnie's voice was cold.

Nate didn't say, "So am I." For some reason he didn't think that would matter much. Instead he said, "Maybe she'll show up."

"Maybe she will. If the person that helped her has any smarts at all he will see that Rudy gets her back," Vinnie said. "Now here's the new password when you see Steve. You contact him yet?"

"No, I wanted to call you first,"

"When you see him ask if Louie found his two shoes. He should answer, 'No, only one.' I don't think anyone has intercepted him but a few years ago we had a problem and since then we're very careful. So, you got that?"

"Yeah, I'll call and make an appointment right after we finish talking."

"Where you calling from?" asked Vinnie.

"A pay phone near......

"That's okay, I don't need to know the exact location. You always call from a pay phone don't you?"

"Yes. If..."

"Call me from another one in ten minutes."

When Nate made the second call Vinnie said, "Now you have the new password, I want you to go back to the second one you used. Remember it?"

"Sure."

"That's in case someone had got to Steve. If you don't get the right response, don't leave the stuff and get out of there. No one there knows what you look like so there shouldn't be a problem. Steve has the new information."

"Okay. "

"Take your time getting to L.A. Dino isn't expecting you for another two or three weeks. Have fun." Vinnie replaced the receiver. Still he had doubts about Nate's story. Something didn't feel quite right. He dialed Steve's number in Denver.

CHAPTER ELEVEN

Carmen missed Nate. She knew she would and as she watched him pull away from the motel she felt the familiar frightening tug in the pit of her stomach ----- will he come back for us? Exactly why should he? Even if he doesn't, she thought, she's away from Rudy, and she has Natalie. The baby now slept peacefully in the car bed Nate had purchased and which he had showed her fitted so snugly in the back seat of the car. Now, though, the bed was placed next to the one she used. Nate had given her two-thousand dollars, had purchased plenty of food, and the motel offered a comfortable and warm place to stay. After a month or so, Carmen reasoned, she could find a job, maybe even here at the motel, or someplace where she could take Natalie and the car bed. It was quite light and folded down like an ironing board. She could easily carry both Natalie and the bed. If Nate didn't come back......

She had met the couple who owned the motel. Harry and Gladys were in their sixties. Harry would be described as wiry, thin, and it seemed to Carmen, very strong. She watched as he built a new walkway along the front of the office handling square blocks of concrete as if they were made of cardboard. He usually wore faded blue jeans and a gray long-sleeved cotton shirt. His working uniform, he laughingly explained. Gladys, on the other hand, leaned toward plumpness and wore dresses well below her knees, plus an apron Carmen found amusing since Gladys manned the motel office most of the time. Nate had called Gladys everyone's grandmother and indeed she did treat Carmen and Natalie as a treasured part of her family.

THE DECISION

"You need anything, you just call," Gladys told Carmen when Nate explained he had a job interview so Carmen and Natalie would be alone a couple of days. Gladys brought Carmen a pot of soup thick with chunks of beef and hearty vegetables, plus a huckleberry pie which she said was so good she would yearn for more forever. Carmen agreed. "You need good food, nursing a baby and all." And she checked in on Carmen several times a day, relating many child-rearing suggestions which Carmen valued.

Carmen hoped Nate would agree to stay at the motel a few more days when he came back. He will come back won't he? What kind of a plan did they have again? Contingency. Yes, that's why she could make it if he didn't come back. She must stop thinking that way. He always came back. He said he always would. She must wash those thoughts out of her mind. Her life is different now. No need to be afraid every moment; no need to be frightened when alone. She had Natalie now, an obligation. A wonderful obligation. Responsibility. A wonderful responsibility.

Then her mind did its regular flip-flop. She remembered the way Nate looked at Natalie, the way he held her. Carmen's eyes wandered around the room, lovingly embracing the baby items Nate had purchased for Natalie. He would be back, she knew he would. Her dark frightening thoughts only surfaced because of the years spent with Rudy. The terror she had lived with everyday. But, those days are gone forever, she told herself.

Or were they?

Carmen smiled as a small cry came from Natalie announcing that she's hungry. She lifted her small baby daughter from the car bed and cuddled her as she held her close to her breast and Natalie sufficed her hunger.

Carmen tapped Natalie gently on the back until she emitted a couple of small burps. "Good girl," Carmen crooned, kissing the tip of the baby's head. She changed the wet diaper, putting the soiled one in a plastic bag and then in a waste basket. She put a clean onecie on the tiny girl and placed her back in the car bed to sleep for another three hours. This routine continued throughout the day and night and it was pure joy for Carmen even though at times her eyelids grew heavy and she longed for a full night's sleep.

As soon as the day ended and darkness claimed the sun, Carmen checked windows once again, made sure drapes were tightly closed, and added security to the locked door by turning a chair backwards and placing it tightly under the door knob as Nate had taught her to do. Just a precaution, he had said. She felt safe and happy as she waited for two days to go by and Nate's return.

CHAPTER TWELVE

Outskirts of Denver

Steve Arson dealt in sports memorabilia and rare coins. His big trade items were anything to do with the Denver Broncos and the Nuggets. People around here were wildly enthusiastic about either team and the closer it got to play-off time, the more bets he handled ---- one of his secret sidelines. Now as soon as he received the "package" he would be in a position to control a whole lot of betting the right way and he would rack in millions. Yessiree. And so easy to get into the team's locker rooms. After all, he told himself, he gave team members a hefty commission for the shirts, caps, baseballs, and any number of small items collectors seemed to prize. In fact, team members just gave him items and only laughed at his offer of commissions. A hundred dollars, what's that when their salaries commanded millions? They liked Steve and he was always welcome in the locker rooms. What a fan. Wish everyone understood, as well as Steve did, when a pass was intercepted, a basket missed, a third strike called, or a homerun hit. Whatever happened, Steve understood and the team appreciated a fan like that.

What about the rare coins? Well did it really matter that most were stolen or fake. He dealt with people who wanted something for nothing. If he gave a false indication that something was genuine and someone challenged him on it, how was he to know the coins were counterfeit? He knew most people would pass them off to their friends as genuine or unload them to another unsuspecting collector anyway. The coins looked great.

113

He got them from Vinnie, back in New York, and Vinnie could be trusted to acquire fake coins that appeared genuine. Almost no one could tell the difference. Almost no one. Except the treasury man who had been nosing around the past month or so. But, not to worry. When Steve had the contents of the "package" and bestowed a drop or two on the treasury man, Steve would have no more trouble from him. And when the treasury man died, people would say, oh, such a nice man, how very sad for the family, and who could have guessed that a little thing as the flu could cause the death?

The call from Vinnie was slightly disconcerting. Playing nursemaid to a delivery person upset his plans. Not exactly nursemaid, Vinnie said, keep your eye on Nate, watch his body language when asking about the girl, and invite him to stay the night with you and Teri. Steve approved the plan with an enthusiasm he did not feel. Whatever Vinnie said is the way it would be.

Great! Teri would hate having Nate as a house guest and that meant a new bracelet or some other pretty bauble for her. He wished he had stayed married to Ann. She never questioned his actions, or pouted to get her own way, or cost him a bundle. Still, Teri is quite a looker and how many sixty-year-olds have a luscious twenty-year-old in their beds? He had no problem getting the pretty baubles she loved. He raised plenty of cash and would soon have more. He knew, no cash, no Teri. Well, she could put up with Nate for one night.

Steve watched as Nate parked his white Buick in front of the shop. Nothing suspicious about him. What did Vinnie mean, anyway? Nate's younger than Steve hoped and better looking. Perhaps Teri wouldn't mind so much. She did enjoy attention.

Nate observed the neighborhood. Not the best, he thought. The air permeated with the smell of pizza, barbecue ribs, onions, hamburgers. Still, he noticed only two restaurants; a store offering to cash all checks for a five-dollar fee; another offered loans with no questions asked; a pawn shop; and a couple of shops stating cards and other games. Nate wondered what other games and he smiled. All kinds of ways to make a living.

THE DECISION

Steve's shop seemed run down in kind of a poor business district.

Nate would have not left Carmen and Natalie parked on a street like this even with the doors locked. He felt, but did not see, eyes watching him.

"Hello, what can I do for you?" Steve asked even though he knew very well this was the person he expected.

Nate gave the password and received the proper response. All fine with this delivery.

"Great, I have your "package" in the car, I'll get it." As he walked back to his car he noticed a wino sitting on store front steps across the street. Another man was trying to help a derelict stand. What a place. Only a few people hanging around, several going into a restaurant for the early-bird special which tonight offered liver and onions for $4.95. Ugh, Nate shuddered, remembering the liver his mother insisted he eat when he was a child.

"Thanks," Steve remarked when Nate handed him the pretty package wrapped in blue tissue paper and tied with a white satin ribbon. What a lovely gift people would remark if they saw it. No one did. "This will bring much joy to my life."

"Mine, too. This is my last delivery, so guess I'll be on my way. Want to get a hundred or two miles or so before I call it a night," Nate said, anxious to be on his way.

"No, I won't hear of it. You're coming home with me," Steve spread his arms in a welcoming gesture. "Teri would never forgive me if she missed meeting you." A lie, but wasn't his life based on lies anyway?

"Oh, no, give her my regrets. I really need to get going." Nate wondered at the contrast in Steve's workplace and his personal appearance. Here is a man, Nate thought, that could be an ad for a successful CEO, or a New York stockbroker. His custom-made gray pin-striped suit, white shirt and gray and black tie, and black shoes so highly polished they mirrored close images, seemed out of place in such dire surroundings. His round face had a pinkish glow, and the rings on both his pinkie fingers had diamonds so large they seemed offensive as if he wanted to show off in an otherwise squalid area.

"Besides, I want to show you my sport's memorabilia. Got a place in the mall right on the way home. Man, the people just flock in there," Steve waved his arms as if he were gathering a crowd. "Ten thousand sweatshirts in two days when the Broncos won the Super Bowl. Ten thousand. Man we had to set up card tables for cash only, checks only. Have two cash registers but we couldn't begin to handle everyone with those. My son's wife pitched in. Teri tried, but she got confused the first hour so we sent her home. Made some real money on that game." Steve's eyes brightened and Nate thought he saw saliva dripping from his mouth. Naw, he guessed, probably his imagination.

"This place is only for coins," Steve glanced around the shop, "and well, you probably knew we do a little betting here. Help a lot of people out," he laughed.

"Some other time," Nate said.

"No, just talked to Vinnie and he said to show you a good time tonight and you know Vinnie. What he says goes and besides we really want you to stay."

Nate got the message, "Sure I won't be putting you out?"

"Naw, I'll just call Teri to let her know we'll be home in about an hour and then go to Ryan's for dinner. It's a great place, fantastic food, you'll enjoy it."

"So great of you to do this," Nate remarked, knowing neither man had a choice.

He followed Steve to the memorabilia store and even though Nate cared little for sports, the extensive display of items was impressive.

"Take a look around, I have to talk to my sons a minute. Hey, I want you to meet them. They run this place for me. Bill and Johnny do a great job. Hey, come over here," Steve motioned to his sons. Both in their mid-thirties, Bill perhaps a couple years older than Johnny, and a younger version of his father, even to the close-set piercing eyes. For some reason Nate felt a chill travel down his back. But why? Both men were friendly and seemed very pleased to meet Nate. And when Steve and Bill wandered off to talk business, Johnny gave Nate a tour of the store. If Nate didn't know what the contents of the package could do, and how receiving it pleased Steve, he would think what a terrific family business.

But Nate did know.

"Okay, let's go," Steve announced, "you can follow me, or better yet, " he paused as if a seemingly incredible thought just occurred to him, "Bill, why don't you ride with Nate just in case he gets lost, and Susan can pick you up at the condo, okay?"

"Sure, I'm ready to leave anyway. That okay with you Nate?"

A quick study, Nate knew when he was being watched. But why? Perhaps wanting to see if he contacts anyone. Is this a duplication of Houston and questions about Carmen? Nate mulled those thoughts around his mind. Lucky he left her at the motel, and lucky all the baby paraphernalia was out of the car and that cute little pine tree covered any scent of Natalie. He was ready!

And that's exactly the reason for the evening's invitation, Steve knew, learn about the girl, Vinnie had demanded.

Teri properly welcomed Nate. She, too, had learned her lessons well. Her only body language, Nate noted, was the way she kept taking a ring off and putting it back on her little finger, and glancing at Steve. Nate smiled, he had seen this scenario with Jaki. By tomorrow Teri would have a new expensive ring. Some play that Nate didn't understand. Perhaps she had had other plans that were canceled by Nate's arrival. Oh, well, Vinnie did have far-reaching control.

Teri's job, Nate guessed, was to distract him enough so that his answers would come quickly ----- too quickly. She almost succeeded since her long blonde hair and smile with white, white teeth, reminded him of Jaki. Teri had dimples in the corner of her mouth and she absolutely knew the effect when she pursed her lips, which she did often. Nate guessed her height at five-feet two, and although she was a little on the chubby side, she used her body very well, very well, indeed. She wore a tight short black skirt and a tighter red top. Steve couldn't keep his eyes or his hands off her. She knew the effect of that as well.

Her blonde hair generated a familiar tug at Nate's heart and her smile sent a thrill reminding him so much of Jaki. Jaki. And he knew she was alone now. Richard was dead.

117

"My, you have a pensive look. Are you thinking about your girl?" asked Steve.

"Yes, as a matter of fact I was," Nate answered truthfully.

"Where is she? Close by?" Steve thought getting the information Vinnie needed maybe easier than he believed.

Nate recovered and brought his thoughts back to Denver. "Actually, she isn't my girl anymore but, once in awhile the memories catch up with me."

"So, where is she?" Steve's voice, low and smooth, invited intimacy, "Is she with you. Do you have her?"

"No, she stayed in Miami."

"Who with?" Stay calm, Steve told himself, you're close to finding out what no one else has ever done.

"Who knows at this point. She's never alone for long. Can always find old friends."

"Where did you leave her?"

"At the beach. She loves being around the water."

"Exactly where at the beach?" Steve asked, sure that these revelations would bring a substantial bonus.

"South Beach. You been to Miami?"

"No, never had the pleasure. Might someday, though."

"Well, it's close to lots of boating activity and she likes that."

"Think she will get a boat back to Cuba?"

"She might, never know what she may do. I certainly can't predict her actions. I'm the last one to know her desires."

Steve's mouth began to salivate. He was excited and could hardly contain his joy. He knew where Nate had taken Carmen! Stay cool, don't let him suspect anything, Steve cautioned himself. Let him think that this is just a casual conversation. Don't let him guess that Rudy will soon have Carmen back.

"If you had to hazard a guess would you say she'll go back to her parents or family?" Steve cautiously asked.

"Never, she'll find another sugar-daddy. One who can buy her whatever she wants. Like all the pretty rings you get for Teri."

"Yeah, Rudy is pretty tight with a dollar I hear." Steve remarked. He wiped his forehead with the sleeve of his shirt.

"Rudy?" Nate asked in all innocence.

"That's who she was with. You know that."

Nate burst into laughter.

"What's so funny?"

"Jaki never even met Rudy and wouldn't give him the time of day if she had."

"Who's Jaki?" Steve asked, puzzled by this new name.

"My ex-girlfriend. The one I left in Miami."

"I thought we were talking about Carmen, Rudy's girl."

"Well, I don't know anything about her. I only know about Jaki. That's who Teri reminded me of."

"Rudy thinks you took Carmen. Vinnie thinks so too."

"So you're supposed to find out where I've got her, is that it?" Nate seemed angry.

"Hey, don't get mad at me. I only do what I'm told." Steve held up both hands as if to ward off a blow from Nate. "I haven't seen or heard of Carmen until now."

"Am I right? I'm here so you can ask me about, ummmm, what's her name again?" Nate hoped he sounded angry and resentful. In reality he had known from the beginning of the conversation Steve's intention. Houston all over again!

During dinner conversation centered around Denver, the Broncos, Teri's interest in performing arts ---- she participated in a little theater group but, so far no one appreciated her acting talent. No one except Steve and he really didn't know she was acting most of the time. Nate told stories of his life aboard the cruise ship, but not in great detail, or for that matter truthfully, although he tried to tell the truth much of the time. Much easier to remember the truth than trying to recall a lie, Richard had told him. Richard. Nate had learned so much from him. He had learned to lie more deftly, to become skillful in deceitful ways, to manipulate, steal, to be shrewd, unfair, all things that Carmen was not. And now he wished he wasn't either. Perhaps the job with Dino would be honest and he could change his lifestyle. Maybe.....

"There you go again, that look. You are far away," Steve remarked. "Teri asked you a question."

"Sorry, daydreaming I guess. This food is wonderful and I'm enjoying myself so much I, well, please ask again."

"I asked why such a handsome hunk isn't married, or are you?" Teri asked, shifting on the seat to make her body move in an enticing way.

Nate, smart enough not to promote a flirtatious exchange merely said," Oh, there's plenty of time. I'll find a wife one of these days."

He turned his attention to Steve and asked, "How long have you been in the sport's collection business?"

Steve smiled. He liked this young man. Not many rebuffed Teri. She began to pout, but, no matter, he would still buy her the tansanite ring she wanted. "Twenty-two years seriously. Before then I collected just for fun, but, now it's a major business for me as well as Bill and Johnny."

"And their wives," Teri added spitefully.

Steve patted her hand as if she were a disobedient child he had to placate. She was and he did.

Despite affection building for Nate, Steve was well aware that he must adhere to Vinnie's desires. Questioning and observations must continue. If Nate knew anything about Carmen, Steve was determined to find out. He doubted that Vinnie pursued anything without reason. Still, he had met Rudy and while he observed the organization's regime, he certainly would have sympathy for anyone in Rudy's power. He winced when he thought of Rudy's hands on Teri, or anyone, he guessed.

"Now it's you with the far away look," Nate remarked to Steve, "and speaking of far away, I'm ready for some sleep."

"Yeah, let's go. We can have a nightcap at home. Right Teri?" She glowered at Steve who knew very well she liked the admiration she received from most of the male diners.

Arriving back at Steve's condo, he said, "Teri, Nate and I have some business so you run off to bed. I'll be in soon."

"Oh, don't hurry. I'm going right to sleep," she said, and flounced off in a pout. Steve and Nate exchanged glances.

"Women," they said almost in unison. Their soft laughter seemed to offer a comradeship between the two.

"Nate, I want to be honest with you and please trust me in this," Steve said as he poured two glasses of sherry.

The "trust me on this" raised a red flag in Nate's mind. Nearly always when that phrase is used it means the exact opposite, he had learned the hard way.

"I appreciate that, Steve, what's on your mind?" Nate offered his trusting eyes look to Steve and hoped he believed that he was being friendly and trusting.

"I can't help thinking why is Vinnie and Rudy so sure you have Carmen?"

"I have no idea. It makes no sense to me. As I may have mentioned to you, I saw her once at Rudy's when I made a delivery, so you can imagine my surprise when Reggie and Cliff ---- you know them? --- in Houston? When they asked me about her. I didn't even know her name until then."

Steve pondered Nate's answer. As a member of the organization, Nate certainly knew how to be deceitful. Is he really telling the truth or not? Steve suspected if Nate wanted to lie, he could, so he must gain his trust, his confidentiality if he was to get honest answers. But how?

"Nate, I've met Rudy and I know if I had a chance to get Carmen away from him I would. He's a monster and nobody should be subject to his demands."

Nate felt a surge of friendliness and hope. How great to have a friend to share his dilemma. Although he believed Teri not a positive roll model for Carmen, she could be a friend and give Carmen someone to talk with. He paused, pondering a response. Steve seemed so sincere and certainly, as he said, Rudy is a monster. Steve knows Rudy. Steve has a family, A family man, a friend. Was he wrong in thinking Steve only invited him to ask questions about Carmen. Steve seems so different now. Sure at first Nate thought Steve devious, but, maybe he picked up the wrong signal. Perhaps Steve really will help.

"I can help you with her. Bring her here. Teri will like that. Rudy can come looking for her and Teri will keep her out of sight. Trust me on this." Steve leaned closer to Nate and put his hand on Nate's knee in a friendly, fatherly manner.

Trust me on this. Trust me on this. The phrase pounded in Nate's head.

"Oh, I would like to," Nate finally responded, "You and Teri are wonderful, just wonderful. I couldn't ask for a better friend."

"Then let's go get her now," Steve's mouth seemed to have that wet saliva look again, and his eyes were bright with anticipation.

"I really want to and I know......." Then Nate remembered the chill he felt when he met Steve's son, and for no reason, a chill. And Bill mirrored Steve exactly. Something wrong here. "I know I would in a heartbeat if I could, but, I have no idea where she is or even who she is," Nate opened his hands as if to say what can he do.

Steve stared at Nate for some time. Nate looked apologetically back at him.

"As much as I enjoy being here, I can't just conjure up someone that isn't around."

"All right, Nate, but I must warn you, and you really can trust me on this, Rudy is looking for you. And he will find you and when he does, and if you do have Carmen, he will kill you." Steve continued to stare into Nate's eyes. "I don't know if you have her or not. You could be telling the truth or one big lie, and if you are, you're telling it very well. I really don't know. But, I told you the truth when I said Rudy is a monster and he will never stop looking for her. I want to be your friend."

Nate remained quiet. If only he could trust Steve, but, he couldn't take that chance. Not with Carmen and Natalie depending on him.

"I almost wish I did have her, Steve. I feel you and I could become great friends," Nate said these words, but his mind he said 'in your dreams old man. Only in your dreams would I become your great friend.'

Nate remained awake long after his head hit the pillow. The talk with Steve unnerved him. So, Rudy still searched for Carmen. He would never give up, Steve had said. And did Steve believe Nate told the truth or was his friendliness a red herring? A means to persuade Nate into telling Carmen's whereabouts. He eyed the telephone on the stand next to the bed. Oh, to hear her voice and to warn her to be extra careful. He reached his hand out to the phone. Then pulled it back as if the machine carried a bolt of lightening ready to penetrate his body. What is he thinking he asked himself, the number could easily be traced and who else but Carmen would he be calling? Well, perhaps he had left a watch, or some such item in a motel room and he contacted the manager about it. That could work, right? No, he rejected that idea almost as soon as he thought of it.

And those thoughts would never had surfaced, had he known that Steve remained awake watching the telephone next to his bed. A touch of the phone from Nate would trigger an alarm to trace any call immediately and if Nate only knew, someone would knock on Carmen's motel room door within an hour. Nate did not touch the telephone and never knew how lucky both Carmen and Natalie were that he resisted. He eventually slept, though fitfully.

Steve planned to prevail on Nate to stay in Denver another day and to bring the conversation around to Carmen again. Nate said no.

"You've been much to kind, " Nate told Steve, "but, I do have a map of Colorado and would appreciate some pointers on what to see."

"Sure."

And when Nate drove away from Steve's condo, he had a list of interesting places to visit, none of which he planned to see. Nor did he plan to take the route that Steve suggested. He did, however, realize that his Los Angeles plans for Carmen and Natalie needed considerable thought. Forewarned is forearmed, an old expression he had heard much of his life, did indeed, cause much pondering for him. Steve had been adamant about Rudy's frenzied drive to find Carmen. Rudy will be waiting in Los Angeles, Steve had warned. Nate could not take her and the baby there. Still, he had to provide a safe place for the two of them. But, where? Those thoughts were on the surface of his mind as he drove south on Highway 25 to Walsenburg. Who, really in his life, could he trust?

CHAPTER THIRTEEN

Kathy, his sister, Kathy.

Always she had run interference for him. Most of his life, always. Ten years older, she went to bat for him when his grades weren't acceptable to their parents. Kathy had pointed out how thoughtful he had been to a neighbor, offering to mow the neighbor's lawn (for a fee, of course) or the time he played catch with Jerry, the handicapped boy next door. Kathy had no idea Nate had planned to stay away from home several hours or at least until his parents forgot about the broken crystal vase. Jerry provided the excuse. And she told their parents they were actually lucky Nate had wrecked their car, taken without permission, because of the lesson he had learned. The speeding tickets could be a lesson as well, since his parents insisted he pay them from the salary he earned from his part-time job at Ralph's. They didn't know that Kathy had slipped him money to help pay the fines.

Oh, yes, Kathy had always been on his side. But would she accept Carmen and Natalie unequivocally? He had to make Kathy understand his plight and without her asking too many questions. Plus he must convince Carmen that he had only her safety in mind when telling her that she and Natalie would be staying in Washington with his sister and not traveling with him to Los Angeles.

This situation requires much thought on his part and an academy award winning performance. Especially convincing Kathy that he is not the unreliable teenager she once knew and sheltered.

Kathryn Wyemark had worked as emergency room nurse for seven years. She was small, five-feet four inches tall and one-hundred fifteen pounds. She wore her short ash-blonde hair brushed back from her face. More for convenience than anything else although when she was younger, friends said it was to show off her vivid blue eyes and dark lashes. She didn't marry a doctor as most nursing students hope to do. At least, her mother always said the students went into nursing to marry a doctor. Instead Kathy married Thomas Wyemark who now practiced law in Everett, Washington, just an hours drive from the Wyemark LaConner home. Thomas, a partner in a three attorney firm, handled civil cases. He would not become a household name, none of the partners would, but each took home a hundred and forty thousand a year and added to Kathy's salary, the Wyemarks lived very well.

Their home, in the Shelter Bay area of LaConner, was modest, compared to some of the homes there. The two-story, four bedroom house nestled among fir trees and rhododendron plants, offered a view of the marina where the Wyemarks kept their thirty-six foot Heritage East Sundeck Trawler, and the Swinomish Channel, gateway to the San Juan Islands and Puget Sound.

The family spent summer weekends cruising, unless Kathy's work schedule interfered, or Thomas Jr. was not up to it. Four-year old Tommy tended to catch colds easily and Kathy attributed that to the day care center. Mothers took their children to day-care sick or not, so other youngsters caught whatever was going around. Tommy got his share.

The nonchalant and really indifferent attitude of the young mothers (young to thirty-seven-year old Kathy) did not surprise her. In fact, nothing much surprised her until Nate's call. Her brother was on his way for a visit. After five years of almost total silence.

A telephone call when Tommy was born, a card or two during Christmas or birthdays. Never writing much. And now he has a surprise. No, he wouldn't discuss it over the telephone, didn't win the lottery, had not been in jail, which in itself was a surprise to Kathy. No more questions. He would arrive the following day. Kathy was elated!

After work the next day, Kathy dashed into Albertson's and bought two roasted chickens, Nate's favorite mustard potato salad, a carton of baked beans, and a lemon chiffon pie, another of Nate's favorites. She picked up Tommy from day-care and silently thanked God that Tommy wasn't coughing or sneezing. Still she wished Jolie would be more careful of her clientele, especially accepting drop-ins and sick children. Oh, well.

Kathy barely got her purchases in the fridge and Tommy settled down with play-doh and a coloring book when the door bell rang. Tommy still smiled when he heard it. It played "Twinkle, Twinkle Little Star," just because he liked that song.

Nate stood at the door and along side of him was a young dark-haired, and Kathy thought a little dark skinned as well, girl holding a very small baby. So, this is the surprise, Kathy thought. Nate is married and has a baby. Hallelujah! She never thought it would happen. But, Mother will just die!

"Oh, Nate, I'm so glad to see you," tears flowed from Kathy's eyes and Nate's eyes glistened as well. They cared deeply for each other.

"So this is Uncle Nate?" Tommy tugged at his mother's legs.

"Yes, sweetheart, this is your Uncle Nate at long last, and this is....... ?" her eyes went expectedly to Carmen.

"This is Carmen, and this is Natalie," Nate said taking the baby from Carmen and turning her so Kathy could see her face.

"Nate, Nate, how wonderful," Kathy reached for Natalie and then to Carmen as well. "Welcome, and a baby. Nate, oh, a baby."

Carmen smiled. It's all right. Nate knew his sister would accept her and Natalie. To have a family again, what more could she ask. And Nate had said he would come for them in two weeks, tops. Until then what joy to share all this love.

Kathy began to cry, causing Tommy to whimper, tears flowed from Nate's eyes, or did Carmen see tears. He looked kind of joyous but with a gleam in his eyes. Yes, that's it, she thought, a gleam, like someone winning the number-one prize. She had never quite seen that look come from him. Kind of strange.

"Are you hungry?" Kathy asked, finally able to stop the tears, although she kept looking at Natalie as if she, too, had won top prize. "I have dreamed this would happen some day. I couldn't be happier. Dinner is ready. Tom won't be home 'til late. This is his day at U Dub."

"The U?" Nate questioned.

"He teaches a class there one day a week. Labor negotiations."

"Ummmmm, Yeah we're hungry. What ja got?"

"You haven't changed. You know what I'd have on your first day here."

"Chicken, potato salad, baked beans and maybe lemon pie?"

"You know it." Kathy laughed and hugged Nate one more time. She included Carmen in her welcoming smiles and Carmen's heart gave a lurch of joy.

"I'll get Natalie's bed. Be right back. Come on Tommy," Nate took the little boy's hand and gave Natalie back to Carmen.

Kathy gave Carmen another hug and guided her towards the kitchen. "I can't tell you how happy I am," she gushed, hardly able to draw her eyes from Natalie. So tiny, almost newborn. "How old is Natalie?"

"Ten days," Carmen smiled at her daughter. The joy of being accepted by Kathy filled her heart. How lucky! During the time with Rudy she thought she would never be happy again. But now, she could honestly say she's very happy.

"That's pretty young for a baby to travel," Kathy said and then added, "but babies are tough," lest she sound critical.

"She's so good and we're so happy with her. It's like a miracle."

Nate and Tommy set up Natalie's bed in the room Kathy indicated.

"All ready for her," Nate announced. Carmen put the baby down for a nap .

"She sleeps three hours and stays awake one. All twenty-four hours," Carmen said.

"How well I know that routine," Kathy said, "and now let's eat, we can get caught up on past years."

"After dinner," Nate pleaded, "I'm starved, but I do want to talk with you, Kathy."

Kathy decided to eat in the kitchen instead of the dining room, "More cozy," she said.

Dinner went well until Tommy asked, "What's the baby's name again? I forgot."

"Natalie," Nate answered.

"Yes, but, Natalie what? I have three names, Thomas David Wyemark. Oh, yes, Junior."

Nate and Carmen locked eyes. Carmen's face showing alarm. Nate quickly looked away and took a deep breath. Kathy observed this and pondered their reaction to such an innocent question.

"She's too small to carry such a load, you're a big boy so we can call you all those names."

Nate's explanation didn't quite erase Kathy's questions. Something didn't sound kosher. She looked hard at Nate but he was busy with his food. Too busy, she thought.

The meal was finished in near silence except for Tommy who chattered about his dog, a dead bird he had seen in the yard at daycare (Kathy shuddered at this, why hadn't the bird been removed) a new boy at day-care who had a large box of new and huge crayons, and Jolie who didn't complete the story she began to read.

"Nate, could I see you in the den, please?" Kathy asked. The request was not negotiable.

"Sure, be back in a few minutes," he told Carmen.

Kathy closed the door of the den and faced Nate, "What is going on. The truth, Nate, no con job."

"You'll get the truth, Kathy. I want to tell you all of it. I, we, need your help."

"What are you into. That girl can't be more than sixteen years old."

"Just listen, Kathy please, and don't interrupt. There's much to tell and honest, this is the truth."

"Start with what happened to you after you got the job on the ship. I've heard from you exactly four times, and that short telephone call when Tommy was born. And your cards told me zip. What," she emphasized the word, "what are you into."

"Not everything right, that's for sure," Nate straddled a chair, putting his arms across the back, "but, I'm on the right track now. I bartended and finally got to be head guy. One day a guy named, well, no names, please. Name doesn't matter anyway."

"Why?" Kathy fairly shouted.

"It's best, you'll see. Anyway, he discovered I kind of kept tips and sort of watered drinks, so we made a deal."

"What kind of a deal and kind of and sort of doesn't cut it. You either did or you didn't. So just say what you did."

"I'll tell you, just listen and don't make a judgment yet, please."

"Okay. "

"Well," Nate shifted his position, "we ... he asked about passengers and I had to go along or he could get me fired." Nate told her about his involvement with Richard and eventually with Vinnie and Miami.

"I delivered things." Kathy's eyes widened but Nate continued, "not always bad, but not always good either. One day I took a package , no, I'll tell you the truth, it was a dead body." Another gasp from Kathy, but she remained silent. "Wrapped in black plastic that I drove to a trailer in a remote part of Georgia. That's when I saw Carmen. The trailer guy had bought her and she literally was his slave."

"Bought her? Where, how?" Kathy was aghast.

"Yeah, bought her, but for now that's another story. She was pregnant and scared to death. That was six weeks ago."

"You mean Natalie is not your baby. Nate what have you done?"

"I'm telling you. This man, this monster. He kills things. He buried his dog alive, he took Carmen's first little baby away. She never saw it."

"She's a child herself."

"I know, but I had to get her away from him. But, he's looking for her and for me cause he thinks I have her. We were on our way to L.A. where I have a job waiting...."

"Nate, this is kidnapping. You're in big trouble here," remarked Kathy.

"I had to do it, Kath, she came willingly. She wanted out. She had to get away, or she couldn't keep Natalie and the baby means the world, means everything to her."

"Let me get this straight," Kathy stared at Nate. "You went to the trailer and convinced Carmen to leave with you? The man didn't object?"

"He wasn't home."

"Then how does he know she's with you?" Kathy had so many questions, still Nate seemed very sincere.

"He doesn't know for sure. No one has seen her with me. They only suspect."

"Who's they, Nate?"

"I had to deliver some other stuff along the way and see some other fellows."

"Another dead body? What exactly are you involved in, Nate?"

"No, not a body. I'm in an organization in New York. It's big, people all over the United States. I work for it."

"The Mafia?"

"Oh, no. Nothing like that." Except Nate knew it was exactly like that. Vinnie controlled, some would say, the country.

"Then what?" Kathy persisted.

"Another organization."

"What do you do?"

"I'm not sure what I'll be doing in L.A. but it won't be like Miami. I didn't want to do that anymore."

"And he said fine, no problem, you can do what you like? Come on, Nate."

"No, he's a nice guy, really. I believe him. I'll be working with his cousin. He owns a printing shop. But our problem..."

"Wait, back up. You convinced Carmen to leave with you. Where was Natalie born? She's only ten days old."

"In Colorado." Nate explained the circumstances of Natalie's birth. And then told about being followed in Houston, the questions from Steve in Denver, and of his fear that Rudy would be waiting for her in L.A. He left nothing out. He knew for Kathy to help him he had to level with her.

"It's something I had to do, Kathy. I had to help her. Now we need your help. We desperately need you to help us."

"What are you asking, Nate?" Kathy knew her brother very well, knew his weaknesses, but she also knew his tender feelings toward the underdog. The lost kitten, the small boy on the playing field, any number of tender and kind actions he had done through the years. Still, she had to be honest with herself, didn't those actions always benefit him. Either by making their parents forget some wrong he had done, or because he actually wanted the kitten. Has he changed? She asked herself over and over.

"Kathy, please, please, let Carmen and Natalie stay here a couple of weeks, until I check things out in LA. and find a safe place for them. I have plenty of money for her care." Nate pleaded as if for his life from a hang-man. Maybe he was!

Kathy was very quiet. Her brother, clearly breaking the law, was asking her to do the same. Her heart seemed to be squeezing inside her body and she felt hot. Certainly she had sympathy for Carmen and Natalie but was she responsible for helping? None of this was her doing. Her life didn't need or want interruptions. This was all Nate's doing anyway. She silently fumed but still..... still he was so sincere in helping the girl. And then she felt such a loss. The baby did not belong to Nate, was not her niece, or Tommy's cousin. Oh, dear, this is a terrible situation. Her mind flashed back to six-year-old Nate. "Kathy help me with my boots. They won't go over my shoes and I want to keep my shoes nice." And, "But, Nate, your shoes are already wet, what were you into?" Familiar words. He came to her after he had done something wrong. He always had. She always fixed it for him. But, this time could she? And more to the point, did she want to?

"Please, Kathy. We need your help," Nate's eyes brimmed with tears ready to spill over at any moment.

"Nate, I can't begin to make a decision on this without talking to Tom about it," Kathy sat forward on her chair, "You are asking us to harbor an illegal alien, shelter her baby from a man we do not know, have never seen, don't even know his name, and is the baby's father. Think a moment what you are asking."

131

"I have, Kathy, I have no one else in the world I can trust her with. I have to protect her. Don't ask me why. I've gone over all the reasons why I shouldn't and it still comes to I have to help her. I can't let Rudy get her back. I can't let him find her. And this is only for a couple of weeks. Please."

"I'll have to talk to Tom first. You can be here a few days can't you?"

"A few. I'm due in L.A. the end of the week. Or I should be there by then."

I'll put you and Carmen in the guest bedroom down the hall. Can Natalie sleep in her car bed?"

"We don't share the same room, Kathy. Carmen and Natalie will be fine in there. I can crash on the sofa."

"There's another bedroom. So it's not even that?"

"Not even that."

"Nate, I have mixed emotions. In one way I'm scared to death for you and in another I'm proud you're helping her. Tom, of course, will be concerned about the legality of all this and talk to you about that. I really have no idea what he will say about her staying here, but, I'll try."

Nate hugged his sister. He had won. Tom always went along with Kathy's wishes. Nate would steel himself to listen to a lecture from Tom. But he had done that before, many times before. Tom liked him but, he is an attorney and stressed obeying the law. A defense attorney would have been better than civil, since in Nate's opinion they didn't always want to know the truth. Still, he felt relieved.

Nate and Kathy returned to the kitchen. Carmen had it spotless. The dishes were in the dishwasher, counter tops and the floor had been wiped clean and dried. She, and Tommy curled on her lap, were intent on a children's book. Kathy stared. Tommy never cuddled with anyone. In fact, she was surprised he hadn't bounded to his room or pounded on the door of the den. Kimo, his favorite stuffed toy, was no where around.

"Mommy, look what Carmen made me. Birds!" Tommy shouted, jumping off Carmen's lap to show his mother little folded paper birds.

"Oh, how lovely. Carmen thank you for the clean-up," responded Kathy.

"Tommy helped. We both loaded the dishwasher. He knows where to find everything."

"Tommy helped? What a good boy." He never even noticed the dishwasher, Kathy thought pensively. "The birds are beautiful. Where did you learn to do them, fold them that way?" Japan is a long way from Cuba, she mused.

"From a Japanese couple that stayed with my parents one winter. I was quite small but always remembered how to do this," answered Carmen.

All of a sudden, Kathy's heart opened to the young, too young mother. Tommy was enchanted. He had never made up with anyone so quickly. This impressed her. It seemed so right to help Nate and Carmen. There's Natalie to be considered as well.

Nate was right. Tom did lecture him about the fallacy of breaking the law, in this instance assisting an alien and falsifying a birth certificate.

"My, God, Nate, if you get out of this you'll be lucky. Keep quiet where they are because," and Tom's stone eyes ground into Nate's, blue trusting ones, "if you don't, Kathy, Tommy, and I will be in deep dog dung. Tommy is the one we have to think about. Two weeks, max!"

"Thanks, Tom. I really appreciate this and it won't cost you a cent. In fact, here's two thousand." Nate opened his wallet and withdrew twenty one-hundred dollar bills.

"See Kathy about that. We don't want paid for this. It makes us even more of an accessory." Tom pushed the bills back to Nate.

The next three days sped by quickly. Kathy insisted Carmen and Natalie be examined by a doctor. She took them to a walk-in clinic and used Olson as their last name. Digging deeper and deeper into the deception herself. Still, Carmen helped so much in the house and without any show of complaint. And Tommy adored her, as she him.

Since Kathy had taken a few days of vacation time, Tommy was home from day-care and spent hours with Carmen. She read to him, taught him games, they drew pictures, and made play-doh animals. Tommy gazed at Natalie and fairly glowed when Carmen placed the small bundle in his arms. All of this impressed Kathy, and Nate as well since he had never seen Carmen in a home situation. But, he was anxious to be on his way. The future lay ahead. He had provided two weeks of safety for Carmen and Natalie, left two thousand dollars with Kathy, supplies he said, and made sure Carmen had sufficient money. Doing the right things, he told himself.

Kathy knew immediately she wanted the two weeks to last forever. Carmen's efficiency astounded her. The house always spotless, Natalie contented and healthy, Tommy happy to spend time with Carmen who taught him something new every day. More than he ever learned at day-care and the pre-school he had attended in the spring. After Kathy's okay, Carmen taught Tommy Spanish words ---- he could now count to ten, say good morning, and thank you, and was eager to learn more. The family settled into a routine Kathy, as well as Carmen, Tommy, and Tom, found very enjoyable indeed.

CHAPTER FOURTEEN

Los Angeles

Los Angeles. City of Angels. Oh, sure, where are they? Nate knew crime was all around, still no place matched Miami for crooks, or so he believed. And wouldn't he know? Working among the very best con people in the world. But L.A. offered the epitome of living. At least for him. Leaving I-5, he drove along to the wild Pacific, the salty air waifed through his nostrils, giving the heady feeling of home. Home to the surfing he loved so much; the beach where he had spent hours ---- many of them contemplating his future. Never did his present situation surface in his thoughts.

He pulled into an ocean side lookout deciding to just think for a half-hour or so, hoping the ocean breeze would clear all troubled thoughts away and he could begin his new profession sharp and focused. He studied his atlas. Marked the route he should have taken. Memorizing names of cities he should have visited, ready to answer questions about a cross-country journey, also realizing one doesn't remember exact travels. His mind saw once again the beautiful coast of Oregon and felt a joy that he had taken extra time to see it. Some day, perhaps, Carmen would..... hey, he had no plans to keep her in his life. Only provide for her until she could care for herself and Natalie. Enough thinking. Get on to south Los Angeles and meet Dino, his new boss.

Dino's office building was located close to Marina Del Rey. Very nice, indeed. Like most buildings around the area, it boasted Spanish architecture. It stood next to a small printing shop. The entire area showed class. Dino's building was very upscale. Nate thought working there a real plus.

As Nate opened the building door, Dino came to greet him putting his arms around Nate as if he were an adored son or special nephew.

"Nate, Nate, here you are. I've been waiting for you. Did you have a good trip?"

"Very," Nate responded, wondering why no secretary, or waiting area. It was as if the entire floor was Dino's office, Then a question flashed in Nate's mind. How did Dino know him? They had never met. He observed the older man who continued to treat Nate as family.

Dino stood about five-feet six, 170 pounds, thinning brown hair, wearing a kind of brownish jump suit that showed, Nate thought, ink spots or smudges. "Now, you must wonder how did I know you? Got a photo from a lady with a lovely voice. Asked as soon as you come in to have you call her in Miami. Jamie, Jaki, or something like that. But, before you do that. Welcome, welcome. Have we got some great things going."

"I'm ready. The phone call isn't important." Is he a mind reader or something, Nate mused.

"Now, you'll need a place to live and I have an apartment building 'bout a mile from here, nice place, one bedroom, or do you need two? Completely furnished."

"One," Nate responded. "What a terrific break. Apartment hunting can be a real drag. Wow! Thanks."

"That's set then. You can move in right away. Been saving it for you. Here's the key. Parking is right by your unit. Second floor, unit 202."

"Great, thanks. Do I pay you or is there a manager?"

"Rent goes with the job and yeah, there's an on-site manager. He looks after the apartments next to your building, too," remarked Dino.

This seems too good to be true, Nate thought. Is it? People always say that if something sounds too good to be true, it usually isn't.

But, keep the negative thoughts away. This is a new job, new boss, not new city, only one he loved very much. A real southern California person, he told himself. He felt a warm glow around his heart.

"Get settled and come in early tomorrow morning. What you'll be doing at first is some printing work we have. Next door is our printing shop, so for a week or so you'll be there. Then we have some exciting projects. Will make a lot of money for us and Vinnie is real high on you for this." Dino paced around the large room pausing often to stare out the window. The room had office doors, Nate noticed, that rimmed the area. There were no visible names or numbers and Nate saw no activity. Strange but, so what? He would learn more in time.

"Looking forward to it," Nate replied. So it will be next door. He had hoped for an office in this building. The plush carpeting felt great. Whatever, he was prepared to do a great job and perhaps a promotion would lead him to work in the super building. He drove away, eager to see his new digs and to call Carmen to check out her situation.

That call was never made.

Associating with Vinnie and Richard had taught him to be distrustful and suspicious. Thus while checking out the apartment he discovered the telephone bug. So, it was too good to be true. His calls would be monitored by Dino or someone reporting to him. Why? Carmen again? Or just a pre-caution with a new employee? It did tell him one thing, be very careful. And if the telephone was not secure, what about mail? Another project! Rent a post office box and check out the mailing shop down the street, especially mail from Washington state or his parents.

Nate chose a post office several miles from his apartment and one with a different zip code. He did believe he should have a few magazines and junk mail sent to his apartment. No need to alert Dino to any unusual actions on his part. Then he remembered that Carmen and Kathy should not call him at the apartment. Must find a safe phone and set up a specific time for calls. Another problem. Would he ever have a relaxing lifestyle again?

The following day he learned about printing new "papers" for well-healed customers. Each set cost five thousand dollars and consisted of a driver's license (any state), three credit cards, (various names), social security card, and basic identification. How convenient, thought Nate. A man named Hugh checked him out on procedures and Nate found the process fascinating.

137

His mind immediately leaped to a birth certificate for Natalie, identification for Carmen and a birth certificate for her as well. The documents were perfect. No name, no test, could reveal that they were false and wouldn't this please Kathy and Tom? Get them completely off the hook. He would tell them that he had done research and found Carmen's background that perhaps she did not know. He decided Carmen's birthplace would be Miami. No one checked anything coming out of Miami anyway, and her age eighteen. He had to keep Natalie's birthplace in Colorado or Kathy wouldn't believe anything else he sent. He decided on a death certificate for Carmen's fantasy husband which made Natalie legitimate. Perfect. And so easy. A social security card for both Carmen and Natalie. America citizens. He made several fake credit cards for them as well, along with a few for himself.

After three days of instruction, Hugh left to do something else and Nate waited another two days before doing the new "papers" for his own use. Always cautious, he knew Dino was maybe watching, although he had carefully checked out hiding places. Plus, he worked on new "papers" for others so it became easy to slip in something for Carmen. And, hey, as a widow, Carmen was eligible for social security payments for Natalie. No, he told himself, don't press your luck. The papers are for emergencies only. And only recently received from Miami, Kathy would be told. She may question some of it, but still would be happy to have legitimate information. What a deal.

And it was. It all worked like a charm. Kathy was in no hurry to ship Carmen to Los Angeles.

"Let her stay longer. It's working out so well," Kathy pleaded. "She's wonderful with Tommy."

It had been completely out of Nate's thoughts to find a place for Carmen and Natalie. He had planned to leave them with Kathy a couple of months at least, maybe longer. So far he had seen no trace of Rudy or even heard his name mentioned but, no fool, Nate did not believe Rudy had given up. Dino had not mentioned Carmen, either. Stay alert, Nate began each day stressing that.

Nate was right in staying alert since two days later Dino arrived at the print shop, a bag of donuts in hand,

and offering a chit-chat. He's having too many of those, Nate mused, observing the extra pounds Dino carried around his waist .

"Let's sit awhile and snack," Dino invited, pulling up a couple of chairs and placing the donuts on a small table. "Want you to know I'm very pleased with your work. Couldn't be better."

"Thank you," Nate responded .

"Yep, Vinnie sent me the best person I've ever had," Dino finished off one donut and, talking with full mouth, reached for another. "Yep, you're the best."

Nate had yet to take even one bite. He avoided empty calories but decided to nibble away at a donut to please Dino. Not that he didn't like them but this meant another hour of bicycling, an activity he now pursued. Who really, could question a nightly bike ride to stay in condition and if the ride happened to go by a post office or a mail handling facility. Well then, who would ever question that?

"I have some great plans for you, Nate. Great plans. Got a long association planned with you. You're like a son to me. Trust you with my life." Dino took another donut shoving it in his mouth.

"Gee, thanks, I really like it here and if you want me to do more or other things, just let me know," Nate offered.

"Trust. That's what it's all about, and I want you to feel free to come to me if you ever have a problem. I can fix just about anything."

"I will. Certainly I will. I appreciate your faith in me and will do all I can to justify it."

Then Dino talked about his children, mentioning several school problems. Minor situations, a lost special baseball, a bully that Dino talked to the counselor about, all things taken care of nicely by Dino. He talked of his wife's shopping habits, just a few tidbits to imply that he trusted Nate to share family secrets or at least personal situations.

Nate felt elated that Dino apparently wanted his friendship as well as being so pleased with his job performance. Nice to have a friend.

Dino repeated this scene the following afternoon. As Dino opened the door to the printing shop, Nate quickly locked the darkroom door. The dark room led to a secure printing area where the illegal papers were processed. The main printing area was clearly visible by anyone entering the shop and showed stacks of job orders. A very legitimate and busy shop.

"You don't have to lock it when I come in," Dino remarked.

"Habit, Hugh said be careful of that. Never know who's coming in."

"Good Job. He's right."

Nate made no move to unlock the door. Dino didn't request that he unlock it, his mission not concerned with printing.

This time Dino talked about his parents, spending his early years on the east coast; the move to Los Angeles; and inheriting the printing shop from his father. Again Nate felt the warmth of friendship.

"Nate, something has come to my attention and I need to talk to you about it," Dino said.

"Yes, sir?" Nate thought possibly a printing order mistake or some minor problem.

"It seems a fellow named Rudy thinks you helped his live-in run away. Now, I hardly know the man. He showed up here a couple of weeks ago looking for you, but when I told him I didn't expect you at any particular time, he left. I did tell Vinnie I'd ask you about her." Dino leaned forward striking a conspiracy pose. "Now you are special to me and I'm definitely on your side, so I told Vinnie there's no one around here that you helped. That seemed to satisfy him. Thing is, if you did, I want to help you if you need it or even want it."

He's so sincere and a real friend, Nate thought, and this maybe a way to find a place for Carmen and Natalie. Perhaps one of Dino's apartments. Course Kathy doesn't want her to leave and maybe if he told Dino that she wants to stay in Washington all would be okay.

"Well, I....." Nate began.

"Trust me on this," Dino interrupted.

Those words again and up went the red flag. He had practice now and no way would he give away Carmen's location or even any indication that he knew her.

"I have no idea and really why he would think so is beyond me. After all the fuss I kinda wish I did know. Solve a lot of problems," Nate felt dejected. Was there no one he could trust? No one on his side. No one believing his, let's face it, lies. And he had almost blown it, chiding himself for not suspecting Dino. After all, his phones were bugged. Why did "trust me" raise such suspicions? He could be wrong, still he couldn't take chances.

The friendly chats and donuts stopped after that day. Nate had no way of knowing if Dino's suspicions did. The telephone remained bugged, mail riffled through after Nate carefully put it in some order. What a life. He knew his apartment had been entered as well.

The pluses came with letters and photos of Natalie sent to the P.O. Box number and then diligently destroyed. Though a photo of Natalie to carry around would be great. It broke his heart, but he ripped the letters and photos to shreds before leaving the post office. Kathy's letters praised Carmen. It seems day-care was out. After pre-school, Tommy spent the time with Carmen. So far, Tommy can count to 100, say his A B C's, print his name, address and telephone number, distinguish and name most colors, draw birds and other animals, say many words and phrases in Spanish. And, she continued, he even loads the dishwasher. "She's wonderful!" They never wanted her to leave. Tom had made arrangements for Carmen to take high school classes at home and she passed a test to receive her GED. Very intelligent, said Kathy, especially in languages and history.

"Did you know she speaks not only Spanish, English, and Russian, but also French and a little Japanese?" Kathy gushed.

Nate was content to leave her in Washington. It made his life much easier. He began to relax and make friends. He surfed most weekends and although he knew he still broke the law in his job, at least he did not deliver dimethylmercury or other drugs, nor did he see any dead bodies around to be disposed of.

Natalie was now three months old and smiling all the time. And one tooth. He wished he could see her.

CHAPTER FIFTEEN

"Okay, Nate, we're ready for the big promotion." Dino walked into the printing shop and this time chewing on a large piece of beef jerky. He went to the Coke machine, banged on the top, and retrieved a can of Coke from the dispenser. "Here's some info you need to memorize so you can talk about it with authority and sincerity." He handed Nate a maroon eelskin briefcase containing a dozen or so typewritten pages.

"These are for your eyes only so don't leave them around," Dino indicated the papers. "Keep the case locked at all times unless you are reading them."

"All right," Nate fingered the briefcase. Very nice and very expensive. He examined the handle which had his initials raised in gold. N.W.O. Nathan William Olmstead. How great, he thought, to be himself again and to not be hiding. At last his job would be in the open and he could even be proud to use his own name.

"The stats will be hard to remember and you will be carrying some info with you at your presentations but learn as much as possible. You'll get some tough questions and I want the answers to be right."

"I understand." Nate responded not knowing at all what he had agreed to do. A presentation? Of what? But, he didn't ask. Dino gave answers in his own sweet time.

"Vinnie says you learn pretty quick so I'm depending on you. Understand?" Dino stared into Nate's eyes and this always gave Nate an uneasy feeling.

"You won't be disappointed," but as Nate glanced at the pages he hardly recognized any of the words. What is this anyhow?

THE DECISION

He would learn more than he dreamed possible about a subject he had never heard of. Working in Vinnie's organization was challenging to say the least. He had observed much more about many things he wished he never knew; he had met people he hoped never to see again. But would he? Coming to Los Angeles had offered a new opportunity for him, but, as he now knew, the old regime prevailed.

CHAPTER SIXTEEN

The New Project

John and Stella

"John, you did it again!" Stella glared at her husband as she slammed the closet door.

"What again?" John gave a belligerent look back.

"Put the garbage in the coat closet," Stella answered, as she pulled a white plastic bag of garbage out of the closet and set it on the floor next to the door.

"I did not. Your boyfriend next door did it. I saw him."

"Oh, John, Rick hasn't been here for months. Not since you threw that rake at him," Stella's voice was soft with sadness.

"He has too. He was right there in that closet waiting for me to go to sleep so he could kiss you. I saw him go in."

"So did you open the closet door and see him?"

"He wasn't in there. He cut a hole in the back so he could get out quick, before I could get to him." John raised his fist as if to strike Stella but didn't bring it down on her. "I know what's going on. You think I don't, but I do. I'm not dumb or blind."

"I know you're not, but you're seeing things and people that aren't there."

"You think I don't see that fellow waiting for you! You think I don't see you get out of bed and go meet him." John slammed his fist on the arm of the chair where he now sat.

THE DECISION

"Oh, John," Stella's voice tender with love and caring. Her eyes began to fill with tears.

"I know he's waiting out there right now, by the bushes."

"Let's go see." Stella moved towards the chair, reaching out to John.

John grabbed her arm, "He's out there, you're not going out. Not this time. I'm getting him." He picked up a hammer he had placed by the living room door, and lunged towards the entry way. "I'll get him now."

Stella slumped into a recliner. What next? she asked herself. What can she do?

John is seventy-four, she is seventy-two. She knew they didn't have many years left and it looked as if what they have will not be happy.

Several times each week, a scene like this happened at the home of John and Stella Stephens. John, as Stella well knew, suffered from Alzheimer's and senility. Many times he forgot his name, where he lived, or even that they had two sons and four grandchildren. And he got mean. Accused her of all sorts of things. But, the thing that hurt most was about Rick, a very nice young man with a lovely wife and three adorable children. They had been such good friends ---the children running to her and John with school pictures and progress reports; being included in backyard picnics; birthday parties; and special celebrations ---- until John got sick and began believing Rick was her lover. She had never, ever, had anyone in her life except John.

Some days he didn't have, what she began to call, his attacks. Sometimes he was almost normal and they talked and laughed about earlier days of marriage and children. But, never did they go next door and the children didn't come to their house anymore. Stella missed them.

She tried, really tried. When his days were good she almost believed all was great again. But then, without warning, the accusations would begin again and he would check closets, the garage, and constantly peer out the window looking for Rick. Stella didn't invite friends over anymore, nor did she accept invitations. Church was out as well, since John once said Pastor Blake kept looking at her. She decided then that they should stay away.

But, she must do something. He could fly into a rage and really physically injure her or someone. He kept the hammer close by and once brought in a crowbar. She did manage to hide that and she had to admit, she lived in fear. Their sons offered no suggestions other than say, "maybe he should go to a nursing home." But, who could afford that? Not the Stephens nor could their children.

She picked up the brochure she had received several days before and read it one more time. Maybe this would work. She dialed a telephone number.

Barry and Sidney

"Barry try a few more spoons of soup, you need to get some nutrition in you," Sidney said beside the bed of his lover.

"Your famous chicken soup. My favorite, thank you," Barry in a weakened condition, managed a slight smile. "And you made the noodles into stars and the moon. How did you do that?"

"My mother always did that when I was sick or when she wanted to surprise me with something special," explained Sidney. He fluffed up the pillow around Barry and helped him sit up a little straighter, hoping he could eat again.

"You know, Sid, it seems to take me longer to shake anything I catch anymore." Barry convulsed into a long bout of coughing and had to lean back on the pillow before he attempted another spoonful of soup. "Someone sneezes and I catch pneumonia."

"I know. You'll have to get more strength before you go back to work. You always go back too soon."

"Maybe."

Both men knew they were lying. Both knew Barry's immune system was failing more and more each day.

Sidney and Barry had been lovers for seven years. Years of pure joy, for them anyway. They could hardly believe their good luck in finding each other. And it had been pure luck. Sidney had entered a race to raise money for AIDS and needed a good pair of running shoes. He wandered into an upscale department store in Horton Plaza where Barry, a high school senior, worked part-time in the shoe department. Later, both agreed they felt a tingle at their first meeting. Barry entered the race as well and the two became friends, talking more than concentrating on running, but it didn't matter, something special had happened.

They moved in together a year later, alienating their families. Barry's parents blamed Sidney, who was three years older, for pursuing Barry and turning him into a homosexual. And it nearly killed his parents when Barry admitted that, indeed, he had been gay since he was twelve and his Dad's business partner had been his first lover. Only to avoid public embarrassment were the men able to dissolve the partnership in a peaceful manner. Barry's parents moved across the country to Alabama where they could stretch their retirement money much further than in San Diego.

Sidney had no such problems with his parents. They knew he was "different" from the time he was in elementary school. They shipped him to live with a relative in San Diego and felt they fulfilled their parental duty with a substantial check each month. The relative didn't know, nor care, how Sidney spent his time. When Sidney and Barry rented an apartment, Sidney's parents used it as a reason to stop sending checks.

Barry got a full-time job at the department store and moved from shoes to men's wear. His commissions were terrific. Sidney worked in construction. They bought a fixer-upper house, remodeled it in their spare time and sold it, making a forty thousand dollar profit. They were now on their fifth house and owned their own home in San Diego's Hillcrest section. Typically, their car had a rainbow strip across the back window, the mailbox was covered in bright rainbow colors, and every Thursday they wore green shirts. They liked being openly gay in a community where it was readily acceptable.

The only sadness came with Barry's inability to fight illness. Each knew it was just a matter of time until Barry could fight no longer. Sidney took the soup dish into the kitchen. As he placed it in the dishwasher, he picked up the brochure Barry had received a few days earlier.

This maybe the best way, he told himself. He dialed a telephone number.

Claire and Ross

"Honey, do you want to go to the play with the group Friday night?" Ross asked his wife.

"Do you mind if we don't?" Claire leaned her head back and pushed the recliner arms so that her feet were raised to a more comfortable position. "It seems I'm sleepy by nine o'clock lately and they always want to end the evening with a late dinner. Maybe next month."

"Is your back still bothering you?"

"It's kind of a nagging pain, down here." Claire put her hand on her lower back, rubbing it gently.

"Here, let me do that." As Claire leaned forward, Ross rubbed her back, giving relief to the, now it seemed, constant pain.

"You need to see the doctor about this. And you need to stop working in the yard so much." Ross admonished.

"I haven't been. Kyle mowed the grass and he's coming again next week to weed the flower beds."

"You didn't tell me." Ross showed immediate concern. Claire never let anyone in her flower gardens. They were her pride and joy.

"I know. You worry too much. This is probably old age aches and pains."

"Old age at thirty-seven?" Ross chided her, "promise me you'll call for a doctor's appointment. Call tomorrow, okay?'

"Okay." Claire hadn't told Ross how many weeks the back pain had persisted or that every afternoon she rested. She had always been so strong, enjoyed the yard work, kept the house spotless. But lately the energy just wasn't there and that dull ache in her back really took its toll on activity. The over-the-counter pain relievers didn't help much anymore.

"I won't take the haul unless you go see what's wrong," Ross stated firmly.

"I will. Where's the trip this time?" Claire asked, not really wanting conversation, but knowing Ross would suspect she tried to hide more pain if she didn't ask questions and show interest in the answers.

Ross owned his large semi and contracted trucking jobs. Actually, he owned two smaller trucks as well and made a good living for his family and his drivers. The only problem was being away from home so much. It put the burden of raising Ryan, Randy, and Molly, and the care of the home entirely on Claire. It was wearing her down, Ross thought. She needs a vacation.

"I'm moving a load of furniture to St. Louis and bringing a load of carpets back from Dalton, Georgia. Be gone about ten days. Ken's going along as relief driver. Be a good payday."

When Ross returned home Claire made her report on the doctor visit. "He wants to do exploratory surgery. Wanted me to go right away, but I told him I had to talk to you about it first. I'm not too crazy about surgery, as you well know."

"Why didn't you tell me? We talked every night?" Ross was a trifle peeved at Claire. She seems to be hiding something, he thought.

"You would have only worried. It's nothing. Maybe an obstruction pressing on a nerve, a bone out of place, or a little fat ball."

Claire laughed or attempted to. She winced instead.

"You're going in today," demanded Ross.

The surgery revealed exactly what Dr. Stoddard knew it would. Claire's body was ravaged with cancer. He told Ross that Claire had six to eight months to live and only if she had chemotherapy.

The couple were devastated. Ross couldn't function, yet he must. He quit driving his truck on the long hauls, designating those jobs to his other drivers. He now worked only a few hours each day, spending much time with Claire. She often heard him crying in another room. And many times hitting a wall, trying to relieve the anger that he would soon lose his wife, his love. His high school sweetheart, the only woman he had ever loved or wanted in his life. The pain of this knowledge became unbearable. He couldn't talk to the children, couldn't play catch, or shoot baskets, or read stories to Molly. He resented anyone else's good health. Why, why God, why Claire? Loving, generous Claire, wonderful Claire. He couldn't attend church or school events. Instead, he would hole up in the garage to vent his anger. He sank into deep depression and began to drink. Staying away from home later and later at night.

Finally one day Claire said, "Ross, I don't want to die, but I can face death much easier than face what is happening to you." Her eyes brimmed with tears. "You come in the house and never even see that Ryan is bouncing his basketball, hoping for a game of horse, or that Randy is hitting his fist in his catcher's mitt, waiting for you to pitch to him. Molly quietly holds her books and I'm sure wondering if you will read her a bedtime story." Claire's tears spilled over, "Ross, they need you. Just .... Ross. They are losing their mother, don't make them lose their father too," she pleaded.

"Claire, my darling Claire. You deserve so much more." Ross couldn't keep the tears away as he buried his head in her lap. Her sharp hip bones showed how much weight she had lost and flesh hung loosely on her arms as she caressed him. "I'm so sorry. I've let you and my kids down so I could wallow in self-pity."

"We were thrown a curve, darling, but we have had so much more than many people ever get. Twenty-one years. My high school hero. And God has given us time to make plans, to ease into this. I could have been hit by a car and been gone instantly, or you could have. We must thank God for our years together and our beautiful family."

"How can you be like that, Claire? You of all people shouldn't have had this happen to you. You're always doing so much for everyone else. You never say 'why me' or complain in any way."

"We don't know why and it isn't up to us to question God's ways. You know that. We have several months to plan our children's future and yours. Let's live them in the right way." Claire smiled and held up a small square of cloth. "I taught Molly how to sew a button on something. Ross, she was so serious and didn't even prick her finger."

"She's only four," Ross quietly remarked and held the cloth against his face. So many memories. Claire, in constant pain, still used her energy to leave the children things she knew they would need to know when she wouldn't be around to help them. The picture in his mind of his small daughter sewing a button on a piece of cloth changed his attitude and burned in his mind forever. No more would he neglect his family. If Claire could face dying without tears or complaints, then he certainly could face living in a responsible way.

That evening he shot baskets with Ryan; pitched with Randy what they both said would be a no-hitter in the majors; and read "Sleeping Beauty," Molly's favorite story, until the little girl fell asleep. He talked Claire into eating a dish of her favorite maplenut ice-cream, but like most of the food she ate, it moved through her system at a rapid pace and she barely reached the bathroom before her bowels exploded and the waste came pouring out. This left her in such a weakened condition that she needed Ross to help her back to the recliner.

Her stomach could tolerate only thin, watery broth with no meat or vegetables. Another time, when she asked for watermelon, she didn't reach the bathroom in time and Ross cleaned a trail of excrement across the floor. This was not the first, nor would it be the last time he cleaned her and would have gladly done it every day for the rest of his life if she could get well.

But, she didn't. He knew her days were ending. He read the brochure once again. This maybe best, he thought, and dialed a telephone number.

Lillian Long, AKA Lily

"Come on, Ron, get me that part. You know I'm right for it." Lily sat on a pink velvet settee in the pink and white living room of her luxury condo in Westbrook. The entire unit was decorated in those colors, which Lily said showed her exquisite complexion best; thick white carpets, marble-topped end tables enhanced with delicate pink etchings spelling out her name; deep cushioned sofas and chairs, all with Lily's beauty in mind when purchased; several large paintings of her decorated the walls. This condo definitely belonged to a movie star. She was reflected in every corner with gold-trimmed mirrors. Lily had graced the screen for almost twenty years now and she wasn't about to give it up.

"It doesn't say you, Lily. Guy wants a dark-haired twenty-year old. A new face."

"Ron, I can be that girl. A dye job takes five minutes and I've played twenty for years."

"Guy is adamant on this. I could ask him to test you, I guess."

Lily began to pace around the room like a caged lion, "Ron, you know I don't test for anyone. No one!" Lily shouted.

"I'll talk to him again, but, I can't promise." Ron averted his eyes from her and stared out the window at the city below.

"You better do more than promise," Lily stomped her foot and pulled another cigarette from a pack. Ron jumped to light it. "Why do you think I pay you all that money?"

"Lillian, listen....."

"And don't call me Lillian. It's Lily, Lily, Lily. Don't you, of all people, forget it!" She angrily crushed out the cigarette and flounced down in a chair, pushing her long blonde hair over the back, spreading it out like a fan.

Ron studied her. She carried five-feet four inches very well, indeed. Never been more than one-ten and all distributed beautifully. Every inch a star. Never letting down for a moment, always looking terrific. Even her long pink crepe jump suit hugged her body as if it appreciated touching such beauty. Still, the little lines around her mouth defied the cover cream she used constantly and the area under her eyes seemed to get a little puffier each week. She was beginning to look her thirty-eight years. Smoking so much didn't help either, he said to himself.

"You know, Ron, I'm an Academy Award winner. That should count for something in this rotten business."

"It does, Lily, it does. But Guy wants a new face and all the hair change and makeup cannot hide those beautiful eyes." Was he laying it on too thick? "You know your fans will recognize you right away, and you have too many of them to think you could go unnoticed."

She walked to a mirror which covered one wall, "I can still do it." She turned right, then left, pulled her chin up and did all the poses she did for hours everyday. "Get me something. I haven't had a big one for four years. I have to get back on top. Sometimes, I think that award is a death knell to a career."

"Spencer asked about you for Alice in "Hunting." Sounds like a good part and you would give it class."

"What are you saying? Alice is the mother of a seventeen-year-old. I can't play that. It isn't even the lead. He sent me the script and I threw it out. Garbage, that's all it is!" She fumed, "and I would never be called Alice. That's so old sounding. Tell him to shove it."

"Sometimes the bit parts are the juiciest."

"Who do you work for anyway? Just leave!"

As Ron left, he tossed a brochure on the coffee table. Maybe this could work. She's been a star too long to accept anything less. Convincing her would be a whole new ballgame. And she's no dummy. Money isn't a problem. Nor is the condo. He had studied the brochure for days. Ever since the certified copy had been sent to him. By whom? He had no idea. He called the number and got more information and mulled the possibilities for Lily over and over in his mind. And no one would ever know.

He dialed a telephone number.

Armon, Harold, Frankie

"You're stupid, Armon. How many times I tell you to wear a disguise? And what you guys doing hitting a stupid bank this close to here anyhow? Did I get you out for that?" Vinnie was furious.

"We didn't think the cameras were that good...."

"You didn't think. You're right, you didn't think, and now your ugly mugs are plastered all over the TV. Lucky my number's scrambled, or the cops would be knocking on my door this minute. Think they can't find you? Think they don't trace your calls? Think they don't know your hangouts?"

"We're not in any of them. Called you first to see where we can hide."

"I oughta send you right back to Attica."

"Please help us with this, we won't blow it again."

"I can't get you out of it. You're escaped cons remember? Dumb for showing your faces like that. And why kill that kid? The public is furious."

"Most of the small banks don't even turn on the cameras."

"That was years ago. Now every place has a camera. A kid in a wheel chair. You're stupid."

"What can we do? Where can we go? You got a place we can hole up?"

"Why the kid?"

"Just got in the way. You know how that is. You been there."

"Hey, don't get arrogant with me. I can put you right back and I might. I thought you guys had more brains. Know what I'd have had you doing? Gonna change your looks and put you on a boat out of Miami. Only, no, you couldn't wait for that. Now all the cops in the country know your names and what you look like. Your ugly mugs."

"There must be some place."

Armon, Harold and Frankie were some of the country's worst criminals. All running from the law, all knowing that if caught they would only be sent back to Attica, if lucky. But, their worst thought was a rebel cop or vigilante shooting them on sight. They were scared of that. All of them could adjust to prison life. They knew how to get along there.

And were their crimes so bad? Sure, society called them monsters, but there's two sides to everything. Right?

Well, wrong. They were monsters and every cop in every town in the United States, Canada, Mexico, and Cuba were on the alert for them.

Armon, and that's all he ever wanted to be called, no last name, just Armon, grew up in East St. Louis, Illinois. Everyone who knew him said he would wind up in jail. He was the kid who put the tail of a cat in gasoline, lit it, and then laughed when the cat howled in pain; or took a younger child's lunch money or even a sack lunch from another if it looked better than what he had, which most of the time was nothing; he stole money from his mother's purse; and made his sister watch while he killed her pet rabbit. And these things before he was ten years old. In his teens he graduated to stealing cars; dealing drugs in the high school which he never attended as a student but hung around anyway; he performed a botched abortion on a girlfriend nearly killing her; and had appeared in juvenile court numerous times. He spent time in a youth detention facility making friends with whom he would continue his life of crime.

In his early twenties, the crimes drew the attention of newspapers whose editorials asked how he managed to stay out of prison. He didn't when he killed a newspaper editor who had reported on Armon and his crimes. Armon testified the killing was during a drive-by shooting in which he did not participate and he had no idea who the victim had been. However, the threats he had made to the editor as well as other solid evidence put Armon in Attica. He was sentenced to life and while there several inmates lost arms, legs, eyes, and one his life, always when Armon happened to be around. The code of silence prevailed and he was never held responsible for any of the deplorable acts even though everyone knew he was.

Harold Prossale had much the same background as Armon. Harold began his life of crime in his early years and mother blindness protected him but left society vulnerable to his acts of violence. His distorted view of acceptable behavior was like a hurricane destroying whatever was in the path he hated. Hate was ever present in his mind and his prison time resulted by him murdering his mother, the one person he could really depend upon.

Harold joined Armon in several violent acts at Attica.

Frankie Adams always sought acceptance. In his early years he agreed to anything any of his so-called friends asked. He gladly gave his lunch money to the school's bully who shared many of Armon's traits. Later, Frankie was a go-between for drug dealers; drove a get-away car for bank heists; watched for cops while prostitutes canvassed an area; he did whatever it took to be one of the guys. He ended up in Attica when he blew off the head of a pretty convenience store clerk when a thug named Joe Boy told him the murder would really make him one of the gang. Frankie never knew Joe Boy had been rebuffed by the girl and wanted to get even.

Frankie reigned as a favorite at Attica ---- willing to do anything for anyone until Armon decided he could use someone so willing to perform. No one argued with Armon.

Armon, Harold, and Frankie got out of prison when an agreement was made with a clerk working in the warden's office to substitute their names on a list of parolees. Who made the arrangements? Who else but Vinnie. Course, the error was discovered but not until the three men were long gone and determined that they needed some quick money.

Now Vinnie made another arrangement for them. He dialed a number in Los Angeles and within an hour the three were on a jet headed to the City of Angels.

CHAPTER SEVENTEEN

"Well, Nate, are you prepared? This is the biggest project we've ever had. Make us a lot of money, but more important to Vinnie, he's sure to get a Nobel Prize," Dino seemed hyper as if he had just won a lottery.

"I've memorized what you gave me and spent some time in the library to learn more. Didn't though. Your material is very complete." Nate riffled through the papers and placed them back in his briefcase being careful to lock it.

"We do our homework. The meeting is set for Tuesday night." Dino continued filling Nate in on the procedures. "Dr. Randolph Ruben will be there to answer technical questions and Max Scidderly will talk on religious issues if any come up. Nossivie Nguyen will handle finances. Try not to use his name too much cause it sounds foreign and people get suspicious of that."

"It is foreign. Isn't he from Vietnam?" Nate asked.

"Yeah, I know, and people don't want no foreigner telling them how to spend their money."

"I have one question and I'm not sure how to ask it," Nate was hesitant, but still needed to be clear on this issue.

"Shoot." Dino had a feeling he knew what Nate questioned. He had some doubts himself when first Vinnie proposed the project.

"Don't get angry, but is this really on the level? Sounds kind of, well, fakery, like a sham, you know, swindle, take the money and run type of thing." There, he had asked the question that had bugged him ever since Dino had given him the papers to read.

157

"I know what fake means, but it's on the level. Real. You asking don't make me mad. I asked plenty of questions myself, but the great part is the organization is doing something for posterity. Think of it," Dino seemed elated to talk about the project, "all the junk people have said or thought, not many would say it out loud, about Vinnie and his business ethics will grovel at his feet because of all the good this will do."

"It sounds terrific," Nate agreed.

"Not sounds, it is terrific and you can put it over," Dino continued. "You're exactly the kind of guy Vinnie said you were. Maybe have to lighten your hair a little and try to spend the next couple of days in the sun to make your tan a little darker," Dino ruffled Nate's hair in a friendly manner. "You look so average and the best part you have a trustworthy attitude."

"Well, I'll be telling the truth so looking the part will be easy," Nate replied. "You know Richard worked with me several weeks so I'd look average. Said it's an advantage 'cause no one could describe me. Nothing stands out." Nate grinned at Dino an innocent expression on his face.

Dino orchestrated the meeting place as if people would hear the most beautiful music in the world. And, indeed, they would. Who wouldn't feel a glow when thinking life could go on forever. In fact, that's exactly what the project is called ---- LIFE, live forever. Nate's job is to explain how.

Dino chose a meeting room that offered a view of a marina and the expansive Pacific Ocean. Floral arrangements scattered throughout the room matched original Monet paintings, of course, giving the impression of flowers forever. Other prints showed children at play, a couple on a sailboat, a man landing a large fish while a smiling woman (his wife?) looked on, and a lovely beach with waves gently lapping the shore. Everything geared to show the good life. Life, that's the key word.

Nate, Dino, Dr. Ruben, Nguyen, and Scidderly, sat in an adjoining room. A middle-aged man and woman, hired for the occasion, greeted the guests at the door and guided them to a seat. Nate had noticed that the chairs were very comfortable, no folding metal chairs for this group. The guests were given a handout with a very brief outline of the program. Nothing specific and distributed only because people expect handouts at a meeting. Later they would be given more detailed information and telephone numbers.

Dino slipped into the meeting room to observe the audience and do a head count. The group was limited to one hundred and he counted ninety eight. Then the final couple entered and as anyone could guess the woman wore a disguise.... sort of. A red wig, dark glasses, and a wide-brimmed hat which did not hide her beauty. Wait 'til Nate discovers who is listening, Dino chuckled. He sat with Armon, Harold and Frankie. "Keep them in line," Vinnie had admonished.

The male greeter, Harry something or other, closed the door and stepped up to a three-foot raised platform.

"Ladies and gentlemen, may I present Mr. Nathan Olmstead," said Harry. Then he and his female co-worker, left the room. They had done their job and weren't involved in any other part of the presentation.

Nate, wearing gray trousers, a blue blazer, lighter blue shirt, and a gray and blue striped tie, entered the room and took his place at the lectern. He glanced at the audience, left for five seconds, the middle for five seconds, and then to the right for another five seconds before moving his eyes back to the middle. He made no eye contact but it seemed as if he had.

"Ladies and gentlemen, I'm delighted to be with you tonight to share with you a scientific breakthrough that will change your lives forever. But, before I get to that, let me introduce my colleagues, Dr. Randolph Ruben, Mr. Max Scidderly, and Mr. Nossivie Nguyen." The three men entered the room and took seats slightly behind and to the side of the lectern. There was a scattering of applause.

"Thank you," Nate continued with a slight nod of his head towards the three men. "As you may know, each of you was sent a special invitation to attend this meeting. You all have a reason to be here, although not the same one. The reason is life, and life as you want it to be." Nate glanced to the window, and several pairs of eyes followed his. The setting sun cast its colors in the sky. The yellows, pinks, and lavenders were impressive. Truly one of the most beautiful sights in the world. Dino's timing of the meeting was inspiring. He knew it would be.

"For years, medical scientists have researched ways to make the aging process stop, to extend lives, to revive life after a terminal illness or fatal accident." Nate made the sweep of the room again, his eyes focusing just above the heads of the audience. "Think for a moment, if you will, if your life could go on forever, you could do all the things you've planned, or always dreamed about, you could spend time with your loved ones." In the audience Barry and Sidney exchanged affectionate looks. "But, you are saying to yourself, only if I have good health," Nate observed the head nods. He had their attention.

"Now, that can be done. This procedure is called 'CRYONICS.'" Nate paused, "A new word to you, perhaps, but not to the scientific world. It has been around for over twenty years and is exciting. Until now, CRYONICS seemed like a pipe dream, but, as you will see, the extension of a healthy life is a reality. So what is CRYONICS?" Nate again paused and his eyes swept the audience, "It's a method of freezing a body after death, a word we don't use anymore but for clarification in this instance I will use the word only once, and then after a period of time reviving the person. To understand how this works, Dr. Ruben will expand on technical information, but, for now I will give you a brief explanation."

Nate flipped a few pages of his notes. "Our bodies are made up of many cells and they are supplied with needed nutrients by the blood stream. When the cells receive what they need, our bodies respond. But, if the nutrients are not provided to the cells, then our bodies, after a short period, quit functioning. This could be minutes and caused by several things, a fatal accident, heart attack, or terminal illness. Still, there is a period when, and you all know what Cardiopulmonary Resuscitation, CPR, is done quickly. Oxygen is forced into the lungs and blood is pumped through the body to the cells and in many cases the bodily functions continue. Now, at low temperatures the cells deteriorate more slowly, so medical scientists researched the theory that freezing the body could stop the process of deterioration completely. Scientists now know that as long as the brain cells in a body are functioning, then life is there as well." Nate's eyes surveyed the audience using the five seconds for each section. "So how is CRYONICS, and what we call suspension, accomplished?" Nate saw the questions in the eyes of the audience. This was the biggie.

"Until a few years ago, CRYONICS could not be used until a medical doctor had determined that nothing more could be done to prolong the patient's life. That is not the case now. People can choose to enter this method of life extension at their own volition. Still, the procedures are the same no matter when CRYONICS is administered. Briefly, it works this way. When the patient decides the time has come to enter into CRYONICS, a technical expert provides nutrients that will shield the cells from injury with a special cooling solution. Remember this slows down cell damage, and then the patient is transferred to a LIFE facility to undergo the entire CRYONICS process."

"But," a member of the audience interrupted, "where... if..."

"Hold your thought and jot down your questions," Nate responded, "we will have a question and answer session following our presentation and we may have answered your question." He smiled at the man and then continued his talk. "At this facility, and," he nodded to the man who had started to interrupt, "we have four in the United States, here in Los Angeles, Dallas, Minneapolis, and Miami, plus Australia, Japan, and Germany." Nate received a nod from the person acknowledging that was, indeed, his question.

"At the facility the patient undergoes the necessary procedures to accept the process. And later, Dr. Ruben will explain that in detail. After the patient is receptive to the CRYONICS process, the patient is transferred to our LIFE long-term care facility. There, and we will be showing you slides of this facility, the patient is placed in a "Dewar" which is a double-walled flask with a vacuum between the walls which are silvered on the inside. This flask is named for Sir James Dewar, a Scot chemist-physicist who lived from 1848 to 1923. The flask is filled with liquid nitrogen . Nitrogen is a colorless, ordorless gaseous chemical element forming nearly four-fifths of the atmosphere. It is a component of all proteins and nucleic acids. And, I have to thank Dr. Ruben for that explanation." Nate put his arm out towards the doctor to include him in the presentation.

"When nitrogen is in liquefied form, it has a temperature of 320 degrees below zero. Therefore, there is no need to depend on refrigeration or electrical power for CRYONICS. The Dewar is monitored on a daily basis and more liquid is added if nitrogen turns into a vapor, provided heat from the environment seeps in. However, this is very minimum and as Dr. Ruben has said, he has never known this to occur.

"Nitrogen is inexpensive, easily available, no complicated storage is necessary, and completely reliable. Therefore, CRYONICS is affordable to almost anyone. Mr. Nguyen will have more on that for you." Nate nodded to Nguyen, who in turn smiled and moved his head forward to acknowledge the words.

"Now," Nate hesitated, giving the audience time to anticipate his next remarks, "LIFE has been developed much further than any other organization or foundation, but, before I get into that, I would like Dr. Ruben to speak on suspension and how a patient is prepared. I'm trying to keep this in chronological order, but, I must admit, it's hard not to reveal our best secret." Nate motioned to the doctor, "Dr. Ruben, if you please."

"Thank you Nate, I'm sure the audience loves a secret, so I'll be brief." He smiled and received smiles in return. "I'm sure you're asking what about people caught in an avalanche, frozen under tons of snow, why don't they survive?" He gazed at the audience as if he had, indeed, anticipated the question. "Quickness is the answer. Remember we slow down the function of the cells at our various facilities and then the patient is flown to our long-term care facility." Dr. Ruben checked his notes, "By the way, the facilities located here in Los Angeles and the other places Nate mentioned, are primarily for research, but, they are located in strategic areas so that people will receive the necessary procedure to slow cell activity in a timely manner. And we have agreements with all hospitals to give the patient emergency care. Patients will carry identification on the procedures needed and you will learn more about that later."

Dr. Ruben took a sip of water and then continued with his explanation, "When arriving at the long-time care facility, and from now on we will refer to it as LTF, the patient receives cryosurgery, an open heart operation so that a circulatory system can be infused, kind of like antifreeze in an automobile's radiator," he smiled, " which will give cells protection from freezing damage as the patient's temperature is lowered. In earlier methods, damage to cells did occur but, our methods have virtually controlled damage and that's our own procedure. No one else has access to it and will not until a patent is received. We use micro-miniaturization which actually is a robot, if you will, small enough to be injected into the blood stream. They clone themselves and follow a procedure to repair all kinds of damage," Dr. Ruben stated.

"Now," he continued, "here's what I want you to think about. How close are we to finding a cure for AIDS, is the artificial heart perfected, cancer almost licked, multiple sclerosis a thing of the past, Alzheimer's, or any number of diseases that decimate life, all gone? Of course they aren't. Nate? Will you tell us your secret?"

Nate took his stance at the lectern, "I'm very excited and humbled by this revelation. Not only has LIFE perfected CRYONIC suspension but now," he paused, glanced at the window once again at the now darkening sky, "we have perfected reanimation ---- bringing a patient back to life. No other foundation or medical facility can make that statement. I cannot, by our patent agreement, reveal to you how this is done. We will, however, by the simple act of humanity, make this reanimation process known to the scientific world. Our founder, Mr. Vincent Corsica, has determined that this knowledge must be shared. He will make the announcement sometime in the coming months. The exact date has not yet been set. Ladies and gentlemen, this is something Mr. Corsica has no obligation to do. In fact, most organizations will question why he does not keep this knowledge for the benefit of his own company. Scientists and medical specialists have been researching reanimation for years.

Now they will have this knowledge due to Mr. Corsica and his belief in fairness."

The applause began slowly and then began to boom like a thunder storm releasing its fury. The audience stood as the applause continued. The four speakers received the accolades by standing, bowing, and giving the universal thumb-finger circle of okay.

"Please be seated," Nate continued, "I have more good news, but first please welcome Mr. Max Scidderly who will talk on the relationship of CRYONICS and religion." Nate took the chair vacated by Scidderly.

"Thank you, Nate, and thank you," he gestured towards the audience, "for that wonderful response to what we believe is the most important discovery in the medical field in a century." The audience applauded once again. Dino smiled.

"Let me tell you a little about myself. After attending college in New Hampshire, I received my Doctorate of Divinity in Chicago. I've been a Methodist minister for seventeen years and presently serve a church in a suburb of Boston. I'm on a three-month leave of absence to explain CRYONICS in relationship to religious beliefs." He put his hands on the lectern and Nate mused that this is a typical minister stance.

"As you know, " Scidderly continued, "Christians believe there is a hereafter, so you may ask why would a Christian accept CRYONICS? That was exactly my question when I was first approached to give a presentation on the connection. Why indeed? I mulled the question over in my mind for many days. Then one day, I was playing golf with a doctor friend of mine ---- on a Thursday afternoon," this got a chuckle from the audience. "He had been late arriving because he had spent the previous eight hours saving the life of a young man severely injured in a motorcycle accident. My friend told me that several times he thought he had lost the young man but he fought, the entire staff fought, for the man's life. 'It's what we do' he told me, 'we keep life going as long as we can.' His words decided me that CRYONICS did just that. Keep life going. That as long as cells are protected there is life. CRYONICS extends life and life is sacred and that's what we do, keep life going." Scidderly took another sip of water and Nate thought it maybe to determine his next words, or to let the audience mull over what he had said.

"CRYONICS and religion work together. I see no conflict," Scidderly continued. "I'll be happy to talk to you individually if you desire. Please mark the second set of handouts you will receive as to your desires."

"By the way, " he said as if a new revelation had just occurred to him, "California was the first state to have the right to conduct CRYONIC suspension, and it will be the first state for reanimation. I hope I'm not telling tales out of school when I announce that in two years our first suspension patient will be reanimated. That will be a time of great rejoicing. Nate?"

"Indeed it will," Nate said, as he took his place at the lectern. "Our patient has been in suspension for five years. He had a problem that is now curable," Nate paused, waiting for the audience to absorb what that could mean to them. "His name and problem will not be made public at this time and never by LIFE. Privacy is intensely protected. In fact," he gave his words special emphasis, "and this digresses for a moment, names are never used. No one, no matter how diligently they try, could ever discover who is in LIFE unless the patient wishes to make it public. And I believe our patient will as many others will, as well. But, it is strictly his decision." This time Nate made eye contact with many in the audience. Eyes met his as well and there was instant trust and understanding. Dino knew that Vinnie had chosen the right man for the presentation. He smiled and dialed his cell phone. Vinnie will like the outcome of this meeting.

"What I want you to think about now is the question Dr. Ruben asked a few minutes ago," Nate continued. "How close are we to eliminating AIDS, cancer, heart disease?" Nate felt the eyes of Barry, Sidney, Ross and Claire, staring intently and listening to his words. "We're close, very close in some areas but we aren't there yet. We will be! LIFE spends millions on research as other foundations and university hospitals do. In five, seven, or ten years we believe a cure will be found and available."

165

Nate waited a few moments before he continued, "If, for instance, a person has the type of heart disease that loss of life is a certainty, and he decided on CRYONICS, the cells are protected, he is in suspension, and artificial hearts are perfected. He is reanimated, receives a new heart, and his life, and the lives of his family, is once again, full.

"Cancer will be eradicated. The cancer-ridden part of the body replaced with new disease-free tissue and life is wonderful again. MS, the very dreaded fear for young people, erased. Answer to yourself," pleaded Nate, his hands, palms up, reaching out, very slowly, and sincerely, "wouldn't you place your body in suspension for five, seven, or ten years to know that your body can be whole again and your lives full of pain-free living?" Nate saw heads nod with the exception of the three men sitting with Dino. Their faces remained belligerent. So why are they here, wondered Nate?

"It is difficult to pinpoint how long before cures are found for diseases that I mentioned and for others just as important to patients and their families. Our best guess is AIDS will be curable in five years. Think of it." Nate glanced at Barry and Sidney who were looking at each other. "Even today, AIDS has been dropped from the top ten causes of loss of life. Heart disease, however, remains number one, followed by cancer, stroke, lung disease, accidents, pneumonia-influenza, diabetes, suicide, kidney disease, and liver disease. AIDS is number fourteen. Those statistics are according to a report released from the National Center for Health Statistics. And as you know, may change from year to year as new cures are found for diseases."

Nate knew he had the attention of everyone in the room. He didn't know how Dino had accomplished it, but each person here had a very personal interest in the presentation and each had been given a special invitation to attend.

"We have told you what CRYONICS will do. I would now like to introduce Mr. Nguyen who will talk briefly about funding." Nate nodded to Nguyen and then took the chair vacated by the next speaker.

As Dino thought, people did not respond well to Nguyen. Only token applause. Nevertheless, Nguyen knew his subject and did command a certain amount of respect for his knowledge.

"We have some very good news in regard to CRYONIC funding. The initial fee covers all aspects of the procedure from the very beginning of medical injections to protect the body cells, suspension, and reviving the patient to once again enjoy a healthy life," Nguyen smiled all through his presentation. A little too much Nate believed. "This can be for a period of five to ten years, depending on the patient's needs. For instance, if a medical procedure is extensive then the costs will be slightly higher, but, for the most part, there will be little difference in the funding for each patient," explained Nguyen. And he, too, seemed to need sips of water.

"First, let me tell you about our long-time care facility. LTF as we call it and I will refer to those initials when speaking of it. We knew we needed a place that would be safe from hurricanes, tornadoes, floods, earthquakes. After all, the patients could not run away from pending disasters." No laughter as Nguyen had expected. "We found such a place in the State of Wyoming. Ever been there?" He paused and waited for the nays and yeas. He heard a few and saw a few smiles as well. "We purchased two-hundred thousand acres almost in the middle of the state. Now, I can hear you say, 'tornadoes, which destroy everything in their paths, do happen in Wyoming' and you are right." Nguyen waited again for just a few seconds before continuing. "Ever been to Japan or Seattle and seen the underground markets?" This time the audience remained quiet and there were no smiles. "If you have, you are aware it's like a small city, everything needed is there. We have done this, the LTF is completely underground and completely safe from the natural disasters that plague so many areas. Here in California, especially."

"Safety is our primary concern, safety every step of the way. We want to see our patients back leading a healthy, productive life." Nguyen paused, hoping for applause. None came. He had not mentioned money yet and that's what the audience wanted to hear about.

"We have slides showing the LTF facility and when you see them, and it's only six minutes, I think you will agree that it's impressive and beautiful." He flipped a switch and photos of the LTF buildings flashed on a large screen that had been placed to the right of the lectern. Members of the audience were very attentive and all eyes were on the screen. Nguyen smiled. The facility was, indeed, impressive. He felt a surge of enthusiasm that, at last, he had the audience interested in his part of the presentation. The interior colors were pink, gold, and apple green with large pots of artificial greenery and cherry blossoms that reflected a soothing, homey feeling. There were several pink leather sofas and easy chairs arranged in small conversational areas. The entire area shouted spring and lovely flowers. Life! Nate noticed a painting similar to one in the meeting room. Were the paintings moved from place to place, he wondered. As he watched the slides, he questioned, why the show? After all, the patients would not see any of this and visitors were not allowed in this area. In fact, visitors were allowed no further than an office and reception room. Another question for Dino, thought Nate.

Nguyen pointed to a Dewar and briefly explained its function once again. "Notice please, that the area where patients will be placed is located behind these steel doors. This is to insure that they are kept from any environmental disturbances. It is, however, monitored by a camera sweeping the facility at all times and physically inspected four times a day. We want all of you to see the care and privacy LTF offers." Several slides of Wyoming's countryside were included and, of course, the cacti were blooming and fields green with spring crops, or so it seemed. No sage brush and sand.

Another slide showed the entry way and reception area which was a partially underground building. No more than eight-hundred square feet set on what looked like the middle of nowhere. The silver and gold colors contrasted nicely with the green of the landscape, and several pots of blooming Black-Eyed Susans. Inside the entry way a pretty receptionist sat at a computer, vase of yellow silk tulips was on her desk adding to the appearance of new-life --- spring flowers, the end of winter. All done to assure that life does go on.

Nguyen flipped a switch to turn off the projector and resumed his stance at the lectern. "Now that you've seen the facilities, I'm sure that you all agree that all possible circumstances have been addressed. You've heard about the research facilities, preparations, privacy, but, one matter, well two actually, we have not touched on." He met eye contact with several in the audience. Nate knew the text of the speech so his mind drifted at times. He, too, observed the audience and wondered their reactions to the proposal.

"First," Nguyen continued, "we have a medical response team that can fly to any location in a matter of hours. The team of technicians carry special equipment ready to assist in the primary CRYONIC procedure--that of lowering body cell temperature and transporting the patient to the facility. This response is done when the patient is not located near our four research facilities, or perhaps is on a vacation and away from the designated location, or if an unforeseen emergency arises." Nguyen paused to make sure all eyes were focused on him, "Now, how much does all of this cost? Less than you may think. The cost of the entire procedure from suspension to reanimation is from seventy-five to ninety thousand dollars, depending on the length of time in suspension and services desired or needed. And I have some wonderful news that most, if not all, of this may be paid by insurance. We can recommend several carriers that now insure patients for CRYONICS." Nguyen smiled. But there were no returning smiles. Dino thought he may need to replace him. The audience did not trust Nguyen, his race perhaps, even though he was an expert in his field.

"We do have an annual fee of four hundred dollars if you want the emergency response team benefit. And there are other ways to finance CRYONICS. You could take a mortgage on real estate, borrow, or use savings. We are prepared to assist you with this and believe me, it is affordable for everyone. We make it so." Nguyen gathered his papers. "I will be available to meet with you on financial matters." He returned to his seat and Nate resumed his place at the lectern.

"Thank you. This is indeed exciting," remarked Nate. "I have just a few more statements before we turn to questions. First, although we do accept last minute patients, we recommend that you make arrangements as early as possible. Several reasons for this. If you wait until there is a health crisis, you may be too late. This is a family decision and if, for instance, the provider has a sudden heart problem, is incoherent, speech loss, then he or she could not make the decision for CRYONICS, and it would be too late for suspension," explained Nate. "You can think of several situations yourself. The patient has to be lucid to make these decisions. The other possibility is Durable Power of Attorney. Of course, making decisions for a minor is a different situation."

"Another reason for making arrangements as soon as possible is insurance rates will be less, legal responsibilities can be resolved, and there is time for planning the future years while the patient is in suspension," continued Nate.

"Now we are ready for your questions and you may direct your inquiries to anyone on the panel." Nate remained at the lectern to act as moderator.

"It seems the brain could be deprived of oxygen before the freezing is done. Would this be true?" A man, wearing a three-piece suit and looking very officious, spoke from his third row seat.

"Dr. Ruben?" Nate turned to the doctor to respond.

"No. Under our procedures, there is no damage from schema because there is no time when the heart is completely stopped. Now, in the early years of CRYONICS, this was not the case. When a patient had to be declared legally dead, sorry Nate, I had to use that word again," Dr. Ruben smiled at Nate who responded with the expected facial expression, "then some deprivation did occur. Now, though, when the procedure is done in the proper situation that is not true, that means, we get heart and lung resuscitation machine into the patient very quickly. The medication reduces brain metabolism." Dr. Ruben returned to his seat.

"Does that answer your question?" Nate asked the gentleman.

"Yes, thank you," and three-piece suit wondered what all those words meant.

Nate gestured toward another member of the audience, this time an older lady.

"Does the money have to be paid all at once?" She quickly sat down and kept her head inclined as if she didn't want her companion to know she had asked the question. The man beside her made no movement or even acknowledged that she had spoken.

Nguyen rose and answered, "We have several payment plans that will make CRYONICS available to everyone. We work on a one-to-one basis and all information is held in strictest confidence." He smiled and the lady gave a slight nod of her head in appreciation.

The man sitting with the beautiful woman who wore a poor disguise, asked, "When a patient is frozen does their body and face get older or look older?"

Nate held back a chuckle since he was sure the question had come from Lily , the movie star Dino had recognized and passed on to Nate and the other members of the panel. Nate knew this answer, but why is she interested in CRYONICS he pondered? To preserve her beautiful body forever?

"No," answered Nate. "Neither the body nor the facial features change or age. A real winner since those not in CRYONICS will be aging all those years."

Lily turned to her companion and he nodded to her. A look of anticipation passed between them. The people's reactions interested Nate and Lily's reaction garnered a whole siege of questions.

"I wonder," the lady who asked the question about financing raised her hand.

"Yes?" Nate pointed to her.

"I wonder if after the person is revived if their memory comes back?" she quietly asked.

Dr. Ruben answered, "This is one of our priorities. Memories that are active, that is the patient has not forgotten and even stays alert to current times, stay in a fixed condition. Our research is for Alzheimer patients whose memory is no longer functioning. We are confident that medical procedures will allow these patients to regain that memory but, that has not been accomplished as yet. It is, however, very possible that this will be accomplished in a few years. Mental retardation reversal is another priority in our research."

Nate wondered. It all seems too good to be true, but then, he only recently learned of CRYONICS and it's been around for a long time. Quarter of a century! He acknowledged a person with the next question.

"If I'm following you correctly," a man near the back of the room said, "when a person has something, say like cancer, that can't be cured now, decides on CRYONICS and after five years or so the cure is found, then that person is revived, cured of the disease, and goes on with life. Right?"

"Absolutely, " replied Nate.

"If everyone does that, isn't the world going to be overly populated? No one would ever die."

"Use the cemeteries to build houses on," a man laughably shouted. Others joined in the humor.

"You would have a point," responded Nguyen. "If everyone participated, which of course, they won't. But, here's what we believe will actually happen and is happening to some extent now. Families are having fewer children. One explanation for that, according to some experts, is that as people become wealthier, family size decreases. Why? We don't know. Plus, areas which now do not lean themselves well to home or business development, will be utilized as technology for resources, such as water and electricity, becomes available. In foreign and third world countries, as well as the United States, there are many undeveloped areas that can handle increased population, if, indeed, that occurs. Look at China, for instance, a limit of one child per family. We could see more of that. And don't rule out another planet. Life there is another possibility. Technology is advancing at a rapid rate. The possibilities are endless." Nguyen concluded his remarks and took his seat. Each of the men stood at the lectern when answering questions.

"I heard that only a person's head could be frozen. Is this true?" asked the officious looking man.

"Yes, that is true. LIFE does not subscribe to that theory, since we believe it is in the best interests of our patients to have full body CRYONICS," replied Dr. Ruben. "Now that reanimation has been achieved, the entire body is restored to provide quality life. Some foundations do suspend only the head, and this is called neurosuspension, and freeze other organs of the patient as well. LIFE does not."

"Is there a chance that a disease will cure itself during CRYONICS and we wouldn't know anything about it since the body is frozen and away in that ---- whatever it's called?" The man asking the question had piercing blue eyes and stared intently at Dr. Ruben.

"I know your concern, but the body does not function as a body, that means, all functions are stopped while in the CRYONIC stage so a cure would not be possible," explained Dr. Ruben. "I do have another bit of research that our facility is doing that I would like to share with you. For many years the medical profession has discussed inserting new genes into the body to counteract a dysfunction. So far efforts in this regard have not been successful, but recent studies have shown that this approach is close to becoming a reality. The procedure is basically inserting therapy genes into the heart which could enable patients to bypass surgery. Like I said, these experimental treatments show great promise. Even successful gene therapy does not negate the need to prepare for CRYONICS, or at least consider that it may be the right decision for you."

"Is the heart the only organ that is being considered for gene therapy?" a lady near the front of the room asked.

"No. Researchers are considering the liver and other tissues. It's very exciting for us in the medical profession. Several foundations and research facilities have announced that they have isolated and grown stem cells and, of course, this opens the possibility for very important new transplantation. You will be hearing much more of this in the months to come."

"It must be costly." stated the same lady.

"Well, all research is and better financing means quicker results," stated Nguyen.

"Will you say something more about Alzheimer's?" the older lady asked.

"As you know, Alzheimer's disease is a gradual deterioration of the brain. It causes forgetfulness, confusion, and personality changes. There are about four million persons with this disease and it isn't confined to older people," said Dr. Ruben. "We have just learned that changes in the brain take place twenty to forty years before the patient shows any symptoms of the problem. These changes include nerve fibers that band together so that nerve cells cannot function effectively. It's a complicated process that will require more time than we have this evening," he continued. "But, I will mention two drugs that seem to be effective in treating Alzheimer's. They are Cognex and Aricept. Both work by adding a brain chemical called acetylcholine, which works with memory. They do not cure the disease, but they do give improvement in some patients. In some patients there has been very dramatic improvements in retaining memory."

"Are there any more questions?" asked Nate. Then, "Yes?" as another hand was raised.

"Have any of you or all of you agreed to CRYONICS?"

"Yes," answered Nguyen. "We have life insurance that will cover costs for us. These are individual policies and I may add that the premiums for Nate are much lower than for the rest of us." The audience gave appreciative laughter for the humor.

Nate thought the premium must be very low since he was unaware of the policy. Another perk of his job perhaps?

"What if we choose CRYONICS and are in suspension and then our spouse wants us to be reanimated? What then?"

"That's why there is counseling and agreement before the patient is in suspension. However, only the patient's wishes are considered regarding reanimation. No one else can change the agreement except for a minor," explained Nguyen.

"Since there are no more questions, I would like to address an important point once again," said Nate. "CRYONICS is a family decision. Although legally, a

174

person may make the decision by him or herself, we recommend that open discussion be made with the persons directly involved in your life. It may be that both husband and wife, or partners, decide on CRYONICS to be done at the same time. If you have parents, children, or other relatives, please communicate with them regarding your plans. Go over the procedures, and we have a handout for this, so there will be no misunderstandings or surprises.

"We have forms for you to review and the four of us will remain here as long as you want to discuss any situations that you need to learn more about or explain anything you may be unsure of. Thank you for coming and please help yourself to refreshments,"

Nate raised his hand, "And no, we do not have Walt Disney in our facility."

The crowd milled around the coffee, punch, and cookie table and several couples broke into smaller groups for conversation. The speakers fielded questions mostly expanding on earlier presentations. Several left immediately including Ross and Claire, who looked very thin and tired; Lily and her companion hurried out, Lily keeping her scarf around her face; John and Stella moved quickly to the door; Armon, Harold and Frankie remained in their seats; Dino mingled with the crowd keeping a low profile so others would not suspect that he was part of the presentation; Sidney and Barry chatted with two other men and hung around the coffee container.

CHAPTER EIGHTEEN

Whew! That's over. Nate couldn't quite relax on the drive to his apartment. Several questions reeled around in his head and he kept seeing the photo of those steel doors. What really is behind them? This all sounds and looks wonderful. Can Vinnie be involved in a benevolent venture? An honest project? Nate had been with the organization two years and had never seen honesty or consideration. How did something change so suddenly? Or did it?

Did those steel doors open to an area that housed CRYONIC patients or, and this thought made him shudder with a stab of fear, were the patients transferred to a remote Georgia hillside and buried in Rudy's "garden" whether or not they were dead? In his mind's eye, Nate saw the graves in Rudy's yard. The ones already there. Mounds of dirt that resembled garden plots, some with little rows of vegetables. Nate knew what was under the mounds. Was the CRYONIC venture only a scam for money and no actual facility existed? Did he know anything for a fact? Still Dino said that Vinnie wanted the Nobel Prize and this project would get it for him. And how often had Nate really been around Vinnie? Maybe there is a good side, an honest side. Maybe Nate had only worked with the dark side of the organization, and now he would see the good side.

But those steel doors kept surfacing in his mind. Steel doors and frozen bodies. Cold steel doors!

Nate switched on the radio, hoping to divert his thoughts. Maybe tomorrow's weather would be great for catching a wave. He could use the exhilarating feeling that surfing always gave him. He caught the last minutes of the national news, and as he listened, nausea hit him in the pit of his stomach.

"Still no word on what caused the death of Texas Governor Russell Blair in Houston yesterday," said the announcer. "The popular politician had been in a coma for two weeks and died with his wife and two sons by his side. Blair's death is the second unexplained death of a no gambling, zero tolerance on crime, politician in recent weeks. Colorado's Jason Sinclair died under similar circumstances in a Denver hospital. Sinclair had been in a coma for several weeks before his death. Reasons for the coma were not known, but authorities are investigating the two similar cases to determine if there is a connection. And now your local weather forecast. Goodnight from the nation's capital."

Nate forgot about the weather and surfing. Two more deaths and in places that only months ago he had delivered dimethylmercury. And who else had distributed the poisonous substance? These two made eight under the same circumstances that he knew about. How many others? And where else? Dino has a vial of the poison. Would Nate soon learn that an important person in this area has lapsed into a coma. Perhaps someone who was blocking a project that Dino promoted. Or maybe a sport's figure that could sway the outcome of a game, giving a huge payoff if bets were put down on prior knowledge. Nate could not let his mind think of such horrid actions of anyone in the organization. But such things had happened. Horrid things.

As Nate opened the door of his apartment, he noticed the blinker on the telephone answering machine, telling him that someone had left a message. Hardly anyone ever left him a message. He was curious. He pressed the button. One word. "Call."

He knew his sister's voice.

CHAPTER NINETEEN

Claire and Ross

Claire and Ross remained silent on the ride to their home, each deep in thought.

Claire, nauseated again, headed for the kitchen hoping a glass of water would be calming and knowing it wouldn't. Nothing would help the almost constant nausea. It kept her awake at night, made her regurgitate any food she attempted to swallow, and took every ounce of her energy. Her time on earth was short. She knew that. Ross knew it. She tried to keep positive thoughts, tried to keep the words, "God's will," and "hereafter," uppermost in her mind. But, how she loved Ross and their children. And her home. Oh, how she wanted her life, her healthy life back. She let her fingers trail over the water faucets; across the stainless steel sink; the recently installed granite counter tops which had replaced out-dated Formica. She touched the blue and white checkered towels, Molly's favorites, since they matched a long skirt Molly had worn in a Thanksgiving Day play at pre-school. Claire's fingers caressed her stove, so many wonderful family meals she had prepared standing on this very spot.

Ross watched his wife, tears brimming his eyes. He wiped his eyes, keeping the tears from spilling over. His heart was breaking.

Claire continued around the kitchen lovingly touching appliances, cupboard doors, making each memory indelible in her mind, or so she hoped. She then walked down the hall to the children's wing. As she quietly opened the door to the boy's bedroom, she stood a moment watching their chests move up and down with steady breathing. She noticed the spit bubble at the corner of Ryan's mouth. He always ejected saliva this way while he slept. Claire smiled. Her wonderful, handsome son. Randy, his arm across his forehead, his habit to ward off dragons, or so he reasoned in his humorous way. He was teased about it by the rest of the family but he only smiled and said they would be glad he did that when he drove the dragons away from them. She tucked the blankets around their feet which were always out from under the covers. What a joy her two sons, and so like their father. She opened Molly's bedroom door. A miniature Claire. What would she be like as a teenager? Shy as Claire had been, or competitive as her brothers were teaching her to be. Claire touched Molly's cheek. The little girl stirred but did not awaken. She's beautiful and Claire loved her dearly. She quietly closed the door.

"Claire, are you okay, dear?" Mother Richards called from the spare bedroom. "I'll be right out."

"No, Mom, I'm fine. Go back to sleep. Ross and I just got home and we're on our way to bed. I only wanted to see the kids for a moment."

"Okay, you need anything let me know." Ross' mother stayed most of the time now. His dad on occasion. Cora Richards always asked Claire's opinion on household and cooking chores making sure the younger woman felt necessary and in charge. In fact, everyone adhered to that, even though Claire would be first to admit that suggesting was all she had energy to do anymore.

Ross guided Claire to the other end of their rambler home, to their private quarters which consisted of a large bedroom, a bath with a Jacuzzi tub, double vanities, and a large walk-in closet. Ross and Claire had laughed many times that this part of the house had sold them.

"Claire, we need to talk about the meeting tonight. You know why I took you there." Ross held his wife's hand and eased her down on the side of the bed.

"Let's get in bed and then talk like we always do when we have a big decision to make. Do you think I could handle a small glass of wine?"

"Maybe. We can try."

"I'll just hold it, not drink it. Like..." Claire's words dropped off. She had to rest and gain enough energy to say what she must. After a short rest she slipped on a blue silk nightgown, Ross' favorite, and leaned back on the soft goose-down pillow.

Ross, too, climbed into bed and fluffed up his pillow. He held Claire in his arms, then said, "Do you have an opinion about CRYONICS, darling? I'd like to think that you will be back with us someday."

"It's lots of money. Ninety thousand would send the kids to college or pay most of it anyway."

"We have the money, sweetheart, and college is a long ways off. I'm talking about us. I want you back. I want our life together, to have you here sitting with me in those rocking chairs we talk about. CRYONICS gives us that chance. As much as we want to deny it, you..."

"I know, I know. There isn't much time. Are you sure, about the money, I mean?"

"I'm sure. I think we can all handle the thought that you will be gone for awhile if we know you're coming back to us." Ross' arm around her shoulder could feel how very thin she had become, even more in recent days. He stroked her thinning hair with his other hand.

"All right, Ross, I'll do it on one condition."

"Anything, sweetheart, you know that."

"I want to divorce you."

"What! Never."

"Ross, ten years or even seven is a long time. The cure for the kind of cancer I have may take that long. I can't let you spend those years alone. You must be free to enjoy life. You can't live in a vacuum."

"Claire, there could never be anyone else for me. I won't divorce you."

"Think of the children. They may enjoy having a mother. After a time when I'm not here, they could love someone, need someone."

"Never!" Ross was adamant. This was completely out of the question. Claire had been his only love and would always be.

"That's the only way I'll sign the papers," Claire firmly said.

"Please, I can't do that."

"You must. I'm not saying you'll find someone else, but I want you to have the option. I know I'll always be in your heart and the kids will always remember me. But, time has a way of dimming memories and today and tomorrow is important too."

"Let me ask you something."

"Okay."

"Think about this for a minute. Say we divorce and say I marry someone and then you are reanimated. Have you thought about that? How would you feel then?" Ross turned Claire's face toward his and looked deeply into her eyes.

"You would have another decision to make." Claire closed her eyes. All energy spent, she needed sleep.

Ross took the never-filled wine glass from her hand and placed it on the night stand. A glass of wine had been a bedtime ritual for them from the first night of their marriage. Until six months ago when she could no longer tolerate wine. He didn't keep up the ritual for himself either. She soon emitted the soft even breathing of sleep.

Ross stayed awake for hours pondering the enormous decision she had asked him to make. Demanded! How could he divorce his love, yet to get her back, he must. Claire was adamant about it. His mind went back and forth. Yes, he would, no he couldn't. Could he? Should he? What would people say? Her folks? His folks? Would the children understand? Would anyone? How could he not be married to Claire? Why did this have to happen to her? Why not some tramp or, or, anyone else but Claire? No, he couldn't do it. He wouldn't say it to her, the kids, to anyone.

And as it turned out, he needn't have stayed awake weighing the decision. The next morning, Claire called both sets of parents and she alone told them of her decision. She had asked Ross and the children to remain in another part of the house and not interfere. After an hour or so of tears and hugs, she convinced them that a divorce and CRYONICS was the right decision for her and Ross.

Then she told the children which they didn't understand all that much, but they knew how very sick she was and had been told she would soon die. The fact that with CRYONICS and reanimation she would be with them again excited the youngsters. Even though they had no concept of the time involved, the youngsters could accept that she would be away for awhile. Ross, of course had mixed emotions. He wanted her back and completely believed in CRYONICS, he just didn't want the divorce.

Claire's decision prevailed. A divorce was immediate thanks to a judge who bent the rules. The day after the final papers were signed, Claire signed another important set of papers. She would soon enter into the suspension of CRYONICS. She was very weak, her body almost a skeleton, she had been in and out of the hospital several times.

The day Ross drove her to the CRYONICS facility, the children stood at the door and waved.

"See you in a few years, Mom," Ryan shouted. Molly echoed him and Randy only watched. At nine he knew how long a year could be. And though Claire was careful not to mention ten years, she did tell them she could be away a few years.

"Get well, Mom," Randy finally said.

If Ross and Claire could have looked into the future, they would have realized that Claire was more astute than even she guessed.

Ross, indeed, did marry again. Molly's first grade teacher, a perky, vivacious, genuine nice lady, gave the Richard's family what they had lost ---- a loving wife and mother. And gave Ross another down-the-road decision. But on that day, the day Claire left, no one could see into the future.

Sidney and Barry

"I have an idea, Barry, that I want to run by you when we get home," said Sidney, steering the car onto the 405 freeway heading south to San Diego.

"Tell me now. I could see you were deep in thought during the meeting, which by the way, I found very interesting."

"Yeah, I did too. Kind of surprised to see Rick and Dan there," remarked Sidney.

"Yeah, me too. Kind of interesting that everyone there seemed to have a specific reason that CRYONICS would work for them. Wonder how that happened?"

"Someone did some homework." Sidney eased into the traffic, which both men agreed, seemed to get worse everyday. Road rage, though, had lessened now that tickets were issued for those undesirable traits.

"So, what's on your mind?" asked Barry. He turned the radio off. Sidney seemed much too serious to have interference from any source.

"We both know AIDS is close to being eradicated, but, the cure isn't here yet. Maybe in five years." Sidney hesitated, "Look, I'd rather talk about this at home and it's only a little over an hour's drive from here ---- traffic is thinning out."

"Sure. What station do you want on?" Barry turned on the radio and began twisting the dial.

"One-oh-one point seven, I guess. We can sing along with Mariah or maybe this is 70's night."

"You'll know it whatever is played. You could have made it with the big bands if you had been born sooner."

"Fun to try anyway. Not that I would have succeeded but who knows? Nice of you to be so supportive." And the banter continued until they were once again in their Hillcrest home.

"Get comfy and I'll get us a glass of wine, " said Sidney. "And then we'll talk."

"Okay, I'm ready and this better be good to make me wait all this time," Barry teasingly said.

"Gotcha." Sidney served the wine and sat beside Barry on the sofa. "Now, we both listened to the presentation tonight and agree it was very interesting. Don't fidget like that," Sidney laughed.

"I'm not."

"Yes you are," Sidney patted his lover's head. "What I want to do is for both of us to go into CRYONIC suspension."

"What?" A shocked Barry shouted. "You must be out of your mind. There's nothing wrong with you."

"I know, but just listen to me a minute will you? I like living with you. I love living with you. I want it to go on forever and it can." Sidney gazed intently into the eyes of

183

Barry. Make him understand he told his mind. "Remember the biggie, a disease can be cured and reanimation can be achieved. So what if I'm not the one who has AIDS, what difference does it make? We can be together."

"You'll be wasting years of your life."

"Hey, didn't you hear the question from the guy with the movie star? Aging doesn't take place. We'll stay the age we are now."

"I donno, it seems like something you shouldn't do. What about our house, your business? You haven't considered this very carefully at all," Barry remarked, an incredulous look on his face.

"Actually, I have. Tonight wasn't the first time I've thought about CRYONICS. When you got the brochure......."

"I got a brochure?"

"Yeah, a couple of weeks ago. That's how I knew about this meeting."

"I never saw it. You didn't show it to me." Barry questioned the ethics of Sidney keeping his mail from him.

"You weren't feeling too great and I wanted you to hear about it from someone else. I'm sorry if I guessed wrong. You know I'd never..."

"I know, I know, it's okay. You always do the right thing for me. You know that I'm sure of that."

"The house will be rented. Stacia can handle it. The business is something I can get back into anytime. Both houses will be done in a couple of weeks and Stacia will list them. When sold, the money will be put in our account. She will have a power of attorney to sign for me. I really have thought this out, I want to do this."

"Have you thought of the timing?" asked Barry. He had taken only a token sip of wine.

"What timing? Let's do it before you suffer any longer."

"No, I mean when reanimation occurs. What kind of a world would we find?" Barry waved his arm in the air as if by some magic the future could be seen. "What kind of products would be there. What will houses be built of? Adjustments. Could we adjust?"

"We can think of it another way. Think of what we will see, the excitement of discovering everything new and discovering it together, with years of good health. I want that, Barry."

"The money. You can't use all your savings." Barry protested.

"That's the easiest part. What good would money be to me without you. In fact, and listen very carefully to me, without you my life is over. I mean it."

"You're very sure today, let's wait a month and see how you feel," urged Barry.

"We may not have a month, Barry. The blood results came back a couple of days ago and it doesn't look good." Sidney draped his arm around Barry's shoulder.

"Sidney, you didn't tell me." Barry looked puzzled, "I can't help but wonder what else is going on that you haven't mentioned."

"Nothing really. And I haven't done anything you wouldn't have done for me. I thought these couple of days would be stressful and you didn't need anything else to think about."

"So what about the blood?" Barry at least hoped he would be allowed to see the results of his own test.

"It's just, you don't have long. I'll show you the print-out." Sidney got a sheet of copy paper from a desk drawer and handed it to Barry. The two men were very quiet as Barry scanned the latest results of the monthly tests.

"You think two weeks tops? Sometimes, like tonight, I've got more stamina. Look how long I've been up."

"Yeah, running on adrenaline, I suspect. I don't know. Anyway, I want to do CRYONICS with you. In fact, I intend to do it with you."

"If I choose not to, then what will you do?" Barry asked, fearing the answer.

"When you die, I kill myself. It's that simple. I won't live without you, but, think about this again. With CRYONICS we will be together forever. When we are both reanimated our lives will be beautiful."

"You're positive this is what you want to do? There's no changing minds a year or two into the program," remarked Barry.

"We won't even know the years are going by. It's like we go to sleep tonight and tomorrow when we wake up and look at the calendar, five years have gone by. And you can be cured of AIDS by whatever method is developed during that time,"

"It sounds wonderful. To be healthy again. To have energy to maybe even play a game of tennis. It's hard to imagine."

"Just a couple of minutes and then you need to sleep," laughed Sidney. "But, when you wake up it will only be tomorrow."

"Okay, what else?"

"The papers are ready to sign giving Stacia power of attorney for me and we need to change yours to her instead of me. That is if you want her to handle your affairs."

"Of course, I want your sister to do this for me. Stacia has always seemed like me sister too. How does she feel about you going into CRYONICS or have you told her all the details?"

"She thought about it for quite sometime and seems kind of excited about it. Said she will miss us but will pretend we are on a long cruise or safari. She said it would make a good book or movie."

"I guess I just want what's best for you," Barry said, barely keeping his eyes open at this point.

"I want what's best for you as well, that's what love is--wanting the best for each other." Sidney drew Barry to him and the lovers held each other.

The decision had been made.

Armon, Harold, Frankie

"Why'd Vinnie send us to this crap?" Armon disgustingly asked his companions.

"Who knows. Hope he doesn't expect us to join those stiffs," answered Harold, who was probably the smarter of the three. And perhaps the most ruthless.

"I won't do it, " Frankie joined in, "I hate being cold. That's why I wanted to go to Florida."

"Well, you wouldn't be cold, stupid, you wouldn't feel anything." Harold explained with a how-can-you-be-so-dumb expression.

"What's the reason for it. What'd Dino say to you about coming here?" asked Armon.

"Only be here," answered Harold.

The three men remained in their seats following the presentation on CRYONICS. They observed the conversations around the punch bowl and though getting in line appealed to them, Dino had told them not to mingle. "Don't call attention to yourselves," he had said. So the three talked among themselves sure they would soon learn why they were there.

"I can think of one reason we're here," Harold remarked.

"Why?" Armon asked.

"Well people getting frozen for a few years certainly are out of sight which is our problem right now."

"Yeah, but look how long." remarked Armon.

"That's the point. Ten years we're out of sight. Everyone thinks we're dead. No one has seen us and the statutes have run out. We're home free."

"Not for that little girl it hasn't. Never will. That was a real dumb mistake," Armon said.

"Can't prove who shot her. Could have been any of us. No one can prove anything. And we all stick together on this," demanded Harold.

"Don't matter who did it. We were all at that stupid bank. I think the courts would say we're all guilty. Besides we walked, courts don't forget that either," Armon reminded Harold.

"Still, ten years could give us a cushion. The thing is if Vinnie and Dino say we do it, we do it and I suspect that's what they have in mind. Maybe we could go to South America," said Harold, looking for agreement from the others who nodded.

Then a smiling Frankie said, "If we do get frozen, and I hope we get boots or something for our feet, ya think we will see anyone we know?"

"Oh, Frankie, you are stupid, this ain't no party," Armon once again showed his disgust.

"I know it ain't no party, but what's wrong with havin' a little fun?"

"Let it go Armon, there's no meat in that sandwich," Harold pacified Armon.

"You got that right." Armon continued to look at Frankie trying to fathom the man's ignorance. Likable, but dumb, he thought. And then had to smile. Let him think it's a party, let him think life's a party.

The men's thoughts were correct. Dino wandered over and quickly said, "Be ready for this at ten tomorrow morning. Take nothing with you, be in front of the hotel exactly ten. Now leave." The three men left as Dino had ordered.

And Frankie later complained, "We didn't even get any cookies or drinks."

"It was fruit punch anyway," explained Armon. "Most of the crowd were hurting it looked like. Specially that skinny one. They couldn't handle anything good."

"See that gal in the big hat, the real looker?" Harold asked.

"Who didn't. She looked like a movie star," Frankie answered.

"I wanted to talk to her, maybe......if," dreamed Harold.

"I was about to go over to her and make her acquaintance and ask for a date," Frankie laughed.

"Maybe she'll be your roommate and you can make a snowman," Armon teased.

"Think she might?" Frankie smirked. He knew Armon was trying to get a rise out of him. He decided to shower and do his hair. Armon always got a charge out of Frankie thinking he was preparing to go out.

"The thing is out of the country sounds nice," said Armon.

"Look at it this way. If we get out of the country no one could find us anyway. I got a cousin still lost somewhere in Mexico, been there five, six years," Harold offered a way out of CRYONICS, or so he believed.

"Mexico ain't that far for Vinnie to reach," Armon replied.

Frankie looked from one to the other ready to agree with whomever got the upsmanship.

"South America or even Europe. I don't want this CRYONIC stuff. We just got out and I'm ready to have some fun," Harold remarked, his mind still on the movie star. He drummed fingers on his chair.

"We all agree on a couple of things," Armon said, "CRYONICS doesn't appeal to us and being out of sight for ten years would be beneficial. You know anybody in South America you can trust," he asked Harold.

"I don't know anyone in North America I can trust, present company excepted." Harold answered.

Frankie snickered. He loved it when his two pals jockeyed for number one decision-maker. He thought Harold usually won, although Armon had good ideas as well.

"I donno," said Armon. "We don't have the money to get lost and Vinnie is really on our case for that bank job."

"We needed money. We walked. What'd he expect us to do without cash." Harold was still agitated at Vinnie for even thinking he would want suspension in CRYONICS.

"I'd like to have a few days here but it depends on what we decide. And if we run we'll have to do a bank or Circle K or something."

"Those small stores don't keep much cash and the clerks can't open the safe. They have a sign that says they only have twenty bucks," said Frankie.

"You believe all that? They only want to scare us. They have to have more than twenty. A bank would work," agreed Armon.

Harold said, "Remember that Becky I was married to for awhile?"

"Yeah."

"Her folks live here and they got a little dough. I know my way around their place."

"You crazy? They'd kill you on sight for the beatings you gave her. You wouldn't get within ten feet."

"I wouldn't be asking for the money."

"I don't think that's a good idea Harold," said Armon. "We have to stay out of sight. Remember that Walsh guy showed our pictures on TV and everyone watches that show."

Frankie rejoined Harold and Armon, "Can't we have some fun tonight?"

"This was our fun," explained Armon. "We may have our future planned for us."

"Well, we know where Vinnie expects us to be for the next ten years," Harold said.

"I don't like it. Vinnie thinks he can run everyone's life," complained Armon.

"You want to tell him he can't run yours?" Harold asked.

The two men stared at each other, "No, I just want out of here," Armon answered.

"We all do," Harold agreed.

"Why don't we think what good it will do. Why Vinnie wants us to do this? Maybe it's a good idea," Frankie, always the one agreeable to anything, questioned.

"You tell us a reason," challenged Harold.

"Well, I just thought of something," laughed Frankie. "Know all those people the cops get to put faces together?"

"Artists," answered Harold.

"Whoever. Hell, they always show people getting older .... like how they might look if they've been on the loose for years. You know maybe bald or fat."

"Sure," agreed Armon.

"We won't look older 'cause we won't be older," smirked Frankie. His remarks brought looks of admiration from his cohorts.

"Frankie, sometimes you come up with something really smart. You're right," replied Armon.

"And we won't feel older either. We could still do all the things we want to do now. Like," Frankie was on a roll, "women, fun, booze.."

"Let's mull this around for awhile. We wouldn't know time is going by. It's not like we would know we're locked up and there could be some advantages of being out of sight," mused Armon.

"What you guys are trying to do is talk yourselves into this stuff. Frankie, call down for some food. The snacks in here are for the birds, we need real nur-ish-ment, and we might as well have the best wine too. If this is going to be our last free night, we might as well enjoy it," remarked Harold.

"This is our last night? I thought we come back from it, after a few years. Re-in-car-nation or something like that." Frankie looked bewildered.

"Come on, Frankie, you know what we mean. Course we'll be back and really make our mark," explained Harold.

"Plenty of time to plan, too. Ten years gives lots of thinking time," remarked Frankie.

Armon and Harold rolled their eyes. Oh, Frankie, you're so dumb, both men were thinking.

"Okay, here's what I think we should do." Armon took a sheet of hotel stationery and with a pen, drew a line down the middle marking each column with either a "for" or "against."

"What are you doing?" snickered Frankie. "Practicing being an artist so you can draw our own pictures."

"Just wait a minute. On this side we put reasons for doing the frozen stuff, and on this column we write why we don't want to," explained Armon.

"I don't like being cold," Frankie chimed in. "That's my biggest reason why not."

Harold and Armon exchanged an exasperating look. Frankie just couldn't understand the procedure, their looks implied.

"You won't feel anything. I told you a hundred times, but, I'll put it down. Harold you go first."

"Okay. Don't hurt to try to make sense out of this. In the for column put, out of sight ten years, stay the age we are now, people forget about us, come back to a new life. Against is that we only got out of Attica and want to have some fun, want to control our own lives. That's about it I guess," said Harold.

"Those are my reasons too," agreed Armon, "we only had three days of freedom and Vinnie shipped us over here. I want some fun for a change. You have any more ideas, Frankie?"

"Only that I bet Vinnie has sent some of our pals here and we might see Raul or Joey. I'd like that. They were great, you guys know that. Remember the Carny we all did one summer? Got lost there for awhile."

"Not only is there no meat in that sandwich, there is no sandwich there either," remarked Harold.

"So, what should we do?" asked Armon.

"The bottom line is that if we run we're dead meat in a week. Dead. Dead, not frozen and I think we all know that. Vinnie doesn't fool around. What I'm saying is, much as we would like to, we really have no choice. We know where we will be the next ten years, and there's no parole," replied Harold.

"Yeah, you're right. The decision is made and not by us," agreed Armon. "Ten o'clock Dino said." He picked up the hotel plate which had held a sumptuous meal. Noritaki, Sweet Leilani pattern, and slammed it against the wall. The three men watched the plate break into pieces. Was the CRYONICS decision a symbol of their lives?

John and Stella

Stella drove home from the meeting with her mind full of conflicting thoughts. John had been quiet throughout the evening and remained still. She wondered what he was thinking. She chatted about the new construction along the freeway, new home developments, an area being cleared that would soon see another shopping mall. John made no response and only stared straight ahead. As she eased the car off the freeway onto a secondary road leading to their home, John gazed out the side window but remained quiet. Stella wished he would say something, but, then perhaps it was better this way. At least he didn't shout and accuse her of driving by some fictional lover's house.

At last entering their driveway, she pressed the garage door opener and parked the car.

"We're home John, remember the day you installed that opener and how happy I was not to struggle with that heavy door anymore?"

John looked back at the door for several seconds as if he wanted to say something, but didn't. At least he isn't violent, Stella thought. So perhaps there could be an intelligent conversation. She would try.

"Let's sit awhile and talk. I'll make some hot chocolate, with a scoop of ice cream, just the way you like it," said Stella.

"All right." His first response in several hours. He sat in an old-fashioned wooden rocker, his favorite chair for years. He rocked slowly back and forth, his hands clenched on the arms. Stella had a fleeting thought of someone strapped in an electric chair about to be executed. Oh, no, she isn't doing that. Never would she deliberately do anything to hurt him. This is the right thing, isn't it. A decision she would question for years.

She pulled a TV tray close to the rocker. John stared at the metal tray, one they had for years, like everything else in house. John and Stella were frugal, things lasted, they made do. She used his favorite mug for the hot chocolate. The light brown one with a picture of a roadrunner going through the sand, purchased on one of their infrequent trips to Palm Desert. They had laughed and enjoyed the tan colored birds with a fairly long tail as they scooted among the cacti.

"Here's your hot chocolate in your favorite mug. Remember?" Stella coaxed a response from John.

Silence, but he did turn his face towards the drink she offered.

"I put chocolate chip ice cream on top, your favorite," she smiled at him.

Silence.

"The meeting was interesting. Didn't you think so?" Stella began the new topic of conversation.

Silence.

"Wouldn't it be wonderful if Alzheimer's could be reversed?" And she questioned for the hundredth time if John really had Alzheimer's or perhaps something else. In all the information she had read, Alzheimer's patients did not become violent ---- mostly forgetful which in itself is certainly bad enough. John became violent at times as well as forgetful. A dilemma she faced everyday.

Silence.

"Can you remember, John, times when you get angry with me?" Is this the right line of questioning? Stella never knew what approach to use.

He stared at her but made no response.

"Do you remember our son's names and their children?"

Silence.

"Wouldn't it be wonderful if you could remember all the things we used to do? The fun we had with the family?"

He only stared at her.

"This new treatment could help. In a few years, cures will be found to reverse the aging process. Remember what that doctor said?"

Silence.

Stella wanted to be anyplace else than the living room of their home trying to convince John that CRYONICS is the best thing for him. Anyplace else!

"John, do you remember what the man at the meeting said about Alzheimer's? Do you remember he talked about new treatment?"

Silence.

"You have Alzheimer's, John. You've had it for several years, maybe more than I thought. But, soon there will be a reversal or even a cure. The man at the meeting told us that," Stella looked at notes she had taken during the CRYONICS presentation, "Nerve fibers clump together and then the cells in the brain can't function. This is what you have, John, and none of it is your fault."

Silence.

"You could be in suspension for a few years until a cure is found and then our life could be great and go on as before." she pleaded.

Silence.

"Do you understand what I'm saying? Or you could take some of the new drugs and they might help. Tell me if you can understand what I'm telling you."

Silence.

"It would only be a few years and it would seem like you are asleep. You wouldn't feel anything, but you are the one who has to say yes or no. I can't sign your name unless, unless you are....... Stella couldn't say unless he was declared mentally incompetent...."unless you are unable to sign your name. You need to know what you are doing. Do you understand?"

She felt it before she saw it --- the cup of chocolate hitting her full in the face. She flinched with surprise rather than with pain. The chocolate had long since lost its heat. BUT, HE HAD THROWN IT IN HER FACE. The insult, the disrespect, and yes, the beginning of terror for the surprising act.

"I know what you're doing," John shouted, half rising from his chair, eyes bulging like a raging bull, "I know.

You think I don't but I know. You want me out of here so he can move in."

"Oh, John, please, that isn't so, I want you well. That's all I ever wanted." Stella wiped her eyes and face with the ever present tissue. It seemed lately she had a tissue box in every room and used them more and more.

John continued his tirade accusing her of taking lovers early in their marriage; that the sons she loved so much were not fathered by him; (and those words hurt more than any other words ever had); that she was trying to poison him; like now with the hot chocolate.

"You think I don't know you put poison in that," he held the now empty mug up and waved it around.

"Please John, don't do this to me. Don't do it to yourself and think about our life. I love you, always and forever. I'm trying to understand."

"You're trying to get rid of me that's, what you're trying. I know it. You think I'm dumb. You thought that all your life. I don't think you are my wife." Stella winced. "You killed her and moved in here. You think you own all this, but you don't. You got rid of her like you're trying to get rid of me." He made menacing gestures towards Stella. "But, I'll kill you first."

Stella was truly frightened. He had never mentioned killing before. She moved close to the crowbar she had stashed under the sofa out of John's sight. This, too, was a new emotion for her. She had known that he could harm her physically, he seemed stronger than ever, but never had he used the word kill. He came towards her, his fist upraised, he had the look of a crazy man. Oh, God, where could she go? She ran towards the kitchen, no, no escape there. The door was locked, so John couldn't leave without her knowing, and the key hidden upstairs. Upstairs! Yes, their bedroom! A telephone! Who to call? Certainly not the police. What would neighbors think? Or say if John was led away in handcuffs? Their sons? But, they lived too far away, more than two hours drive. Was John following her up the stairs? She listened. No sounds. Did she dare open the bedroom door? No, John's very cunning. Many times she had seen him silently watch her doing such innocent tasks as washing dishes or folding clothes with a mean hateful look in his eyes. She pushed a chair under the knob of the door hoping that could stop him entering and knowing it wouldn't if he was determined to get in. She heard nothing. She tip-toed to the telephone. Who actually could she talk to about this. The brochure from LIFE lay just under the bedside lamp. She dialed the number she had called only days ago.

"LIFE agency, how may I help you?" A very pleasing, confident voice answered on the first ring of the telephone.

"I need to talk to someone. I'm scared. We were at the meeting and it set him off." Stella's voice trembled. She was very frightened.

"Hang on. Please stay calm. We can help."

Then another voice came on the life. "This is Doctor Newsome, please talk to me. I can answer your questions."

"My husband has gone wild and wants to kill me, I need someone and I don't know who to call."

"You are in danger now?" Newsome asked, all the while signaling for someone else to listen.

"I don't know. He threatened to kill me and I ran upstairs. I don't know where he is."

"Are you in a safe place?"

"In the bedroom with the door locked and I don't hear anything but he could get in. I'm scared." Stella was sobbing now.

"You were at the meeting and when you got home your husband got violent. Is that what happened? The Alzheimer's patient?"

"Yes."

"Give me your address, I'll have someone there in a few minutes, fifteen at the most. You probably aren't in any danger. Alzheimer's patients aren't violent, but he may have something else. Where do you live?"

Stella gave the address and telephone number. Fifteen minutes. She could handle anything that long and there was still no sound from John. No pounding on the door or yelling to be let in.

"I'll stay on the line and talk with you. Can you see your driveway from your bedroom window?"

"Yes."

You'll see a car drive in, a blue one. There will be no sirens or flashing lights. When the two men walk to the door, you go down and unlock it. Stay out of your husband's way, though I don't anticipate a problem. Your husband will be taken to a safe place and LIFE will pick him up within an hour." The voice calmed Stella somewhat. Now something will be done.

"Then you will be brought to our facility to sign papers and make other arrangements. It should be all done by morning and you can relax."

"Could I come there in the morning? I'm exhausted."

"No, it must be done tonight. We've handled these cases before and this is the better way to do this. You'll understand when it is done."

"All right. I'm okay now." And soon she saw the blue car pulling in. She felt a tremendous relief. She was safe. The two men walked towards the door. Stella crept down the stairs and unlocked the door. She did not look either right or left, kept her eyes firmly fastened on the door.

"Where is he?" a tall heavy-set man asked.

"I don't know which room. I was upstairs."

"Okay, we'll find him. Why don't you just sit here. He hurt you at all? You need medical attention?"

"No, I ran." Stella began to cry. What had happened to her life?

John was found asleep in the spare bedroom. "Come on big fella, wake up. You gave your wife a fright so we'll take you for a little ride." One of the men shook John awake.

"He drunk?" the other man asked.

"No, a patient of Dr. Newsome that got violent."

"Looks pretty calm to me."

"Still we take him in. Newsome said he is very deceiving and will try to show he is sane."

"Dr. Newsome said that? You know him?"

"His spokesman. Guess the doctor was talking to the wife. I've worked with him before, several times. We just take the husband to a safe house for the night. In the morning he will be transferred to CRYONICS lab or someplace." Handcuffs were put on John.

"Let's go. You okay now?" the tall man asked Stella. "Someone will be coming for you in a few minutes."

197

"Yes, I'm okay. Why the handcuffs? Is he, will he be all right?" Stella was concerned about John.

"He's in good hands. The cuffs just a precaution. Take them off in the car. Don't worry. Probably only needs a good night's sleep."

But was John in good hands? Why did the men not wear uniforms? Why the car not have official markings? Or was it too dark to see? Stella was too upset to ask these questions.

A smiling Nguyen met Stella as she was brought to the LIFE office near Marina Del Rey. A very long night but, hey, here's another ninety thousand dollars. Dino will be very proud of this case. In less than one-half hour an exhausted and emotionally drained Stella had signed John into CRYONICS suspension; signed John as incompetent to handle his affairs or make decisions regarding his health; gave the title to the Stephen's home to LIFE to pay for John's care; and found herself almost destitute because of other expenses Nguyen explained were coming up. She didn't remember that from the presentation but, then had she heard every word?

In a month she was told that she had to move, the house had been sold. Now, at seventy-three, she had no home and needed a job. Her sons asked why had she made those decisions and offered no financial help and very little emotional solace. They blamed her for the loss of their father.

Stella found a job as a greeter at Wal*Mart; rented a studio apartment near her job, the only dwelling she could afford; and daily pondered her decision she made with the person she called that tragic night.

She never again saw her husband.

Lily

"Why did you drag me to that?" a furious Lily yelled at Ron. If she had been anyplace but in the car, she would be stomping her feet and throwing whatever she touched.

"Come on, think about it," Ron's voice soft and cunning as he tried to placate her." Just listen for a moment."

"What are you trying to do. You're fired, you know that, fired!"

"Lily, hear me out. I've worked it out and it could be terrific." Ron glanced at Lily almost as often as he watched the highway.

"You are saying my body should be frozen for ten years. Now tell me, what would that do to my career? Ten years. Are you crazy. I hate you. Get out of my life!"

And why didn't he? She treated him like a dirt bag, always had, sometimes even becoming physical. But, he loved her, understood her moods and besides, she made him a lot of money. This new deal could provide millions. And, of course, they were married. She couldn't fire him; couldn't survive without him.

"I'm listening, not that I would ever agree to it. Give me a cigarette and this time light it for me," she demanded.

"Okay, say you are away for ten years and then resurface. The media would go wild. Where has she been? What happened to her? And the beauty of it, you won't have aged ten years. Your magnificent body will be the same. And don't think that won't cause an uproar in the media. Won't be able to keep TV away. Everyone else will look ten years older, but not you. Think of it!"

"I'm thinking no one will remember me."

"Of course they will. I'll see to that," Ron waved his arms as if to encompass the world. "All of a sudden you'll be back. All your films will be re-released. The crowds will pour in."

Her eyes narrowed as she stared at him, "And what will you be doing all that time?" Suspicious, she mistrusted him anyway.

At home Lily stomped into the condo yelling as Ron continued to talk about the advantages of his proposal.

Lily listened while pacing around the pink and white living room, sometimes shouting, "Never," or "No way." Even for Lily she was reasonably quiet. Well aware she hadn't been box-office since her Academy Award, and very knowledgeable on the benefits of publicity. Still, still ten years.

"Lily, you have no idea what this will do for your career. You won't be ten years older. You'll be exactly the age you are today. Think of it," Ron pleaded, "Julie, Melanie, Sharon, will all be and look ten years older."

"Melanie hasn't looked ten years older since she was twelve. She always looks young, and besides, you didn't answer my question. What will you be doing all that time?"

"Waiting for you and planning your return." Ron gazed into her eyes, hoping the look coming out of his showed sincerity and concern. In fact, he did have plans. A twenty year old, every bit as lucious as Lily, and not nearly as demanding, by the name of Kimmie, was "waiting in the wings." An old show business expression came into his head. Course he didn't love Kimmie as he sincerely loved Lily, but what the heck, variety is the spice of life, as the old saying goes. Lily seems more responsive to CRYONICS and he truly believed he could do wonders for her with this new idea.

"By the time I work out all the publicity for you......."

"Like what? I won't be here you say," questioned Lily.

"I plant articles every few months, what happened to Lily and so forth. On the six month anniversary of your disappearance we start to run all your movies. At the one year date we do it all over again and we keep it up every six months with updated articles. We have a contest on who can solve the mystery of where you are. Then when you show up better than ever..... "

"How can I be better than I am now?" Lily walked to the mirror and patted her hair.

"Because you will be the same lovely you and everyone else will be older."

"How about the younger ones? They're always waiting to pounce when someone isn't looking."

Did she read his mind? "No one can match you in anything, Lily. No one ever will. Only sometimes we need a new gimmick and this is it. I'll be terribly lonely without you. But, I'll be busy planning the big blow for your return."

"Doesn't ninety thousand seem like a lot?" Lily, having grown up in poverty, watched what was spent. Ninety thousand would buy some very nice jewelry - for herself. The only person she spent money on and CRYONICS wouldn't give her anything tangible.

"Not for you, baby. Nothings too expensive for you."

"When would we do this?" Lily seemed resigned to at least consider CRYONICS.

"Tomorrow." Ron beamed at her. What a joy living in this lovely condo with Kimmie. Think of all the perks he will have.

"I need time to tell my friends good-bye for awhile," said Lily, her face mirrored on all four walls. She always patted her hair, clicked a speck of dust, someway drawing attention to herself

"Lily, Lily, that's just what you can't do. This all has to be a secret. You'll be missing. No one will know. Think of the publicity. I'll be interviewed, be inconsolable. We can milk that for months."

"Let me think about it. Publicity every week, a new story every week? I demand it."

"Of course, in all the major magazines and newspapers. You'll be on everyone's lips. Get Lily back. We'll put that on billboards across the country. Use that head shot you like so much."

"You like it too."

"Of course I do. It's beautiful. Leland did a great job capturing your beauty. Course, that isn't hard. You have no poor angles." Not too thick, Ron cautioned himself. She's not stupid.

"This better be on the level and work out how you say." Lily glared at him.

"Honey, it's perfect. And if the clammer is hard to handle, I'll bring you back in five years."

"Five years, at first you said ten. Five years is better, except what about Melanie? She won't look any different in five years. Probably not even in twenty."

"I'm thinking publicity. And that gives me time to get new material for five or more movies. Contact new writers, fresh ideas."

"You should have been doing that now if you had any smarts. You don't seem to recognize all the talent I have."

"I do, but the scripts around now don't do justice to you," continued Ron.

"You got that right." Lily kept pacing the floor getting another cigarette, taking a few puffs and then grinding it out. "I need some wine, get it will you?" which wasn't exactly a request; she expected her desires to be filled immediately. And Ron jumped to do just that.

"I want to do a musical. Like the Doris Day movies. And you know that shot of Betty Grable looking over her shoulder, you know the one I mean?"

"Sure, during the big war it was the most popular photo, still gets raves."

"Well I want a shot like that only in a bikini. And one like Farrah had and I want a singing part."

"You've never been in a musical, but, I know you can sing, though. I've never heard you, so what do you like?" Ron hoped he showed genuine interest. Of course, he had heard her sing and she couldn't.

"Those romantic-comedies like Doris and Rock made. Get me some of those," demanded Lily.

Kimmie is the one for those, Ron thought, but only said, "Perfect for you if I can get a good enough writer to come close to your talent."

"You better be telling the truth and you better work hard at this, I'm still not sure I'll do it."

Ron inwardly groaned. He had already promised Kimmie she had a great movie part and a lovely home with him. He could handle Lily, make her think she may be right, don't do it, lose all that publicity.

"Well, if you don't want to, I'll get Melanie to do it."

"She won't. She's too hot right now."

"She knows the value of terrific publicity and knows a winner when she sees it."

Lily fumed awhile, Melanie getting all that press coverage. No way! She lighted another cigarette stamped it out, poured another glass of wine, drank it down in a couple of gulps, preened in front of the mirror; sat on the loveseat, paced again. Ron waited. He knew the acquiescence signs.

Ron began to daydream about Kimmie. The day he met her, she was carrying a tray of orange juice around to serve the movie set crew. She reminded Ron of the cute cigarette girls of the 40's movies, though she wore tight jeans and a white tank top. No bra. A younger version of Lily. Dressed for attention and she got it. The eyes of all the males followed her moves and Ron led the pack. Who cared about the juice? Ron only wanted to watch her walk. The first day was like being thirsty and receiving a nice cool drink. The next time he saw her she remembered him, "You really like orange juice don't you? I'll bring you all you want." And she did. She sought him out each day. Not hard to do, he watched for her as well.

One day she gave him a small replica of his automobile - a white Mustang. It gave him a lift to know that she found him interesting. Not bad for a fifty-year old, he told himself. Kimmie continued giving Ron small attentions and if being a Hollywood agent was the reason, he certainly didn't care. He did help her career along by getting her a walk-on now and then and several times she even got to say a word or two. She was very grateful. And now with Lily going away, the relationship could develop into something very nice indeed.

"Why are you smiling?" Lily was thumping his shoulder with her fist, bringing him back to the present with a jump. "Your thoughts were a million miles away."

"Seeing the publicity. It will drive everyone nuts. Melanie's mom can milk it too."

"She's not getting it. Give me those stupid papers," Lily stomped her foot. Competition will spur her on everytime. Ron smiled.

"You're sure? I don't want to push you into something you don't want."

"You can't push me into anything," Lily antagonistically said. "I need to get out of this rat-race awhile anyway. A good rest will do wonders for me, not that there's anything wrong."

"Okay, we'll do this tomorrow. What newspaper do you want the article to be in first?"

"I'll make a list and use the photo on the piano, and you do a lot of crying. That's good for copy too." Lily got a pen and paper and began to write names of newspapers and magazines. All of a sudden, she became excited about the project.

"Baby, this will put the world into a frenzy." Ron needed to handle this right.

"I know it will. Save all the clippings. This can be terrific. I can just see the looks when articles about me push everything else off the front page."

"Beautiful!" Ron smiled. Everything was falling into place and Lily clapped her hands like a school girl being elected queen of the prom.

"You know how Susan likes to borrow my jewelry? Don't let her. Put it in the safe deposit box with our other important papers."

"No one will even dare to ask about borrowing anything" Ron promised, not intending to keep the promise at all.

"Here's a list of what I want you to do. And these newspapers first. Make a big splash all at once and keep the pressure on. By the way, I'll close the condo."

"It wouldn't work. It has to look spontaneous or everyone will know it was planned and it will fall apart." Please make her see that.

"Yeah, you're right. I disappear right away without anyone but you knowing we planned it." Lily gave him a very hard look. Does she suspect something, wondered Ron.

"Got to be that way for it to work. It could be a kidnapping, a murder, loss of memory, anything to keep people wondering." Then Ron got a lonely feeling. Could he really live without her for ten years or even five? They had been together for twenty years. Lily had been a seventeen-year-old starlet just beginning to get noticed and Ron an agent looking for clients. He became her agent and manager, guiding her career to her Academy Award. They had been married eighteen years now.

CRYONICS and the publicity of her disappearance would boost her career to astonishing heights, but, really, he would miss her dreadfully. Miss the fights and making up; miss her demands and the shy smile when she got her way; miss her spectacular way of getting attention especially at an opening; miss the attention he received because of her; but, most of all he would miss her being part of his life everyday. He couldn't let her go.

"Lily, I can't let you do CRYONICS. I can't stand to be without you ten years. Not even ten days." Ron was contrite.

"Well, too bad, I'm doing it. You told me yourself on how much it would boost my career. I know this is a gimmick no one has ever used. It's priceless. Now tell me, isn't that so?"

"Yes it is. But...."

"No buts, and listen to this. I'll tell everyone where I was and become a national spokesman for, what is that again?"

"CRYONICS." Ron was almost speechless. Lily was on a roll and now he couldn't stop her.

"Yeah, rake in millions doing that, and, my dear husband, if you don't want to do the publicity, I can do it all or get Stan's agency to do it. He's always had a thing for me anyway."

"I'll do it. I'll miss you like crazy. But, I'll do it if you insist on going through with this."

"It's the best idea you've had for years. The other gals would kill for it." Lily laughed.

And suddenly Ron did not see Kimmie here in Lily's condo, did not see her wearing Lily's clothes, or her jewelry, or preening in front of Lily's mirrors, or riding beside him to an opening or anywhere, or in Lily's bed. All of a sudden he saw Kimmie as the grasping, selfish, fluff-head that she was and he wanted no part of her. He wanted to be with Lily forever.

He decided that he, too, would go into CRYONIC suspension with Lily. They together would milk the publicity when reanimated. They spent the next several hours working out the details of their disappearance and neither knowing the other had capitulated to the other.

The decision made, they spent the rest of the night in each other's arms.

CHAPTER TWENTY

Nate heard Kathy's voice: "Call."

Just one word but it shouted apprehension. Is it Natalie, Carmen, something else? Kathy would not call his home unless there was some kind of an emergency. Since she knew about his bugged telephone, calls were made at another place at a predetermined time. This call sent shivers down his spine. He left his apartment and jogged to a safe phone.

Kathy answered on the first ring, "Hello."

"What's wrong?" Nate fairly shouted.

"Calm down, we are all fine here. But Mom and Dad's place was broken into."

"They all right?"

"Yes, they weren't home. But the reason I called, the break-in was strange. Nothing was taken. Stuff, pillows, end tables, lamps, were piled in the middle of the living room but the scary thing, on the bathroom mirror written with Mom's lipstick was 'I know who you are' that's all."

"Sure nothing was taken. How did he get in? Their place is pretty secure I thought."

"Didn't even look like a break-in. The cops thought it might be a joke and I told them it looked like that to me too so they wouldn't be afraid but I told them to get the locks changed anyway." Kathy was nearly out of breath.

"When did this happen?" Nate's apprehension was immediate.

"This afternoon."

"Where were Mom and Dad?"

"Their bridge day at the club house."

"Had they locked the doors?"

"She said she thinks so, but you know villas, all so close together and everyone knows each other so they probably get careless about locking doors."

"So someone walked in and left a message."

"What are you thinking, Nate?" Kathy caught something in Nate's voice that scared her.

"Did you talk to them again tonight? They okay or shook up?" asked Nate.

"I talked to them around eight. New locks and neighborhood watch out in full force. In fact, a couple of neighbors are staying with them. They kind of think it's a joke now, I think. Do you?" Kathy's voice trembled.

"I'd like to think so, but the message 'I know who you are' scares me Kathy." Nate's voice grew very quiet. "I think it might be Rudy. He's tracking my family and if he knows where Mom and Dad live, then he will soon know where you are, if he doesn't already."

"But, he hasn't been around Los Angeles. You haven't seen him have you? In what? Five months since you heard anything about him."

"He was here a week before I got here and Dino apparently convinced him that he could handle it so Rudy went back to Georgia. That was more like six months ago, no, I guess closer to seven. Six and a half. And as you know my phone has been bugged and well I think I am being watched. Course she isn't here, so I hoped he had given up on me. I don't mind the bug or being watched. I'm not doing anything, anyway."

"What about now? Are you at home?"

"No, I'm okay. This is safe and I can see if anyone is around and there isn't."

"Any ideas?"

"Let me think about it. Keep your eyes open. Use caution and talk to your neighbors about watching for anything suspicious."

"Lucky Dan and Janet live across the street."

"He the retired sheriff?"

"Yes, and our best friends. They like...."

"Never mind. No more names. Always be cautious."

"Okay. Will you call me tomorrow after you think more about it?"

"Yeah, the usual and don't worry. It still maybe a joke or some promotion from a company or something."

"But, you don't think so?" Kathy could always know when Nate tried to hide something.

"No, and listen, I want you to be prepared to do whatever I tell you. No questions."

"All right."

"Bye then,"

"Bye."

So, Rudy again. Nate was sure. Why doesn't he give up? He treated Carmen like dirt. Really only wants her back to prove a point. She's his possession, or so he believes. Still, the problem has arisen again, if it had ever subsided a few months. Maybe only to make Nate get over confident and less observant. Nate pondered his action and decisions he must make. Certainly since his parent's home had been entered, it was just a matter of time until Rudy would make a connection with Kathy if he hadn't already. Nate must again warn Kathy and Carmen to be extremely careful, until, well, forever it seemed.

CHAPTER TWENTY-ONE

Dino's spirits were soaring. Seventy members of the audience had opted for CRYONICS. That meant, Dino had said, that it was almost one hundred per cent successful, since in some cases, a spouse or friend had attended with the patient and would be participating in suspension themselves.

"Can you believe how popular corpscycle is? Over six million from a two-hour presentation."

"Corpscycle? Is that a new word we will be using?" asked Nate.

"It's Vinnie's word. Frozen corpses. Not very nice," laughed Dino. "But, when you think about it, not far off the target."

"Speaking of target, it seems everyone there tonight was either a candidate or a supporter of the patient. How did that happen?"

"Homework. Actually we work with a few doctors who give us names of people who are terminally ill or would be a good CRYONICS candidate. We do the rest," explained Dino.

"Is that ethical of the doctors to do that?"

"Who cares? Their names are never used or made public. And we would never admit we get names from them. No one in the organization would even mention it -- -- course you know that. And, besides, think of the good it does. CRYONICS is the way to go so to speak," laughed Dino.

"It sounds great." Nate regretted his words about ethical doctors. Can't be critical of the organization he told himself. Dino didn't appear to take offense, however.

"Soon CRYONICS will be discussed more openly. When our man is reanimated you can believe people will come flocking to be a corpscycle," boasted Dino, waved his arms as if to encompass the world.

"Another thing..." Nate was hesitant to ask. although Dino certainly was in a talkative mood.

"Shoot."

"It looked as if the people there weren't much concerned about money. Except that one old lady who asked if it had to be paid all at once."

"That's another part of our homework. Everyone there, including that old lady, can afford CRYONICS. Vinnie has a team that checks finances. He isn't in this for charity."

"Lots of time and work goes in this. I had no idea." Nate was impressed, though a little disappointed that money once again ruled.

"Vinnie has about thirty guys working full time on this. Background checks, who's a candidate, a group to set up presentations, do advance work like sending out brochures, and then you guys who do the presentations. After that, another group takes care of getting the patients to the LIFE facility and into suspension."

"And people at the facility," added Nate.

"Yeah. It's quite an organization and really Vinnie's baby. He's sure to get the Nobel."

"Yeah, it's quite a deal."

"So, what's on your mind? You look like you don't believe all this." Dino, very astute at reading expressions and body language, asked.

"Everyone I know in Vinnie's organization borders on, well, shading the law," Nate explained his questioning.

Dino laughed, "Crooks you mean. Well, he is using questionable personnel, like you, for instance. But, hey, we can do good things too and this is a money-maker for the organization, no question about that."

"About the space for the facility. Is that place in Wyoming the only one or will there be more in other states?"

"Here's something I'll tell you and this is for your ears only." Dino leaned forward as in a conspiracy with Nate.

210

"Sure, our conversations always are," agreed Nate. And he was right. He had never told anyone the truth about Dino's business.

"Vinnie, not Vinnie himself, but a couple of his guys, are working with the Cheyenne to use their burial places to build another facility. They have miles of reservation in Wyoming."

"But, they get real uptight if someone even looks at those places where their ancestors are buried," remarked Nate.

"Money talks again and the good doctors, Hall and Hernandez, convinced them their ancestors would like CRYONICS. Hernandez being an Indian and highly respected since he's a doctor," laughed Dino. "And the promise that tribe members will be accepted at no charge."

"That could fill the facility. Where's the profit in that?" asked Nate.

"You're right. That would fill up the facility if, and don't even let this linger in your mind, if they are placed in suspension LIFE."

"You mean their bodies would be buried someplace else?"

"Naw, cremated. No space for the pine boxes. A real beauty isn't it? Boy, Vinnie is a jump ahead of everyone on this. The Indians are convinced their lives will go on forever, and like early day Cheyenne, will be head honchos again," gloated Dino.

"So, the Indian bodies will be cremated. Any others," Nate thought it would be safer to laugh at this new idea. New to Nate anyway. "To save space?"

"You never know. But, Indians always believed in reincarnation. Look at all the eagles they carve. Probably believe it's their grandfather," smirked Dino. "If they get antsy about reanimation, Vinnie will point out an eagle and tell them that's how the body came back and they'll believe it. Always have."

Nate felt a little nauseated. What is he into anyway? Is any of this on the level?

"When's the next presentation?"

"In Chicago next Thursday. We leave Tuesday to check out the stage. We have almost two hundred people coming."

211

"If this keeps up won't we run out of space?" asked Nate.

"Vinnie calls it freezer space. He has another three hundred acres in Wyoming, about fifty miles from the first one and also engineers working on units that more than one patient can fit in."

"Instead of individual Dewers?"

"Something like in a morgue when trays are pulled out. Could stack a lot of bodies on top of each other."

Nate shuddered. What was really going on? How could he have been in the organization two years and just now learn of CRYONICS? Then again, he had only made "new papers" a few months as well. How far did Vinnie's organization reach? And in what?

"Hey! Guess what?" Dino suddenly changed the subject and smiled in what Nate recognized was his devious way.

"What?"

"Your old friend Rudy's in the area or soon will be. Vinnie said Rudy's had business out our way and may stop in."

Nate could play this game very well. "Great. When you see him send him up to my place. He can see for himself that I don't have his girl friend."

"He knows that. I told him she's not living at your place and it maybe other business anyway."

"Thanks for telling him. You must be the only person in the world who believes me. Course maybe he found her already. Or her body." Nate hated to imply that Carmen could be dead but, it seemed safer for her.

"He hasn't. He told me he's still looking for her and has some ideas where she may be."

"Good for him." Nate hoped he sounded totally uninterested. In fact, his heart was pounding. Where is Rudy?

Nate called his sister from the safe telephone. "Kathy, Rudy is in the area and still looking for her. Can you get out of there until he either decides she isn't with you or I get to him?"

"Nate, what are you planning?" Kathy was apprehensive, her brother could be so impulsive.

"Something has to be done about him, Kath. She can't live in fear for the rest of her life."

"But, what if we do stay away for a few days? What good will that do? We still have to come back sometime," protested Kathy.

"Kath, I don't know. I need some time to work something out in my head. I want to find out where he is and I'm not sure how to do that. Stay on the boat for a few days."

"The boat is only a block from our house. We wouldn't be out of sight."

"Take it to the islands or to Coupeville. Do this for me and for your own protection. And hers and the baby. I need some time and need to know you are safe. And be careful and keep an eye out for trouble."

"All right. You have our boat number so give a call."

"Yeah, the regular time," agreed Nate, and breathed a sigh of relief that he had convinced Kathy of the need for the family to be away for a few days at least. And why this seemingly renewed interest in Rudy looking for Carmen? Several months had gone by without an inkling and then his parent's house broken into. Rudy never gave up.

CHAPTER TWENTY-TWO

Rudy

Rudy was not the most likable person in the world and could well be the most ruthless. He believed Carmen was alive and with Nate, even though Dino said that Nate definitely lived alone.

"Why do you think Nate helped her?" asked Dino. The two men had met at a restaurant in El Segundo, Dino promising the best Mexican food anywhere. He was right.

"I live in a very isolated place, you know the reasons why. This past year there have been five drivers there that Vinnie arranged. The only other visitors were a couple of gals that I took up there. Nate was sent by Vinnie. The last one. He drove a white Buick. A white Buick was seen leaving my place the day Carmen disappeared."

"But, what about the other drivers?" Dino asked, still hoping to believe that Nate was innocent. "Couldn't she have wandered away and got lost in the woods and had an accident? That's what Nate says he believes happened, when he talks about it at all and that's only when he's questioned."

"That's the way I'm supposed to think. But..." Rudy punched his fingers on the table, "her black sweater was found in Nate's car."

"Sure it was hers?" asked Dino.

"Reggie described it to me. Exactly like hers and hers is gone," continued Rudy. "And that's not all. A photo album with pictures of her parents, her brother, and I guess their home in Cuba, was missing, and an old bag, made of denim that she had some other stuff she looked at, is gone too."

"What was in the bag?"

214

"Oh, junk. A rock, an envelope with a lock of hair, said it was hers when she was small, a small piece of cloth, a few coins, a picture of a kitten. Just junk."

"Treasures to her, I guess," remarked Dino, thinking of the things his children collected and kept in an old cigar box he had around for years. Each of his children had such an old box and thought the boxes were treasures as well.

"I guess. But, they were gone. She wouldn't take them for a casual walk," explained Rudy.

"No, it doesn't seem so."

"Nate paid attention to her the day he came up."

"Like how."

"Oh, friendly. Asked about the baby. Thanked her for the cupcakes." Rudy remembered the day so well, the same day he buried his dog.

"He is friendly though, and very polite," said Dino. "I questioned him about her and if he helped her at all, it would have been to get her back to Cuba. Only, he denies it and I tend to believe him."

"I don't." Rudy maintained his story and he stared intently into Dino's eyes with a look that would have frightened anyone else.

"Look at it from his standpoint. Why in the world would he burden himself with a pregnant girl, maybe face criminal charges, and what about the kid? Makes no sense to me," stated Dino.

"It happened. You ever been to his apartment?"

"I have his phone bugged. Vinnie asked me to do that, and you can listen to the calls. Only talks to other surfers, ordering a pizza, surf reports. That's all he seems to be interested in. That and keeping in good physical condition. Riding his bike and jogging."

"I'm going through his place. Maybe I can pick up a clue. I got a letter from his parent's place. He has a sister up in Everett, Washington. I'm headed there after I look around his apartment. I can get information out of her. Out of anybody!"

"Tuesday would be a good time to see the apartment. We're going to St. Louis for another presentation. Nate will be gone and Ray will let you in."

"Ray your man? How many of these things you done now?"

"This is our fourth presentation and yes, Ray is our man. They're stashed all over. Ray has managed that complex for years and has no suspicion of Nate."

"Everyone seems to think Nate's a Boy Scout. But, tell me, what is a Boy Scout doing in Vinnie's organization?" sneered Rudy.

"You have a point. I asked Vinnie the same thing."

"Richard brought him in. Said Nate was greedy, cheated on drinks and tips, when he worked on the cruise ship. Richard thought him a good candidate for Vinnie and tell you the truth, Vinnie is high on him. And let me tell you, Nate is absolutely terrific at the cryonics presentations. He's smart and a quick thinker."

"And he took Carmen," added Rudy.

"Donno. It would seem out of character for him," remarked Dino, as he savored the Mexican sampler plate.

"If it turns out he did, what will the organization do to him? Since we're both part of it. Loyalty and all." Rudy wanted the pound of flesh knowing all the while he could get it himself and more fun!

"Well, Vinnie would be livid no doubt of that. Nate would be one unhappy person. Anything else that makes you suspicious of him?"

"Followed his paper trail. Usually got two or three thousand cash at a time except once in Walsenburg, Colorado, then he got five thousand."

"Well, like most of us, he deals on a cash basis so what's the big deal 'bout that?" asked Dino.

"Seemed all of a sudden he needed more than usual. Maybe a hospital or something," stated Rudy.

"You have any ideas on how he spent his money?"

"Used a credit card sometimes but mostly it must have been cash. Not too easy to trace cash especially if you don't know where someone is. Shouldn't have cost more than a couple a hundred a day, motel, gas and food. So why so much that time?"

"He could have done some fun things along the way. He wasn't on a schedule or anything," Dino continued to defend Nate.

"I think he knows something about her and I'll find out," promised Rudy. It wasn't an idle threat.

"Search his apartment. No problem for you to do that. I've been in it a few times and didn't see anything suspicious. And here's another thing. Why don't you contact someone in Walsenburg to see if something happened to anyone that would require that kind of money." Dino wondered why Rudy hadn't done that before. But then, Rudy isn't that bright.

Rudy knew better, though, than to contact the police department, so he opted for local newspapers to be sent to him. He asked for two weeks of papers during the time the cash had been withdrawn. A small article caught his eye about a baby born during a fender-bender. The young couple were named Olson. Mr. and Mrs. Nathan Olson.

While waiting for the newspapers to arrive, Rudy searched Nate's apartment. He began by listening to telephone messages. Pondering Kathy's "Call," he dismissed it as a surfing pal. Other calls, as Dino had said, were about ordering pizza and getting surf and weather reports. Each of Nate's books, and there were very few of those, were gone through page by page; drawers were emptied and frames searched for hiding places; backs of the always generic prints in an apartment and perhaps used as a place to hide photos or a letter, were removed; linings of clothing were gone over; every inch of space was diligently covered and ultimately rejected as hiding any trace of Carmen. Disappointed, Rudy arranged the apartment exactly as he had found it foregoing an inclination to leave his calling card.

Maybe she isn't here living with him. But, he's sure to know where she is. Perhaps he should check out that Walsenburg place. But rejected that. They wouldn't stay there anyway and even though Nathan Olson could certainly be Nate Olmstead, Nate was smart enough to leave no trace of where they were now. And if he left Carmen there, which he wouldn't, she could be lone gone now. No, better to find Nate's sister, Kathy. Everett, Washington. Just where is that anyway? No matter, Rudy was on his way there.

His flight from LAX arrived at SeaTac airport in Seattle on a windy and rainy afternoon. What a place! It seemed nearly every passenger raced to an espresso bar and carried a container of, it looked to Rudy, coffee with whipped cream on top, all the way to the luggage pick-up area. The containers were like a badge of acceptance and people in Seattle didn't even discover coffee, they only thought they did and hey, in this weather, coffee was a basic necessity. Another thing, the sky was gray, the rain seemed tentative, more like a light mist that couldn't decide whether to stay or go. But, he guessed it stayed more often than not since outside was very green.

At the airport, he rented a light blue Taurus, a little snug for his big frame, but indistinguishable. A pickup suited him better, an old pickup. He wisely determined he received too much attention by his sheer size to add more by driving a truck through a residential neighborhood. And wasn't he expecting too much from just a name on a note? There must be hundreds of Kathys in Everett. He realized his research was inadequate. Still, since he was there, he would try to find her. The only clue must be at the local Post Office.

Leaving SeaTac, Rudy drove north on I-5 through traffic and wild drivers that rivaled Atlanta or Miami. Why is this place getting so much attention as a great place to live? And is this the only highway through Seattle? He glanced to his left and saw a domed structure.

So, he thought, that must be the Kingdome, home of the always ineffective Seahawks. Seattle's claim to a pro football team. He laughed. Small dome like that, why would the good players consider coming here? The skyline boasted a couple of dozen tall buildings, one very tall, and in his mind's eye he envisioned it crumbling to the ground like the one in Oklahoma City. He laughed again, learning more about explosives was high on his list of fun things to do. He drove through an underground highway that looked as if structures were built on top of it. This would be a nice disaster, too, he mused.

Traffic continued to be heavy although it looked as if he was leaving the city. Apartment buildings and shopping malls dotted the area with exit signs pointing to various suburbs or so Rudy guessed. Lake City, Edmonds, Lynnwood, Bothell. Interesting names and finally an exit denoting Whidbey Island to the right and downtown Everett to the left. Nearing five o'clock, he guessed rightly that the Post Office would be closed and his quest postponed until the next morning. He spotted a steak house adjacent to a bar and wheeled in. Like most bar-grills, this looked like a greasy spoon, but so what. The coffee was hot, steaks large and surprisingly tender, rare and juicy, french fries crisp, beer cold. Altogether a very satisfying meal to an airline-food empty stomach.

Rudy's eyes canvassed the area. A bar stood at one end, stools covered with brown imitation leather, fairly new job, he thought. Two men were playing pool being watched by three women wearing tight jeans and sloppy sweat shirts. One of the women, a chubby bleached blonde, eyed anyone entering the bar area and Rudy surmised the other two belonged to the pool players and the blonde was hoping for some action. He considered her and filed the thought away for the moment. Booths ringed the walls of the restaurant; several tables with chairs taking the floor space. Room for about thirty people Rudy guessed and about a fourth of them full. Several men sat on the bar stools. His kind of place, he smiled.

He finished his steak dinner and ordered another. While waiting, he sauntered to the bar and watched the evening news on the big TV screen above the counter, prevents an argument being controlled by the bartender, at least most of the time, Rudy surmised. Patrons glanced at the TV periodically. There was a smattering of interest in a report about the coach, quarterback, and running back of last year's super bowl champions apparently getting the flu or food poisoning and now in a comma. Rudy wondered if it was Vinnie at work again.

The blonde watched Rudy wander to the bar area and casually pick up a post card, look at the framed prints on the walls, and then cast his eyes around the room. Their eyes met in the mirror behind the counter, she smiled. He raised his eyebrows and asked, "You had dinner?"

Her chest tightened, she wondered what he was offering. Should she join him and where will it lead? Is she ready for that? Again?

"Go for it, Betty, you deserve it," said one of the women at the pool table. "He looks nice."

Betty glanced at the woman and smiled, then at Rudy. "No," she answered, "I haven't had dinner."

"Care to join me?" Rudy asked. "Anyone here to object?"

"No, no one to object. Sure, " Betty replied and went with him back to his table.

"What you drinkin?" Rudy asked, "Wine okay or order whatever you want."

"Oh, I don't care. Yes wine," Betty was already impressed with Rudy taking care of her. No one had done that in a long time.

Rudy definitely had plans to take care of her.

They exchanged small talk. Not one word of Rudy's being the truth. Betty, not adept at deceitfulness, told him her life story. A northwest person, she had grown up in Darrington, Washington, a small town in the foothills of the Cascade Mountains. She married young and dropped out of high school. Her husband, Kenny, worked off and on in the timber industry, Darrington's major employer, and Betty waited tables. The young couple barely got by financially. Then the babies came. Three in three years. Not difficult to understand why the marriage failed. Young, broke most of the time, crying babies, and a husband who spent most evenings drinking with his friends and weekends playing slow-pitch. Betty watched soap operas every afternoon dreaming of a life like the beautiful actresses. She would never get it.

After four years of non-bliss, Kenny left for Alaska leaving Betty and the babies with her parents. The grandparents kept the children when Betty moved to Everett and through a job training program got a job in a convenience store. She eked out a meager living, married and divorced twice, saw her children during holidays, and drifted in and out of relationships. Then Rudy came along flashing a roll of hundred dollar bills and she thought, why not?

Rudy, of course, did not use his real name. Indeed, he used a stolen credit card and driver's license easily obtained from Dino. His steel blue eyes were covered with dark brown contacts, a hair piece added bulk to his sparse hair, and with a thin mustache, his looks were dramatically changed. He planned it that way.

He told Betty that he grew up in abusive foster homes, being hungry much of the time running away and being returned to more abuse. Until one year when he was twelve, a foster family liked and enjoyed him, turning his life around in a warm trusting direction which he has followed ever since. He smiled at her. She smiled back. The steak was good and it saved her the price of a dinner which in any case would not have been steak. More like a package of Top Ramen.

"I have an idea, " Rudy announced, his steak eaten and the bottle of wine nearly empty.

"What?" Now the proposition she thought. What does he have in mind? Expect her to stay with him for a steak dinner. Well, why not? She had done it for less.

"Let's go shopping tomorrow. You've got to get rid of that awful sweatshirt," he smiled.

"I guess I don't look so great," apologized Betty.

"You look great. Only you should be in something pretty, something to match your eyes. I'd say let's go now but I'm kind of tired. Think I'll just find a motel and crash. Can you suggest a place?"

Here it comes she thought, "There's a couple close to here or nicer ones further out."

"Which one do you recommend?"

"I don't know. Any of them I guess." Betty began to fidget with her napkin. Rudy watched her.

"You got time to show me around the area. Those tall trees are beautiful. Are there any close by that I could get a closer look?"

"Sure, not much to see, but, sure," answered Betty.

"I've never seen such tall trees," remarked Rudy.

"To really see the big ones you have to drive further up to the mountains," Betty explained.

"How far?"

"Oh, it would take an hour or so."

"Still enough light to see some," Rudy remarked, feigning interest he did not feel.

"Yeah, we have long twilights here and it's only six-thirty. But, you know, there's a tree at a rest stop that a car can drive through. It's not far from here, about a half-hours drive."

"A half-hour there, look around a few minutes, then a half-hour back. I have time if you do."

"Sure," Betty was breaking her own rule. Never get in a car with a stranger, but, he seemed nice and hasn't once mentioned her staying the night with him. She felt a glow of anticipation and he had talked about shopping too.

"You have a car here?" Rudy asked. "We can drop it off and I'll drive you home."

"No, I came with friends."

"Let's go then."

"I'll just tell them you'll take me home. Want to meet them?"

"Naw, I'm in kind of a rush. Want to get back early." Of course, Rudy, who called himself Arnie, didn't want to meet anyone. He did, though, wave to Betty's friends as he guided her through the door and to his rented car.

Her friends waved. They were happy for her. She needed a man in her life. Maybe this time. Maybe not!

Early the following morning, Rudy walked into a Post Office pushing himself in front of a line of customers. "I need to see the postmaster," he said, ignoring comments about waiting your turn or hey don't push.

"Sir, these people were here first. Please stand in line and you'll be helped as soon as possible," a clerk, with Susan on her name tag, quietly suggested.

"I don't have anything to stand in line for," answered Rudy. "Where's the boss?"

"Sir, I can't let you do this. Please wait your turn. It will only be a few minutes," a forty-something clerk, name tag Helen, said.

"Which door is his?" demanded Rudy, looking toward several doors in back of the counter.

A bald-headed man, around fifty, short and much over weight, appeared from a side door, "Can I help you?"

"You the boss?" asked Rudy.

"Yes, sir. Would you like to talk to me?"

"Yeah."

"Please come in." The postmaster stepped aside to let Rudy enter the office. "Helen, order more fifty-cent stamps please," a suggestion that would bring a security man to the front of the office. The man conferred quietly with Helen and Susan.

"Ladies and gentlemen," the security man said, "we're asking that you please vacate the building quickly and quietly until we determine if we have a problem here."

"Hey, come on, I've been here in line a half an hour already," a man near the front of the line complained. He shoved a small package and a five-dollar bill on the counter and stalked out.

"You get change sir," Susan reminded. But the man was out the door. The others were pushed out by the security man amid mumblings that they wanted to conclude their business and although had heard the large man's disturbance, were not unduly concerned. And they had no reason to be. Rudy had no intention of causing a problem. Information was all he had in mind. Finding Kathy his only desire.

"What can I do for you sir?" The postmaster's name tag read Robert Swenson.

"Well, Mr. Swenson, I want you to tell me where this came from." Rudy produced the envelope and note from Nate's sister Kathy.

Swenson took the envelope, turned it over, then back to the front. "There's no return address on this. I have no idea. There's no way to tell where it came from," he explained.

"It says Everett, WA. That's here ain't it?" Rudy asked in a belligerent voice. "Where in Everett?"

"There's no way to determine where it was mailed. It doesn't even say it was mailed here, only postmarked here. And mail from all the surrounding towns have the Everett postmark." His telephone rang. He answered and briefly said, "No, it's okay."

"You mean there ain't no code or something to say which part of town this came from?"

"No, like I said, it could even be Mount Vernon or Snohomish, many places. There's several collection centers in the state. It's been a long time since each city or town postmarked its own mail. Course, if someone asked that a certain postmark be used, then the request is honored."

Rudy picked up the envelope from the desk and stared at it. He had been so sure information that he wanted could have been found here.

"I would suggest you contact those people, " Swenson indicated the envelope, "and get the address you want from them. Perhaps a telephone call...."

"So you can't help me?"

"I'm sorry, no I can't." Swenson rose from his chair dismissing Rudy.

Rudy knew a telephone call would garner no information from the Olmsteads. Indeed it would only alert Kathy. But, he knew ways to get information. Knew these ways very well.

And he was long gone, back to Palm Springs when "The Heralds" front page story revealed that an unidentified woman's body had been found near a rest stop north of Marysville. The rest stop where an old tree stump, large enough for a car to drive through, was located. According to the news article, the woman was twenty-five to thirty-five years old, blonde hair, five-feet eight inches tall and weighed one hundred and sixty pounds. If anyone knows a missing person matching that description please contact the Marysville or Everett police departments.

The following day, a photo of Betty appeared with an updated article. The photo had been touched up so the bruises around her face were not as horrible as reality showed. This was due partly to ease the pain of any relative seeing the photo, plus as one policeman explained to reporters, no one could have identified the swollen face whose eyes had been gouged out. The body had been left in a horrible condition, but it was determined that she had suffocated and then her body mutilated.

Why?

Law enforcement officers pondered that question. They contacted the Green River task force in Seattle to see if perhaps this woman had been murdered by the same person or persons that had murdered so many women and left their bodies near the Green River in Washington state. Other areas where serial killers had operated were contacted, but there was no connection to other crimes.

Betty was identified by her mother. She had seen the newspaper article, read it with interest, then received a shock when the following day Betty's photo appeared. It took an hour or so before Mrs. Anderson was calm enough to call the police department. A horrid experience for her and Betty's children. Betty's friends from the bar also called to identify the body and gave the police their first solid lead.

"She left with this man, tall, very tall, dark hair, very nice teeth. Seemed okay, nice, had a thin mustache. Rene offered a description of Rudy, such as it was. Of course she would identify him, she said.

"Ever see him before?" asked the police officer.

"No, just that night. He asked her to have dinner with him, seemed to be having a good time," said Rene.

"You live in the same building. Did she often go out with strangers? Weren't you concerned when she didn't come home?"

"She went out sometimes, we didn't always know who with, and she would visit her kids in Darrington so she would be gone a few days. She always came back," added Ralph.

With the friend's information and description of Rudy, the case could be solved very soon. Someone had heard Betty call the man Arnie; someone had seen them leave in a blue Taurus; someone added the type of clothing Arnie wore; and although eyewitnesses are known to be unreliable, the police felt encouraged. These people were sure and their descriptions matched. And when the investigation turned up a rental car agreement from the SeaTac airport with Arnie's address and driver's license number, the Los Angeles police were contacted immediately.

Of course, no one in Marysville knew the documents had been stolen. Arnie turned out to be a seventy-five year old bed-ridden stroke patient who didn't even know the documents were gone. The investigation had come to a stand-still. No leads. Add this to another unsolved murder. Another vicious act by Rudy who seemed to enjoy inflicting pain on the unsuspecting.

Before Rudy reached Palm Springs, Vinnie summoned him back to Georgia for another "business" burial and the Olmsteads were safe. At least for awhile.

CHAPTER TWENTY-THREE

Nate glanced around the Chicago hotel meeting room which looked much the same as other places CRYONICS presentations were made. On the walls hung the same Monet prints; floral arrangements matched the colors in the prints; the view from windows being the only difference in the setting from one presentation to another. Members of the audience had been hand-picked for need and ability to pay. Need being a supposedly incurable illness that CRYONICS would offer a welcome way to once again live a full and healthy life. Nate saw anticipation and hope reflected in the eyes of the audience. He could recognize the very ill who, for the most part, seemed uncomfortable, perhaps wishing to be in bed at home. They looked resigned as if accepting whatever fate had in store. Nate wondered, what indeed, does fate have in store for them. Is CRYONICS the answer for them? For anyone? Ever since Dino had told him about bilking the Cheyenne Indians out of property and cremating the dead instead of suspension in CRYONICS, Nate had doubts about the entire program. What, exactly, is going on?

The hope etched in the anxious faces produced an unidentified emotion around his heart. Why now did he care if people were swindled? Was there really any difference in watering drinks to cheat, stealing employee's tips, promoting prostitution, delivering dimethylmercury, which causes an anguished death, or convincing heartbroken people to enter into CRYONICS if, indeed, it is a fraud? Cheating and lying is, after all, cheating and lying. Does he have a conscience now when he never seemed to before? Before Carmen, is that it? Then again, does he have any proof that this project is fake? Information he had gathered maintained that CRYONICS is being done. But, are Vinnie and Dino on the level about it?

The meeting, based on the same information and presented by the same personnel as earlier ones, garnered nearly the same questions from the audience. Is there a cure for cancer? AIDS? Alzheimer's? Multiple sclerosis? Or any number of fatal diseases now reaching the curable stages? How many years away? And the cost? Nate determined that the women asked more about cost and men asked more often how many years before loved ones could be reanimated. He pondered the reasons and guessed that women thought about children and their inheritance while men envisioned lonely years ahead without their mates.

Nate's mind wandered while Dr. Ruben, Nguyen, and Scidderly presented their portions of the program. Where was Rudy? Is Carmen safe? How many teeth does Natalie have now? Can Kathy keep them safe? Then his mind jumped to the present when Dr. Ruben said, "We all like surprises and Nate has an important one to share. Nate? Nate?" Scidderly nudged Nate.

"Yes, yes, indeed." And Nate explained once again that in a little less than two years, a patient at LIFE will be reanimated and would be sharing his story with the world. At that time it is expected that CRYONICS will become popular and prices rise. There could be no better time than now to consider a CRYONICS program. Nguyen explained finances including insurance policies and again laughed when he mentioned that Nate's policy cost less because of his age. This brought expected laughter from the audience and though they were unaware, it planted a seed in their minds to get insurance now. Or at least consider finances.

The presentations were all the same. Nate could do them almost automatically and this program was no exception. The audience of three hundred responded with intelligent questions and there was no resentment shown towards Nguyen. Apparently Dino had schooled him on presentation pointers.

227

Still, Nate felt apprehensive. These people trusted him. As Carmen does. Had she influenced his life so much in such a short amount of time. Natalie is seven months old now. Oh, oh, his thoughts were drifting again. What did the woman near the back ask Dr. Ruben. She wanted a more specific date on when a cure for Alzheimer's will be found. Well, Nate thought, who knows?

Dr. Ruben gave a very diplomatic and accurate answer. Basically, research was on-going and positive results could be available in the near future. What did that mean exactly, Nate asked himself. Just as he thought earlier, who knows?

The woman was visibly pleased. In her mind's eye her husband's mental state returned, allowing him to drive and maintain their car, mow the grass, check the furnace, do all those jobs once again that she had been doing. The past few years had been lonely, memories unable to be shared, indeed, even a short walk had become an ordeal. Her husband had no idea where he lived. He could never go out alone. She wanted him well again and, according to Dr. Ruben, it could be soon. Had Dr. Ruben said that? Never. She only heard what she wanted to hear. Like many people.

The presentation over and talking with people during the reception, Nate once again felt an emotion that questioned the CRYONICS project. These people were hopeful. All their dreams will come true ---- a long healthy life together ---- they thought. Nate knew that someway he must see the LTF facility in Wyoming. See for himself if all this is true. But how? Dino would never allow it unless he could convince him it is necessary for the presentation.

And Nate did just that!

"All right, Nate, fly to Salt Lake City and get a commuter to Evanston. Rent a car there. It's an easy drive to the facility. I'll call ahead to give you the okay to look around. You'll need to see Ralph when you get there," said Dino.

On the drive from Evanston, Nate was surprised by the dry sagebrush and sand. He thought the countryside quite ugly. But then he was used to palm trees and ocean beaches. He stopped along the highway and tore a small piece of sagebrush from a larger plant. He held it to his nose. The aroma was wonderful and he saw the area in a more pleasing way. The wind was tossing a barrel-size tumbleweed around, making it touch the ground and then quickly hop and scoot across the flat terrain.

Reaching the LTF facility, the magical greenery shown on the video used in the presentations was nowhere to be seen. The token greenery being indoor-outdoor carpet at the entry of the so-called office. The beautiful interior on the video was reduced to a room with a desk, chair, a six-foot wide filing cabinet, and containers of artificial flowers. Dusted and washed, the flowers could look real on a video and on closer inspection Nate recognized the floral bouquets that were, indeed, on the video of the LTF facility. An adjacent room was named "Reception Area" and housed two sofas, a loveseat, and several occasional chairs which circled a large oak-veneer coffee table. Several books depicting flower and vegetable gardens, trees in bloom, and scenes of a sprawling countryside featuring lovely homes and families enjoying togetherness. So, Nate thought, this is actually where the video is shot and it looks as if visitors do come here. Otherwise all this enjoyable living propaganda would be wasted. He guessed, though when visitors were expected, fresh flowers and general sprucing up would hurriedly be done. He felt encouraged. If the reception room could be ready for visitors, then perhaps his suspicions were wrong. Why else would anyone come here than to see for themselves where their loved ones are cared for?

Yet, it wasn't that easy to tour the facility.

"Oh, no, this is as far as you can go," a swarthy-looking Ralph said. He wasn't a big man as perhaps Nate expected a watchman to be. Instead, he stood about five-feet seven and weighed one-hundred sixty, tops. He wore faded jeans, a black and white checkered flannel shirt under a denim jacket lined with sheep's wool; cowboy boots and hat completed his Wyoming look, or as Nate believed the way men in Wyoming dressed. Most didn't, he later learned.

"Dino said I could look around at whatever I wanted and I'd like to see behind that steel door," Nate said.

"No way," answered Ralph.

"Well, I'll just have to call Dino about that."

"You do that," sneered Ralph, as he walked towards another part of the building and out the door.

Good, Nate muttered to himself. I'm alone here and I'll get that door open and answer all my questions. A small library was adjacent to the reception area and a quick glance showed Nate that most books were on gardening and cooking. All for show, he believed. Going down several steps from the reception area he could already feel the chill in the air. Underground, he remembered. Visitors were not allowed in this part of the complex, he knew.

A telephone rang, startling Nate. Ralph appeared briefly talking on his cell phone. From the gist of the conversation Nate believed a picnic was planned and Ralph was expected somewhere and was already late. Good, Nate thought, nice to be rid of him.

Alone once again, Nate tried the steel door. It was locked. No surprise, how else could it be secure? he told himself. The lock had a combination of numbers which, if he chose the right ones, would magically open the door. He listened for the clicks. Richard had trained him to open almost any lock. Not this one, it seemed. No sounds. He tried several more times. Nothing. He needed the combination. Well, he surmised, it wouldn't be kept in this room. Yet, just a portion of the complex was above ground and certainly this door must be opened to reach the underground facility ----- his major target. He searched the room feeling along the baseboard and ceiling seeking a hidden storage unit. Then again, would such important information be found so close to the source? There must be a key room.

He felt before he saw eyes boring into him. He turned slightly. Ralph stood just six feet away. When had he come in so quietly? Nate had heard nothing. Not a good sign.

"Whatever you are looking for, you won't find it and I strongly suggest you quit snooping around," Ralph quietly said.

"Not that it's any of your business, but I'm here under Dino's direction and have full authority to look wherever I choose," responded Nate.

"I just bet you have," sneered Ralph as he began to stalk away.

"You don't have as much to say about things as you think." Always accuse the accuser. Richard had taught him that. Throws them off guard.

"You think!" Ralph stomped out, no doubt to call Dino, Nate thought. He was right.

"Let him in," Dino told Ralph, "but be sure he has all the gear on."

The gear consisted of a heavy silver-colored insulated suit complete with a helmet covering his entire head. His body was completely encased in the suit which had air pockets inside the lining next to his body. The air pockets, as well as spaces around his feet and hands contained warming pellets.

"This is to keep you from freezing to death and keep your body heat from altering the inside temperature. Up to you, you could go in without it," Ralph said, hoping Nate would opt to not put on the suit. "You can be in there ten minutes if you want to stay that long. There's an alarm bell just inside the door if you want out sooner. Otherwise I'll open the door in exactly ten minutes. It can be open only five seconds so be by the door. You have a watch on the palm of your hand, that piece covered with Plexiglas. Watch it. You won't want to miss those five seconds. You wouldn't last another ten minutes in there. Ralph's remarks sent chills down Nate's spine and he hadn't yet set foot in anything colder than an air-conditioned supermarket, which in itself was always much colder than it should be. He was frightened and what if Ralph chose not to open the door. What is that temperature again? Low enough to freeze to death in he guessed thirty minutes or so. And is there really anything behind those doors and all this preparation just a sham? Why this interest anyhow? What difference can it possibly make in his life? Ralph's sinister smile chilled him even more. And now Nate thought, he may freeze to death out of curiosity.

"Sure you want to go in?" Smiling Ralph asked quietly and this made Nate even more frightened.

"Actually Vinnie..... you know him, don't you? Big boss on Long Island? He's waiting for a report. Let's see, it's around three now isn't it?"

"Yeah, quarter to."

"You know him. Got to call on the dot. Don't know why he chose me for this."

Apparently Nate chose the right man. Ralph's face colored slightly and he wiped his brow. Hasn't learned to hide his feelings, Nate mused. He will open the door. Vinnie's name spoke volumes. Opened many doors and certainly this one. He watched as Ralph pressed buttons to open the steel door. Ralph quickly drew back apparently feeling a rush of cold air. Entering the large cavernous room, Nate in his insulated covering, felt nothing except prickles like stinging nettles. He felt these on his arms, legs, and back, and wondered if it was the cold penetrating. Certainly a new sensation causing him to shake involuntarily. He quickly checked the time on the unusual watch set deep in the palm of his hand. He felt like a man from outer space and fear permeated his body. Fear of what he may see as well as what may not be there.

And he would never in his lifetime forget what lay behind those steel doors.

CHAPTER TWENTY-FOUR

"So now you know." Dino looked directly into Nate's eyes. "You've seen what only four other people have been allowed to see, and you know you mention this to no one. With only five people with this knowledge, leaks would be easy to trace. Understand?"

"Yes, I do, perfectly." Nate met Dino's eyes with a steady gaze. And he did. This thought was heavy on his mind ever since he had left the LTF facility. This knowledge added pressure to an already tense-filled lifestyle. Now, more than ever, he would be expected to perform all the duties assigned to him by either Dino or Vinnie. Would he ever be free of the organization?

"We have another presentation in Minneapolis next Friday, a week from today," announced Dino. "But for the next few days I want you to work on new papers. Got orders for fourteen and probably get more today. Brian's bringing a load in from Mexico."

New papers meant Nate would provide a social security card, credits cards, driver's license, birth certificate, and depending on the customer, perhaps a marriage license, divorce papers, or death certificate. Complete identification change including photos if desired and paraphernalia to change one's looks. The photos were altered to match credit cards or other identification papers. Each set netted Dino five to ten thousand dollars. Most customers wanted two or three sets; a very lucrative business, indeed, since Nate managed several sets a day.

Since Nate had not done papers for several weeks, he practiced on new identification for himself. He became various people, and just for fun, Carmen got the same new identifications. He stashed his practice work out of sight.

233

Course, he couldn't keep the papers around the print shop or his apartment. He added them to his already large supply of cash he kept in a safe deposit box several miles away. For no reason he could identify, he needed easily obtained cash. Richard had taught him to be constantly prepared for any eventuality.

The only addition to the presentation in Minneapolis was a segment on brain implants. Dr. Ruben gave a spellbinding talk on this new medical break through.

"A brain implant will help patients with Parkinson's disease as well as other tremor sufferers," said Dr. Ruben. "It is a pacemaker type implant and the treatment can decrease tremors in many people. It is something like this," he continued, "a hole drilled through the skull and an electrode is implanted into the thalamus, a small region in the brain that controls movement. A wire runs under the scalp, down to the collarbone where a pulse generator is implanted. This implant sends constant electrical shocks to the thalamus and tremors are blocked." Dr. Ruben had the attention of the entire audience. "This is a very simple explanation of a very dramatic procedure." He had captured their attention and never let it go.

Nate, impressed as always, observed members of the audience as they digested this new information. What it would mean to them was unclear to him, but Dr. Ruben certainly knew his stuff. Dino couldn't suppress his smile. Signups for CRYONICS reached an all-time high. Over nine million dollars and more to come when couples discussed the alternatives. The basic cash outlay ---- new equipment, personnel salaries, property purchases, took a big chunk, but still leaving a hefty amount for Vinnie and Dino. Nate's share amounted to fifty thousand of which a good portion was taken to the safe deposit box. He couldn't begin to spend all the money he made. Also in the safe deposit box, although he had vowed not to, was a few photos of Carmen and Natalie. Natalie was now sitting up by herself, had six teeth, and a beautiful smile which was a carbon copy of Carmen's. He missed them.

And now with all the new information he had learned recently, he wondered, more than ever, would he ever see them again?

CHAPTER TWENTY-FIVE

It wasn't too difficult locating Kathy. Vinnie's network reached every nook and cranny in the world and Rudy decided to utilize it. He had hoped to find Nate's sister, which he was sure would lead to Carmen, without Vinnie's help. It was one thing to look for Nate, and even okay to scare the Olmsteads in Palm Springs, as long as it was only a scare. But Vinnie frowned on too wide a range involvement, especially for Rudy to be seen in too many places. After all as an escaped felon, law enforcement officers constantly were on the look out for him even though most would be glad to have another jurisdiction capture him. And Vinnie needed Rudy and his burial ground. Not that someone else couldn't do it, but Rudy enjoyed it so and knew the program perfectly. Vinnie liked long-time associates. The more he knew about them, the easier to control. That's why Rudy got the nod over Nate. Members of the organization were not treated equally as Nate would learn someday.

It distressed Rudy that when in Everett, Washington, he had been close to Kathy's home in LaConner, in a development called Shelter Bay. Once again Rudy flew to SeaTac, the international airport between Seattle and Tacoma in Washington state. He rented a Lincoln Town Car, no more small cramped automobiles for him, and drove north on Interstate 5. Driving through Everett, his mind flicked to Betty and his great evening with her. That she resisted him and the eventual results was her own fault. She shouldn't have scratched his face. He touched his cheek with his hand. The scratch barely visible now, still he grew angry thinking about it. A few miles past

Marysville was the entrance to the rest stop with the drive-through tree. He considered driving in, relive the memories. Her body, no doubt, had been found weeks ago. Didn't need to hide it very well A few branches broken from small evergreen trees did the job.

Better judgment prevailed and he drove past the rest stop. Why tempt fate? Someone may have caught a fleeting glance of him even though he certainly looked different now. He had changed into a suit and tie in the men's room at SeaTac. Looked as if he belonged in an affluent neighborhood. Quit daydreaming and get moving. After all, finding Carmen has top priority not reliving an enjoyable incident. And was that all Betty was? Rudy's enjoyable incident.

His map showed a highway leading out of Mount Vernon with a turn off towards La Conner. He stopped at a small store called "Jack's" and asked about the Shelter Bay area.

"Just go down this road, follow it across the orange bridge, then hang a left and you're right there. There's a gate, but it's always open during the day. Has a security guy but he just waves people through," explained a clerk in the store.

"Thanks, I guess I don't have time now, have a plane to catch, maybe another year," said Rudy, knowing he would go back a block, take a parallel road and find Shelter Bay out of sight of the man in Jack's. The man certainly knew the procedure. The security gate was open and the security man waved him through.

Kathy's street had an Indian sounding name and he soon noticed that all the streets were named some kind of an Indian name. As he drove along Shelter Bay Drive, he came to an office near a marina. A helpful lady gave him a map of the area and asked if he needed a specific location. Suit, tie and expensive automobile worked wonders, thought Rudy.

"Just told some friends I'd drive around and give them my impression. They want to move here," he explained. And she had no idea it was another of his lies.

The woman gave him several brochures and explained the amenities of the development. Swimming pools, golf course, tennis, She did scrutinize him a little more than necessary, he thought, and he knew why. After all, six-foot five, on large frame, and scraggly face, brought stares of apprehension from almost anyone, in spite of his smooth shave and business-like appearance, or as he perceived a business man would dress.

"Drive around all you want and if your friends are boaters be sure to tell them about our wonderful marina," said the woman.

"Oh, yes, a great perk. So no one will question me driving around, maybe parking awhile to get a feeling of the place?" asked Rudy.

"No, and if they do, tell them to call me."

"Thanks. You're a great asset here." Is he laying it on too think? Rudy asked himself.

"Thank you." She beamed, but still paid attention to his questions and his body language. She would remember all about him.

Rudy did drive around the various streets. Didn't want to drive directly to Kathy's. He walked a few yards by the marina, stopped along the golf course as if to survey the area for his fictional friends. Along Shelter Bay Drive, Rudy saw the homes were nice enough and it seemed to Rudy that there must be strict covenants since no boats, trailers, or garbage cans were in sight. In fact, no residents were around either. What do these people do, he wondered. Then he noticed a man walking a small dog. Great he thought, at least this isn't an extension of the old cemetery he passed just before entering the so-called security gate. The golf course was on his left, several people taking token shots. Further to his left he looked again at the marina. Many upscale yachts as well as a few smaller cruisers. A very affluent area, thought Rudy. Maybe he would burglarize a few homes before he left just to leave his mark and keep in practice, show these rich bugs what it's like to come home and find something gone. Like Carmen. He would find her. His major goal in life.

Kathy's house had numbers prominently displayed on the curb as did other homes in the development. The place looked as if no one was around. Drapes partially drawn, no vehicles in sight. Rudy parked a few doors away to observe his surroundings. He stayed only a few minutes. Then he drove to another spot on a street parallel to Kathy's. This gave him a view of her back yard. He noticed what appeared to be a sand-box with bright colored toys: buckets, shovels, empty milk cartons, plus a swing set with a small slide. Kids, here anyway, he thought. Could scare her with a child missing. Get any information he needed if he had her kid and it could be fun if the kid was a little girl. He liked older ones better, but hey, he was due for some fun. Boys were okay, too. He watched longer than he should have and knew it, but his mind couldn't let go of his desires.

Rudy jumped when someone rapped on the window of his car. How did that happen? Someone walked right up and he was unaware. Not good! His fantasizing must stop. Pay attention! He turned the key so he could open the car window.

"Hello there," smiled Rudy. Be friendly no matter that he wanted to smash the stranger's face.

"Noticed you parked here and wondered if I could answer some questions for you?" the stranger asked.

Rudy thought it was just a polite way to ask what are you doing in my neighborhood? Okay, conjure up any charm you might have, Rudy told himself. "Thanks, I'm getting a feel of the area for a friend who's thinking of moving here or around here someplace. Since I had business in Seattle, I offered to check out a few places for him. The gal in the office was kind enough to fill me in on a few things and gave me a map. Said it was okay to take my time and look around." There, that should give credence to his being here and satisfy the creep.

"Oh, " the man visibly brightened, "there's some great things to do here. My wife and I enjoy life here very much. Quiet, but still quality and friendly."

"This looks about what he and his family want only are there many younger people around. Say kids sixteen or so. Close by here? I see things for young kids." asked Rudy, off-handily he thought.

"Teenagers? Your friends have teenagers?" No teenagers wanted in this neighborhood, at least not by this person, the man's tone clearly indicated.

"Have a niece I believe. No, I'm only observing the area and know they want a quality neighborhood."

"Shelter Bay is quality."

"I can see that. Still I know they want to know how many kids are around and their ages. You ever see a teenage girl around. Someone their niece could visit with once a year?" There, Rudy thought, that should bring out some answers.

"Well, there's a few school kids but mostly we're retired around here," the man replied.

"What about this place?" Rudy pointed to Kathy's house, "Looks like a few kids there."

"Yeah, a fairly young professional couple. A little boy. They have a life-in sitter with a young baby. Very nice, quiet family," the man definitely promoted the area.

"Doesn't look like anyone's around." Rudy was fishing for information about Kathy and her family. Live-in sitter with a baby? Could it be Carmen. Did she have the kid? Too much good luck connected with that idea.

"Well, I don't know, parents both work. He let the answer hang, after all this is a stranger.

Rudy picked up on the man's apprehension and immediately decided to leave. "Enjoyed talking with you and I think my friends will like my report."

"Got a house up the hill I want to sell. If you got time I could call Doug, he's my Realtor, and he could show it to you. One more thing to tell your friends about."

"Sounds great. I can't today, how about tomorrow?" Rudy was jubilant. This would give him another excuse to be here. The man had fallen into his trap, like Betty had. A con man, always a con man and really people were so dumb. Smart guys, like himself could steer any conversation around. He had learned this very well from his so-called lawyer. The creep didn't get him off. Maybe pay a visit to his family someday. His lawyer had a daughter too. But for now, only concentrate on finding Carmen. Get rid of her and whoever helped her and he knew it was Nate, then find another squeeze. Good cook, great looker. A keeper if she played her cards right, which Betty didn't. Someone like Carmen.

He drove back into the town of La Conner and then decided to explore other surrounding areas. He turned toward Anacortes. Marveled that such a nice area would also have an oil refinery with a couple of tankers at the end of a long dock. A great place for boating, except for that smelly refinery. No wonder that marina at Shelter Bay was full. Look at all the water around here. Rudy had never been in the northwest until his quest for Carmen brought him here. He liked it. The highway leading into Anacortes had a spectacular view of the water and mountains. A snowcapped mountain out to the right. He laughed when he saw a sign denoting that the freeway ends. After Atlanta this is a freeway? Get real. Commercial Avenue. A long street with small businesses as well as several homes, a church, and a nicer business district strung the length of it, plus a couple of fairly large grocery stores. Probably large for this town. The residents should see Atlanta if they wanted to see big.

Deciding to stay the night Rudy spotted an acceptable motel with a nearby restaurant. Several bars looked inviting and he briefly considered another Betty, then reconsidered. No need to make waves and draw attention to himself even though he now wore a different disguise than he wore while talking with the man at Shelter Bay. That man would never recognize Rudy except for his size. Rudy couldn't alter that. Easy to change one's looks, though, and fool most of the public.

Rudy hadn't spent much time in a small town. He walked along downtown Commercial Avenue noticing the trendy shops geared, in his mind, for tourists. The grocery stores sought local trade he guessed, and espresso stands, like in Seattle, were major interests. He felt out of place not carrying a container of Starbucks or Seattle's Best and stopped in a coffee roasting place to get a container of coffee to sip along the way. The street was nearly empty and he guessed the bars supplied the nighttime action. After a walk which took him all the way to the end of Commercial and a large waterfront docking facility, he thought about snooping around for something to steal, a basic instinct for him. Nothing. He retraced his steps and sauntered along the other side of the street. Most of the shops were closed, not that he intended to buy anything anyway. He decided on Mexican food at El Jinete's and was pleasantly surprised. And he thought only southern California served great Mexican food. The evening loomed ahead as very boring. Still, he told himself he must keep focused on his decision to find Carmen. Bar hopping only, no women. Tomorrow the search for Carmen would continue.

And it did. Driving on the Highway 20 spur out of Anacortes, Rudy glanced across to the refineries. Why then was gasoline so expensive in this area? The tide was out and the air permeated with a rottenness smell. Ugh! Could anyone ever get used to that smell? Glad to turn on Reservation Road toward La Conner which took him through an Indian Reservation. Indeed, Shelter Bay itself was located on lease-hold lands. Interesting driving on Reservation Road, Rudy wondered at the trashy homes and did everyone have a black or brindle-colored dog? One yard boasted large totem poles and wooden carvings of eagles and fish. Looked like his kind of people along this road. Those fancy houses in Shelter Bay left him wanting to torch a few. Jealous and vindictive Rudy hated anyone who in his mind, had it easy.

The gateman waved Rudy through and to not arouse suspicion, Rudy drove along Shelter Bay Drive to the office and spoke to someone named Clarice. She, like the lady the previous day, told him of the amenities and touched briefly on activities. One difference between the two women, and Rudy picked up on it immediately, Clarice paid more attention to him, studied his body language more intently, and gave out little, other than basic information about the area. He turned on whatever charm he could muster, which wasn't much, and after a few mundane questions and a feigned show of interest, quickly left the office.

No one seemed to be around Kathy's home again the second day of observation and Rudy wondered where they could be. He drove around Shelter Bay three times a day and on the fourth day found a small community beach at the very end of the development. Picnic tables, barbecues and great relaxing spot. He could kill a few hours and be out of sight. No one seemed to use the beach or facilities. Then he hit on the idea of staying until dark to take a look inside the Wyemark home. An easy walk and with the large trees and foliage plus no street lights, it was a snap to get around unseen. Twilight lasted forever, or so Rudy thought, but by eight-thirty it was dark enough to move around undetected. He was home-free from any nosy resident or security person.

Being a master at sneaking through woods, Rudy made his way to the Wyemark home. As he expected, it was locked tight. He chuckled. He could enter any house in a couple of minutes. Those locks, what a joke and the security. Well, who could see him anyhow. The neighbor's dog loved the rest of his sandwich and the "Halt" spray he always carried kept the dog away. Yes, that little, what he called his survival kit, really made his "work" easy. He entered through a day-light basement window and wouldn't you think the Wyemarks would have trimmed the rhododendron bushes. And those evergreen trees that had been topped made them bushy and a very nice hiding place. He laughed out loud. He quickly disabled the security alarm, and staying close to the walls, he searched the basement which was more of a recreation room. Pool table, small fridge, card table and chairs, fireplace, and a make-shift bar. Rudy made himself a drink, then smashed the glass against the fireplace. Kathy would realize that someone had been here ---- he could care less. Let her worry. He slipped up the stairway careful to shine his penlight only in front of his feet. The Wyemarks did have night lights installed along the baseboard of each room. Were these people cooperative or what? They had angled the Venetian blinds up to help give privacy and in his case complete freedom to walk around. The drapes were only slightly open. His actions unobserved by anyone outside.

And that's how he discovered that Carmen did, indeed, live with Kathy. A small bedroom definitely belonged to a baby and through an adjacent door, there for all to see, or at least Rudy, was a larger room and on a vanity, prominently displayed, was a photo of Carmen holding a small baby. The kid. So she did have it. Bonanza! He had found her! The closet held clothes that absolutely would fit Carmen. Not many, she never wanted anything for herself. Crazy. Stupid really, he thought. He searched through drawers but found nothing special, not that he expected to. And really, he only wanted to find her. Back in the baby's room he noted many little dresses and toys. Whatever money Carmen got, and he guessed from Nate or Kathy, unless she had a job which he doubted, what could she do, prostitute maybe? Naw, too scared for that. Anyway, whatever money she got went for the kid. Well, that would soon change. He wanted her, not the kid! And he would make Carmen stand and watch. He became sexually aroused when he thought of how the kid would die. Abuse her first. Carmen standing by, screaming. Rudy laughed. He could hear Carmen beg. The kid screaming in pain.

It was clear the family was away. Vacation perhaps? He listened to over a dozen telephone messages. Several reminding Kathy of a sale she supposedly contributed her famous brownies to; a dinner invitation from Becky; could Tommy spent Saturday afternoon at Kyle's house; bridge invitation; but nothing from Nate and nothing for Carmen. This surprised Rudy. It seemed the family had left in a hurry and didn't inform friends. Rudy pondered this. Why? And for how long would they be away? He zapped a large pepperoni pizza in the microwave, opened a Bud Lite, and sat in front of the TV for a late night snack. He felt perfectly at ease. His shoe broke a glass insert in the coffee table. So what? And if pizza stained the beige and white sofa it didn't matter to him. In fact he smeared the sofa and matching chairs with the remaining pizza. He laughed. Then sobered immediately. Did he really want Kathy and Carmen to know he's around? Stupid of him and no way to clean up the mess. Make the entry and destruction look like a random burglary. Grabbing a bath towel he silently broke a side window allowing a so-called burglar to reach in and unlock the door. Although he had already disabled the security system, he pulled a few more wires making it look as if the entry door system had been broken. Then he scattered a few things around the living room, emptied contents of drawers on the floor of the bedrooms, and broke glass and spread ketchup and jam around the kitchen. He took pieces of jewelry (very few real gems he noted) so he could drop an item or two outside. Several rolls of coins would work well to make it look like some kids had broken in. They always took stupid rolls of pennies or nickels. Rudy was satisfied it looked like a burglary by an inept young person.

He was right and days later when Kathy talked to Nate, he assured her it couldn't have been Rudy. "He knows how to get in and out of a place and leave no evidence. Wasn't him. Probably some kids looking for some quick cash."

Rudy, though, kept his vigilance of the Wyemark house. And entered each night to set up an inside hiding place. Each day he drove by. And on the sixth day, he saw that the drapes were open. Bingo! He knew that sooner or later they could come home. Now to implement his plan. He knew exactly what needed to be done. He watched as the home was cleaned, erasing all traces of the "burglary." Several cops had been to the home and Rudy guessed that they, too, had determined it to be a random burglary by teenagers.

Then his plan!

He had utilized a little-used basement closet for his hiding place.

He had stocked it with food items and beer taken from the Wyemark kitchen. Not much. He didn't plan to be there long, perhaps even less than a day. As Rudy had learned from his snooping, both Kathy and Tom were employed. Tom an attorney and Rudy hated attorneys, Kathy, a nurse, and could be gone at various times not necessarily during the day. Course he could always kill her and her little kid. Maybe the husband as well. That cutsey family photo in their bedroom made him sick.

Rudy waited through the night, only slipping out to use the basement toilet, never flushing. Give her more to clean. He was smart, he thought, to wait until Kathy had the house cleaned before he took up his "residence" in the basement closet. No hurry now, he had found Carmen and never would she get away again. And Nate had helped her, he had been right all along. Wouldn't Dino be surprised ----- Dino's fair-haired boy. Rudy got a real high fantasizing about their meeting. Her pleading. He played the scenario over and over in his mind. Her begging for the kid's life, maybe struggling to save her own life. Such fun. A little, or maybe a lot of torture along the way. She deserved it.

Early the next morning, Rudy watched through a crack in the closet door as Carmen came down the basement stairs carrying a basket of laundry. She carefully measured detergent into the washer, turned on the water, and added clothes. Always the perfectionist, Rudy angrily remembered. White clothes alone, never with colored. What a crock. This wasn't the opportunity he needed. Kathy was upstairs. He waited. Carmen came down once again and put the clothes in the dryer. She looked good, Rudy thought. filling out in all nice places. He wiped saliva from his mouth. She returned to the upstairs. Rudy jumped as Carmen came down again. How long had he been thinking of her ---- the clothes couldn't be dry yet, but they were. He watched as she meticulously folded the clothes and placed them in the basket she had carried down. She held a small dress to her nose, savoring, he thought, the aroma of the freshly laundered garment. She seemed happy. Very happy. This, too, made Rudy angry. He thought of the stack of dirty clothes he had in his trailer. In fact, one room had been designated as the dirty-clothes room. His dirty socks alone would fill the basket Carmen had placed the clean folded clothes in. It had been several months since Rudy had washed clothes and even the deodorant spray he had used almost daily, couldn't mask the loathsome odor emitting from the room. He needed her home!

Rudy had no opportunity to snatch Carmen that day. She, Kathy, and the two children left the house in the early afternoon. While they were away, Rudy once again inspected crannies he had ignored previously. He found photos of the baby and a small boy in Kathy's bedroom. He thought how much like Carmen the baby looked, as much as a baby could look like anyone. A post card from Nate stating all was fine in California, getting in lots of surfing, and will call on Saturday. The cancellation showed it had been mailed weeks before. Would have been fun, Rudy thought, to be on an extension when Nate called.

After snooping an hour or so Rudy grew tired of the game and decided to replenish his food supply and then slip out and return to his car. He had no desire to sleep either in the car or closet. Still with only one road out of Shelter Bay, he was cautious about leaving until it grew dark or he was sure Carmen and Kathy had returned home. He watched from a wooded area and around four o'clock saw them return with bags of groceries. Hope they had bought more beer, he muttered to himself.

And he chuckled wondering if people realized what great cover a green belt offered, in more ways than anyone could imagine. While residents only saw the green evergreen trees or thick bushy cover, opportunists like Rudy saw great hiding places for many things. Maybe a body!

Rudy's hiding place in the small closet held boxes of Christmas decorations and other seasonal paraphernalia and it was unlikely that anyone would want anything in the boxes except during a particular holiday. He was quite comfortable. Apparently no one had missed the chair and table lamp he had garnered from the living room or perhaps they believe the burglar had stolen them. He had heard no conversation about the missing items and he laughed. Stupid people. He waited. The game exciting to him as he fantasized about the capture of Carmen. He kind of hoped someone would open the closet door. His knife was posed and ready to do a job without making a sound. He opened the closet door a little wider. Perhaps Kathy would need something from the basement, see the open door and give him a little fun. She shouldn't have Carmen here anyway. Her own fault when he killed her. Maybe he could call Carmen down and make her watch. Then she would know how many lives she had snuffed out by her actions. Betty for one and he decided to return to Palm Springs and do the Olmsteads. Certainly kill Nate. He wished Carmen would see it. Maybe...... still he must return to Georgia soon. Vinnie had another job waiting. Let's see, in one week Vinnie had told him.

Rudy heard excited talking. A young boy shouting, in a hurry to go someplace. Do something. Kathy saying, "Okay, okay, calm down. You won't be late." She came down the stairs and grabbed a dark blue nylon jacket from a hook by the clothes dryer. She glanced Rudy's way, saw the open door.....

"Come on Mom," the little boy seemed almost in tears, "come on."

"All right, I'm coming." She glanced at the partially open door again, frowned, started over, then apparently changed her mind and ran up the stairs. The small boy had continued pleading which, for the moment, saved his mother's life. Rudy had his switch-blade in his hand. He popped out the blade. Click!

Kathy hesitated before opening the door at the top of the stairs. She glanced at the closet door again. What was that click. She listened. She felt a chill and the hairs on the back of her neck seemed to be standing up. Don't be silly, she told herself. Probably that mouse trap Tom had set a couple of days ago. Oh, well, no time to check it now, Tommy is itching to be at Robbie's party. Still, why the apprehension? She'll have Tom recheck all the windows and locks tonight, just to ease her mind and take the fearful feeling away. Course the burglar had entered by the front door, the broken glass a dead give-away. And the locks had been changed. Lighten up, she scolded herself and called to Tommy, "Let's go."

Rudy crept to the doorway ---- listening. Would Carmen leave with Kathy? Maybe this is the time!

"Carm, we'll be back around five. Remember I'm having lunch with Ceil and then after I pick up Tommy I promised Gwen we'd stop by. She's studying for her boards and I said I'd help. Only a couple of hours, Tommy can play with Kyle."

"Shall I make the chicken casserole for dinner?" Carmen asked.

"Terrific!"

"Have fun Tommy. Give me a hug," Carmen put her arms out and the little boy ran and jumped on her. Carmen laughed. Kathy smiled. Carmen is such a treasure.

Rudy heard this exchange and felt a rush of adrenaline. At last! Carmen and her kid in the house alone. Should he play cat and mouse awhile or get her and take off. No real hurry, he has six or seven hours before anyone knows she's missing. What a break! He silently opened the door that led into the kitchen. He paused and listened. He heard Carmen singing softly something about loving a baby girl. He saw her cuddling the kid while dancing around the floor. The kid laughed. Carmen kissed the baby's cheek.

"How about a bath and a little nap before lunch? Does you little dolly need a bath too?" Carmen fairly cooed to the baby. It made Rudy sick. He continued to watch. Had she danced toward the kitchen area, they would have been face to face. Soon he thought. He stepped into the living room.

"Hello," Rudy's voice was low and menacing. It would have chilled Satan's soul, if he had one.

Carmen quickly turned. She screamed and ran to the door. He stepped in her way, grabbing her arm.

"Please, please let us go," she screamed and ran towards the kitchen where she knew a telephone hung on the wall. He blocked her way.

"Give me the kid," Rudy demanded, holding on to Carmen's wrist and twisting.

"No, Rudy, no. She's just a baby. No, let us go. I could give you money," Carmen pleaded, her fear making her stutter and cough. Rudy laughed.

"Money? I don't want money."

Carmen had never been so frightened. Oh, God, and no one else was home. No one expected. She and Natalie were alone with this monster.

Quietly Rudy said, "Give me the kid, Carmen."

"No, never, she's mine. I'll die first. Rudy, please don't hurt her, I'll go with you. Leave Natalie here. Take me. I'll go back with you. Do anything you want with me. I'll never leave again, just leave her here. Please," begged Carmen.

"I think I'll take her with us, Carmen. Your little girl'l come in handy."

"How, how did you know I was here?"

"Easy. You can never get away from me."

"I won't, I won't, just leave Natalie here. We, I , we could have lots more fun if she isn't with us. Leave her."

"Well," Rudy used a fake drawl, "that's just what I had in mind at first. I only wanted you, but now seeing what a pretty little thing she is, I think I'll take you both. She looks like fun."

Carmen held Natalie so tightly she squirmed to be loose and began to whimper.

"She can't do that. I like quiet girls," and then his voice grew lower, "I know how to keep her quiet. You know I do."

Carmen began to cry. Huge sobs, "Not my baby. Please, please Rudy. Have mercy."

"Oh, I have mercy, Carmen. That's why I'm taking you both. Get whatever she needs to keep her quiet and let's go."

"Where? I have to tell Kathy. And, and Nate. Nate will find us."

"Oh, yes, your boyfriend Nate. Well, I hope he does find you. Save me the trouble of finding him, which ain't hard since I already know where he is. Didn't want you with him did he? Has a nice little apartment and making tons of money. Sent you any?"

"Let me call Tom and, and, and...."

"And what. Come on!" Rudy jerked Natalie out of her arms causing the baby to cry and reach for her mother. Carmen tried to take Natalie back only making Rudy hold her even tighter causing louder cries. He put his large hand over Natalie's mouth startling her. The crying stopped and Natalie stared up at Rudy. She stopped squirming. He removed his hand . The baby did not make a sound, only looked at Rudy, her big brown eyes never blinking.

Carmen knew the power Rudy held. Her mind flew to Nate and what he had taught her. Contingency plan. Her gun. There is no plan. No one ever thought Rudy could find them. Especially after all this time. And the gun had long since been taken out of the house. She and Natalie at the mercy of a man so ruthless he buried animals alive and put men in a snake pit. What chance does she and Natalie have with such a person? Think Carmen, think. What did Nate teach you? If she could convince Rudy to leave Natalie here, the baby would get hungry and have soiled diapers, but, would be alive. If Rudy took both of them, he would eventually kill Natalie. He hated children. She knew what happened before. She must stay calm. She must protect her baby.

"You know, Rudy, someone will be here soon and find us. If you want me back in Georgia we better leave. I'll just put Natalie in her crib and you and I can get out of here," Carmen reached for her daughter.

"You're sweet, Carmen, real sweet, but stupid. I don't actually want the kid." Carmen's hopes rose. "But with her along, you'll do exactly what I say. Get her bottle or whatever it takes. We have a long ride," Rudy said. "Two minutes. I'll hold the kid, you get some stuff ready. Last warning and don't think you can get cute or make a call."

"I won't." Carmen filled a baby bottle with milk, two with water, grabbed a few small cans of orange juice and jars of baby food. Although Natalie drank from a cup and had her own little plate of food at the table, Carmen grabbed as much as she could since who knows if Rudy would allow any food purchases along whatever way they were going. Or where for that matter. She was sure it was back to Georgia. She knew what he had there. She kept her eyes on Natalie. Rudy held her under one of his arms, like a football. Natalie made no noise and lifted her head to watch Rudy

"Can I hold her now?" Carmen asked. "I only need to get a blanket and some diapers."

"You go get the stuff, you have thirty seconds. Get a cell phone and book, too," he demanded.

"Let me have her." Carmen hoped he would tire of this game and she also hoped Natalie would stay quiet and not soil her diaper. Rudy would hate that!

"Get this straight, when you do something I hold the kid. You know why don't you?" Rudy snarled.

"Yes, I know why and I'll do whatever you say." Quietly, Carmen answered still trembling, but willing herself to remain as calm as possible. Never had she been more frightened or felt more helpless. She needed to protect Natalie. And think! Think! She must go with Rudy. Better if Natalie could be left behind, but Rudy was adamant. She must keep Natalie's protection uppermost in her mind.

"Come on. The car is at the beach and I want you to walk along like you don't want to be anywhere else. We go through these woods and I carry the kid. You make one word I don't like and the kid gets it. All of a sudden you see she isn't breathing. Know what I mean, sweet Carmen?"

"Yes, I know."

The trail was, indeed, hidden. And as in previous days, Rudy did not encounter any other person. Kathy's house was just a few short blocks and then down a hill to the beach area where Rudy had left the Lincoln. Perfectly safe and out of sight from a casual visitor who may have decided to go to the beach for a few hours. Apparently the car had missed the scrutiny of the security person. No notes on the windshield. Probably no one had even been around.

"Get in," snarled Rudy.

"We should have brought her car seat. It's the law," explained Carmen, thinking of Natalie's safety. Then she gasped, she shouldn't have said anything. Rudy gets angry so quickly.

He glanced at her. "You better learn quicker than that. You forget the rules already?"

"No, I'm sorry. I wasn't thinking. I do remember the rules and I will follow them only, do you really want Natalie with us? We could leave her on the church steps or at any store downtown."

"There's all kinds of things I could do to the kid and all in due time I will," Rudy sneered and his tone sent chills down her spine once again. She must get Natalie away somehow.

"You hold the kid, I'm making a call and practice smiling. You look scared or try to send some kind of a signal, like you did Nate that day, and the kid is history but not before a little fun for me. You got that?" Rudy ran his fingers over Natalie's leg. Carmen felt a lurch in her stomach. She became nauseous. Those hands on her daughter.

"Yes." Don't argue, don't plead. Stay alert and keep Natalie in her arms. Carmen tried to think what Nate would tell her to do.

Rudy called the small regional airport at Bayview located fifteen miles north of Shelter Bay. Carmen heard him negotiate to rent a plane and hire a pilot. Emergency, children in an accident, no time for a commercial flight, money no concern. Twenty thousand to rent the plane, ten thousand for the pilot. Five thousand for the pilot to fly them to Georgia, five thousand for the pilot's return.

Not a bad salary, Carmen thought, and for so much money would the pilot be loyal to Rudy or would she have an opportunity to speak with him, perhaps enlisting his aid in an escape for Natalie and herself. She listened very intently to Rudy's conversation. The plane, a model 36 Lear Jet, will be ready in an hour. It belongs to a former airline pilot who Rudy apparently talked with for the arrangements. A restaurant adjoining the little airport will provide box-lunches for a small extra cost. Rudy agreed to all fees, but Carmen pondered whether he would actually pay or find another way. She shuddered. Rudy ruled. He didn't submit to any demands. Ever.

Rudy guided Carmen to the plane, his large hand on her elbow, squeezing hard enough to make her know there was no escape at this time. She carried Natalie in her arms cooing to the little girl hoping to keep her calm. Natalie kept her eyes on Rudy as if to read his mind that she too, like Carmen, must be on guard. But how could a baby have such thoughts? Carmen marveled that this little person belonged to her. She vowed to protect her from this monster. Rudy pushed Carmen harder. Could he have read her mind? Rudy placed Natalie beside him and Carmen across the aisle.

"She will stay quieter if she's near me," Carmen said, hoping Rudy would agree to let Natalie be close to her.

"She likes to be by me. I know I like to be by her. Really like it," Rudy looked lasciviously at Natalie. Carmen grew nauseated once again, she began to shake and perspire. Stay calm, stay calm, she willed herself. Swallow, count to twenty, don't look at him. That's what he wants, to get a reaction from her. She looked at her fingernails, rubbed her thumb along the ends. This kept her hands moving so he couldn't see them shaking. She hated him. If she had her gun she would kill him and once she had thought she could never shoot it. Or a knife. She could stab him if she had a knife. He had one. She had seen it, he made sure of that. She knew there could be no confrontation on the plane, they would all be killed including the innocent pilot, but perhaps the pilot would be observing enough to guess what is happening. Maybe. Maybe not.

And she prayed, promising God, anything to keep Natalie safe. Then she knew God didn't do things that way. She prayed for direction on how to keep the baby safe. How to get them both away from Rudy. Are you listening God? Will you help?

As the pilot taxied the plane along the runway, Rudy turned to Carmen, "Here, you take the kid, don't want her getting sick and throwing up all over me." He handed Natalie to Carmen across the aisle.

"Okay." Carmen was elated. Her baby in her arms once again.

Still don't look too pleased, she cautioned herself. Rudy can change his mind quickly enough.

The pilot asked them to be sure their seatbelt was securely fastened and the seat upright. Just like an airline flight. Rudy smirked at his smart actions in hiring a private plane instead of trying to keep Carmen in line on a commercial flight.

"We will be stopping three times for fuel but you can remain on the plane or get out and stretch your legs. To keep on schedule, our stops will be only for a few minutes, so if you get out it will be only for a minute or so. The trip will take ten hours and I'll radio ahead for additional food at a stop in Indiana. If you have any allergies or dislikes of certain food let me know. Otherwise I'll get KFC. What should I get for the baby?" Steve, as the pilot had introduced himself, asked.

"More milk would be nice and the potatoes and gravy," replied Carmen, pleased with Steve's concern. Maybe he will notice her discomfort, she hoped. Carmen held Natalie on her lap. Still the baby had twisted around so she faced Rudy. Her big eyes never wavered from looking at him.

"Why is that kid staring at me like that?" Rudy questioned in his snarly tone.

"Children have a sixth sense or something," Carmen answered. "Maybe she can feel that you are her father. Do you feel anything for her?" She hoped to instill some kind of bonding so Rudy would like Natalie a little, perhaps saving her life.

"Oh, I feel something for her all right. You may not like what it is. You want to see?" His hand moved toward his crotch.

Oh, God, Carmen almost cried out. Not my baby. He wouldn't do that to my baby would he? Even Rudy. Is he that horrible? Then she remembers Goldie, Rudy's favorite dog, that he buried alive just because Goldie got old. She watched Rudy bury Goldie that day. Watched out the window and that was the day Nate had come there. He saw it too and their eyes met and held for a few seconds. It must have been then that Nate made the decision to rescue her. He had never said. How very grateful that she had these lovely months with Natalie. The happiest she had ever been. Gladly she would give her life to save her baby. How could she accomplish that? Could she convince Rudy to let her little girl live? Carmen's heart felt heavy with anguish and she was terrified. She needed Nate or Kathy and they had no idea what had happened to her and to Natalie. How could she contact either of them. She heard Steve talk on the plane radio. The only words she actually understood were, "No, no names. John and Jane Doe, and a baby. I guess it doesn't matter," silence, then, "Late, I'll give the plane a good checkup," Silence. "Macon. Love you. Talk to you tonight." Oh, how Carmen wished she could talk on that radio. Her wishes were to no avail. Steve remained focused on the business of flying the plane and offered no conversation during the flight.

Salt Lake City was the first stop for fuel. Rudy said to remain on board and eat lunch. Carmen was starving but knew better than to say so. Rudy would keep the food from her if he knew. However, Steve distributed the box lunches and warmed something for Natalie before he began checking the plane and refueling. Rudy caught on that Steve was paying attention. Watch what you say, he warned himself. Perhaps he should be nicer to Carmen, especially when Steve is in earshot. Ask her if her arms are tired holding the kid --- what's her name again, Natalie, girl's name for Nathan, Nate. Rudy grew angry again. And she said his kid. Well yes, he knew that was true, but he had no parental instincts if there were such things. As far as he was concerned the kid was just in the way. Good insurance, though to keep Carmen under his control. The kid's history as soon as they get to the trailer. But for the benefit of Steve, Rudy decided he could be a concerned relative or good friend. Steve hadn't asked any personal questions and certainly Rudy didn't offer information.

"No, my arms aren't tired and she's falling asleep so it's okay. Thank you, though," Carmen answered.

Steve glanced at both Rudy and Carmen. He felt that something is going on and he, indeed, was curious, but, also cautious. After all it's business and thirty thousand dollars ain't hay for a trip that cost less than three thousand. A nice payday. A nice chunk of cash to help pay off the loans. Keep the customers happy. It could result in more jobs. A few more like this and he'd have his plane free and clear. If there is a problem back there, it wasn't his business. The gal look frightened, but maybe she's afraid of flying. Not his business. Still it doesn't hurt to listen and be visible. He pulled open the curtain his wife had made and installed just behind the cockpit. The curtain mainly to give passengers a little privacy. Now it was to ease his conscience and the girl gave him a grateful glance. Fleeting glance, she's scared of that man, Steve determined. Oh well, get them where they're going and his job will be done. What happens after that is up to them. Keep everyone's emotions under control. The man seems a little friendlier to the girl. Just let the miles go by. Steve's thoughts jumped around. All was quiet in back, the baby asleep. The young girl had her eyes closed but Steve knew she wasn't sleeping. The large man with the mean eyes and manner, gazed out the window, his jaw set in a firm non-smiling way. Hate to tangle with him, Steve shivered. And he had left his gun in his locker. Well, maybe there won't be trouble. Play it by ear. Concentrate on flying the plane.

The weather became a little rough so Steve took the plane up a little higher to smooth out the ride. A tail wind will shorten the time to nine hours and another fuel stop, plus dinner from KFC. Steve checked the radio once again. The flight was going very well.

The baby stirred and the young girl readied a bottle of juice. The baby turned her head and stared at the man across the aisle. The man's eyes flicked to her and then away. He seemed to have no interest in the child except to taunt the girl. Steve hadn't heard all the words they had exchanged, only enough to be concerned for the girl. He pondered the relationship.

Father-daughter? Granddaughter? No blood ties? Then what? Not your business Steve, don't get involved. He felt eyes boring into his back. Dare he turn around to discover which one is staring? He reached up and adjusted the mirror . He could see the man, not the girl. The man still stared out the window so it must be the girl. Steve turned and met her eyes but only for a moment. The man's head turned from the window. The girl immediately dropped her eyes.

"Just wanted to say we'll be refueling again in about an hour and have dinner." Steve wondered if he had said that before. For some reason he felt very apprehensive. "I've called for dinner and then the rest of the flight will be completed in about three hours." He began to relax. Flight talk always gave him confidence and really, why had the man upset him? There had been no reasons, only a feeling. And the girl's eyes had pleaded for help.

"Get on the radio and rent me a car in Macon. Here's a credit card," demanded Rudy.

"Any particular agency. Avis, Alamo? And what kind of a car?" asked Steve.

"Get a......."   Rudy thought awhile.   Can't be too obvious so a pickup is out. "Make it a Chevy Blazer."

Steve took the credit card which did not have the same name as the man had used to rent the plane. Plenty of time to verify it, though. But why two different names? Keep cool Steve, he told himself. Not your concern. The card for the plane had gone through immediately.

On a whim, Steve decided to eat dinner with the passengers. He marveled watching the baby wolf down the potatoes and gravy and milk. Fresh fruit, apples, pears and grapes had been added to the KFC dinners and Steve received another grateful glance from the girl whose name had never been mentioned. He wondered why. And he wondered if she would have been allowed dinner if he hadn't joined them. He didn't trust the man, whatever his name was.

The last leg of the journey went quickly. The landing in Macon smooth and uneventful. The girl had long since placed the baby's and her articles in a small bag. The man had no carry-on. Interesting situation, Steve thought. However, his job was over as soon as he escorted them into the terminal and rental car desk. He already had been paid for the plane and his time. A fleeting thought once again on different credit card names but he had checked the man's identification very thoroughly and felt confident the money was there.

It wasn't though. Rudy's identification was as false as any positive emotion or concern he may show. Steve was out thirty-thousand dollars and the car agency would lose four hundred. Even when credit cards are scanned and showed approval, they were part of Dino's paper scheme that bilked thousands of dollars from accounts. Fake papers did wonders for members of the organization. Rudy had several sets. Nate had made them, though he had no idea who they were for.

Rudy used fake identification, he used knives, he used guns, he used dimethylmercury. Whoever got in his way, got in his graves.

Natalie was in his way.

CHAPTER TWENTY-SIX

Nate completed another presentation and added fifty thousand to his secret bank deposit box. Now he had close to three hundred thousand. He told Dino he had loaned money to a friend; had lost a little on poor betting habits; and was saving for a condo on the beach someday. He wore expensive clothes and used fake credit cards to purchase them and other items including expensive jewelry some of which he wore and others placed in the safe deposit box. He lived well and treated his surfer friends very well, indeed. He sent quite a sum to Kathy and Carmen. Still, he liked to see the cash add up. And the presentations were easy.

In fact, his life was terrific. He didn't think too deeply about his involvement in the organization. There was hardly any pressure from Dino. Requests now and then to work on new "papers" for someone and he always added a few for himself and he had fun adding Carmen's and Natalie's names. Course these "papers" went into the safe deposit box . No special reason, he had no plans to ever use them, he just didn't want Dino to find them and he had no other safe place to put them. Even waste baskets were inspected. The episode with his parent's home a month or so ago nearly forgotten. No other contact by the intruder had been made, so Nate dismissed it as, indeed, a burglar. His parents were now on a cruise and then a longer vacation with friends in Arizona anyway. Dino had not mentioned Rudy lately. Kathy and family were spending several days cruising the San Juan Islands (due back in a couple of days) so life seemed calm and Nate relaxed for the first time in years. True he was involved in, let's face it, crime, but no murders, no delivering dead bodies, no pretty-wrapped packages of dimethylmercury. He rationalized that printing fake "papers" for whomever wasn't such a crime. He didn't think too deeply about that either nor the presentations. They were kind of fun and he loved the money.

The thing he did every morning without fail, was study the weather reports and decide where to spend a couple of hours surfing. Dino never minded and he used this time to check his out-of-the-area mailbox always hoping for a letter or photo from Carmen or Kathy. He admitted to himself that Carmen and Natalie surfaced on his mind more often than he ever believed they would.

A short note from Kathy told him that they were arriving back at Shelter Bay in a couple of days and as he glanced at his watch, which noted calendar days as well as time, they had arrived home three days ago. Not a scheduled telephone call day, however, so a report on the vacation would have to wait until the weekend ---- four days away.

The surfing report looked good and he was eager to get out on the water. First, though, he needed to review information on the next presentation scheduled for Cleveland. He always learned something about the city he visited so he could appear knowledgeable of the surroundings. This pleased Dino. But it was a trick he had perfected while a bartender on the cruise ship. A little information made such a huge impression. Nate was one smart man! And his life was coming together.

Except soon it would completely unravel and another decision be made.

CHAPTER TWENTY-SEVEN

Steve walked his passengers from his plane to the rental car desk. He wished he could at least ask the girl if she was okay, but the man stayed alert to any conversation and opportunity soon ended. And later he would ask himself why he had been perhaps too frightened of the man to answer the girl's pleading eyes. Could he have changed lives?

Rudy rented a Blazer. He held Natalie while he signed for the vehicle. "This is so you won't decide to run with her," he said.

"I won't. I'll stand right beside you and hold her so can have your hands free, if you want me to," lied Carmen. She would run in a heartbeat if she had Natalie in her arms. Instead, she stood close to her daughter. So frightened, the knot had been in her stomach ever since Rudy had appeared at Kathy's home.

"I make the rules. You roll your eyes or give any more pleading looks and the kid gets it. My thumb on her throat and....."

"Please Rudy....."

"Be quiet, the guy is coming back," admonished Rudy, as the attendant returned with the contract for the vehicle, and Rudy's credit card, which, of course, had a fictitious name. The procedure went quickly since Steve had called in the reservation and card number from the plane.

"Come on Carmen, we're on our way home," Rudy held Natalie. Once in the Blazer he handed Natalie to Carmen. "You jump out, she dies."

"Rudy she's, innocent. None of this is her fault and she's only a baby. Do what you want to me. Let me leave her with someone, please, I'll do any thing, you know I will," pleaded Carmen.

"You said all that before and what did I say? Remember? Huh, what did I say?" He squeezed her arm. She willed herself not to wince, but he did hurt her so. He knew all the places to press to cause excruciating pain and leave no marks. He could do that to Natalie so easily. Carmen held her baby closer.

"I remember. I shouldn't have asked again. I'm sorry," Carmen quietly said, tears so close to the surface of her eyes. She must protect her child but how? She and Natalie were Rudy's captives and he was ruthless. Carmen knew that.

The highway out of Macon was unfamiliar to Carmen. She guessed she may have been on it with Nate. She remembered the names of most of the cities they had gone through. Atlanta must be the other way.

"Tell me, my little slave, which you are you know, didn't you have a clue I would find you? Don't you know I own you? I bought you!" Rudy asked and not really expecting answers.

"I thought you might want a prettier girl than me or one who knew how to do more things to make you happy."

"Don't try to con a con man. I know why you ran. To keep the kid. Forget it. Soon as we get home, and I have some fun with her, she goes or maybe sooner if I feel like it," laughed Rudy.

Carmen's tears ran down her face, she couldn't keep them back. Every few seconds a loud sob escaped. He laughed again.

"I like to see you cry. Cry Carmen, cry. Beg Carmen, beg. Not that it will do any good," he pounded the steering wheel with his fists and loudly shouted, "Whoopee."

"Rudy, if any of your friends come over, I'll never refuse them again. They could come everyday and I'll never cry about it again, if you'll let Natalie live someplace, not even with me. She's only seven months old."

"Oh, I'll keep her around a little while. Would you really want me to do that? So you can watch what I do to her?"

Carmen decided at that moment that she would rather see her daughter dead than in Rudy's hands. She knew what he planned to do. Could she open the door and throw her out? But what if she didn't die? What if no one found her and she starved to death? What if she cried for her mother or what if animals got her? Carmen could not throw her out the car door.

"It's locked," Rudy quietly said, glancing at Carmen with a look that sent more chills down her back.

Oh, God, will you answer my prayer. She had prayed, silently --- Rudy would never allow spoken prayers --- that she could save Natalie. But, she had no answers on how to do that. Now she prayed that Natalie die in her arms before Rudy got her. She felt defeated. Sorry, Nate, she said to herself, she couldn't save the baby. Then she thought she knew where Rudy kept his guns and maybe she could get into the trailer before he did and get a gun. Maybe. Or maybe she could smother Natalie. That would be painless for the baby and Rudy couldn't --- Carmen shuddered. Then he would kill her, there was no doubt in Carmen's mind.

Carmen put her hand over Natalie's mouth and nose. Her heart was breaking. She loved Natalie so much but she couldn't let Rudy abuse her. The pain for Natalie would be unbearable and Carmen made to watch, tied to a chair so she couldn't reach the baby. Rudy knew that Carmen would die to protect Natalie so he would tie her and make her unable to reach Natalie. Carmen knew his actions so well.

Natalie squirmed, pushing her hands to her mouth, fighting for oxygen, eyes wide with panic staring at her mother. Carmen removed her hand. She gathered Natalie close to her heart and kissed her. She could not take her daughter's life. Not that way.

"That won't work either," Rudy laughed, "you don't have the guts. You might as well realize that you'll see what happens to her when I decide it. I've been thinking I'm tired of her eyes staring at me and what does she need eyes for anyway?"

"Rudy, don't. I beg you, don't hurt her. She's a baby. Your baby, too. You take care of your own, you know you do," sobbed Carmen.

"Yeah, I take care of my own. You should have thought of that when you made the decision to run. Remember Goldie? The dog I loved so much? Well, that's what going to happen to you. First, my little Cuban runaway, you'll watch me with the kid," Rudy snarled. "Want me to tell you step by step what I plan to do? Do you?"

"No, no, I can't bear it."

"First, I said she doesn't need eyes, or ears, and I don't know about her mouth. Is it big enough for what I want to do or not. What do you think?" he laughed. "But, I'll let you see for yourself, we'll be home in less than an hour and then the fun begins. Remember the day I brought you there? Wasn't that fun?"

Carmen didn't respond. Her pleas had fallen on deaf ears. He had no compassion but, she had always known that. She spent the last few miles praying, asking God to guide her, show her the way to help her baby. Save Natalie, save Natalie, save Natalie, the words pounded in her ears as the miles went by. She began to see familiar countryside. Her heart seemed to jump louder and louder. Could Rudy hear it? Natalie remained quiet, her eyes wide open staring at her mother. Anything could set him off. Keep him calm, at least, thought Carmen. Save Natalie, save Natalie, save Natalie.

Rudy drove through the small town where he nightly frequented the local bar. He slowed the vehicle and craned his neck to observe the clientele. Soon be back on his preferred schedule, he told himself. He felt a lift being back on his home turf. It had been a tense-filled seven months looking for Carmen. He had focused on finding her, and now that he had, he wondered why had he bothered. The fact is, he needed the space Carmen and the kid's body will take for someone else. Vinnie had four more bodies on the way. He might dump several in together. Hey! Then a terrific thought surfaced in his mind.

"Remember the snake house, Carmen?"

"Yes," quietly she answered, thinking of the men Rudy had placed in with the snakes. They lasted a few minutes, minutes of sheer torture. Oh, God, not that!

"Well, look here we are. The driveway to our beautiful home," laughed Rudy. "Did you miss it?" He kept looking at Carmen, hoping for a reaction.

She shuddered but remained quiet. The nausea was rising from her stomach to her throat. She swallowed. Natalie turned and stared at Rudy with somber eyes, no smiles as if she knew what he planned. Rudy drove the Blazer fast up the dirt and gravel road to the trailer. He hit every chuckhole possible making Carmen and Natalie bounce around the seat. He enjoyed any discomfort he could inflict on anyone. A fleeting thought crossed Carmen's mind ---- does he like anyone or anything? Her thoughts quickly returned to her dilemma. Could she get in the trailer and locate a gun before Rudy saw her. That was her only hope.

Rudy stopped the vehicle, "Give me the kid and don't get smart or she dies quicker than you blink those big brown eyes."

"Rudy, I really need a drink of water and Natalie does too. Can we go in and get some. We're here now. I can't run away. I won't."

"No, you aren't going in. Do you think I'm crazy? Give me the kid." He grabbed for Natalie, nearly pulling her out of Carmen's arms.

Carmen heard a low growl like a rumbling of thunder and saw a blurring flash as the three dogs ran towards Rudy and jumped on the big man. Killer grabbing Rudy's throat in his large mouth, Demon knocking Rudy to the ground, while King began pulling at Rudy's arm.

"Carmen get a gun and kill these damn dogs." He tossed a ring of keys to Carmen as he pulled his arm away from King's mouth. He screamed a horrid guttural, gasping sound beginning low and increasing into a piercing cry of anguish. Blood began to spurt from his throat and from his legs where Demon was pulling flesh away from the bone. Rudy twisted and turned, trying to get away from the dogs.

"Carmen, help me! Call them off, they listen to you," screamed Rudy. He flung his arm over his face but King seized his hand and tore off Rudy's fingers.

Carmen grabbed the keys and ran toward the trailer holding Natalie tightly in her arms. She fumbled with the key and finally unlocked the door. She looked back at Rudy and heard him call her name once more, "Carmen, I love you, I'll take care of you and Natalie," he did know her name, Carmen thought. "Kill the dogs." She met his eyes and held them for a few seconds. Her emotions were indescribable. The dogs were tearing him apart and he is a human being, she thought. All three dogs were tearing at his clothes; blood flowed like creeping thick mud painted red. She opened her mouth to call to the dogs, but no words escaped her lips.

Carmen rushed Natalie into the trailer shielding her from the horrifying scene. She locked the door. She sat Natalie in a large easy chair and faced a kitchen chair to the door back side under the knob . This will keep him out for a few minutes while she found a gun. She hurriedly looked out the window, Rudy screamed her name again, "Caaaaaarmen." The dogs were still tearing at him ----- his clothes torn to shreds, blood covering his body. The dogs made no sounds. It was as if they were working in unison to destroy him. As if in a trance, Carmen couldn't tear her eyes away from the carnage. Her heart pounding in her ears as if it would jump out of her chest.

Then the dogs growled, stood back, looked at Rudy, then attacked again. They were killing him. She stood frozen. Then Killer looked towards the trailer and it was as if he smiled. The same look as when she had gone away with Nate. Carmen shuddered, her body jerking, she reached to remove the barricade from the door. She knew in her heart that she could stop the attack on Rudy. She left the chair in place.

She turned from the window. Call 911, she told herself. She picked up the telephone, heard the dial tone, then put it back in the cradle. The gun, where's the gun?. Not for the dogs as Rudy had demanded, but for him if he came towards the trailer. She checked the chamber of the Colt Anaconda .44 Magnum. Loaded. She knew it would be. Rudy always kept the guns loaded. "Always ready to kill," he had told her when spinning a gun in his hand. He never should have told her where he kept the guns on that day so long ago. She had watched and learned and remembered. Now she held the gun in her hand as she crept towards the window once again. Rudy lay still, the dogs standing as if on guard. Killer standing by Rudy's head, King, at his feet, and Demon a little back by Rudy's side. Rudy was covered with blood and the dogs as well had blood dripping from their fur. It was a shocking, ugly scene and one which Carmen would live over and over in her dreams for years. But, she and Natalie were safe. Safe from Rudy, but, was the dog attack for him only, or had they gone mad? Would they attack her?

The dogs then began to pull Rudy towards the "garden." There, as Carmen could barely see from the window, was a partially dug grave. Rudy must have left in a hurry ---- he never left such a situation unless ----- but how could she have such a mundane thought as that? Did it really matter? Yet, she could not pull her eyes away from the scene in the yard. The dogs nudged Rudy into the hole and began to use their back legs to scatter dirt over his body. Carmen ran to the bathroom and threw up ---- her stomach could not hold the nausea any longer. She had just witnessed the most horrid event she had ever seen, still she could not stay away from the window. Carmen knew Rudy was dead, yet, she must make sure.

Natalie had fallen asleep in the large over-stuffed chair. Carmen thanked God that the baby was too young to understand what had happened and she had not seen any part of the dog's attack on Rudy.

Now, did Carmen dare leave Natalie inside the trailer while she viewed the outdoor situation?

Then she heard Killer whimpering at the door. Carmen tentatively opened it a few inches. All three dogs stood there, wagging their tails, and giving that, what could only be described, as a smile. It was then that Carmen began to cry. Cry with relief and joy. She and Natalie were, indeed, safe!

"Come in, come in, let's get you all in the shower," she joyfully shouted. She didn't care that they dripped blood on the floor, or that blood got all over her when she hugged each of them. Her friends. They had not forgotten her. She turned on the warm water, poured liquid soap over each of the dogs as they jumped into the shower, and then got into the shower herself washing Rudy's blood down the drain . Washing him out of her life, and Natalie's life, and yes, Nate's life.

The dogs had done it for her. This, she believed, was God's answer. She thanked Him everyday for the rest of her life.

Prayers are answered in strange ways.

EPILOGUE

Carmen isn't called Carmen anymore. Nate has a different name, each is called various names depending on where they live. Natalie (not called that) has a little brother. He is two years old. Natalie is five.

Carmen, Nate, and the children live in a small midwest town. At least they did last year and maybe still do. You may know them. Carmen volunteers at Natalie's kindergarten class. I won't tell you the name of the school or the name of the town. Remember all those fake "papers" Nate made? They use them. Nate will always be looking over his shoulder. The organization never forgives nor forgets.

Oh, yes, Nate took a chance one day and located Carmen's brother, Carlos. Only he isn't called that anymore, either. He lives in the same town as Nate and Carmen and will be getting married soon. Carlos knows the code of the organization and is just as careful as Nate.

I should describe the town so you can look for, I guess, the Winters family. Except they aren't called that, either. It's a small, friendly town. No ocean around for surfing and Nate misses that at times. There is a municipal swimming pool where Natalie and her brother take swimming lessons. Natalie also takes dancing lessons and her little brother jumps up and down pretending to dance, too. The family attends church, but I guess I won't mention the denomination. Carmen helps with Sunday School and Nate helps around the grounds.

They meet with Kathy and her family once or twice a year in a remote location. Whenever they have contact, the meeting place is always in code. Letters and telephone calls are in code as well. They do not send E-Mail. Nate learned the organization's lessons very well.

You're wondering what really was behind those steel doors. Vinnie's CRYONICS program was for real and Nate saw hundreds of Dewars, ready for frozen bodies. But the thing that frightened him was another steel door at the far end. He didn't get to see inside, but he did smell something. Vinnie did, indeed, receive the Nobel Prize for Humanity. Which goes to show that no one knows everything. Nate learned about it, well, I won't say what newspaper he read or what TV station he watched. Sometimes he hears of a famous athelete or political figure suddenly dying after lapsing into an unexplained coma, Nate knows. And he feels responsible.

Nate, Carmen, and the children eat at McDonald's sometimes. Natalie and her brother play in the playplace. Carmen still shoves the french fries in her mouth and Nate laughs. Or sometime they go for Mexican food, but favorite dining is their backyard barbecues. Carmen will make Cuban food once in awhile, but only for her family or Carlos and Becky (real name, but not if they move.)

Nate's parents were killed in an automobile accident. He didn't attend the funeral, Kathy told him about it and mentioned a couple of strangers that stood in back of the church. The strangers left before the service was completed, only she had noticed them sitting in a car about a block away from the church. So, they're still looking for us, Nate told Carmen. So, they moved again. The same type of small town.

Do you know them? This young family with the cute little girl and boy? If they live in your town, don't ask too many personal questions. they don't want to lie, but, protecting their real identity is vital to their lives. Ask, instead, if they want to volunteer in some way to help the community or school. They'll say yes in a heartbeat!

I almost forgot, Carmen is pregnant again. The whole family is overjoyed!

Oh, and I forgot this too. You probably want to know that happened to Killer, King, and Demon. The man working on his fence --- remember the one Rudy thought at first took Carmen? Well, he has the dogs. They smile at him, too. You may wonder how the dogs survived when

Rudy was looking for Carmen. He kept the dogs watered by an artesian well and a food dispenser filled with 500 pounds of dog food. Rudy was very resourceful.

Oh, I guess I can tell you this. Nate and Carmen are buying a home. Three bedroom, two bath rambler, with a kitchen Carmen says it's to die for. The backyard has a place for a garden where they can raise vegetables and flowers. A different kind of garden than the one they knew in Georgia.

You may wonder how Nate could go from fifty thousand dollars a month to less than that in a year. When he sees Carmen's eyes light up after they purchase a new appliance or they go to Natalie's dance recital, or he plays hide and go seek with his son, Nate knows that money, indeed, does not buy happiness.

When he pats Carmen's swollen stomach, he says, "The best Decision I ever made was when I stopped for you."

It's a wonderful life for this small family! And you know what? It stays that way.

About the Author

Mary Syreen is a Pacific Northwest native and considers herself an island person. She lives on an island in Puget Sound, spends time on Kauai, and vacations on pretty Anna Maria Island in Florida.

Kevin Cox is an Air Traffic Control Chief Petty Officer in the United States Navy. He edits manuscripts and provides photo-ready copy for book production. He lives in San Diego with his wife Marilyn, and two daughters, Jennifer and Stephanie.